The Fall and Rise of Ronni Fairweather

Gina Hollands

To Shirley,

Congratulations on winning the Sussex Local competition. & I hope you enjoy the book!

Love, Gina x

Stories that inspire emotions!

www.rubyfiction.com

Published 2022 by Ruby Fiction

Penrose House, Crawley Drive, Camberley, Surrey GU15 2AB, UK
www.rubyficiton.com

A CIP catalogue record for this book is available
from the British Library

EPUB ISBN: 978-1-912550-68-5
PRINT ISBN: 978-1-912550-71-5

For all the teachers who taught me at Sherburn High School 1992–1999, with special mention to Mrs Angela Harding, Miss Claire Burdett, Mr Dave Brewster and Miss Kirsten McKay. You gave me so much, including knowledge, time, patience and confidence, and I will be forever grateful.

Acknowledgements

The biggest of thank yous to my lovely friend and talented author, Juliet West, whose mentoring skills and unwavering faith in Ronni helped this book be far better than it would have been without her valuable input and advice. Thanks also to Alfie Collens whose eagle eyes saved me from making several embarrassing errors.

I'm enormously grateful to my editor, who patiently corrects my (at times, ridiculous) mistakes without so much as a tut, and of course to the Ruby Fiction team for helping me bring my dream to life.
A cheeky apology to everyone whose real-life experiences and jokes I have nicked and presented as being from my own imagination. I owe you a drink or two.

To the Choc Lit and Ruby Tasting Panel, I very much appreciate the time you generously give to read my and my fellow authors' manuscripts and provide us with the valuable feedback which helps us to make our books the best they can be. Thank you: Isobel McIlwraith, Emily Smeby, Reverie Black, Jill Leonard, Hilary Brown, Yvonne Greene, Dimitra Evangelou, Nicola Whittaker, Bee Master, Shona Nicolson, Lorna Baker, Gillian Cox, Honor Gilbert, Ruth Nägele, Alma Hough and Sharon Walsh.

Without any one of you, there would be no Ronni Fairweather.

Part One

Chapter One

19 June 2018 – Guildford, Surrey
Raegan

'Dead?'

'I'm very sorry, Mrs Kent-Walters. Is there anyone you'd like us to call?' The policewoman's eyes are swimmy, and her hand trembles as it reaches out to touch my wrist. She and her colleague gave me their names at the door but, like a bubble that's burst, they've popped out of my head.

I blink a few times, willing myself to cry. Why can't I? If she's welling up, I should be too. He's *my* husband. My eyes sting with the strain, but remain bone dry despite my best efforts. I raise a hand to my cheek, just to make sure a tear hasn't escaped without me knowing, but my steady fingers feel nothing, only the smoothness of my skin after my last derma-peel. Costs a small fortune for a half-hour treatment, but then, Matthew doesn't care about me spending money. He's a very generous soul.

He sure won't care now. Not now he's dead.

Six feet under.

Pushing daisies.

Brown bread.

He likes brown bread, does Matthew. I toasted him a slice this morning. I smoothed a thin layer of low cholesterol margarine over it. His favourite brand, the one with the heart on the tub. I know why I'm not crying – because Matthew is not dead.

I look up at the two police officers. 'He can't be dead,' I say, relief surging through me. 'He only eats low-fat marg.'

Matthew must be alive and well. He's a member of Surrey Park Golf and Health Club, for God's sake. A hundred-and-fifty quid a month membership. But he makes the most of it with his thrice weekly power kettlebell class. Always comes home revived. If that doesn't keep his arteries as clean as a freshly irrigated colon, nothing will.

The policewoman shoots a glance at her older, male colleague and frowns. She's got a lovely empathetic manner, but the poor girl's got it all wrong. It's another woman's husband who's lost his life, not mine. It can't be. Around now, Matthew will be climbing into his E-class Mercedes, and heading home from the Surrey Park Golf and Health Club. He'll be here in a minute, then she'll see.

'I'm afraid your husband didn't die of natural causes.' The male police officer pulls out the kitchen chair beside me, angles it in my direction, and sits down.

'This might be difficult for you to take in, love,' he says.

Love? Are police officers allowed to call people that these days?

'Matthew's body was found this morning in the woodland near Silent Pool. It appears he hung himself.'

'Hanged,' I correct him gently. 'No one ever gets that right, even sometimes on the BBC.'

He pulls his lips into a thin line in an expression of pity. Poor man should really be more concerned about the state of his grammar than worrying about me when there's no need. Sadly, that's a phrase he might have to say again to someone one day, like the wife of the man who really did take his own life, and I'm sure he'd prefer to know the correct way of saying it.

He turns away and says something about sugary tea to his colleague. As if calling me "love" isn't over-friendly enough, now he's ordering a brew in my kitchen without asking me first. I consider objecting, but hold back. I'll have to handle this one gently. I can't imagine how awful it must be to have to turn up at a stranger's house and break the news that their loved one is dead. I admire them. I know I couldn't do it.

He turns back to me and I smile, shaking my head a little. I'd do it more vehemently but I don't want to embarrass the pair of them. It's not their fault someone at Surrey Police has made a monumental screw-up.

'I'm sorry. You've got the wrong house. The wrong wife. Matthew would never take his own life. We're going to Barbados next week, you see. To a five-star Meredith hotel. We've even made a booking at Louis Vermont's restaurant – you know, the celebrity chef from *Kitchen Kings*. 'Anyone in their right mind, who wanted to kill themselves, would at least wait until *after* that kind of holiday, don't you think?'

The female police officer puts a mug of tea on the table in front of me.

'Drink it, love,' the policeman says, and slides it further towards me. 'There's a bit of sugar in it for the shock.'

'I don't take shocker.' I realise it's come out wrong, but don't bother to correct myself. He must know what I mean.

He carries on staring at me. He's not going to be happy until I drink the damn tea. I shrug, pick up the mug, and sip. The syrupy hot liquid slips down my throat a treat. It's wonderful. I haven't had anything this sweet for years. The calories mean I'll have to do fifty burpees before bed tonight, which is a pain, but necessary. It's organic red bush tea, so tastes a bit gone-off, but the sweetness makes the roof of my mouth zing, and I carry on sipping. A proper cuppa would be better, but Matthew doesn't like me buying real tea, and he's probably right – the rooibos, as Matthew calls it, is a more refined flavour. He always pronounces it in a South African accent. He's never been to South Africa, but informs me Garth from the office is from Zimbabwe, and that's how he says it.

Once the policeman's satisfied I've thrown enough liquid down my gullet, he pipes up. 'Matthew doesn't appear to have left a note, but we still have officers searching the area. We'll certainly let you know if we find one.'

'That just goes to prove it's not him,' I say, smiling as I think of my risk-averse, check-everything-over-ten-times husband. 'Not that Matthew would, for one second, consider killing himself, but if he did, he'd write a note, have it proofread, laminated and delivered by registered post just to make sure I got it.' I let out a laugh that comes out higher pitched than I intended. It lingers in the air. I don't seem to be terribly good at knowing what to say to these poor people who are trying so hard. I take another sip of my tea.

Out of the corner of my eye I see the female police officer mouth something to the man. I can't tell what she's trying to say, but he seems to get the message because he clears his throat as if preparing to comment on something he doesn't have the appetite for. I hear his phlegm crack and suddenly feel like it's in my throat and I want to gag.

'I'm afraid we will need someone to identify the body,' he says. 'It can be a distressing experience but it is an opportunity to say goodbye and gain a level of acceptance.'

I sigh, unsure of what it is I have to say to get the message across that my Matthew is not the man they found at Silent Pool. How can I possibly identify the body of a man I'm unlikely to know? Maybe the only way of proving it's not Matthew is to humour them and go along to the identification.

'Mrs Kent-Walters. Raegan. Do you mind if I call you that?'

I shake my head.

'Do you think you're up to that this evening?'

'This evening?' I mentally flick through the pages of my diary. 'No. No, I can't tonight. I've got my dynamic hot yoga class.' *That reminds me – where did I put my new three-quarter length leggings?* I remember buying them online, unpacking them and putting them somewhere; I just can't quite remember where. Then of course there's those pesky fifty burpees.

A fuzzy sound followed by a distorted and largely incomprehensible woman's voice distracts my train of thought. I look for the source of the noise, and my gaze unfortunately settles on the policeman's crotch. He reaches for the walkie-talkie strapped to his belt, touches a button, and the voice is silenced.

The only sound now is coming from the radio in the far corner of our kitchen. The room is big enough that, although it's on fairly loud, I can barely make out the song that's playing. It's something modern, something Sabrine would like.

'Who's Sabrine, love?'

Had I said her name out loud?

'Our daughter.'

'Is she in?'

'No. She's a sixth-form boarder at Felbury Girls. It's her last day today. Matthew and I are picking her up tomorrow.' I hear the pride in my voice.

'Would you like us to wait while you call her?'

'Why do I need to call her when I spoke to her yesterday? I've got nothing new to say. She hates it when I phone for the sake of it. She'll be busy with her friends, anyway.'

The policewoman's sitting on the other side of me now. When did she sit down?

I'm half aware of the officers talking quietly between themselves, something about a doctor. It's a bit late for all that since they said themselves the poor man was found dead this morning. I don't profess to be a medical expert but I do believe even doctors have their limits.

I close my eyes and let their voices wash over me. When I snap my eyes open again a few seconds later, the police officers' heads are bowed in conversation. Their mouths move and I hear the words, just can't make sense of them.

I look around at the kitchen walls that we recently had painted "truffle grey", the shiny white kitchen units – soft close of course; the tall breakfast bar chairs, and my new all-singing-all-dancing quadruple oven that has more dials than a cockpit. A welcome warmth fills my tummy at the home Matthew and I have created – with a little monetary assistance from his parents in the early days, admittedly, but that was a long time ago. It's all down to Matthew these days. His job as Business Development Director at one of the biggest corporate insurance companies in the City, is exceptionally well paid and means I haven't had to work since having Sabrine. I'm so proud of Matthew. My Matthew, who is currently on his way home from his thrice-weekly power kettlebell class at Surrey Golf and Country Club. Because it's Tuesday, and that is what Matthew does on Tuesdays.

Any second now, he'll walk through the door and the dynamic policing duo before me will realise their mistake. They'll apologise profusely, and Matthew and I will tell them not to worry, mistakes happen. Then we'll all laugh about it over a cup of organic red bush.

'Now, are you sure you don't want me to stay over with you tonight? It's really no problem. It's not like I have to go far to get my toothbrush.'

She presses down gently on my shoulders until I sit down. The last time I sat in this chair was yesterday, when my life was perfect. I look up at the kind, crêpey face of my next-door neighbour. 'Lynn?'

'Yes, dear.'

'How long have we been neighbours?'

'Ooh, quite a few years now. I remember seeing your young lady when she was a little girl.'

'Don't you think it's strange that we only learned each other's names because the police asked if you'd come with me to the mortuary?'

She smoothes my hair away from my face. An intimate gesture from a woman whose name up until several hours ago I didn't even know. 'Well, everyone's so busy with their own lives these days. There's not a lot of time to talk for you youngsters.'

'What about your husband? I often see him gardening. He must see lots of people passing-by and talk to them.'

'John?' She lowers her pale blue eyes, and I follow her gaze to her wrinkled hand, peppered with brown age spots. Her skin looks so delicate and thin. I want to reach out and feel its velvet softness. Instead, I watch her twist the thin gold band on the third finger of her left hand. 'John passed away last year.'

A slice of sympathy for the old lady cuts its way through my own searing pain. 'Oh, I'm sorry. I didn't realise.'

'It would have been our ruby anniversary this year. I can't complain though. For thirty-nine years I had the most wonderful husband I could have dreamt of.'

Since when was I the kind of person who didn't know my neighbours' names? Since when was I someone who didn't notice when the old boy next door stopped tending to his garden because he was dead? Since when did I not realise the sweet woman who lived metres away from me was nursing a broken heart?

'I'm so sorry,' I repeat, not knowing what else to say. She looks up at me, reaches for my hand and strokes the back of it.

I look around me. The remnants of my sweet potato and tuna salad lunch are by the sink, waiting to go in my three-tier dishwasher. I must get that moved before Matthew's home. He hates dirty crockery being left hanging around and will make that annoyed clicking sound with his tongue.

But Matthew's not coming home.

Not tonight.

Not any night.

Realisation hits me like a bowling ball in the chest. I saw his body. Just now. Down at the mortuary. I saw it with my own eyes. But somehow, even that wasn't enough to get me to understand I'll never see or hear my husband again. Even the dark brown mole on his shoulder, the one I always thought was the shape of a tiny dolphin, didn't hit home. It took a state-of-the-art kitchen appliance to do that – to get me to realise that I am the forty-three-year-old widow of successful, ambitious, handsome and loving Matthew Kent-Walters.

I stare over at the bowl with the dried-on tuna. The remnants of my lunch; the remnants of my life. The rough, inedible end of the sweet potato and some sad leftover flakes of fish. Not long ago, that fish was swimming around in untinned salt waters under the glorious illusion it would be happy and free forever. Then along came fate with its strangling net, and that was it. Game over.

A surge of panic rushes through me. 'How am I going to do all the banking? And the insurances? I don't have a clue about all that.' I look at Lynn. She must have had the same issues when John died. A worse thought occurs. 'And spiders? How am I going to deal with spiders? I'm terrified of them! Why did he do it, Lynn, why? Why did he kill himself? He was happy. *We* were happy. We've got everything we always wanted.' I gesture around at the beautiful newly-fitted kitchen. 'He didn't even leave a note. Was living with me so bad? Was it? I really did love him, you know. Didn't he love me as much back?'

For some reason Lynn's not giving me the answers. She just keeps on looking at me with her gentle, watery eyes. 'And what if the boiler breaks down?' Not that Matthew could have fixed it, but he'd know who to call, and how much things should cost. How will I cope with all that stuff now that I'm a woman on my own?

A woman on my own. I breathe in deeper and deeper but can't catch my breath. I stand up quickly. Too quickly. My head spins. 'And what if something goes wrong with the Range Rover? I don't even know which garage Matthew uses.' I flatten my palms against the table for support. My lungs feel like they're withering up through lack of air. Is this what Matthew experienced as he drew his final breaths?

A grotesque vision enters my head. Matthew's feet, still in the leather Italian brogues he keeps fastidiously polished, are kicking at nothing as he dangles above the ground. He's clutching at the noose around his neck, and his light brown eyes – the very ones I looked into as I said my vows – are bloodshot and bulging like they might any second pop out of his skull. His face, that he probably moisturised this morning with the men's skincare set Sabrine bought him for Christmas, is bright purple. Was he thinking about our daughter as the life seeped away from his body? Was he thinking about me?

'Why did he do it? Why?' I repeat. 'I loved him so much. Didn't he know that?'

Lynn has hold of me now. She's got a mighty firm grip for a petite woman in her seventies. I know my voice is somewhere between a screech and a wail, but I can't stop. I don't want to stop. I want it to get louder and louder until someone somewhere finally gives me some answers.

'I'm going to be sick.'

She loosens her hold on me, but I lack the energy to do anything other than sink to a crouched position on the floor. My stomach flips and gurgles. Something's definitely on its way out, I'm just not sure which way. The reality is I might be about to lose what's left of my dignity, right here, right now, on my newly tiled kitchen floor as my kind neighbour, whose name I've recently discovered is Lynn, looks on.

Chapter Two

18 November 1987 – Haxton, Yorkshire

Ronni

'Mum, can Ronni stay for tea?' Laura doodles a heart on top of the "i" she's just written in her exercise book, and looks up hopefully from her seat at the Baileys' kitchen table.

Pammy Bailey closes the oven door and adjusts her apron over her generously proportioned bosom. Her plump face is red and shiny from the heat, and when she smiles over at us, two ruddy cheeks shine like polished apples. 'Course she can, love. It's Wednesday. We always have Ronni over for tea on Wednesdays. I've got a Viennetta in the freezer especially. I know how much you lot like them.'

A stab of something – I'm not sure if it's love towards my best friend and her family or envy that they have something I don't – plunges into my chest.

Lance stabs a finger at his calculator. 'Never mind Wednesday, we have Ronni over for tea almost *every* day.'

My heart sinks and I feel an urge to cry. I won't cry though. I never do. Not any more. There's no point. It doesn't achieve anything. Lance has a point though. I am here a lot. Because they pity me. I'm always told I'm too young to understand things, but I understand that.

Laura glares at her brother who, at fifteen, three years older than us, is going through a rather unfortunate gangly stage of looking like his limbs are far too long for his body. 'Why don't you piss off and play on the A1, you big wanker. You're just jealous I've got a friend over and you haven't.'

I put my hand over my mouth to conceal an explosion of laughter. She's being mean, not funny, but laughter is better than tears. We all look over to see if Pammy has heard Laura swear, but she's too busy singing along to George Michael on the radio and buttering bread to be paying any attention.

'Piss off yourself, you stupid slag.' Lance's face grows so red that the pus of his many meaty whiteheads glow, like a luminous dot-to-dot.

'Lance!' Pammy places a plateful of buttered white bread in the centre of the table, and swipes Lance's spiky-haired head with a tea towel. 'Enough of that language. You're not too old to have your mouth washed out with soap and water, you know.'

He jabs a finger across the table at Laura. 'She started it!'

'I did not!' lies Laura.

'You two always manage to find *something* to argue about,' says Pammy. 'I'll never forget that time me and yer dad took you three-hundred odd miles down to Brighton, and you were arguing over one pebble. One bloody pebble! There were millions of the things on that damned beach, and you two wanted to fight over one!'

I attempt to stay well out of this argument by double underlining the title I've just written in my exercise book. As soon as I sense any sort of conflict, I duck straight out. I've heard enough arguments to last me a lifetime and even though this one's just harmless sibling rivalry, I don't want any part in it, especially because it centres around me. Just like the ones I used to hear at home. Too quickly, I move my ruler away from the line I've just drawn, causing the fresh ink to smudge.

'He's been 'orrible, saying we have Ronni around all the time for tea. It's 'cos he fancies her and he doesn't want her to see all his zits.'

I feel my cheeks heat and I daren't look at Lance because if he sees me blushing, he'll think *I* fancy *him*. I don't. I just don't want him to think I do.

Pammy swipes Lance and Laura in turn with the tea towel.

'Mum, give over, you'll knock over my Vimto,' protests Lance.

'Laura, be nice to your brother. He's got some special facewash now. It just needs time to work, then he'll have skin like a baby's arse. And you—'

I risk a glance upwards just in time to see that Lance's face has turned from red to a dark shade of beetroot.

'Ronni's having a tough time at the moment and she can come for tea whenever she fancies.'

I squirm in my chair as my woollen tights suddenly start to itch my thighs. Pammy means well, and it's not like what happened is a secret, but I wish she wouldn't bring it up. I wish we could just forget it ever happened.

'Hell,' she says, oblivious to my thighs that are screaming with discomfort, just like they always seem to do whenever the topic is raised. 'She's better behaved than you two put together – she can have both your bedrooms if she likes and you two can move into Barnardo's with them poor kids who've got nowt, then you might realise how lucky you are.'

'That's the only way Lance'll get a girl in his bed—' Laura teases, 'if *he's* not in it.'

'I don't want a girl in my bed!' he blurts back, then looks quickly down, instantly regretting it.

'Yeah, 'cos you're a big gay,' Laura hisses across the table.

'Shut up, you!' shouts Lance.

'Enough, or I'll slipper the both of you.'

At the mention of their mother's slipper, Laura quickly picks up her pen and Lance suddenly becomes highly interested in the contents of his textbook, as if he's just discovered it contains the secret cure for acne.

'Right,' says Pammy. She throws the tea towel over her shoulder and heads back towards the oven. 'Five more minutes of homework, then you'll have to clear the table. Tea'll be ready as soon as yer dad gets home.'

'What we having?' asks Laura.

'Beef casserole. Plenty of goodness. Just what you growing kids need.'

Laura screws up her face, scrunching up the freckles at the sides of her nose until they merge together to form two big brown patches over her pale skin. 'What the chuff's *casserole*?'

'Stew,' says Lance, without looking up from his textbook. 'Mum thinks she's posh if she calls it *casserole*, 'cos that's what that bloke on telly calls it, who's always pissed. Kiefer Lloyd, or whatever his name is.'

'Oi, you, cheeky!' Pammy, peers around the side of the cupboard door she's opened to get out the plates, and narrows her eyes at her son. 'It's Keith Floyd. And watch your language. This isn't Fairhills Working Men's Club. Besides, he's not pissed – he's French.'

Pammy's head disappears back behind the cupboard door, and Lance chuckles. 'French, my arse,' he says, although this time he keeps his voice down low enough for his mum not to hear.

Laura huffs and rests her head on her hand. 'God, I bloody hate stew.'

So do I. The way the stringy meat gets stuck in your teeth and you spend the rest of the night trying to prise it out. And those horrible soft bits of cooked celery Pammy likes to put in it by the bucketload. Eurgh. The icky aroma of fried onions floats past my nostrils and my stomach turns over.

I eye up the thickly sliced Mighty White on the table and resolve to mop up as much of the stew as I can with the spongy dough. If I can fashion a stew sandwich, then it might be just about edible. One good coping method I've discovered when eating around at the Baileys is to hold my breath as I chew. Mrs Reader said in biology that taste is mainly smell, so last Wednesday when it was stew, I tried not breathing while eating and it worked, in the most part.

I'd never complain though. Obviously, I'm very grateful to the Baileys for having me over so often. They have me round every Wednesday, most Mondays and some Thursdays because that's when Dad's working. I haven't told Laura he sometimes does extra hours the other days too, because there's only so much of Wednesday's stew, Monday's Crispy Pancakes with oven chips and Thursday's chops and mash I can take. If I hold my breath any more I might pass out.

I know this means I sometimes have to eat cereal on my own at home because Dad hasn't had a chance to go to Safeway's – sometimes I eat the cereal dry if the milk's turned – but I don't mind; I like cereal, even when it's dry. And I like being on my own sometimes. It gives me a chance to think things through. Make plans. It will be years of course before I can actually do any of them, but just thinking about them makes me feel better. Gives me a sort of escape.

A blast of cold air rushes in from the hallway as the front door opens. 'Hell-ooo!' a jolly male voice calls. The owner of the voice closes the door behind him and the whole house seems to shake with it.

'Oh good, yer dad's home. Just in time.' Pammy clatters around in the cutlery drawer, pulling out a handful of knives and forks.

The long strings of beads hanging down from the kitchen door frame clatter as Gus Bailey sweeps them aside and enters the kitchen in stockinged feet and black-spattered overalls. 'Hi-de-hi, campers!'

'Ho-de-ho!' Pammy's the only one to reply, and does so without looking up from the kitchen counter where she's ripping pieces of kitchen paper from the roll. Her voice is light and easy, but is tinged with mundanity, as if this is a line she's uttered many times in her married life. From the amount of time I spend at the Baileys, I know this to be true.

Even though Gus is at the far side of the kitchen, I can smell the engine grease on his skin and mechanic's overalls as it cuts through the stench of the onions. That stab is back. It cuts deeper this time, now the family scene is complete.

He presses a kiss to his wife's cheek and calls over at us, 'Ey up, kids.'

'Hi Dad,' Laura and Lance chorus.

I smile and give a little wave. 'Hiya Uncle Spud.'

He's not my uncle, but that's what I've always called them – Uncle Spud and Aunty Pammy.

'Ah, evening, Ronni. Nice to have you over again.'

A surge of gratitude and love towards Spud and Pammy makes my spine tingle. I've known them my whole life. They've always been there for me, but never so much as in the last few months.

Spud scratches his long, ginger beard and flakes of dirt float down onto the kitchen tiles beneath. He unzips his overalls, revealing an oil-stained white T-shirt over a paunchy stomach.

'Not there, Gus, for goodness' sake.' Pammy shoos him towards the door. 'How many times do I have to tell you not to take yer mucky overalls off in the food preparation area! Go and get yersen showered while I serve up.'

He pulls a mock-frightened face. 'All right, Pammy, all right, calm down. I'll do whatever you want, just keep yer slippers on!'

Laura, Lance and I all laugh as he pretends to rush out of the room, one leg out of his overalls and one still inside them.

'Ooh, one thing first.' He stops at the doorway and some of the long beads are draped over his shoulder, making him look like he has Boy George dreadlocks. 'Ronni, yer dad says he's going to be home late tonight. He's picked up a couple of extra fares, see. He asked if you could stay round ours, and I said no bother.'

Extra fares? On a Wednesday? Liar.

Pammy looks at her husband out of the corner of her eye and raises an eyebrow. He meets her gaze but, for my benefit, I'm sure, is careful not to change his expression.

'Oh, yes, great idea.' Pammy flicks her head around to look at me and pastes on a smile. 'Why don't you nip home to get your duvet straight after tea, Ronni? Go with her Laura, there's safety in numbers.'

Lance guffaws. 'She only lives next door.'

'Well, you never know what funny fellas might be knocking about at this time o' night.'

In a rare scene of sibling harmony, Lance and Laura exchange glances and snigger at their mum's dramatisation. I force a smile too. It requires so much effort that it makes my face ache. I'm too busy thinking about the look Spud and Pammy exchanged to see the funny side of anything. It was a look that confirmed my suspicions that Dad's got himself into bother. Again.

Chapter Three

20 June 2018 – Felbury, Buckinghamshire

Raegan

I turn off the ignition and the Range Rover's engine slips into silence. Its low hum still buzzes in my ear as I look out of the windscreen up at the formidable old stone building before me. A nausea seeps over me. I've always hated this place. From the very first moment I saw Felbury Hall Girls School seven years ago, with its dark stone frontage and foreboding turrets, it had the power to make me feel cold and inadequate, like it knew all my secrets and was silently threatening to expose them.

If I'd had my way, Sabrine would have gone to the comprehensive school down the road. It got good results and meant she could have come home every evening to sleep in her own bed. But Matthew had insisted that Felbury Girls, with its world-class reputation and machine-like efficiency for pumping young women into Oxbridge, was the school for our one and only child. Plus, Matthew's sister, Melanie, and his mother, Elizabeth, were both former Felbury girls, so practically from the moment Sabrine came into the world, he had her name down on the waiting list. I never argued. To do so would have caused such a stink with Matthew's family – a stink I couldn't afford to cause when I was so desperately out of favour with his mother already.

I grab my Prada shoulder bag from the passenger seat and reach for the car door handle. I pause, squeeze my eyes shut and wonder for the millionth time this morning whether coming here to break the news to Sabrine was the best idea. Should this really be the place she learns of her father's death?

I lower my head, rest it against the leather steering wheel and let out a frustrated groan. Come on, Raegan, come on. You're her mother. You *have* to be the one who tells her. But here? Yes. Better here than at home. I can't spend an hour and a half in the car with her and pretend everything's fine, only to tell her once we get through the front door. Anyway, she'll think it's strange Matthew's not with me. We always said on her last day we'd both come to pick her up, then stop for lunch on the way home for a celebration. *Oh, shit! Shit, shit, shit!*

I sit bolt upright and slam the palm of my hand against the steering wheel. It hurts and I'm glad. It's nothing compared to the hurt I'm going to inflict on my daughter, who right now will most likely be happily packing her bags thinking she's coming home to two loving parents. Little does she know, her life's about to change forever. Just like mine did yesterday.

I think back to that tuna swimming around contentedly. I'm the proverbial net about to swoop down and strangle the happiness out of my daughter until she can barely breathe with the pain. After I tell her, will she be able to look at me ever again without associating my face with the worst news an eighteen-year-old can receive?

But I'm her mother and it's my duty to tell her. I flick the handle with so much force I'm surprised it doesn't break. I kick open the door and climb out before I lose my courage and drive away, leaving my daughter in ignorant bliss.

'Ah, Mrs Kent-Walters, you've arrived.' Petula Hargreaves places a hand on my shoulder and ushers me through a door marked in swirly gold font with her name and "Headmistress". She can't be much older than me, and yet she has the air of someone who's found her calling in life and has the confidence and authority to show for it. A stab of envy shoots through me.

Far from being the archetypal head of a girls' boarding school that harks back to the days of the Ark, Petula Hargreaves, with her short crop of auburn hair, houndstooth trouser suit and rainbow brooch that she wears on her tie, is an out and proud lesbian.

Matthew had been so stunned when he met her at the open day, I thought I'd have to manually shut his jaw. It wasn't that he had anything against lesbians, he'd said later – which I didn't comment on, but I knew to be true from his internet history – just that, as he'd phrased it, he'd been *a tad surprised*. It hadn't been a big enough surprise to dissuade him from sending Sabrine to Felbury though, but he always kept the headmistress's sexual persuasion quiet from his mother. Elizabeth Kent-Walters, for all her airs and graces, had a strong distrust of anyone who wasn't exactly like her: conservative, straight, white, upper middle class, and with an accent so plummy you could make jam out of it.

'I'm so sorry for your loss,' Petula says, in a soft rhotic accent which suggests Cornish roots. She guides me over to a small sofa at the far side of her vast office and gestures for me to sit down. 'Rest assured, I haven't said a word to Sabrine since your call yesterday, just as you requested.'

'Thank you.'

She sits in an armchair across from me and as she does so, her trousers ride up slightly, revealing brightly-coloured Christmas socks. It's

June. I almost laugh at the absurdity of the situation, but I suddenly remember why I'm here, and the unfunny reality hits me like a slap across the face.

'I thought you might like to use my office to talk to Sabrine. I will of course make myself scarce to give you two some privacy.'

'Thank you,' I repeat, and even now, with my husband dead and my daughter on the verge of finding out, I'm worried about whether Petula Hargreaves thinks I'm a dunce and that "thank you" is the extent of my vocabulary.

'I'll let Sabrine know you're here.'

I want to shake my head and shout at her that no, I'm not ready, but instead, I nod silently.

As if reading my mind, she leans forward and places her hand on top of mine. 'Perhaps you'd like a cup of tea first?'

I take a deep breath in and speak as I exhale. 'Thank you.' *There I go again with my favourite words.* I don't want another cup of bloody tea and know I'm procrastinating, but I just want to give Sabrine a few more minutes of happiness before I beat the crap out of her sweet world.

Petula Hargreaves smiles and pats my hand, as if I've just made an important decision on something that matters – such as where to dig for oil – rather than agreeing to a hot beverage. She stands up and makes her way over to where a silver tea set is sitting upon an antique-looking sideboard. 'Do you take sugar?'

'I'm sweet enough, thanks lovie.' My hand flies to my mouth. 'I'm so sorry.' I feel the heat from my face, which I know must be lobster-red. 'I don't know where that came from.' I let out a small, nervous laugh, then concentrate on breathing to calm my furious blush.

'Perfectly understandable,' says Petula Hargreaves as she sets teapot, cups and milk jug onto the side table next to the sofa. Her movements are swift and precise, as if she's used to dealing with verbally-challenged morons who talk to her like she works in a truckers' cafe. 'I expect you're all over the place at the moment, what with the terrible news of your husband's death. Once again, on behalf of all the teaching staff, I'd like to offer my sincere condolences, and if there's anything any of us can do for you and Sabrine, you only have to say the word.'

A lump rises in my throat in response to her kindness, and I quickly swallow it down. I need to stay strong for Sabrine, not crumble into a blubbering mess. She needs to know I'm here to support her rather than worry I'm crippled by my own grief. I open my mouth to thank her, but quickly rethink my words and tell her that's very kind.

I fumble with my delicate china cup, trying to get my fingers into the stupidly tiny handle, and ponder what Petula Hargreaves *could* do to help. I could ask her to pop over to the house and run the Vac round, but don't think she'd be up for that. So, other than to serve tea in a decent sized mug, there's nothing. There's nothing anyone can do. It's all down to me – telling Sabrine, sorting our finances, ending Matthew's Country Club membership. No point paying for that now. And … *Matthew's work! Shit!* They'll be wondering where he is. I'll have to call them. What do I tell HR? *Sorry, my husband won't be showing up for work today, or any other day for that matter because unfortunately he hanged himself.*

All down to me. I swallow a mouthful of tea and it tastes like a dose of loneliness – stewed, bitter. I tip the cup up and throw the rest of the scalding hot liquid down my throat. I want it to burn so much I can't talk. Then maybe I wouldn't have to be the one to tell Sabrine.

Petula Hargreaves gives a single nod. 'I'll go get her now.'

Oh no. She's taken my empty cup as a sign that I'm ready to face my daughter. But it's anything but. As she passes the sofa I act on instinct. I grab hold of her jacket and look up at her, hoping my imploring eyes tell her I can't go through with it. Maybe she'll feel so sorry for me she'll tell her instead. My chin trembles. I haven't felt this out of control since my first day at school at five years old. I grabbed hold of my mum, refused to let her go, and begged her not to make me go into the big, scary building. But this is much bigger and scarier. Petula Hargreaves doesn't exactly shove me in and tell me not to be so silly, like my mum did that day. Her approach may be more refined, but it amounts to the same thing.

She bends down and kneels on the carpet beside me. Her face is so close I can feel the warmth of the tea she's just drunk on her breath. 'You *can* do this, Mrs Kent-Walters,' she says.

I shake my head so hard I hear my brain rattle inside my skull. 'No, no, no.' I repeat the word over and over and know a candle of thick snot is working its way from my nostril towards my top lip. Not wanting it to flick off and hit Petula Hargreaves, I cease the shaking, and don't try to stop her when she prises my hands from her clothes.

'I wish you had a choice, Raegan,' she says, her voice even gentler than usual. I guessed it was the tone she used when dealing with upset students, and now I understand, more than ever before, why this woman has the top job. Rather than pushing me into the situation, she's coaxing me, cleverly slipping in my first name to make it all the more real and personal. Although her way doesn't make it any less big or scary, acceptance starts to creep in that it's going to happen anyway and no amount of my begging or pleading is going to change that.

I sniff the trail of snot back inside my nostril, making a disgusting sound. Under any other circumstance, I'd be horrendously embarrassed, but my husband's just died, so I figure I'm allowed to be ungainly.

I mutter a pathetically weak 'okay', and she pats my hand as if those oil digging decisions have paid off. 'I have every faith that you'll articulate this news to your daughter in a way only her mother can. I'll be just outside if you need me.'

I watch her leave and wonder what I've done to make her think there's anything remotely articulate about me – although I did double my vocabulary by managing a few hundred "no"s as well as a million "thank you"s, so maybe that was it.

I hope she's right to have faith in me, because right now, sitting here in the headmistress's office, waiting for my daughter to walk through the door, I have next to none in myself.

The corners of her pretty pink lips fall and part. Her lightly-freckled fair face fades to a white shade of ghost, and her blue eyes widen, glistening with tears. Her young, smooth skin on her forehead creases into ridges I've never seen there before, and I'm sad, so very sad that I've done this to my own daughter.

'No, Mummy!' She throws herself into my arms and I clutch her slim, shaking body. It's not her grief that's making her call me "Mummy". She's eighteen and she's always called us Mummy and Daddy. Matthew likes it – *liked* it – because it's a Felbury thing, apparently; a sort of show that our daughter goes to an exclusive school. I liked it because it made me feel that even though we sent her away from home, she's still my baby.

For the first time, I question how good a thing it is. As of tomorrow, she'll no longer be a Felbury girl. And she'll only have a "Mummy", not a "Daddy". For the first time in her life, our little girl has some serious growing up to do, and what have I done to help her get there?

'But *how* is Daddy dead? He's not old. He's fit and healthy. There's nothing wrong with him.'

I smooth her long hair away from her face as tears spring from her eyes. Even though she's my daughter, I can look objectively and know she's beautiful. With her long legs currently concealed with well-worn jodhpurs, her even, white smile and peachy complexion, she's a much more attractive woman than I could ever hope to be. She has my cheekbones, but most of her other features, including her height, naturally blonde hair and athletic figure, she inherited from Matthew. On a normal day, she could easily pass for early twenties, but with her face blotchy and lips quivering, she looks like an over-sized little girl. *My* little girl. My heart creaks, and I make an instant decision not to tell her that Matthew ended his own life – that he chose this for us.

'It was his heart, darling. It was an underlying heart condition he didn't know about.' The lie trips off my tongue easier than I expected.

'Were you there when it happened, Mummy? Was he in pain?'

'Yes, sweetheart, I was right there with him. And no, there wasn't time for him to suffer. By the time the ambulance arrived, it was too late.'

'Did he say anything?'

Oh God, I should have thought this through. 'Yes. He said he loves us both. Very much. And he's sorry.'

'Sorry for what?'

'For having to leave us.'

'But it wasn't his fault.'

'I know, sweetheart, I know, but I imagine he was so devastated he'd never see us again.'

'I can't believe this is happening.' She breaks away from me and paces the room. Every few steps she stops and either screams, tears at her hair or buries her face into her hands and sobs.

I cry too. Not for my husband this time but for my daughter. Because I know what it feels like to lose your father. I know there won't be a day that will go past without her thinking of him, and today is only day one of thousands.

Eventually, she sits down on the sofa where I'd sat earlier. She pulls incessantly at a loose thread on the arm, and every few seconds I hear the stitching rip. I want to ask her to stop because Petula Hargreaves is not going to be happy to find her furniture threadbare, but every time I open my mouth to say the words, she beats me to it with another question.

Where did it happen? When did it happen? Yesterday? Why didn't you tell me yesterday? When's the funeral? Did they try to resuscitate him? Where is he now?

I answer every question as best I can, having to lie sometimes to cover up the suicide. Then she stumps me.

'Does Grandma know?'

'I haven't told Grandma yet.' The heavy brick of dread that makes an appearance every time the thought occurs, re-emerges and promptly sinks to the pit of my stomach. I look over at the door, willing Petula Hargreaves to come in. I want to grab her lapels and hear a vote of her confidence telling me I'm strong and articulate, because the last thing I want to do is visit Elizabeth to tell her that her son is dead.

As if by magic, there's a knock on the door and Petula Hargreaves enters. 'I'm so sorry to interrupt, ladies, but Cressida and Olivia are leaving, and they're very keen to say goodbye to you, Sabrinc. I haven't told them anything, but thought you might like to see them.'

Sabrine wipes her eyes and heads out the room. I stay put, but can hear her telling her friends through fits of tears that her father is dead. There are lots of "Oh my God"s and "I'm so sorry, Sabby"s going on. Sabrine's crying becomes muffled, I imagine due to consoling embraces. An older woman's voice filters through. I assume it's one of the girls' mothers. She asks if there's anything she can do. She could do our dusting. What with her, and Petula Hargreaves hoovering, I could sack the cleaner.

I don't want to go out there and face their pity, so I sink myself into the sofa and focus on wrapping the thread Sabrine was pulling around a loose button on the arm. If I do a good job, Petula Hargreaves will barely notice the crime against furniture.

After several minutes, Sabrine comes back in holding a soggy tissue to her face, with Petula Hargreaves behind.

'Can we go home now, Mummy?'

'Of course, sweetheart.'

Eager to get away, I stand up too quickly and my head spins. I seem to be making a habit out of that. I blink hard and rub my forehead.

'Are you sure you're okay to drive, Mrs Kent-Walters? You are most welcome to stay here at Felbury tonight if you like. Many of the girls have already gone home, so there are plenty of rooms vacant.'

Her well-groomed auburn brows are knitted together. I note she's gone back to using my surname and take it to mean that the earlier connection between us is broken. She's back in headmistress mode. Despite her offer of us staying, I sense she wants us to go, and I can't blame her. There's only so much misery anyone can take, even when it's not their own. Sadness is infectious. It's only a matter of time before someone else's seeps into your soul and sucks it dry of all its joy.

'No thank you. I think it's best we go back home.'

'Of course. Whatever you think is the right thing for you both.' She turns to Sabrine. 'It's been a pleasure having you here over the years, Sabrine. I'm sorry your last day had to be like this, but I hope you'll take with you all the wonderful memories you have of Felbury.'

'I will, Ms Hargreaves.'

Petula pulls Sabrine into a hug, which sets Sabrine off on a fresh batch of tears.

'Keep in touch. And do let us know how you get on.' Petula Hargreaves pulls away from the embrace, but leaves her hands on Sabrine's shoulders and looks at her with an expression full of empathy but also firmness. 'And don't worry about Whitey. We can keep him here as long as you like. The equestrian team are working all summer to look after our international students' horses, so he'll be well cared for until you can find the time to pick him up.'

Oh God, I'd completely forgotten about Whitey. That bloody pony. How the hell am I going to sort that out as well as everything else? Panic rises inside me. The list stored in my head of things I have to do is getting so long I'm spinning desperately out of control. Organise the funeral, visit the bank, tell old Mrs Kent-Walters her son is dead, transport a pony across half of the Home Counties.

We bought Whitey when Sabrine returned home after her first term at Felbury, distraught she was "the only Felbury girl without a pony". It was fine, all the time Sabrine was at school – well, apart from the astronomical stable charges, but Matthew sorted all that out – now, though, where would we put the bloody thing? Matthew had said something last week about hiring a horse box, but at the time I'd been serving up a nice piece of grilled sea bass with Chantenay carrots and, while I'm sure I nodded and mmm-hmm'd in all the right places, I hadn't been paying all that much attention.

Why would I? I never normally needed to.

Chapter Four

24 June 2018 – Guildford, Surrey

Raegan

'Just to warn you, you might get a bit of a shock when you see her. Elizabeth's dementia has worsened quite a lot since your last visit. Don't be surprised if she doesn't recognise you.'

I follow Julie, the senior carer at Treetops Nursing Home, up the sweeping staircase. A cocktail of flowers and bleach pervades my nostrils. It's all very well this place being private, but no amount of lilies can overpower Toilet Duck used on this scale.

'Really? She wasn't too bad last time we came and that can't have been, what, more than a couple of weeks ago? A little confused, perhaps, but she definitely knew who we were.' *It might have been better if she hadn't.*

We reach the landing. Julie stops and turns to me, breathing heavily from the exertion of walking up the stairs. She rearranges her tight white tunic over her large bosom and gives me a sad smile. 'Dementia can suddenly escalate at any time. For many clients, it isn't a gradual deterioration like you might expect.'

Julie's one of the few genuinely good people in the world – with a heart you wished you had, but couldn't hope to, not even after a faceful of G&Ts. We've known her almost two years, since Elizabeth moved in to Treetops, and we both think a lot of her, but I wish she wouldn't call the old folks *clients*. Clients are people in suits who choose to enter into a deal. These shells of human beings, whose cries and screams echo in the tastefully decorated corridors, do not have a choice. These are not clients; they're patients – sufferers, shadows of their former selves waiting to die. And as much as it makes me a bad human being to think it, I hate being here.

Julie reaches out and touches my arm. 'It's difficult to say, Mrs Kent-Walters, but I don't think Elizabeth will see Christmas. It could even be sooner. I'm glad you're here today – I was going to phone you. You might want to give your husband a call. It's probably a good idea he pays his mum a visit.'

'Oh, right.' I lick my dry lips and reach into my handbag to retrieve my phone to call Matthew. Only when my fingers touch its smooth, slippery surface do I remember that he won't answer. I pause, my hand still in my bag. For some reason, I can't bring myself to tell Julie that he's dead; that the real reason I'm here is to tell Elizabeth her son has perished.

Julie's looking at me. She's waiting for me to call Matthew. Her eyebrows raise in expectation. For a moment, I consider having a pretend phone call with my dead husband as it seems preferable to informing Julie that two days ago he took his own life.

'Oh, I've just remembered'—I try so hard to smile it hurts my face—'he's in a meeting till three. I'll call him then.'

Julie nods, satisfied with my explanation, and we continue to walk along the corridor towards Elizabeth's room.

'What should I do?' I ask. 'If she doesn't recognise me, I mean?'

'You might be all right. Although her condition's deteriorating, she does have moments when she seems as right as rain. I haven't popped in on her for a couple of hours because she was napping on my rounds earlier. You might just catch her on a good moment.'

'Oh, right. And if not?'

'Best to go with it. No point arguing with a dementia client – it tends to upset them more. It's just nice for her that you're here.'

I somehow doubt that Elizabeth will share that view.

Julie stops at a freshly painted bright white door and raps gently on it. 'Elizabeth, darling,' she calls. 'Visitor!'

Only Julie could get away with calling Elizabeth Kent-Walters "darling". I doubt she's ever been given a fond name in her life before moving into Julie's wing in Treetops. Most people would be terrified at her reaction – and that's before the dementia set in.

Julie swings open the door. I can't see Elizabeth's face yet, as Julie's ample form is obstructing my view, but I can see her feet, nestled in the pink Shepherd of Sweden slippers with the white pom-poms I bought her last Christmas. They cost almost as much as a starter home. She beamed at Matthew when he gave them to her as if he'd stitched the bloody pom-poms on himself. She didn't bother to look in my direction, even though I was the one who ordered them and Matthew hadn't known what was in the box until he watched his mother open them.

'Raegan's here to see you, darling.' Julie spoke at twice her natural volume as she bustled into the room and adjusted the blanket draped over Elizabeth's lap.

I can see the old woman now. She looks tiny, sat in a high-backed armchair by the bay window. She's always been thin, but she can't weigh much more than six stone now. Her skin is heavily wrinkled and her pure white hair, that must have been freshly done today if the tightness of those curls is anything to go by, is even thinner than I remember. It looks like someone's emptied a bag of candy floss on top of a skeleton.

'Who?' It doesn't seem possible that such a clean, crisp voice could come out of something that frail. That prim sharpness always did have the ability to put the fear of God into me, even now that she looks less duchess and more living dead.

'You know – Raegan.' Julie's voice reaches dangerously high decibels. It's no wonder half the residents have hearing loss. If they didn't before moving in, they would soon after. 'Your daughter-in-law.'

Elizabeth screws up her face like an old chamois leather. 'No. I don't want to see *her*. She's a filthy, common, gold-digging whore!'

Just my luck. In a week when she doesn't know Pope Francis from Kim Kardashian, she has no trouble recalling me.

Julie continues tidying the coffee table as if her *darling client* accusing her daughter-in-law of being a sex-worker with hygiene issues is perfectly normal. 'Now, now. That's not a very nice thing to say about Matthew's lovely wife, is it?'

'Matthew!' Elizabeth sits up in her chair, and her wizened face instantly brightens. For a fleeting moment I see the attractive woman she must once have been. 'Is he here?'

No. He's dead. I try to imagine myself saying the words and can't, so instead I pretend to admire the view from the window.

Julie plumps a cushion and places it back on the bed, then comes towards where I'm standing by the door. 'Don't take it to heart,' she says, her voice hushed. 'She doesn't mean it – it's just the illness talking. Actually, this is the most lucid she's been for days. At least she knows who you are.'

'Yeah, lucky me.'

Julie gives a sympathetic smile, and heads for the door. 'I'll bring some tea up.'

The door clicks shut. The room seems to shrink – the walls close in. It's just me and Elizabeth now. Two women who've despised each other since their first meeting. The only thing that ever linked us together – her son; my husband – has gone. I know it. She doesn't.

I meet her eyes and a cold shiver runs down my spine. I don't know if it's because I'm alone with her, or because I'm here to tell her that Matthew is dead and I don't know where to start.

'Matthew. Where is he?' She peers at me with deep-set blue eyes and wrinkles her nose as if just becoming aware of a terrible smell in the room. Those eyes search me, pressuring me for an answer. I force a smile to stretch across my face, and walk towards her on shaking legs. Not once does she tear her stare away from me. I perch on the chair across from her and open my mouth, waiting for the words to fall out. God knows what I'm going to say, but I figure if I just let them fall, the right thing might magically come out.

And then clarity explodes in my head. I *can't* tell her. *Of course* I can't. And I don't need to. Julie said herself that she's dying, and is getting more and more confused. She won't be wondering why Matthew hasn't visited if she doesn't even know what day of the week it is. I've already broken the news to Melanie and even through her devastation, I could hear the relief in her voice when I offered to tell her mother. She said with her being in New Zealand and all, it was the kindest thing – for me to do it face-to-face. But Melanie's a spiritual soul. She'll understand why I couldn't go through with it. She'll have to.

Relief washes over me, quickly followed by utter desolation. The man Elizabeth and I both adored is dead, and I have no one to share my grief with. Even sharing it with Elizabeth Kent-Walters seems better than no one.

'Matthew couldn't make it today, unfortunately,' I say. 'He had to, um, work, but he sends his love.' My voice catches in my throat, and my words are barely audible, but there's no doubt she's heard.

She humphs, and slumps back into her chair. 'Then go!' she says. 'I don't want a dirty trollop like you anywhere near me.'

'Yes, right. Okay, I'm going.' I don't know why I say that, but in the prettily decorated room, with the orchid on the windowsill and the still-life fruit painting over the bed, it seems only appropriate to agree with her.

I get up to leave, but she suddenly lunges forward and slaps me hard on my arm so that I leap back in my chair in defence.

'I always hated you,' she seethes through gritted teeth. 'I hated you for taking my son away. He deserves better than *your kind.*'

If Elizabeth were a sweet lady, whose personality had been robbed by the ravages of dementia, that comment wouldn't have the power to reach into my chest and smash my heart to pulp like it did. Elizabeth's inner filter might have been destroyed by her disease, but I know full well she means every word.

Anger roars inside me for everything this woman has put me through over the last twenty-five years. I want to tell her how many times she caused me to cry myself to sleep; how she made me feel that I was never good enough to be the wife of her precious son and the mother of her only grandchild. But as I open my mouth to speak, a waterfall of guilt crashes over me. Maybe if Matthew had married someone more suitable, he would be alive and happy. Maybe his death *is* my fault. I drove him to it because our marriage should never have been. Maybe she was bloody right all along and I never listened!

'I'm sorry,' I gasp, as the realisation takes my breath away. 'I'm sorry for all of it – for everything.'

She purses her thin lips and reaches forward, grabbing my wrist with a strength a woman in her condition should not possess, and digs her nails into my skin so hard I cry out.

She starts to talk and I freeze in disbelief at what she says. She's hanging on to me just as tightly as before but with the shock of her words, I no longer feel the pain. She finishes speaking and smiles, her eyes narrow in triumph.

All I can do is stare at her. Then I remember she's still clenching my wrist, and I wrench my arm from her vice-like grip.

She sits back, clasps her knobbly hands together and rests them in her lap like she's at tea with the vicar and has just commented on the moistness of the Victoria sponge. She turns her head away from me to look out of the window at the manicured gardens below. I know this is the last thing I'll ever hear Elizabeth Kent-Walters say. She always was going to have the last word. I just never thought it would be that one.

Chapter Five

24 October 1991 – Haxton, Yorkshire

Ronni

'Mi lady, your chariot awaits.' Chopper spins the shopping trolley around and bows with a flourish.

I notice an old cabbage leaf hanging limply over one of the metal rungs, and scrunch up my nose. 'You what?'

'You said your feet are 'urting, didn'ya? So jump in and I'll push.'

'What – you'll push me all the way home? It's miles. Where did you get that battered old thing anyway?'

He shrugs. 'Found it by the trees when I went over for a wazz. 'Spect someone nicked it from Kwiksave when they couldn't be bothered to carry their shopping 'ome.'

'What if the police see us? They might think *we* nicked it.'

Chopper throws his head back and laughs. 'I wouldn't expect Lenny Fairweather's daughter to give a toss what 'pigs thought.'

Before I have a chance to answer, he scoops me up and pulls me to him. 'If we 'ad twenty mile to walk, I'd push ya all the way, because you, beautiful, are mine.' He lands a kiss straight on my lips, then pulls away and flashes me a gorgeous grin. He looks just like Alex James from Blur, which was why I noticed him on registration day at college. Good job we got together in the first week, because it ended up being Chopper's first and last in further education.

I giggle. I love it when he calls me "beautiful", which he does all the time, even though I'm not. Not really. I know I'm not grotesque or anything, but I'm just a mousy-haired, short-arse, average weight, average-looking lass if I'm honest. Not like Laura with her petite figure, porcelain skin and glossy, dark hair. The lads all go mad for her, but for some reason, which I haven't quite fathomed, Chopper only seems interested in me, even though there are plenty of lasses who'd happily take my place.

The remnants of his beery kiss still linger on my lips and I breathe him in. He's all leather jacket, Hugo Boss and a trace of Benson & Hedges.

He lifts me into the trolley, despite my squeals, and the cold metal stings my legs. It's freezing and I hug my knees to my chest, thinking I should have worn tights, and wriggle my tight mini skirt as far down my thighs as it will stretch, which isn't far at all.

''Old on, Ronni, I'm taking you for t'ride of your life.'

Chopper charges forward with the trolley – and me inside it. It has a dicky wheel which makes it shudder so much my screams and laughter have a robotic quality.

'What's the rush?' I yell.

'I wanna get back before pubs start turfin' out. Otherwise it'll be trolley dodgems.'

He bumps me down a kerb and the trolley leans over so far I think it's going to tip. I grab on to the metal rungs and laugh so hard I'm sure my lungs are about to burst.

'Jesus, Chopper. You're gonna kill me if you're not careful.'

'No chance, beautiful.' He stops just long enough to give me a long, lingering snog that makes my insides tingle. 'I promised yer dad I'd get you 'ome safe and what I promise, I deliver.' He starts running with the trolley again and I swivel around on my backside to face him. His curtain hairstyle flops in front of his eyes as he runs, and he flicks it away with a toss of his head.

'You scared of my dad, by any chance?' I shout over the din of four flimsy wheels bashing over tarmac.

'Nah.' He pants, grinning down at me. 'He likes me, does yer dad. Doesn't give me any grief for taking you out, doesn't seem to mind if you stay round at mine. I don't wanna let him down by not getting you 'ome in one piece.'

'Oh, aye?' I say, touched at his decency. Chopper doesn't have the greatest reputation around Haxton for being a man of upstanding values, but I know him better than most, and I know he's got a heart of gold.

'Why do you think he likes you then?'

''Cos I'm tall, dark, 'andsome and gentlemanly. And a good Yorkshire lad n'all. It all makes for perfect breeding material.' He waggles his eyebrows, making me laugh out loud.

'That's bollocks. It's because he likes you coming round on your motorbike, so he can drool over it.'

'Yeah, that and t'fact I've got money. Keeps his daughter in a manner to which she deserves.'

'Money?' I laugh. 'Are you joking?'

He's breathing harder now as he runs up Syke Hill. 'Got more than most our age now I'm out grafting instead of that college bullshit. And it keeps you in lager 'n' black and a packet of cheese 'n' onion every Saturday night, dunnit?'

This is true, but while Chopper's laying bricks, I'm building my own future by studying at college. It might not be paying off now, but it's not now I'm so bothered about. I'm biding my time till the year after next when I can go to uni. I'm about to tell him so when his eyes widen and he swerves the trolley as quickly as it will go with its dodgy wheel.

I'm thrown to the side but manage to cling on and stay inside.

'Fuckin'ell, Chopper, you and your lass nearly went for a right burton then!'

I spin around and see a group of young men and women pouring out of The Royal Oak. I recognise some of them from school even though they were a few years older than me. The girls are all in heels and low-cut tops and the lads have smart shoes and bomber jackets. It's like they're dressed in their own Saturday night uniform. I look down at my own get-up and realise I'm pretty similar.

'Today, Kwiksave trolley, tomorrow top-of-t'range Kawasaki,' shouts Chopper without slowing down.

'You sure know how to treat a woman, Chopper!' shouts one of the girls.

We turn the corner into Gladbeck Road, *my* road, and their laughter fades into the distance.

''Ere we are, mi lady. Told you I'd get you back in one piece.'

He helps me out of the trolley and places me on the pavement, then pulls me in for a long, sexy kiss.

'Are you coming in, then?' I ask when we finally come up for air.

'Depends.'

'On what?'

'Is yer dad in?'

I laugh. 'So you *are* scared of him.'

Under the orange glow of the street light I can tell he's blushing. And Chopper doesn't do much blushing.

''Course not. Just don't think he'd like me so much if I keep him up all night banging 'is daughter.'

I slap my arm against his leather jacket. 'Do you mean *making love*?' I know this thing I've got with Chopper isn't love, but it sounds rough calling it "banging".

He shrugs. 'Call it wha' you like. So, is yer old man in then, or what?'

'Or what, I expect. He spends most weekends round Donna's these days. Says they're just mates, but I don't shag *my* mates. He must think I'm daft.'

'I wish you *did* shag your mates.' He cocks his head to next door's house. 'I wouldn't mind seeing you and Laura Bailey copping off together.'

'Oi, you.' I slap his other arm.

'Just jesting ya.' He squeezes both my buttocks and nuzzles his face into my neck. His hot lips are on my skin making me want more of him on more of me. I only lost my virginity a month back – to Chopper, of course – and now I'm seeing what all the fuss is about. Sex, at least with Chopper, is definitely *not* overrated.

'Come on then, let's get inside,' I say, grabbing his hand and tugging him towards the front door.

'Be there in a sec,' he says, pulling away and steering the trolley over to the road. Just gonna get this in mi van.'

'What do you want that for?'

'Might come in useful when mi mum's delivering her Avon stuff around t'estate.' He opens the back doors of the rusty yellow Transit van, jumps inside and heaves the hunk of metal into the back.

'Good job it's empty in there. Where are all your tools?'

'Take 'em out on a night, don't I? Mi brother's van got done over last week so I'm emptying mine every night now. Can't afford to buy 'em all again.'

'Did you forget that?' I nod towards the solitary bucket tucked into the corner.

'Nah, can't take that inside 'ouse. Mi mum'd go spare. It's the one I use if I need a shit when I'm on a job.'

I pull a face. 'You shit in a bucket? Why not use the toilet?'

''Cos there aren't any bogs on 'alf of the sites I'm on.' He jumps down from the van and throws the doors shut.

'Oh, shit!' I shout into the still air.

'Yeah, and I piss in it n'all,' he says.

'No, I mean *shit* – I forgot my house key.'

'No problem, beautiful.' He ruffles my long hair which must be a right mess now after the trolley dash. 'We'll 'ead over to mine.'

'But you live halfway across town and I'm not getting in that death trap again.'

'I'll drive.'

'You can't, you've been drinking.'

'I 'ardly touched the stuff tonight – only 'ad four pints and a couple o' shots. I'll be fine.'

'Are you sure?'

He walks around to the passenger door, unlocks it and pulls it open for me. 'Safe as 'ouses,' he says, gesturing for me to climb in.

I step up inside the van, and Chopper takes the opportunity to put his hand up my skirt and tickle me over my knickers.

'Stop it, I'll fall out!' I laugh, and slap his hand away.

'Can't 'elp myself. You're just so sexy. Can't wait to get you into my bed.'

He shuts the door and I blow a kiss at him through the glass. He responds by thrusting his pelvis forward. I spot old Mr Keyton walking his dog on the other side of the road. He's watching Chopper with a frown. I clamp my hand over my mouth. Chopper thinks I'm laughing at him so he makes a show of doing more pelvic thrusting. I can hardly contain myself and by the time he's climbed into the driver's seat, tears are running down my cheeks.

'What?' he asks, turning the key in the ignition and pulling away.

'Never mind,' I say. 'God, I'm gonna miss this when I move away.'

He gives me a sideways glance. 'Move away?'

'When I go to university.'

'Don't talk soft, Ronni. You're not off to university.'

'What do you mean?'

He changes gear and leans his elbow against the window. 'How many kids from 'axton go to university?'

'I don't care how many go. *I'm* going.'

'Well—' He breaks off his sentence and I turn my head to look at him. His jaw is set making him look uncharacteristically serious.

'Well what?' I prompt.

'I just don't get why you want to move away from 'axton. Yer dad's 'ere, yer mates are 'ere. *I'm* 'ere.'

I let out a surprised laugh, then stop when he doesn't join in.

'What's funny?' he asks without taking his eyes away from the road. 'I thought we 'ad something special, you and me.'

'We've only been seeing each other a couple of months, Chopper. I thought we were just having fun. That's what you said.'

'Yeah, at the start maybe.'

I look down at my hands, not sure where to take this next. We're getting on great, but not for one second do I think this is a long-term thing. Chopper, as funny and sweet as he is, doesn't form part of the future I have planned for myself.

'I like ya, Ronni. A right lot.'

'I like you too.'

'No, I mean, I *really* like ya. I think I might love ya.'

That makes me look up at him.

He meets my gaze and I half expect to see his lips flicker as a sign he's having me on, but they don't.

'Chopper—' I begin.

'You're the first girl I've felt this way about, Ronni.' He reaches over and lays a warm hand on my knee.

Neither of us says another word for the rest of the short journey. The only sounds are the chug of the van's unhealthy engine and the faint hum of Bryan Adams on the radio singing "(Everything I Do) I Do it For You". We pull up outside his house and he turns off the engine, plunging us into an eerie quiet that pierces my ear drums.

He shifts his body around so his shoulder is leaning into the seat and he's facing me. He stretches his arm over to me and strokes my hair. 'I wasn't shitting about when I said I love ya.'

I risk a glance over at him and really, really don't know how best to react. I wasn't expecting this tonight, or ever, from Chopper Wallington. He's a lovely bloke and I don't want to throw his heartfelt words back in his face, but nor do I want to lie and tell him I'm staying when that's never, ever going to happen.

I do the only thing I can. 'I love you too,' I say. Maybe it's not a lie – maybe I do love him, I just don't recognise the feeling because it's not something I've had before. Maybe we can continue being *in love* for another year before I go off to university, and in that time he might get bored of me, fall out of love and that will be that. No broken hearts, no hard feelings. Job's a good'un.

He beams, pulls my hand up to his lips and kisses my knuckles. 'One day you and me are gonna get wed, Ronni Fairweather. I want loadsa kids n'all. We'll be a proper 'appy family.'

I force a smile and glance over his head at the council house where he lives with his mum and brother. An image of an older me aged about thirty living in that house flashes behind my eyes. I'm picking up grubby underwear that's been strewn on the floor and am almost knocked flying by a bunch of our brood thundering past. Chopper's shouting at the footy on the telly in between swigs from his can of lager. The Chopper in my fantasy lets out a loud, raspy fart, congratulates himself, then resumes shouting at the TV.

'Plenty of time for all that,' I say.

He leans forward and kisses the end of my nose 'Can't wait, beautiful. Now 'ow about we get you inside so I can put this to good use.' He rubs his crotch and gives me one of his grins that normally makes me melt. This time though, my heartbeat remains regular and my tummy doesn't somersault. I'm going to have to put my acting skills to good use tonight because, with all his talk of marriage and kids, my libido has completely timed out.

Chapter Six

29 June 2018 – Guildford, Surrey

Raegan

'Why didn't you tell us, Rae?'

Lucy curls her jazzy lycra-clad legs under her pert bottom, making barely a dip in my white leather sofa. 'We'd have been round like a shot to look after you and Sabrine,' she adds, taking a tissue out of her Mulberry handbag and dabbing her eyes. 'I can't believe Matthew's been gone over a week and you didn't feel you could come to us.'

'Sorry,' I say, rubbing my forehead to try and clear the dull ache that's festering there from all the crying I've done. 'I've just had so much to get my head around and yet I can't think straight. I've been with Matthew for so long that now he's gone, I feel like I've lost a massive part of myself – like a couple of limbs, or something. I know it sounds stupid …'

She shakes her head. 'No, it doesn't. Not at all. It really makes you think, doesn't it? You think you're going to live until you're old and grey and then someone you know just drops down dead from heart failure at forty-four. I still can't believe it.'

I swallow, guilty at the lie I've told. Even though Lucy and Charlotte are my closest friends, I'm too ashamed to tell them it was suicide. They'd wonder why he did it and soon come to the conclusion it's all because of me.

'And there's been so much to do,' I add, changing the subject. 'Picking Sabrine up from Felbury, organising the funeral, telling Matthew's work – and I still haven't managed to visit the bank. God knows what's going on with our accounts.'

'Whatever you need, we'll help,' Charlotte announces as she enters my living room carrying a tea tray. She hands each of us a mug of Rooibos and gives me a sympathetic smile with a whole lot of mouth. Her lips have gone up a size again. I have a lot of time for Charlotte. I love her matter-of-fact attitude and her quick-wittedness, but at fifty-eight, her love for cosmetic surgery is making her look more and more like an ageing Jessica Rabbit.

'That's really good of you, girls,' I say, 'but there are some things I just have to take care of myself.'

'And what about you, Rae?' Lucy flicks her long, blonde hair over her shoulder. 'Who's taking care of you?'

I shake my head. 'To be honest, I can't think of that right now. I need to focus on Sabrine, and making sure she's all right.'

'How's she taking it?' asks Charlotte, her lips engulfing an M&S Finest shortbread finger.

'As to be expected.' A whiff of steam from my mug floats past my nostrils and the herbal blend reminds me of the day of Matthew's death. I lower the mug to my lap. 'She's cried a lot. We both have. Neither of us is sleeping much. She's been coming into my room most nights. Sometimes we just lay awake, hugging each other until it's a respectable time to get up.'

'Oh, poor darling. Is she still planning on going travelling?' Lucy hands me the biscuit tin and I shake my head at the offering.

'Yes. We've talked about it and I've said I think she should still go. It'll help her take her mind off things and she's been planning it for months with the other girls.'

'A whole year away.' Lucy sighs. 'How wonderful to be young. But will you be alright without her, Rae? After what's happened?'

'I can't hold her back. I'll just have to get together with you girls more often.'

There's a duet of agreements and thoughtful tea-sipping.

'With your friends around you and some professional help, you'll have all the support you need,' says Lucy.

'Professional help?' I ask.

Presumably you and Sabrine are seeing counsellors?'

'Oh. I haven't thought about it, actually. Not since the police gave me the leaflets.'

Lucy pulls a sleek-looking phone out of her bag and taps a long and perfectly polished nail at it a few times. 'I can highly recommend mine. She's *fabulous*. There. I've sent you the details.'

'Thanks. I'll have a look.'

'Grief counselling'—Lucy clicks a button on the side of her phone and slips the device back into her bag—'is vital.'

'My sister-in-law's a counsellor,' says Charlotte. She hovers her hand over the biscuit tin and wriggles her fingers before making her choice. I don't know how she does it – manages to stay a size eight with her sweet tooth. 'When Cyan died, she recommended that we share memories and look at old photographs together as a family.'

'Who's Cyan?' asks Lucy.

'Our Lhasa Apso.' Charlotte sniffs. 'I was absolutely heartbroken when she passed.'

If anyone other than Charlotte compared the death of their dog to that of my husband, I may have been offended, but having known Charlotte for twenty years, since we lived close to one another when I first moved to Surrey and she invited me to join the local book club, I know how much she adores her pets. The love she has for her dogs far outweighs that she feels for her current husband, or the three before that, come to think of it.

'I knew something was wrong, I just *knew* it,' Lucy says, seemingly unperturbed by the passing of Cyan. 'When I went to get my extensions done, Lydia mentioned you'd missed your root touch-up appointment. I should have realised then that it had to be something serious.'

I reach up and touch my parting. It's slick with grease and I can't remember the last time I washed my hair, or even had a shower for that matter.

'Well, I thought there must be something going on when you didn't show up for Hot Yoga on Monday,' adds Lucy. '*And* Tara Grunwald said she'd seen you in Waitrose the other day without any make-up on. That didn't add up to me. The Raegan Kent-Walters I know wouldn't be seen dead putting the bins out without make-up, never mind—*oops*.' She slaps her hand over her mouth. 'Sorry.' She cringes. 'I'm just so desperate not to say the *d-word* that it comes flying out of my mouth.'

'Don't worry about that,' I say. 'It's me who should be sorry, for not letting you both know sooner.'

'For goodness' sake, Luce.' Charlotte raises her eyebrows but her forehead remains frozen in place. 'Poor Rae is about to bury her husband and you're talking about her not wearing make-up to the supermarket.'

Charlotte looks at me out of the corner of her eye, testing the water to see my reaction, and I can't help but laugh. Charlotte looks relieved and joins in, so does Lucy, but with reddened cheeks.

'Oh, I didn't mean it like that. If it were Tesco I wouldn't think twice about it, but Waitrose is a different matter. I'm surprised they let you in.'

'Luce!' Charlotte almost spits out her tea, which sets me off laughing all over again. Thank God for these women.

'Sorry, I'm sorry!' says Lucy. 'There I go again, shooting my mouth off. I just feel like such a bad friend. I should have texted to check you were alright as soon as Tara said. The signs were all there, that's all I meant.'

'Me too,' adds Charlotte. 'I just wished we'd have come over sooner, you poor thing. You must think we don't care.'

'Don't be silly. Of course I don't think that.'

'Gosh,' says Lucy. 'I can't imagine what you must be going through. So much to have to sort out, on top of dealing with your own grief.'

I manage a nod. I don't want to start talking about my grief. At least if I stay on the topic of practicalities, it helps me function somehow. Delving into the part of my heart where my loss for Matthew is felt the deepest isn't something I'm comfortable doing right now, not even in front of my best friends. If I start diving into that, I really don't know how deep it could go.

Lucy stretches her arm out along the radiator on the wall beside her and sighs. 'Such a big house to manage all on your own too.'

'Oh God.' I press my fingers to my forehead again as the pain darkens. 'The central heating. I don't even know how it works. Matthew did all that too. The fuse board – where is it if something trips? The Range Rover – where does he take it if something goes wrong? Our Wills – I think he had them updated when Sabrine was born, but I can't remember. And I can't even remember which solicitor they're with.'

A pair of toned, tanned arms embrace me in a Chanel-fumed hug.

'We'll help you sort it,' whispers Lucy against my ear.

'Don't you worry, Rae,' says Charlotte. 'Together we'll get it all sorted.'

I rest my head on Charlotte's shoulder and smell the faint biscuit aroma of fake tan. 'I don't know what I'd do without you girls.'

Lucy strokes my hair and soothing sounds are issued by my friendship duo.

'Pardon me for saying so.' Lucy breaks away from the group hug. 'And I'm only telling you this because I love you, Rae. You stink.'

There's a few seconds of silence, before we all burst into giggles through our tears.

'I haven't even thought about having a shower,' I admit, grateful for the moment of comic relief.

Charlotte stands up and makes shooing gestures at me. 'Get yourself upstairs now, you. Have a shower, wash your hair, and put on lashings of hideously expensive moisturiser. I'll fix you some lunch.'

'But—'

'No buts, do as you're told. You don't look like you've eaten all week either. You're even skinnier than usual and that's saying something. You look like a matchstick with the wood scraped off.'

'Thanks, Char.' I'm so grateful at my friend's concern, my eyes fill up with tears all over again.

She puts her hands on her hips. 'Don't start all that again, or you'll set me off. Go. Sort yourself out. Take your time. I'll cancel my Power Pilates class so you've got me for the whole day if you want me. We can make a list of things you need to do and start working through them.'

'I'll catch you later, Rae.' Lucy presses a kiss against my cheek. 'I need to pick Jenson and Casper up from nursery in an hour. Then I'm going to afternoon tea up at Carlton Lodge with the school gate brigade.' She hooks her Mulberry over her arm. 'God, I hate that lot. Such massive bitches.'

'Why are you going then?' I ask.

Lucy and Charlotte stare at me for a second, then burst out laughing. I hesitate, then laugh along. I'd never normally say such a stupid thing. I silently berate myself. I'll have to get a grip because I'm not prepared to lose all this. Not even now Matthew is gone.

'Thanks Char', you're a diamond.'

She looks over from where she's wiping the sink and winks. 'Don't mention it. I know how much you love a cheeky fish finger sandwich.'

'Don't tell Matthew. He'll lecture me about the horrors of carbs.'

It's only when she pauses to look at me that I realise what I've said.

I drive my fingers through my damp hair. 'Oh, Christ. I keep doing that. I keep forgetting he's dead and think I'm going to see his car pull up in the drive or hear his key in the lock.'

She sits down beside me at the kitchen table and squeezes my hand. 'I know. When I lost Cyan, I kept thinking I could hear her shaking her little diamanté lead wanting a walk. It took months before that stopped.'

I feel a rush of fondness for my friend, even though she's going on about that flipping dog again. 'Listen, Char. I really appreciate you looking after me like this. But get going if you need to. Roger'll be wondering where you are.'

She waves a hand as if batting away a fly. 'Oh, bugger him. He's *working* late.' She makes quotation marks with her fingers. 'He's never home much before ten when he first starts seeing a new floozy.'

'What? Not another?'

She gives another flap of her hand. 'Don't worry about that. I don't. In fact, I'm grateful to whichever poor woman it is this time. At least it saves me from having the great lump wanting to have sex with me all the time. Watching that hairy gut jiggling on top of me is such a turn-off that last time I insisted on reading my book while he did what he needed to.'

I pull a face. 'Um, did Roger not mind you doing that.'

She shrugs. 'Didn't seem to. Did his usual push, push, squirt and seemed happy enough if his grunting was anything to go by. *And* it meant I got to the end of the page before falling asleep, which is more than I normally manage.' She flashes a very pleased-with-herself smile.

'Why do you put up with it?'

She raises her eyebrows. 'Put up with what?'

'Your husband being unfaithful.'

She bursts out laughing and I wonder if I've asked another stupid question. Two in one day would be a very bad performance indeed.

'You of all people should know that.'

I blink and my mind whirrs. 'Should I? Why?'

She stops laughing and searches my eyes. She seems confused. 'Well, the same reason you do, of course.'

I look from left to right, thinking the answer must be out there somewhere, but I'm struggling to find it.

'You *know*, with Matthew, I mean,' she continues, but doesn't look so sure of herself any more.

'What about Matthew?'

Her lips part, at least, I think they do. It's difficult to tell with the size of them. 'Come on, Rae. You know what men are like.'

'Not all men have affairs.'

'No,' she says, quieter this time. 'Maybe there are one or two out there who don't.'

'Matthew never had an affair.'

She looks down at her hands.

'Charlotte?'

She doesn't respond.

'Charlotte!'

Finally she looks back up at me.

'Matthew was never unfaithful,' I insist.

'Okay.' Her voice is meek. It doesn't belong to the sassy woman I know.

My heart starts to pound in my chest. 'Are you trying to tell me something?'

'No, darling.' She stands up and crosses the kitchen to the sink, where she picks up the dishcloth and wipes the same spot over and over. 'Just ignore me.' She laughs, but it's more of a strangled sound. 'I'm just cynical because of my own experiences. Not one of my four husbands could keep it in their pants. What are the odds of that? Now, shall we start making that list?'

The fish tastes bitter in my mouth. I force it down, and stand up, sending my plate wobbling and crumbs scattering across the table. 'If there's something I should know, then please tell me.'

She spins around and leans against the kitchen counter. 'I always thought you knew.'

'Knew what?'

'About Matthew.'

'About Matthew's *what*?' I'm shouting now, but I'm so desperate to get her to spit it out that I can't stop myself.

'About his other woman.'

Blood pounds in my head. 'Wh-what?' I feel myself swaying and am only vaguely aware of Charlotte rushing over and guiding me back onto my seat.

A million questions all get stuck in my throat, and all I can do is stare at her with wide eyes.

'It might be a load of rubbish,' she says, although I know she doesn't really believe that. She's just saying it to make me feel better. 'I don't know for sure, it's just that a woman I know from the tennis club works in Matthew's office and she mentioned that, well – it's probably not even true.'

'Mentioned what?' My voice is steadier than my nerves feel.

'Well, just that she saw Matthew a few times going out for lunch with one of the secretaries.'

My racing heart calms. 'Is that it? Going to lunch with someone doesn't mean they're having an affair.'

'No, of course not, but apparently they've been out for dinner together a few times too.'

'On work dinners with the whole department? Yes, I know about those. Matthew always tells me – *told* me – if he was going to be home late.'

'No, Rae, not with the whole department. Just the two of them.'

'Probably to discuss sensitive work issues that only he and one of the department secretaries could be aware of. Matthew had a lot of important clients who insisted on non-disclosure agreements. I know that. He did actually talk to me, you know.'

'And last year,' she continues. 'He went away with her for a week. That's how I thought you must definitely know something was going on.'

'Yes, the seminar in Geneva. I know all about that, Char. Half the company went. Matthew really didn't want to go because it was my birthday weekend, but he couldn't get out of it.'

Charlotte shook her head. 'There was no seminar, Rae. It was just the two of them.'

I let out a laugh, thinking the world had gone mad and this was some sort of weird joke. I expect Charlotte to shout *gotcha* and laugh along, but her face remains straight.

'Wait a second.' I place both palms flat against the table. 'A week ago, my life was perfect. Normal. I had a loving husband, who was alive and well, and now he's dead, his body barely cold, and you're telling me that he was having an affair?'

She shakes her head. 'I shouldn't have opened my big mouth.'

'Who is she?'

'On the other hand,' she says, more to herself than me. 'It's bound to get out sooner or later. Maybe it's better you hear it from someone who loves you.'

'Who is she?'

'I don't know.' She shuffles her feet. She's lying.

'Who *is* she?' I demand.

Charlotte lets out a deep lungful of air. 'I think her name's Isobella or Annabella, something like that. I don't know her surname.'

I storm over to the corner of the kitchen where my handbag's sitting on the counter, and rifle through, searching for the cold metal of my car keys. 'Right. I'm going over to the office now to ask her outright.'

'No, don't do that, darling.' Charlotte's next to me, gripping me by the shoulders.

'I have to!' My voice sounds high-pitched and desperate even to my own ears. 'If everyone in this bloody city thinks my dead husband was a cheat, I need to clear his name. I owe him that at least'

'You can't.'

I stop searching and glare at her. 'I can, and I will. I won't have my husband's memory ruined when he's done nothing wrong.'

'Raegan—' Charlotte's stroking my arm, but I won't let her put me off.

'I need to do this, Charlotte. I need to know the facts, then that woman at the tennis club will maybe keep her mouth shut in future before she spreads rumours about some other poor, innocent soul.'

'You can't go to the office, Rae.'

'I can and I will.' I plunge my hand back into my handbag but all I can feel are crumpled up old tissues and loose lipsticks.

'She's not there.'

'Then where the hell is she?'

She pauses, as if she's about to say something, then stops herself.

'Charlotte,' I say, in as calm a voice as I can muster. 'Where the fuck is she?'

Her shoulders sag and she looks at me with sad eyes. 'You won't find her at the office because she left a few months ago. She's on maternity leave, Rae. She had a baby boy.'

Chapter Seven

13th July 2018 – Farnworth, Surrey

Raegan

If the last two weeks have been the worst of my life, I'm not holding out a great deal of hope for today, the day I cremate Matthew. The only consolation is at least it will soon be over. Up until only a few days ago I thought I was going to have to postpone the funeral; the post-mortem they were insisting on still hadn't been carried out and the bloody coroner couldn't even confirm the date until the last minute.

They managed it, finally, and found nothing other than he'd died of asphyxiation. I don't understand why they wanted to cut up his body. I don't have a white coat or a science degree but I could have told *them* the cause of death – he'd been found hanging with his belt, the police had confirmed that. Doesn't take a genius to figure out what did it.

The police paid me another visit last week, asking me a load of questions. They even brought Matthew's personal belongings back, including the belt. Like I'd want that back! It was the black leather Gucci one I'd bought him for his fortieth birthday. That's the bit that hurt more than anything.

It was a relief Sabrine had been out at the time the police visited. I know I'll have to tell her the truth soon, but I can't face it yet, and don't think she could either. The only people who know the truth are Melanie, Elizabeth and Julie at the care home. It helps that Melanie couldn't make it for the service, too busy running her yoga retreat on the other side of the world to attend her brother's funeral. After my aborted attempt to tell Elizabeth, Melanie broke the news over the phone to her mother herself. Julie told me she was so confused she thought Matthew was her old classics teacher. Probably for the best.

Julie thought it would be too upsetting for Elizabeth to attend the funeral, which I'm beyond grateful for as it means I don't have to deal with her calling me a dirty, common whore, and also that we should get through the day without Sabrine or anyone else finding out the true cause of Matthew's death. Another plus is that Sabrine says she's too upset to go and see her grandmother, as she likes to remember her, not how she is now, but how she was. I personally don't get this, because as far as my memory goes back, she's always been a bitch, but I told Sabrine I understood entirely.

It works for me. It means I can tell her the truth about her father at another time. When we're both ready.

A strand of Sabrine's hair tickles my nose as she sobs silently on my shoulder. I'm glad she can't see my face because my eyes are dry as the celebrant waxes lyrical about Matthew – loving husband and son, dedicated father, ambitious career man, blah, blah, blah. She doesn't mention anything bad, like the fact he chose to die. I made her promise she wouldn't. She said it wouldn't be appropriate anyway; the service was about celebrating life, not commiserating death.

Even though I know she's only going to say good things, I'm still half waiting to hear the part where she tells the packed crematorium Matthew was a lying, cheating shit who got another woman pregnant, but it never comes.

It never comes, because it's not true, I remind myself. I thought Elizabeth's words the other day had the power to shock, until I heard Charlotte's, whom I notice has thought better of coming today after our little spat. I've thought about little else other than our conversation since we had it, and have turned it over and over in my mind until it all finally started to make sense. Charlotte, who I thought was my friend, is judging my marriage by her standards and assuming we all have the same warped deals with our husbands as she does with filthy rich and even filthier-minded Roger. Yeah, he has more money than God, but can he keep his dick in his trousers? Like hell he can. And that's the trade-off. She, of course, is fine with that, as long as her allowance is generous enough to afford weekly salon appointments at Oliver James, three cruises a year and Lakeland's top-of-the-range spiralizer.

Well, the same is not true of my Matthew. Matthew *was* a loving husband, a dedicated father and an ambitious career man. One thing he definitely was not was an unfaithful bastard. Telling myself that over and over is so exhausting, I have no energy left to cry.

I endure the rest of the service in a daze and focus my efforts on comforting Sabrine. We lead the mourners out of the crematorium and as the bright daylight of the outside engulfs me, I feel like I can finally breathe again. What seems to be a never-ending stream of people offer their condolences. I nod, smile and mutter my thank-yous until I feel like an automaton. I'm at the end of a pity production line and must remember my phrase: 'Please join us for sandwiches and drinks at Carlton Lodge. Please join us for sandwiches and drinks at Carlton Lodge. Please join us for dandwiches and shrinks at Larlton Codge.' I correct myself and glance down the line, my heart sinking as I see the stream of mourners before me doesn't seem to have diminished. It's the first time I've not been happy Matthew is so – was so – popular.

The crowd finally thins out as a convoy of executive saloons and four-by-fours file away out of the grounds headed for one of the most refined hotels in the county; a fitting send-off for a refined man like my Matthew.

'Ready, Mrs Kent-Walters?'

I nod at the undertaker and put my arm around Sabrine, guiding her to the car. That's when I notice a pretty, young, slim woman with long blonde hair that reaches halfway down her back. She's standing by the entrance to the crematorium looking directly at me. Her make-upless face is red and blotchy from crying, and she has one hand resting on an object beside her. At first I think it's a suitcase, but then I realise it's a pram. My heart bangs inside my chest as I hear Charlotte's voice in my head. *I think her name's Isobella or Annabella, or something.*

'Mummy?'

'Sorry, sweetie, did you say something?' I tear my gaze away from the woman with the pram to look at Sabrine, who instantly looks over at the blonde.

'Who's that?'

'Oh, I don't know, just someone Daddy knew, I expect.'

'I've never seen her before.'

'No, me neither. Maybe she came to the wrong funeral.'

She knits her brow. 'She looks pretty upset.'

'Well it would be annoying, wouldn't it, turning up at the wrong funeral.'

Sabrine looks at me like I've just landed from Planet Crazy.

'Oh well, I don't know,' I say, flapping my hand, wanting the conversation to go away. 'Maybe she and Daddy worked together. He was well-loved. He knew a lot of people. It really doesn't matter. Let's just get this day over with so you and I can move forward.' I kiss her forehead where the skin on her brow is still puckered in a frown.

The interior of the funeral car is spotless and smells of leather and furniture polish. It crunches over the gravel drive, straight past the woman and her pram. The car windows are tinted and even though I know there's no way she can see me, her eyes still burn into mine as we pass.

Chapter Eight

25 December 1991 – Fairhills, Yorkshire

Ronni

''Appy Christmas, Ronni, love.'

'Happy Christmas, Dad.' I smile back at him. He's got a couple of teeth missing from fights he's been in over the years. He was meant to go back to the dentist to get false ones put in. They said they'd do it on the NHS, but he didn't show up for the appointment. Said he didn't want to miss valuable pub time, so now he's got two gaping holes where teeth should be. Not that he seems all that bothered. "Lager's not crunchy", he says.

'It's nice to spend Christmas Day with mi little 'un. Not that yer all that little now. Don't s'pose it'll be long before you bugger off int' big wide world and don't give a toss any more about yer poor old dad.'

'Don't talk soft, Dad.' I pluck the plastic mermaid from my glass and take a slurp of orange squash.

'Ah, take no notice of yer daft dad,' he says, flicking open his rolly tin. 'I'm just getting sentimental in mi old age. I 'ope you *do* go off to university, love – a clever lass like you should. Go and show them posh twats 'ow it's done. Nice to come out for Christmas, though, init? It's not been the same at 'ome, ever since yer mum, well, ya know.'

I nod, and knock back a cube of ice. I crunch the freezing block with my teeth and wince, although I'm not sure if it's from the cold or the words Dad can't bring himself to say.

'I know it's not exactly t'Ritz, like, but it's all right 'ere, init?'

I look around the room. Even the garish brown and green patterned carpet can't hide the amount of beer stains. The ceiling brandishes yellow cloud-shaped stains from all the fags that have been smoked in here since the dawn of time, and the whole of the clientele put together doesn't possess enough teeth to make one complete mouthful. This place isn't all right; it's the armpit of the world.

'Yeah, it's all right,' I say, and shift along the pub bench to let an elderly couple sit down at the next table. The palm of my hand catches on the bench, where a piece of the upholstery is torn and some scratchy stuff is spewing out.

Dad winks at me and licks the edge of his cigarette paper, before rolling it around the tobacco path he's lined up.

For all Dad's misdemeanours and all that he lacks in dental work, he's an intelligent man. No way on earth does he think that Fairhills Working Men's Club is anything but a complete shithole. When he says "all right", he means the beer's cheap and that if Donna's working not only does he get an eyeful of her massive tits, but she'll often slip him a free packet of Mini Cheddars for me.

I come to the pub with him less and less these days. It's easier doing homework in my bedroom than in the corner of a pub – although after several years of practice, I'm pretty adept at switching out the background noise and concentrating on conjugating verbs or deciphering algebra. The downside, of course, is that if Dad's out on his own, it's more likely he'll get into bother. Me being there doesn't mitigate the possibility entirely, but it does minimise the chances. Depends how tanked up he is.

'Oh, look.' He nods across at where a sparkly-corseted Donna's distributing something among the tables. 'Bingo cards are coming out. Love a bit o' bingo, me. Wanna play?'

No. 'Yeah, why not.'

With his fag in his mouth, he shifts over to one buttock and delves in his pocket for change.

'This one's on 'ouse, Lenny,' says Donna, as she places a handful of bingo strips on our table. One of her fleshy breasts looks in grave danger of flopping out of her top and into Dad's pint. ''Appy Christmas.'

He gives her a wink. 'Ah, thanks, Donna love, and 'appy Christmas to you n'all.'

Donna makes her way to the next table, and Dad blows out a stream of smoke.

'Aye, it's all right this Christmas malarkey, init? You get stuff for nowt. It's normally a quid a book.'

'Grand,' I say. 'How do we play this, then?'

''Ere you go, love. You can use one of my dabbers.' The old betty on the next table hands me a short, chunky pen. 'Just dab it on t'number when they call it out. Be careful though, you don't need to press on too 'ard otherwise you'll get yersen in a right mess.'

'Thanks very much,' I say, pulling off the lid and inspecting the red spongy tip.

Donna calls out the numbers far too fast for my brain-dabber co-ordination. Just as I start getting the hang of it, the game gets interrupted by a fight between two women. It seems that the girl behind the bar won't serve some lass because she's too pissed. The lass shouts a racist insult at her while lunging across the bar, declaring she's going to "smack her head in". The bingo is held up by about six seconds and all the old betties in the place are well miffed, because we haven't even been playing long enough for anyone to get a line yet.

Some of the blokes manage to break up the fight and everyone cracks back on with the bingo as if nothing ever happened. We even get a line and Dad wins a mug that has "Jesus Saves ... at the Bethlehem Building Society" emblazoned across it. He's right chuffed with it. He pours some of his pint in it and slides it across the chipped wooden table to me.

'There you go, lovie,' he says proud as punch, as if it's the Holy Grail. 'Yer first Christmas tipple.'

It wasn't my first, and he knew it. He's been letting me have tipples – and not just for Christmas – since I was a kid. Not that I like it all that much. A couple of halves of lager 'n' black on a Saturday night when I'm out is my limit. I'd still rather have an orange squash, but when I ask for one, Chopper sneaks vodka into it, thinking I won't notice, and I can't stand vodka.

I don't go down the park much with Laura these days because all she and the rest of them want to do is sit on the swings and drink White Lightning. Waste of time. I'd rather be studying for school. It might not be fun but at least it should get me somewhere; somewhere hopefully a bit better than Fairhills Working Men's Club.

Later on, we all get a free party popper. Some folk even get a cracker, but me and Dad miss out on them because there aren't enough to go around. My party popper backfires and burns my finger. I end up having to stick it in the Jesus Saves mug to stop it from blistering, although the lager inside is warm now so I'm not sure it helps much. At least it gives me an excuse not to have to clap along to the turn. June Ashfield's on doing all the Christmas classics. I've seen her before when I've been out with Dad. She does all the working men's clubs around Leeds. Massive woman, she is. *June, July and August*, Dad calls her.

Dad's puffing away on his rolly and ash is flying everywhere as he's singing along to whatever June's belting out. And that's when it hits me. It's like I've been slapped in the face by that angry lass who couldn't get served. It's nearly time. My time. Never again will I have to spend Christmas Day playing bingo in the arsehole of Leeds pub land. It's not long now before the highlight of my week will not be when Donna liberates a packet of Mini Cheddars for me. And in a few months' time I'll no longer be the girlfriend of a bloke who craps in a bucket in the back of his van.

Just thinking about what my life could be is enough to send a fizz of excitement through me. Energised with hope, I pull my still sizzling finger out of the lukewarm lager and take a few big gulps from the mug. Warmth floods through my veins. I smile over at Dad, who lights another fag, then ruffles my hair. I throw one arm around his neck, and another around the betty who gave me the bingo dabber and is now three sheets to the wind, and together we sway in time to June Ashfield warbling about seeing Mummy kissing Santa Claus.

Chapter Nine

24 July 2018 – Guildford, Surrey

Raegan

'And you say you only have the one account?'

'Yes,' I say, feeling the temperature of my blood rise another degree. The bank employee who, according to his name badge is "Andrew Tanner" and is "here to help", is really starting to get on my tits. He's asked me the same thing three times and so far still hasn't managed to produce an answer to my question of how much money is in our account.

He clicks his computer mouse with one hairy-knuckled finger and uses his other hand to stroke his hipster beard. In the reflection of his glasses I can see the white glare of his computer screen and rows of numbers flying past as he scrolls.

'So, you and Mr Kent-Walters only have one joint current account and—'

'And one Maxi-Saver account, yes, that's right,' I say, finishing his sentence off for him.

'You said you thought there was about a hundred thousand in the Maxi-Saver, is that correct?'

I stifle a sigh. 'Around about that, yes. As I said, I'd just like you to confirm the exact amount please, and also the precise figure that's in the joint account, which I think should be around seven thousand.'

More scrolling, mouse-clicking and beard-stroking, but no answers.

'I'm sorry, is there a problem?' I say, leaning forward and not even trying to hide my agitation this time.

Andrew Tanner lets go of his mouse, steeples his fingers and, so the beard-stroking doesn't have to stop, rests his chin on his fingers and moves his head up and down. 'I'm very sorry to say this, Mrs Kent-Walters, but according to my screen, the balance of your Maxi-Saver is three pounds and fifty-one pence.'

I blink, trying to make sense of what he's telling me. 'Three pounds fifty?'

'Fifty-*one*.'

'I don't understand. We always kept it at a hundred grand.'

'When was the last time you checked the account?'

'What? Oh, I never check it. My husband always dealt with the banking.'

'I see.' He moves his fingers up to his lips and starts stroking them now. 'Could it be that your husband might have moved the funds over to another bank?'

My heart rises in my chest. Of course, that's it! Thank God for Andrew Tanner and his quick-thinking logic. Matthew's moved accounts and didn't think to mention it to me. Why would he? He did all the banking. 'Can you check please? Presumably your screen will tell you if he's made a big transfer to another bank.'

'Yes, certainly.' He pushes his glasses up the bridge of his nose and turns back to his computer. 'Hmm, that's interesting … oh, there's one large transfer … and another … ah yes.'

'Oh, so you've found it, good. Which bank did he move it to?' I edge forward in my seat, trying to peer round at his screen. I hope it's not Lloyds, because I don't much care for the colour of their new debit cards.

'Yes, I mean, no. What I mean is, I've found the transfers, but they weren't to another bank in his or your names.'

'What then – a building society?'

'Not exactly.' He turns his screen around to me and points a finger at a number on the screen. 'On the third of February there was a transfer of just over twenty thousand to a Miss A Pentecost. That's the first big one. Then—' He scrolls the wheel of his mouse. 'There are a series of payments to Luxus Casino in London. One for three thousand, this one on the eighth of March for two and a half thousand, one two weeks later for a similar sort of amount, then another …'

He's still talking, listing dates and the huge figures that were siphoned out of our joint bank account to some casino I never even knew Matthew went to and a person I've never heard of. I'm losing track of the amounts, and all I can hear is Luxus Casino this, Miss A Pentecost that. With every number he calls out, my lips grow drier. It's like I've died and ended up in the bingo hall of Hell. I thought anything was better than listening to him stroking the scratchy bristles of his chin, but how blissful that was in comparison. Any second now, the list is going to end, but I can't wait that long. 'Can you tell me how much in total went to this Pentecost person and how much to the casino?'

'Erm, yes. I'll just do a search … just shy of forty-four thousand to the Pentecost payee, and the remainder to the casino.'

My heart thunders in my chest. 'You mean, there's nothing left?'

'Oh yes, there's something left.'

'How much?'

'Three pounds—' He squints at the screen. 'Fifty-one pence.'

For Christ's sake. 'And the joint current account? Is there more in that?' There should be. I've hardly spent anything recently, not even for the funeral which, I found out when I finally hunted down the solicitor who had sorted our Wills, Matthew had already paid for years ago when we first bought our house. Just as I'd expected. Well-planned, methodical Matthew.

He turns the screen back to him and hits a few keys. 'Oh yes, there's more in that.'

'Thank God. How much?'

'Eighty-seven pounds ninety-two pence.'

'What?'

'Eighty-seven, ninety-two,' he repeats, slower this time, like he's realised he might be dealing with a moron who's struggling to understand.

I clutch the edge of the desk. 'Please. Tell me. Are there any more accounts in either Matthew's name or mine?'

He looks uncomfortable and starts to scratch at different patches of his head. 'Erm, no, sorry Mrs Kent-Walters. I'm afraid not.'

'Are you telling me that my husband has bled our only two accounts dry to a casino and a woman I've never heard of?'

He licks his lips and his Adam's apple bobs as he swallows. 'It seems that way, yes.'

My mind's whirring and I dart my eyes from side to side, trying to fathom what all of this is about. Matthew doesn't gamble. I didn't even realise he'd ever set foot into a casino. He doesn't even bet on the Grand National. And who the hell is A Pentecost … Pentecost … the name doesn't even ring a bell.

'Wait!' A thought occurs to me, which immediately makes everything a lot less scary.

My exclamation makes Andrew Tanner jump back in his seat.

'Life insurance. We both took it out when we first got our mortgage. I can't remember how much it's for. Enough to cover the mortgage and a six-figure payout, though, I'm sure.'

'Ah, yes.' He looks almost as relieved as I feel, and starts clicking and scrolling again in earnest.

I sit back in my chair. Whatever Matthew's been doing, I'll think about later. I just need reassurance today that me and Sabrine will be okay.

'Sorry to ask a sensitive question, Mrs Kent-Walters, but what did your husband die of?'

'He took his own life.' My voice shakes. I still can't say those words to anyone I know, but strangers like Andrew Tanner – it's somehow cathartic to say it to them, like I'm using them to test the response.

Andrew Tanner's face pales by several shades. At first, I'm touched by his empathy. It's only when he speaks that I realise the true cause of his pallor.

'I'm afraid the insurance doesn't pay out for instances of suicide.'

A noise, somewhere between a sob and attempt at words, escapes my throat. 'Please tell me you're joking,' I manage at last.

He bites his bottom lip, taking some bristles in his mouth with it. 'I'm afraid not.'

'Oh my God,' I whisper. None of this makes sense. I can't think of anything else to say, so I say it again, and again, and again, louder each time. Andrew Tanner keeps the beat to my repetitious blaspheming by stroking his beard, which he does so vigorously I fear he might start a fire.

'Eighty-one pounds, ninety-two pence now,' I say to myself as I pick up the bottle of Chardonnay on *special discount*. My preferred Sancerre it isn't, but it's wet and alcoholic and right now that's all I'm bothered about.

With the news I've just been dealt still spinning around in my head, I make my way down the aisle towards the till, and stumble into an unsuspecting shopper. I mutter an apology and she spins around to face me, wafting me with a cloud of expensive perfume.

'Raegan, *darling*, however are you?'

I search the hazy cells of my brain for where I know this woman who's about my age and wearing a designer label T-shirt tucked into pastel blue capri pants. Her expensive highlighted bob swings perfectly back into shape as she waits for an answer and displays a row of pearly white teeth.

'Tara.' I blurt out as soon as recognition hits. Tara Grunwald, owner of luxury travel firm, wife of extremely handsome and sickeningly wealthy city banker and queen of the yoga mat. This woman spends so much of her time at Surrey Park Golf and Health Club in a downward dog position that it's a wonder she hasn't started barking.

'You'll never believe this but there's a condolence card on my kitchen island waiting for a stamp so I can send it to you.' She transfers her laden shopping basket into her other hand and clasps my wrist. 'Might I just say how sorry I am to hear about Matthew. How are you and that gorgeous girl of yours coping with everything?'

'Fine,' I say automatically. 'We're doing fine.'

'Not taken to self-medicating, have you?' She peers at the bottle in my hand, which I self-consciously shove behind my back.

'No, no. Just a present … for a friend.'

'Oh, look at you. Thinking of others in your hour of need. That says so much for your character. I know you're putting on a brave face, but I can't imagine how hard it must be for the two of you. If there's ever anything I can do for you, anything at all, you just have to say the word.'

'Thank you.' I give a weak smile and turn to go.

'And to take his own life like that.'

I stop in my tracks and turn back to her with a quick sideways glance to see how many people might have heard her not-so-quiet exclamation. Thankfully, other than an elderly woman squinting at the herb shelf, the aisle is deserted.

Tara's words are an unwelcome reminder that I'm going to have to tell those closest to me how Matthew really died before they find out from someone else. If Tara Grunwald knows, it's only a matter of time before the rest of Surrey finds out.

'News travels fast,' I say, unable to keep the bitterness out of my voice.

She takes a step closer to me and slaps a hand to her cheek. 'Oh, I'm sorry, Raegan, darling. I didn't mean to upset you. It just came as such a shock. Richard heard at the country club a couple of weeks ago and I couldn't believe it. Apparently one of the chaps in the kettlebells class works in the coroner's office and recognised Matthew's name. He assumed it was common knowledge. You must miss him so much. I know Richard does. He says Matthew was such a great workout partner, but then he hadn't been to the Country Club for a few months, so we did wonder if something wasn't quite right.'

Despite clutching the chilled neck of the discount wine bottle, my palm prickles with sweat. 'Hadn't been for a few months?'

'Well, no,' she says, her eyes twinkling with an interest she tries to disguise by rubbing her glossy lips together. 'Did you—I mean, far be it for me to pry, but did you not know?'

'I … um, no, it's not that. I, well, he didn't report to me his every move.'

'Oh no, darling, of course not. He was most likely busy at work. Do you know why he did it? Did he leave a note? You weren't the one to find him, were you? Oh my, that must have been *awful* for you. Depression can be a terrible thing. My second cousin suffered for years and tried a couple of times to take an overdose, and in the end—'

'Depression?' I interrupt. 'Matthew wasn't depressed.' *Was he? If he'd been depressed I would have noticed, surely. Then again, I didn't notice him slipping off to spend thousands in a casino, him getting another woman pregnant or emptying our bank accounts.* I'm beginning to wonder if I noticed anything about my husband at all. In the absence of a suicide note, I assumed he'd done it to escape me – that it was my fault somehow. But now, with everything I'm starting to find out … I'm so confused it hurts.

Tara was talking again, onto her next line of enquiry. I can't bear to hear another word. I mumble something about having to go and pick up Sabrine, then hurry to the till.

I step out of the automatic doors of the Co-op and gasp for air. Somehow I manage to put one shaky foot in front of the other and walk down the street. My mind's a jumble of today's revelations: Miss A Pentecost … depression can be a terrible thing … Miss A Pentecost … another payment to the casino … three pounds fifty-one pence … depression can be a terrible thing … Miss A Pentecost …

I'm panting now; can't get enough air into my lungs. I stop and lean against the window of *Londres*, my favourite boutique – the one I wouldn't normally think twice about popping into and blowing a few hundred pounds on a new silk shirt and pair of bum-hugging jeans, or whatever they had in stock that would be *just the thing* for our next cruise, brunch with the girls or even the weekly Waitrose shop.

I press my forehead against the cool glass window and catch a glimpse of the price tags next to the immaculately dressed mannequins. *Gilet £180.00, jeggings £165.00, handbag £260.00.* I have enough in my bank account for precisely half a jegging. I imagine myself sipping cappuccino up at Surrey Park Golf and Health Club wearing only one jegging leg, and burst out laughing.

I laugh, despite being the widow of a man who, for a reason I haven't yet fathomed, chose death over a life with me, despite having eighty quid to my name because my husband blew everything we had at a casino and on a woman I don't know, and despite the only thing I have to look forward to is a night in front of the television with a bottle of *special discount* plonk. I laugh because I don't know what I'm meant to do.

I wipe away the laughter-induced tears and realise I'm standing across the road from Oliver James, the salon where I've been having my hair done for the past decade. Over £200 for a full head of ash blonde highlights every six weeks. 'That's going to have to change,' I say to myself. That's when something inside me budges. A shoot of strength sprouts within me. It's tiny, but I'm in no doubt it's there, and I like the way it feels.

I'm broke – in both senses of the word, but I still have my daughter, my health and my brain. The latter is something I haven't used for a while – not properly, not to anywhere near its full potential. That's something else that needs to change. I adjust my handbag over my shoulder. On feet that are now steadier, I trek across town to the area I normally avoid; the area where the pound shops and charity shops are, and where ValueKutz is located.

'So, a drastic change then?' says Elle, Bell, Nell, or whatever she said her name was.

'Yes. Short and shaggy. Get rid of all the blonde please. I'd like it back to my natural colour, which is a sort of mid-brown.'

'Are you absolutely sure?' she says, fastening the press studs at the back of the extremely unflattering bin bag-style cape she's covered me in, which has the bright pink and gold ValueKutz logo emblazoned on the chest. 'This ash is such a gorgeous shade. It must have taken ages for you to get it like this. And it's a great length, very versatile.' She places a strand of my hair between two of her fingers and pulls it down to just below my shoulders.

'I'm sure,' I say, wishing Elle, Bell or Nell would just get on with it. 'I want it as easy-to-manage as possible.'

'Well, the thing is—' She pulls a comb out of the tool belt around her waist and starts de-tangling my hair. 'The ash blonde platinum blend you've got now hides the grey regrowth really well. You'll find that a warmer colour will emphasise any grey unless you have a regular root tint.'

The comb's fine teeth struggle to get through my wind-swept tresses and the constant snagging on my scalp makes my eyes water. It makes me realise how much I've let my standards slip over the last few weeks and heightens my resolve to chop the whole lot off.

'I don't *have* any grey,' I tell her with a tinge of smugness that although I'm not a natural blonde, nor am I a natural grey.

She peers at my roots. 'I can just see a few here starting to creep through, but you're right that it's not too bad. Most people your age have a lot more.'

My smugness evaporates. I look at her properly for the first time. She's pretty, slightly plump and has a small gold hoop through one side of her nose. She must be about the same age as Sabrine. She probably thinks I'm ancient. I eye her hair, which is pulled up into a messy bun and secured with a silver-sequined scrunchie.

She catches me looking and smiles, misinterpreting my scrutiny as admiration. 'Cute, isn't it?' She points at her scrunchy. 'Claire's Accessories. Can I get you a coffee and a mag?'

'Yes please. Both would be nice.' She hands me a well-thumbed gossip magazine. It's the kind I'd never choose to read – the pit of the celebrity press, with faces on the front cover I don't recognise. I consider asking for a *Good Housekeeping*, but don't, as I'm quite pleased that despite most people *my age* being grey, at least she considers me young enough to read this stuff.

'Got any plans tonight?' she asks, as she mixes my dye in a plastic pot. 'Hot date maybe?' She laughs as if the thought of an ancient creature like me being attractive to a man is the most hilarious joke she's heard all year.

'I'm putting my house up for sale,' I say, realising for the first time that is exactly what I'll be doing this evening. Straight after I break the news to Sabrine that there will be no globetrotting, no pony and no more living in the most expensive county in the country, that is.

'Ooh, that's exciting.' She pastes the gloop onto my hair. A shiver runs down my spine and I'm not sure if it's the cold of the dye or the dread of telling Sabrine.

'What?' Sabrine's mouth hangs open where she'd been about to pop in a spoonful of yoghurt. 'Sell the house? But it's where we've always lived, Mummy. It's where *Daddy* lived. All our memories of him are here. We can't just *leave*.'

'I know, sweetheart, and believe me, it's the last thing I want, but I'm afraid we don't have much choice.'

She drops the spoon into her bowl and a spatter of yoghurt lands on her black top. 'There must be something you can do. Why don't you just go out and get a job?'

'It's not quite that simple. I spoke to the mortgage people this afternoon. We're so behind on payments we have to sell as soon as we can or they'll repossess it and we'll lose everything. Even if I got a job tomorrow, I wouldn't earn enough to pay for this place.'

'Why not? Daddy did.'

'Daddy didn't give up work eighteen years ago, sweetheart. I've been out of the working world for so long, my skills are practically zero. I don't know anything about computers. I can't see anyone wanting to hire me any day soon. I'd have to retrain first and we just don't have time for that.'

Sabrine presses her fingers to her temples. 'I can't believe you expect me to move when this has been my home for my entire life. Don't you know how much I love this house?'

Her pretty face crumples and I cross the kitchen to embrace her. 'Of course I do. And I love it too. If there was any way of keeping it, I would, but we just can't, Sabrine. I'm so sorry, I really am.'

She clutches my arms that are wrapped around her neck. 'Surely, if you just explain to the mortgage people the situation – that Daddy died – they'll understand. Maybe they can reduce our payments for a while until you do get a job.'

She doesn't get it. She doesn't get it because she doesn't know the half of it. Telling her we have to move house is bad enough. I can't break her heart even more by explaining we're on the breadline because her father paid thousands into some strange woman's account and all evidence points to him gambling the rest away. The Matthew I knew and loved would not do these things. He wouldn't put his family's livelihood at risk. I need to find out the truth, but making sure my daughter has a roof over her head is the priority.

She turns around in her chair and looks up at me with big, watery, blue eyes. 'As long as we can stay in Guildford, then I suppose it's okay.'

I shake my head. 'We can't, sweetheart. It's just too expensive around here.'

She springs up, sending me jumping backwards, and stamps her foot. 'I can't *believe* this, Mummy! My daddy's gone and now you're taking me away from all my friends. What next – we have to sell Whitey?'

I look down.

'Oh my God. Oh. My. God! You're kidding me?' She clenches her fists and holds her arms stiffly by her sides. She looks like a giant toddler.

I reach out to touch her arm, but she jolts back. 'I don't know what's going on with you, Mummy. First you come home with this … this weird haircut!' She gestures to my new brunette choppy style that's about as far removed from my usual sleek, shoulder-length blonde hair that's possible to get. 'Then'—she throws up her arms—'you announce I have to sell the pony that I've loved since I was a little girl, *and* that we're moving to some godforsaken hellhole away from all my friends.'

My heart sinks to the shiny tiled floor. I hadn't expected this to go well, but a part of me hoped she might see it as an opportunity for a new start – to get away from the bleakness of Matthew's death. I haven't even got to the hardest part yet.

'Where are we going then?' she asks. 'If we can't stay around here, where is it you're expecting me to live? How about we give Syria a go? There's probably a couple of refugee tents we could afford. Or what about Afghanistan? I've heard it's pretty cheap there at the—'

'I own a house,' I say, interrupting her crass monologue. 'It belonged to my dad. He left it to me when he died. It's all paid off, so we wouldn't have a mortgage to pay.'

'Why don't you just sell *that* house then, and use the money to pay for this one?'

'It's not worth nearly as much as this one. It wouldn't even dent the debt.'

She's shaking her head and her chin's wobbling. 'No, Mummy. I'm not going there.'

'You've never been, Sabrine. My dad died when you were tiny.'

Her head-shaking slows, then stops. A flicker of brightness appears on her tear-stained face. '*I* don't have to live there,' she says, so quietly it's almost to herself. 'I'm going travelling in two weeks for a whole year, then when I come back I'll get a job in London and move into a flat with Bridie, or Octavia or Millie.'

'Listen, sweetheart—'

'You won't sell it in two weeks. I'll be gone first. Oh, thank God.'

'You can't go travelling.'

Her smile fades and she stares at me. 'What do you mean I can't go travelling?'

I lick my lips and hold on to the back of the now vacant chair for support. 'I hate having to say this, but the money Daddy and I were going to give you … it's gone.'

'Gone? Gone where?'

I take a deep breath in. 'On, um, bills and things, I suppose. Expenses. Even if the money was still there, I'd have to use it for the mortgage repayments.'

She slaps both hands down onto the table and her face reddens. 'How could you? How could you do this to me? What am I going to tell Octavia and Bernie? We've made plans to go into town tomorrow to buy new bikinis. I can't tell them I'm now not going travelling. They'll think we can't afford it.'

'We can't, sweetheart.'

She pushes her hands into her hair. 'Mummy, don't say that!' She begins pacing the floor. 'What about if once we've sold the house, I go then? It won't take long to sell – everyone wants to live in this area. It should only take a few weeks, then I could catch up with them in Thailand.'

Although I knew this conversation wasn't going to be easy, I'd hoped that, at eighteen, however much the news disappointed her, she might at least try to understand. I swallow my irritation, telling myself her reaction is to be expected. She's just lost her father and now I'm worsening the situation.

'No, Sabrine,' I say. 'I'd love for that to be possible, but there won't be enough money, even after the sale. We owe so much, and anything that is left over will have to help pay our bills before I can get some sort of job.'

'All I'm hearing from you, Mummy, is no this, no that, no the other. Don't you ever have anything *positive* to say? There's no wonder Daddy's heart failed living with someone like you. You probably depressed him to death.'

'Sabrine!' I can't believe those words came from my own daughter. I expect a hand to fly over her mouth and for her to apologise for saying something so hurtful. Instead, she storms out of the kitchen and into the hall. I follow, pleading with her to stop and talk.

She ignores me and stamps up the steps, pausing and turning to me when she reaches halfway up. 'No, Mummy, I don't want to talk about it. You've obviously made up your mind which is why I *hate* you so much!'

I clamp my mouth shut, stunned. She *hates* me? She's never said that, not through toddler tantrums or the early days of puberty. She hates me.

'Don't say that, sweetheart,' I say. 'You don't really mean it. We're just going through a very difficult time at the moment. Things will get better, I promise.'

'Things will never get better,' she spits back. 'Everything's ruined now that Daddy's gone. I wish you'd have died instead!' With that, she stamps back down the stairs, pushes past me and heads for the front door.

'Where are you going?'

'To Octavia's house, to tell her I won't be going travelling with her and Bernie. I'll sleep over at hers tonight so don't expect me back, not that you probably care.' She shoves on a pair of flip-flops, grabs her bag, and slams the door shut behind her.

I stand, stock-still, for a few seconds, just breathing and listening to my heart thudding inside me. Then I release an almighty scream louder and longer than anything my lungs have produced in my whole life. I hold onto the scream as long as I can until I've wrung every last bit of air out of my body.

In the hallway, right above my head is a photo of our wedding. It was taken as we're coming out of the church, hands clasped and arms aloft in a cheer. Delighted smiles make our young faces glow. A single flake of confetti is positioned in front of Matthew's mouth making it look like he's missing a tooth. That's why we gave that photo pride of place – it always made us laugh.

It's not making me laugh now. I tear it off the wall, slam it to the floor and grind my bare foot into Matthew's face. The glass cracks but it doesn't stop me grinding. The sharp shards cut into my skin. Blood seeps over the photo and trickles onto the wooden floor beneath.

I gather a ball of saliva inside my mouth and spit it out, aiming at the photo below, but instead of hitting the bullseye of Matthew's face it trickles down my chin. 'You fucking fuckety fuck-fuck!' I scream, swiping the gobby mess from my face. 'You lying, cheating, scheming, dirty fuckwit. I hate you, I hate you, I HATE YOU!'

I skid on the blood and land in a heap on the floor next to the smashed glass. I pick up what's left of the photo and frame and scream the questions that are eating me up. 'Why did you do it? Why, why, why?' The handsome man in the morning suit doesn't answer; he just keeps on grinning back at me.

'You bastarding coward, why did you do it? How could you leave me? How could you leave our daughter? How could you leave us with nothing?' I shake the frame, desperate to jostle answers out of it – answers I so desperately need. A chunk of loose glass slithers to the floor and the man I thought loved me is still grinning.

'Were you really shagging that woman – were you? Is it your baby? Please, God, say it's not your baby.' I hug the photo to my chest and choke out big, fat tears accompanied with spluttering coughs, hiccups and animal-like roars. Even to my ears, I sound like a wild beast in its final throes. But I can't stop, and I don't want to. I need to get it out. I need to express my pain and fury at the man I'd had but somewhere along the line had lost, and my fury at myself for not having a clue it was all happening right under my nose while I was poring over kitchen tile colours.

Now Matthew, the arsehole love of my life, is free from all this. I love him and I hate him, and I hate myself for loving him.

The knock at the door silences me mid-sob. I make out long, blonde hair through the half-circle of frosted glass on the front door. *Sabrine.* She's come to apologise for wishing me dead. I've forgiven her already, of course I have. She's my daughter and she's just lost her daddy. She didn't mean it.

Another knock.

'Hold on!' I pick myself up off the floor, not realising I've pressed the heel of my hand on a broken piece of glass until a warm stream of blood trickles down my arm. I wipe my arm on my jeans and suck the broken skin, stemming the flow of blood with my mouth.

I don't want Sabrine to see me like this. I must look a total mess, but I can't leave her standing on the doorstep, alone and distressed. I drive my non-bloodied hand through my hair, then wipe a finger under both eyes in turn to wipe away any telltale mascara smudges.

'Just a minute, sweetheart!' I use my non-bloodied foot to shove the broken frame and as many shards of glass as I can to the side of the door. She might not see it when she comes in and I can clean it up later.

'Oh.' I say when I open the door. Instead of Sabrine, another girl who's just as pretty and slender and only a few years older stands in front of me. I've seen her before, but I can't think where. She's probably one of Sabrine's friends. 'Sorry, I thought you were … uh, never mind. I'm afraid Sabrine's out at the moment.'

She frowns. 'Who?'

'Sabrine. She's out. I assumed you must be looking for …' I don't bother finishing my sentence because I now realise, with a thump inside my chest, where I've seen this girl before – the crematorium after Matthew's funeral.

My brain aches with the recall of how her gaze burned into mine through the blacked-out windows of the limousine, and how she had a pram by her side. Then I see that two sets of eyes are on mine. It seems odd I haven't registered this before but the shock of it not being Sabrine at the door, followed by the realisation it's the girl from the funeral, are making things difficult to compute.

The small boy in her arms can't be any more than a year old, and yet I've seen those eyes before; that mouth – the way it turns down slightly at the corners. It's the mouth I knew for twenty-three years, and the mouth from which now I know for sure lie after lie gushed like Niagara fucking Falls. It's the mouth of my husband on the face of a baby.

'Oh my God.' My hand slaps against my lips and the world spins. If there had been before, there is now not one shred of doubt in my mind that Charlotte was telling the truth. The son Matthew always wanted, he finally got. Not from me. No, not from me because, despite trying, I never fell pregnant a second time. But it didn't matter in the end to him. He got what he wanted. He always got what he wanted, Matthew did.

'You're bleeding.' The girl, for that is what she is, looks at my wrist from which blood is flowing freely.

I don't care. I don't care if I bleed to death. Matthew managed to escape it all, leaving me to pick up all this crap. Why shouldn't I get off lightly too?

I ignore her comment. 'You're so young.' My voice comes out as a genteel whisper, though inside my mouth it tastes like day-old puke.

She adjusts the baby, who has started to squirm, on her hip. 'I'm twenty-three, actually,' she says as if that's the age of a worldy-wise woman.

Twenty-three. Five years older than our daughter. My husband was cheating on me with a girl who was born two years after we met.

'What do you want?' My throat tightens. I can barely get the words out. I can't believe – cannot *actually believe* – this is happening.

'This might come as a surprise to you,' she begins, pulling her hair away from the little boy's chubby-handed grip. 'But your husband and I were in love. Oscar'—she nods at the child, who grins back at her—'is Matthew's.'

I lean against the doorframe and wrap my arms around myself. It's a hot day, but I'm suddenly freezing.

'He was going to leave you, you know,' she adds. 'As soon as the time was right.'

I can tell by her accent that she isn't from one of the posher parts of town. And her clothes scream cheaper end of the high street. What was Matthew thinking?

'Leave *me*? For *you*? And when might that have been?'

'No, Ozzie, don't pull Mummy's hair.'

Oscar giggles, turns his upper body to me and holds out his podgy baby arms for a cuddle. My husband's love child wants me to cuddle him.

The girl transfers him to her other hip, and Oscar grizzles in objection.

'Once you got used to the idea and stopped begging him to stay with you.'

I widen my eyes. 'What?'

'I don't know why you couldn't just accept that he didn't love you any more.'

I want to be angry. I want to hate her. I should hate her. Perhaps I should even hold her responsible for Matthew's death. Maybe it was *she* who drove him to it, and not me after all, but my heart does not beat rapidly with rage as I want it to – it simply sinks to my navel.

'He never said he wanted to leave me,' I say. 'He never even said he was unhappy.'

'If he'd been happy he wouldn't have gone and killed himself, would he?' Her lower lip quivers and the tip of her nose reddens.

'How do you know about that?'

'Mamama.' Oscar lays his head on his mother's shoulder and wraps his arms around her neck.

She doesn't answer me, just holds her son's dumpy little hand.

'Oh Jesus, you poor girl.' I don't know where that comes from; don't know why I feel only sympathy towards my husband's mistress, but I do. Maybe it's because she's not far off my daughter's age, or maybe it's because she's a victim of Matthew's lies as well.

'It's your fault,' she says as her tears begin to fall. 'It's your fault he's dead. Now Oscar's lost his daddy and we'll never get married like we planned.' She's full-on crying now. So is Oscar.

'Whatever reason Matthew had for killing himself, I can assure you, it had nothing to do with me begging him to stay, because that conversation never happened.'

'Well, why do *you* think he did it then?' she chokes out between sobs.

'I don't know, but I imagine having a wife, a mistress, a love child and debts up to his eyeballs causes a man a lot of stress.'

'Debts?' She sniffs. 'But I thought … he said …'

'Debts.' I nod. I'm enjoying the strange sense of calm that has taken over me. 'So many in fact that I'm being forced to sell the house.'

'B-but, I need more money. *We* need more money. Bringing up a child is expensive. I can't be expected to do it all on my own.'

'Is that why you're here – for money? Well, maybe you should have thought of that before sleeping with a married man.'

She at least has the grace to avoid my gaze. 'It's money we're owed,' she says. 'Ozzie is Matthew's responsibility as well as mine.'

'*Was* Matthew's responsibility,' I remind her, somewhat cruelly, but if it's me and my daughter against this girl and her son, then I have to protect my own. I *will* protect my own.

She glares at me, then kisses Oscar on his tufty blond head.

The sight makes me want to cry. Half of me hates her and him; despises their bloody guts – but the other half of me pities her and her innocent little boy.

'I don't know how we'll manage.' She pulls the boy around to her front and hugs him to her.

She's weakening, I can feel it. I just need to hold my ground and get her out of my hair. Anything I say now is self-defence. It's to protect me and Sabrine. I'm the wronged woman in all this. I deserve to have the upper hand. I take a breath and complete clarity washes over me. I know what I have to do next.

'You are, I take it, Miss A Pentecost?'

She nods. 'Arabella.' Her voice is smaller now, like a little girl's. Her earlier bravado must have taken effort and rehearsal.

'Arabella,' I say and stand up straight, relieved to find the world has ceased wobbling. 'My husband paid you over forty thousand pounds over the last year. That, plus his gambling debts, and God knows what else I'm going to find, have left me—well, let's say – totally broke. Even after the house has sold—'

'The money he gave me,' she cuts in. 'It was for all the baby stuff. And my rent, and the car. It's all gone now. There's nothing left. I've got no money coming in now that my maternity leave has ended, and I don't know how I'll ever be able to afford to go back to work, not now that Matthew's …'

'Can't your parents help you?'

'There's only my m-mum, and she h-hasn't got enough for herself, n-nevermind us too.' She can barely get the words out through her tears.

Oscar pauses his grizzle and shoots me a grin. Poor kid. He has no understanding of the fucked-up world he's been born into, and the tragedy is that none of it is his fault. Long may he not understand.

'Well,' I say, determined not to let any hint of the sympathy I feel for the wretched pair on my doorstep show in my voice. 'That's really not my problem. Just don't think you'll be getting another penny out of us. And another thing, if you dare come anywhere near me or my daughter again, I'll pay a visit to my solicitor and start proceedings to claim back the money Matthew gave you.'

'You can't do that!' she says. The hand she has on her son's back trembles, and I know I've got her. My father taught me the signs to look out for – signs of weakness; giveaways that your opponent fears you – and that was one of them.

'My father is an expert in law, Miss Pentecost. If you so much as come within a mile's radius of us, I'll do all I can to ensure that money finds its way swiftly back into my bank account. Now, do we have an understanding?'

She moves her head in the smallest of nods.

'Good. And while we're discussing terms, who else knows?'

'Knows what?'

'About you and Matthew and your sordid little affair.'

'No one. Well, not really, I don't think. There were rumours at the office, I suppose, but nobody knows anything for sure. Matthew wanted to keep it that way, until the time was right. He wanted to tell you about us himself, not have you find out from someone else.'

'Wow, what a thoughtful man he was.' I fold my arms across my chest and glare at her.

She glares back. I'll be damned if I'm the one to look away. We stare at each other so long I start to think we'll still be here at sunrise. A rumble from the direction of Oscar's nappy-padded backside breaks our silence and our stare-off.

'Come on, Oscar,' she says. 'Let's go home.'

Chapter Ten

17 September 1993 – Haxton, Yorkshire

Ronni

I scan my bedroom – a last-minute check before I go. It seems bigger than before. Now I've packed most of my stuff, it feels weirdly unfamiliar. I always thought this would be a sweet moment; the moment I leave. It's the moment I've been dreaming of for a long time. Now it's here, though, a lump has lodged in my throat. This has been my home, my bedroom, for my entire life.

There's a square of dusky pink carpet that's brighter than the rest. It's where my beautiful chest of drawers, with the individual painted knobs, stood. As soon as I emptied it, I gave it to Laura, who has always coveted it. I can't take it with me and didn't want to leave the job of shifting furniture I'll never use again to my dad.

He thinks I'm coming back for the holidays. I won't be, but I haven't the heart to tell him. Not now. I'll deal with that later, most likely using a holiday job as an excuse. There's bound to be plenty of seasonal jobs for students in Bangor.

So as not to dash his hopes, I've left the rest of the furniture. The thought pulls my gaze to my dressing table in the corner of my room. It's a kid's dressing table really, but it reminds me so much of when I was a little girl, when life was still good, that I never wanted to get rid of it. I vividly remember getting it for Christmas. It was too big to wrap and had a huge red bow around it. I could only have been around five or six, but it's still my favourite gift of all time.

I haven't had a wrapped present for years, never mind a bow. I don't think Dad knows how to wrap. Even on the odd occasion he remembers my birthday, he'll just hand me a gift. Sometimes it might be in a plastic bag, but not always. Not if he's bought it off one of his cronies down the pub, like the knocked-off computer he got me for my eighteenth. It didn't work properly but I was happy enough that he'd remembered.

'Ronni, are you ready to go, love?' Dad shouts from downstairs.

'Yep, just a sec',' I call back.

I cross the room to the dressing table, and perch on the tiny stool. The face looking back at me in the heart-shaped mirror looks older, more sophisticated than it has before. I figure moving away, starting afresh, is a good opportunity to be who I really want to be, which is why I've invested in my first lipstick and a new black eyeliner for the occasion.

I stare at myself and after a few seconds, my face seems to contort. It becomes slimmer and longer. It's not my face any more, but the face of my mother. She's sitting on this tiny stool – much too small for an adult – and a little girl is behind her, brushing her long, glossy brown hair.

She raises a hand to her head. 'Ooh, Ronni'—she laughs—'you're a bit rough, lovie.'

'Sorry, Mummy. Just getting the knots out.'

'Well, you might need to be a bit gentler if you're going to be a hairdresser when you're older.'

'I think I will be a hairdresser. Then I can make all the ladies beautiful.'

'You can be whoever you want to be, Ronni. Don't you ever forget that.'

I reach out and touch the mirror. The little girl disappears and my mother's face fades away, becoming mine again.

'I haven't ever forgotten it, Mum,' I say.

'Ronni!' My dad's voice breaks into my reverie. 'You'd better look sharp, love, or we'll never get there.'

'Yeah, I'm coming!'

I sniff back the emotions, stand up, and hurry to the door.

I cast my eyes around the pink box that has been my bedroom – my sanctuary – the past eighteen years. The faint jasmine scent of Avon's *Far Away* perfume, that Chopper gave me for my eighteenth, hangs in the air.

'Well,' I say, to the almost-empty room. 'Thank you for your service. You've seen a lot, and heard a lot, over the years. We've had our adventures, haven't we?' Will I miss those pastel pink walls and swirling artex ceiling or will I never think of them again?

Without looking back at the dressing table again, I leave the room, and close the door behind me. Dad looks up at me as I head down the stairs. He's got a suitcase in each hand and a fag dangling out of the corner of his mouth. He sees me, puts down the cases, pinces the fag, which is little more than a stubby tab and a stretch of precariously arcing ash, between his thumb and fingers, takes it out of his mouth and blows out a stream of smoke so long I wonder how he's got the lung capacity.

The ash falls to the floor like burning snowflakes, and Dad rubs it into the carpet with the toe of his knock-off Adidas trainer.

'Somebody's 'ere to see you, love.'

'Are they?' I ask, my heart soaring in my chest. 'Who is it?' I can only think it's Chopper come to say goodbye. I finally finished with him last week. There was no point hanging on any longer, what with me going off to university. He cried. Shed real, fat tears, he did, the daft lump. He held me to him really tightly and wouldn't let me go. I had to push him off in the end and walk away. I left him in the pub on his own, sobbing. I didn't know what else to do. If I'd have stayed he'd only have tried to convince me to stay, and that was never going to happen.

'It's Donna,' says Dad, breaking into my thoughts. 'She's come to say ta-ra.'

'Oh, right.'

'She's brought you something.'

'That's nice of her.' I wanted it to be Chopper. Don't know why, because I'm not staying, but I wanted him to try to convince me one more time. Maybe just for my ego's sake. I try to cover my disappointment with a bright smile.

Dad lodges the fag, that's now nothing more than an orange tab, between his remaining teeth, and grunts with the exertion of picking back up my suitcases. He says something I don't catch because he's hardly moving his mouth to ensure he doesn't lose the cigarette, but I know from his sideways head cock he means that Donna's outside.

There's one remaining bag waiting to be loaded into the car. It's a huge rucksack, packed so full I can almost hear the stitching protesting with the strain. I heave it onto my back and follow Dad outside.

Summer should be in its dying throes by now, but no one's told the sun, for its heat beats down, its warmth seeping into my shoulders. The brightness compared with the shady depths of our house has me squinting, and through my narrow slits I see Donna. Or rather, I see two flesh-coloured mounds spilling over a too-tight top and assume it's Donna.

The sound of her voice confirms I'm right. 'All right, Ronni, darlin'? I brought you some of your favourites, so you'll never go 'ungry.'

As my pupils become accustomed to the assault of light, the cardboard box she's brandishing comes into focus.

Donna tucks the box under one armpit, causing her left breast to swell like a squeezed stress ball. 'Pork scratchings, scampi fries, Mini Cheddars, crinkle cut prawn cocktail …'

With her other hand she's rifling through the box, picking out random packets and swinging them in front of me.

'Oh wow, Donna,' I say, unsure of whether having a reputation at uni as the woman with an endless supply of bar snacks is a good thing. 'That's really kind of you. Thank you so much, there's loads there.'

'Ai, well, Dave dun' know I've taken 'em, but they're all out of date, so it's not like he can flog 'em or owt.'

I hold out my hands and accept the box from her. God knows how all this stuff's going to fit in Dad's cab.

'Ronni, love.'

I tip my head to look past Donna at Dad, who's halfway through loading the suitcases into the boot.

'Yes?'

He raises his eyebrows and shifts his gaze to something behind me.

I turn around, slowly, because the heavy rucksack and huge box of salted snacks prevents any sudden movements. When I finally manage the full one-eighty, I'm looking into the intense dark eyes of my now ex-boyfriend.

'Chopper. I didn't think you'd come.' I try not to look as happy about him being here as I feel, but my lips curve upwards into a smile before I have time to tame them. I don't want to be in love with Chopper, and I'm not really sure if I am or not. I like him. A lot. And I'll miss him, just not enough to dilute my ambitions.

'I'm on mi lunchbreak,' he says. 'I told t'gaffer I was nippin' out t' shop.'

'That's nice of you. I don't want you getting into trouble, though.'

'I didn't think you'd really go, Ronni,' he says, shifting his feet.

'I told you I was going. I've been telling you that for a long time.'

He sniffs and twitches his nose. 'Yeah, I know, but I thought it was just a load of old crap you were spouting, like what you lasses do. I didn't think you'd ever really go through with it.'

I'm about to answer when bounding footsteps and a call of my name stop me.

'Ronni! Ronni!' I tear my attention away from Chopper and see Laura running towards me just before she embraces me into a tight hug.

I laugh, trying to keep my balance while holding the rucksack and the box of liberated bar snacks.

'You weren't going to go without saying goodbye, were you?' She pulls away from me, a strand of my hair still caught on her lip.

''Course not.' I tease the hair away from her mouth. 'I was going to get all my stuff loaded in the car, then give you a knock.'

'Mum and Dad want to say goodbye n'all.'

Laura moves aside and there are Uncle Spud and Auntie Pammy in front of me. They hug me, in turn, and wish me well, telling me I deserve it because I'm clever and work hard.

'I wish my two were a bit more like you sometimes,' Auntie Pammy says and rolls her eyes. 'They could do with a kick up t'arse 'arf o'time.'

I laugh and tell her I'll miss her stew and dumplings.

'Let's be off then, lovie.'

I nod at Dad and make my way over to the car to load the rucksack, the weight of which is starting to eat into my shoulder.

''Ang on a minute, will ya, Ronni?'

I turn back to Chopper.

He looks from side to side at the small tribe gathered, then finally back at me. Everyone falls quiet, waiting for him to speak.

His face is paler than usual, and he rounds his shoulders making his skinny body appear even skinnier.

'What's up, Chopper? Are you okay?'

'Yeah, fine.' He swallows hard, his bobbing Adam's apple a dead giveaway of his nerves, and shoves his hands into the pocket of his cement-spattered joggers. His eyes dart around as if he's not sure what he should do next.

'Well, see you later, then,' I say, when he makes no attempt to speak.

Before I can take a step, he strides over to me and bends down right in front of me. I think it's a joke and he's going to pretend to cling onto my ankles so I can't go. I laugh in anticipation of whatever prank he's got up his sleeve, but when I look down he's gazing back up at me, not a hint of a smile on his lips.

It takes me a few seconds to work out that he's down on one bended knee and has a blue velvet-covered box in his hand. He flips open the lid, and a burst of light, like a flash from a camera, explodes from inside as it catches the sunlight. His hand's shaking and, as it moves, the light gives way to an object. I blink, splashes of green and yellow appearing behind my eyelids, and when my normal vision returns, I see that the object, which is nestled within the groove of a tiny cushion, is a ring.

'Chopper,' I whisper. What's he thinking? Is he actually proposing to me at age eighteen on the day I leave for university? In front of Dad, Auntie Pammy, Uncle Spud, Laura, Donna and Donna's cleavage, which is enough flesh to make another human being? Is this really happening? I ease the cardboard box to the floor, but end up dropping it as the weight of the rucksack unbalances me. A sole packet of scampi fries skims off the top and lands by Chopper's feet.

'Chopper, I—'

'Marry me, Ronni. Don't leave. Marry me. Please.'

There's a crack on the *please* and I know it's the sound of his heart, rather than his voice, breaking.

I look up. The first person I see is Donna. She has a hand rested on her chest and a soppy smile on her face. There's a tear in the corner of her eye. She bites her bottom lip and nods at me, willing me to accept. In Donna's world, a world where dentally-challenged punters leering down her top is the height of romance, Chopper's Gladbeck Road proposal is the stuff that dreams are made of.

I shift my gaze to Laura who, in stark contrast to Donna's reaction, has a hand over her mouth, and is stifling a laugh while, beside her, Auntie Pammy and Uncle Spud try to pretend they haven't noticed what's going on, in the same way you might try not to stare at a crazy person shouting in the street, whether out of politeness or embarrassment.

I catch Dad's eye in the hope he can give me a sign of how to handle this. He shrugs and cups a hand over the cigarette in his mouth to protect it from the elements as he lights it. He wouldn't mind if I didn't go to uni and married Chopper instead. I know he doesn't want me to leave Haxton, not really, but he'd never say so. He never tells me what to do, my dad, which I appreciate more than he'll ever know. But on this occasion, it's not helping.

'I'll make you 'appy, Ronni, I promise I will. I'll work 'ard for ya. You'll never want for nowt, not wi' me looking after ya.'

'I know, Chopper. It's just—'

His eyes are wide and wet. 'What?'

'I don't *want* looking after. I want to be able to look after myself. That's the point.'

He stands up, wraps warm arms around my waist and pulls me into him. He lowers his head and presses his forehead against mine. His eyes are squeezed shut. His body starts to shake and, although he's so close to me his eyes have merged into one like a cyclops, I know he's sobbing.

'Don't Chopper, please,' I plead.

'I can't 'elp it, Ronni, I don't want you to leave. I love ya.' His voice is high-pitched and broken.

Pressure starts to build up behind my eyes. 'You're not making this easy for me, Chopper. It's hard enough, you know.' I try to laugh through my words, to ease the pain that's building inside my rib cage.

What am I doing thinking I can escape all this – that a girl like me, made-in-Haxton, will ever amount to anything? Whatever fancy letters I might get after my name, it won't change who I am, what I've seen or where I come from. I'd be an idiot to think anything else.

Suddenly, I feel like a massive fraud, a pathetic wannabe. I have a gorgeous boyfriend who loves me, and I'm breaking his heart. What if no one ever loves me this intensely ever again? What if we only get one chance and I'm on the verge of blowing mine?

And Dad? What kind of a state is he going to get himself into if I'm lording it up at university? He's a liability as it is, even with me around. In the last six months alone, the pigs have locked him up overnight three times for getting into scraps, and on at least as many occasions he's come home bleeding or with his shirt ripped after getting involved in a punch-up at the pub or coming a cropper having been pissed-up on his way home.

This is my life, my fate. Ronni Fairweather – Lenny's young'un, Chopper's lass. That's who I'm meant to be. Wanting anything else is greedy, stupid, and proves that I'm a silly little girl with ideas far above my station.

I hold the sides of Chopper's face, close my eyes and plant a kiss on his forehead. He smells of beautiful familiarity. Leather, Hugo Boss, Benson & Hedges. 'You daft apeth,' I say. 'I love you n'all.'

He raises his head up, and looks down at me, hope dancing in his eyes. 'Does that mean it's a yes? You *are* going to marry me?'

Everyone around us is silent, ears creaking with strain to hear the tiny one-word answer which will determine the rest of our lives.

Chapter Eleven

18 September 2018 – Guildford, Surrey

Raegan

'What the—? I'm not getting in that.'

I lock the front door of Ambleside, Goring Drive, for the final time and join Sabrine on the driveway. She's staring, open-mouthed, at the white Ford Transit that's driving us, and what's left of our possessions, halfway up the country. 'Why not, sweetheart?'

'Mummy, it has "Hire Me For Ninety-Nine Pounds a Day!" written all the way across the windscreen.'

'Oh yes, well I know it's a bit pricey, bearing in mind we barely have a bean to our name these days, but it's the cheapest they had at the van hire place.'

'I'm not talking about *that*! I'm talking about the fact that you expect me, after everything I've been through, to live through the humiliation of driving past all my friends' houses in a rust-bucket with the hire price emblazoned above our heads. Oh my God, I can't believe you'd do this to me.' She covers her face with her hands.

I rub her back and steer her to the passenger door before she notices that "Hire Me For Ninety-Nine Pounds a Day*!" is* sign-written in bright red on both sides of the van and the rear doors too.

'I don't get you any more, Mummy,' she says, as I pull her seat belt across her and click it into the fastener. 'You used to be so normal, but ever since Daddy died you're acting all weird.' She turns her head to look at me as if a thought has just occurred. 'Do you think you might be having a breakdown? I mean, it would be understandable after all the stress we've been under.'

I stifle a sigh and remind myself that Sabrine does not know the half of it – not of her father's affair, love child or gambling habit. 'I'm fine, sweetheart, honestly. And I'll be even more fine once we're settled in our new home.'

'Oh God, don't remind me.'

'Look, Sabrine,' I say, feeling my blood pressure start to rise. 'It's not like we have a lot of choice at the moment. Consider yourself lucky that Granddad left me the house. At least we have somewhere to live. It could have been a lot worse.'

‘Hardly,’ she mumbles, into the collar of her denim jacket. ‘It is temporary though, right? Once you manage to get a job we can come back to Surrey, can’t we?’

‘I hope so, sweetheart. That’s my plan. I just don’t know how long it’ll take.’

She closes her eyes and harrumphs.

‘I’m just going to nip this across to Lynn to thank her for, well – to thank her for something.’ I pull a bottle of Dom Pérignon out of my Louis Vuitton handbag. Matthew always kept one in the fridge for special occasions. We hadn’t got round to drinking this one, and I can’t imagine having a reason to celebrate any time soon.

‘Who’s Lynn?’ asks Sabrine.

‘The lady next door.’

‘Oh.’ She looks decidedly uninterested, takes her phone out of her pocket and starts to fiddle with it.

‘Right, be back in a minute, then,’ I say, although I’m talking to myself, as Sabrine is shoving headphones over her ears – a present last Christmas, which cost more than it would to hire this damn van for a whole week.

I throw the passenger door shut, and head across to Lynn’s.

I ring the doorbell and wait, admiring the perfectly trimmed topiary on her front lawn. I don’t wait long before a neatly-dressed Lynn appears, shoes and all, at the door.

‘Oh, hello Raegan dear. How nice to see you. Do come in.’

‘Hello Lynn. Thank you, but I won’t.’

She maintains her smile but I notice that, behind her half-moon spectacles, her eyes fall slightly at the edges. This woman is lonely. It takes one to know one.

‘I’d love to,’ I add quickly. ‘It’s just that today’s our moving out day.’ I point in the direction of our house.

‘Oh, I see. That’s come around so quickly.’ She leans out of the doorway until she spots the van on our driveway.

‘Is your car already at your new place?’

I shake my head. ‘I’m afraid I had to sell it.’ I don’t elaborate. Lynn doesn’t need a rundown of how I appear to have become piss-poor overnight.

She’s too polite to ask any questions, but she must sense there’s an undertone to my voice, for she reaches out to clasp my hand.

‘You and your girl will be fine, Raegan. In time.’

‘I know.’ I nod, and swallow the lump that, since the day Matthew died, has formed in my throat anytime someone expresses kindness towards me.

‘It seems so silly,’ she says. ‘Me, rattling around on my own in this house that’s far too big for me, and you—’

She doesn’t say it, but we both know what she means. I haven’t told Lynn about Arabella Pentecost, or about the gambling, but the rumours are out there, I know they are. I don’t even care if she’s heard them, as long as Sabrine hasn’t. I’ve been counting down till this day – not because I want to leave Ambleside, which I most certainly do not – but because at least if she’s hundreds of miles away, Sabrine’s less likely to find out about what her father was up to.

‘I brought you this.’ I pull my hand gently away from Lynn’s, reach in my bag and pull out the bottle of champagne.

‘Oh, my.’ She accepts it from me with a grin that makes her look years younger. ‘I’m going to visit my daughter in Kent next weekend, and this will be just the thing. My grandson’s just turned eighteen, you know.’

I smile back, delighted Lynn has a special occasion of the type this bottle was intended for. She deserves some happiness. ‘Have a lovely time.’

She clutches the bottle to her chest. ‘Thank you, dear.’

‘You’re very welcome. It’s a thank you for looking after me that night.’

She reaches out and strokes my cheek with her thumb in a way only mothers do. It’s been a long, long time since I’ve had that done to me, and I really have to battle not to cry.

‘No need to thank me,’ she says. ‘It’s just such a shame we didn’t get to know one another earlier. It’s nice to have neighbours who are friends.’

I give her a hug, tell her to keep in touch, and hand her a piece of card on which I’ve already written my phone number and forwarding address.

I head back down my own drive with a smile on my face. I’m imagining Lynn, surrounded by her family, toasting her grandson’s leap into adulthood. I don’t wish to budge from the warm, cosy daydream back to the reality of my day: my daughter, who currently despises me, sitting with her arms folded in the “Hire Me For Ninety-Nine Pounds a Day!” van, waiting for me to drive her to what she perceives as purgatory. And although I’d never say it to her, I feel exactly the bloody same.

‘Rae, Rae, wait a minute!’

I am wrenched from the cosy daydream by a familiar voice, coming from familiar lips on a familiar body which is tottering down the road as quickly as her five-inch stilettos will allow her.

'Rae, I'm so glad I haven't missed you.'

'Charlotte.'

'Darling, listen.' She peels a long strand of perfectly-tonged hair away from her lips, where it's stuck to a streak of pearlescent gloss. 'I know we haven't spoken for ages, but I don't want us to part on bad terms. We've known each other so long.'

I nod and look at my feet. Guilt snakes down my spine as I recall how Charlotte took me under her wing when Matthew and I first moved into this street.

'For what it's worth,' she continues. 'I'm sorry I said anything about Matthew and that woman. I genuinely thought you knew.'

I look back up at her. 'It's okay. I would have found out soon enough anyway, and it would have been worse coming from someone else. I'm glad you told me.'

She presses her lips together and smiles. 'Friends?' she says.

I nod, and throw my arms around her neck. 'Of course we're friends. It's just been so hard recently, you know, Char. What with Matthew's death, then finding out about—'

'I'm so sorry about the money, darling, and that you had to sell the house. And the suicide! Rae, why didn't you tell me about that? Oh my goodness, it's all just so awful.'

I pull away from her. 'How do you know about all that?'

'Tara Grunwald said she saw you in the supermarket looking upset. She let it slip that Matthew had … you know, taken his own life—'

'Let it slip, my arse!' I cut in.

She rubs my arm. 'When I heard your house was up for sale I assumed that there must be some financial problems somewhere along the line. I know how much you love this house and would never sell it through choice – even with Matthew gone. I called a few times and left messages, but you never called back.'

'I'm so sorry, Charlotte. It's not you I was angry with. It's Matthew, and that woman he was shagging and, and—'

'Men. Always arseholes. Even cause you problems when they're dead.'

Only Charlotte can say the most offensive, inappropriate thing without being offensive and inappropriate. I laugh and give her another hug.

'Listen,' I say. 'I've got to get going. I've left Sabrine sulking in the van.'

'Go, but you might want to avoid heading down Silver Lane. Tara will be on her way to the Country Club about now and if she sees you driving around in this monstrosity,' she nods at said monstrosity, 'Then it'll be all over Surrey before you get to the M25.'

'Thanks for the tip.' I hand her a card like the one I gave Lynn and tell her to keep in touch.

'I'll come visit,' she says, reading the address. 'I've heard the men there are *hot*.'

As I reverse out of the drive, I wave in turn at Lynn, who is still standing at her door, and at Charlotte whose enormous lips form a kiss that she blows at me.

'So, a new adventure,' I say, with a sideways glance at Sabrine.

She scowls and pulls one side of her headphones away from her ear. 'What?'

I repeat what I said, and she mumbles something I can't decipher and goes back to listening to her music. A split second later, she knocks the headphones off her head onto her neck and screeches, 'No, Mum, not Silver Lane. This is where Octavia lives. If she sees me in this thing, I'll never live it down. Go the other way, the other way!'

'Sorry, sweetie, I just wanted to wave goodbye to an old friend.'

Sabrine groans, and adopts the brace position.

'What are you doing?'

'Hiding my face!'

I don't argue, because at that moment, I see Tara Grunwald in the Country Club car park, getting out of her glossy black Mercedes with her mobile phone clamped to her ear. Spreading more gossip, no doubt. She catches sight of me and abruptly stops talking into her phone. I do a quick check to make sure Sabrine still has her head between her knees, then I wind down the window, stick my arm out and flick Tara Grunwald the bird.

Chapter Twelve

21 February 2000 – Leeds, Yorkshire

Ronni

'Now then, little'un, aren't you a sight for sore eyes?' Dad's eyes shine as he grins at the sleeping bundle in the baby carrier. 'Who'd have thought it, Ronni love, that daft fella of yours being capable of helping to make something so ruddy lovely.'

'He's got his good points.' I laugh.

''Ow is 'e anyway? 'Aven't seen 'im since the wedding.'

'He's fine, Dad.'

Dad leans forward from his wheelchair and strokes my baby's chubby, pink cheek. His permanently bent finger doesn't look capable of a touch so delicate, but he succeeds in brushing the surface of her impossibly soft skin without causing her to stir.

It's the first chance he's had to touch her and I know it will also be his last. She's ten weeks old and making the journey here felt like an enormous mission. Unpredictably lactating breasts, seemingly never-ending feeding times and extreme exhaustion has meant that today was the first day since her birth that I have felt able to function for long enough to visit Dad in the nursing home.

'Can't believe you've left it so long to come and visit your old dad, Ronni,' he says, as if reading my mind.

'It's knackering, Dad! You wouldn't believe the amount of stuff I have to carry with me everywhere.'

'All right, all right, woman, don't get yer knickers in a twist. We had a baby n'all, you know. I'm looking right at 'er.'

I say nothing, but know that while Dad was my only parent after the age of eleven, in the early days, my upbringing had been left mainly to Mum.

'So,' I say, eager to change the subject. 'Are they looking after you in here?'

'It's a right bloody dive,' he says. 'And it stinks.'

I sniff the air and must admit there is a faint cabbagey aroma.

Dad rummages in the pocket of his stained jogging trousers as best he can in his hunched-over sitting position. He produces a packet of cigarettes, flips the lid open and pulls one out with his teeth.

'Feeling flush, are you?' I nod down at the packet.

'Can't roll mi own now with these buggered fingers,' he says with the cigarette still in between his lips. 'Gotta light?'

'No, 'course not. I don't smoke, do I?'

He takes the cigarette out of his mouth with two gnarled fingers. 'Oh, ai, I forgot you're boring.' He laughs and I can't help myself – I laugh too, as I shake my head.

'Right, well, let's get out of this shit'ole for ten minutes while I have a fag. 'Lass at reception will have a lighter. She's much more fun.' He winks at me and I take this as the signal to pick up the baby carrier and follow him towards the exit.

I walk slowly behind him as he steers the wheelchair by the wheels. It's such a sad sight. My dad, who I remember as tall and strong, now spends his days slumped in a wheelchair, smoking even more fags than usual in the hope the Grim Reaper will finally show him some mercy. Despite two weeks in intensive care and a stint in a hospice, this long overdue visitor has, to Dad's disappointment, proven so far elusive.

'Is it really that bad this place?' I ask, once we are settled on a bench at the front of the home. It overlooks the main road and I have to raise my voice to be heard over the constant stream of traffic.

He looks at me out of the corner of his eye as he takes a drag, then exhales a dragon's breath of grey smoke. 'Well, I wouldn't recommend you checking in anytime soon.'

'Well, no, obviously. I was actually meaning the care side of things. And the staff – are they nice to you?'

'Aye, they try their 'ardest, but they've got their work cut out. Have you seen the state o'folk what's in 'ere? Someone ought to put a gun to their 'eads. That's not living.'

'They do all seem rather ancient.'

'You're not kidding. Do you know, at fifty-nine, I'm the youngest in 'ere by almost twenty years.'

'Jesus.'

'Mike's all right though. I like 'im.'

'Who's Mike?'

'The bloke who does the night shifts. He 'elps get me ready for bed. We 'ave good chats, 'im and me.'

'That's good.'

'Ai. Rest of it's shit though. Wish I was back in t'ospice.'

'Why can't you? Have you asked? Maybe if you—'

'Because I didn't die quickly enough. They don't want you there more than six weeks. Too expensive. So if you haven't kicked t'bucket by then, they ship you to a shit'ole like this to speed t'job up.'

'Well, at least it's clean here,' I say, with the distinct feeling that I'm clutching at straws in my bid to stay positive. 'It's a far sight better than Farehills Working Men's Club.'

'It bloody isn't! There's no beer and none o'lasses have got tits like Donna's.'

'Dad!'

'Sorry, love, but for a clever lass you say some fucking stupid things.'

'I'm just trying not to be mournful, that's all.'

He pats my knee. 'I know, love, I know. There's no point dressing it up, though. You can't polish a turd n' all that.'

'Yeah, s'pose.' I rock the baby carrier with my foot. I can't believe she's sleeping this long. Dad will never see how beautiful her blue eyes are at this rate. It will also mean she'll probably scream all the way home in the car. I'm contemplating waking her up, when Dad's voice interrupts my thoughts.

'I'm exceptionally proud of you, you know, Ronni.'

I turn my head to look at him. Dad has never said anything like that before. That I'm clever, yes; that I'm a good lass, yes, but proud? Never.

'Are ya? Why's that?'

He throws his tab end onto the ground and fishes another cigarette out of his pocket.

'All these folk in 'ere.' He rotates a skinny wrist, his finger pointed, illustrating that he means the residents of the nursing home. 'When you speak to 'em – the ones that aren't completely cuckoo, that is – they go on about their kids and grandkids, saying this, that and t'other about how bloody great they all are.' He puts on a mock female voice. 'Our Linda's such a bright girl – got her own hairdressing salon 'n' everything.'

I laugh and dig my elbow into his arm.

'Point is,' he says, his tone more serious. 'However bright Linda might be and however good she is at perming, I know none of 'em – and I mean not one of 'em – has done what you 'ave.'

'What have I done?' Warmth floods my body. It's good to hear him compliment me, but at the same time I'm slightly uncomfortable with the notion. Because it's so unusual – at this intensity, at least – and it feels depressingly terminal. Like Jerry Springer's *Final Thought* before the closing credits appear on screen.

‘What ’ave you done?’ He tries to lift his head, but his hunch prevents him. He has to make do with straining his eyelids so he can look up enough to see me. ‘What ’ave you bloody done?’ He takes a drag and laughs-splutters-coughs as he blows out the smoke. ‘Don’t you even know?’

I shift my gaze from side to side as if the answer’s about to creep up on me. ‘Um, no, actually.’

‘Let me ’elp you out then, Ronni, love. You’ve always been dead clever and worked so ’ard. You were determined to go off and do something with yer life and look at you now.’

I look down at my beautiful, sleeping baby, swaddled in a yellow woollen blanket and topped off with a white pom-pom bonnet. ‘I’ve had a baby,’ I say quietly. ‘I’m glad, and I absolutely love her, but anyone could do that.’

‘Anyone can have a young’un, yeah,’ he says. ‘But not everyone can give them the life you and that chap of yours have made for yourselves.’

Now the pieces of the puzzle slot into place like a Tetris game on overdrive. I know what he’s getting at.

‘I know things weren’t always easy for yer, when you were a kid.’

I’m surprised at this. He’s never before even hinted that he thought my childhood was anything less than charmed.

‘Me and yer mum didn’t have a lot, but we loved you a lot.’

‘I know,’ I say. I’m not sure where he’s going with this. Half of me wants him to carry on, but the other half is finding this all too out of character to deal with.

‘I know what happened with yer mum wasn’t ideal.’

I almost burst out laughing at his understatement, but manage to stop at a strange smile.

‘But I ’ope you know I did my best after she’d gone,’ he continues.

I pat his knee, in the same way he’d patted mine. ‘Why are you getting all soft on me?’

He doesn’t smile back. ‘I just want you to know, Ronni, that I love ya, that I’m really, really fucking proud of ya, and I’m sorry if I might have made some mistakes. It’s ’ard being a parent. You’ll come to realise that.’

I think of my stretch marks, sore nipples and infected stitches. ‘Yeah, I’ve figured that out already.’

He smiles and shakes his head at the same time. ‘You think you ’ave, lovie, but you ’aven’t seen nowt yet.’

We sit in companionable silence for a long time. Dad chain-smokes. I rock the baby carrier with the toe of my boot.

'I'd better get going,' I say, through a yawn. She slept for five hours solid last night, but the exhaustion's creeping up on me.

'Already, love? You've not been 'ere two minutes.'

'It's been three hours actually, Dad. I want to get going before the traffic gets bad, plus this little one will be wanting a feed soon.'

'Ai, well, I s'pose. Shame I've not got to see yer 'ouse yet. Bet it's well posh.'

'It's nice,' I say, wishing with all my heart he was well enough to jump in my car and come over for a visit. I've told him what our house is like – described the garden, the kitchen, the nursery, showed him plenty of photos I took and had developed specially. Told him what a far cry it is from Gladbeck Road. It's not because I want to brag, but because I want him to know his daughter has made something of herself, and that he had a big part to play in that.

'Bet you've got that fancy scented bog roll.'

'We have n'all, you know.' I laugh.

''Allo Vera.' We both turn to each other and say it at the same time. Dad hoots with laughter.

'Not to worry,' he says, once he's calmed down. 'I'll visit soon enough.'

I raise my eyebrows. 'And how do you think you're gonna manage that?'

'I'll haunt ya,' he says, his eyes twinkling.

'Don't you bloody dare. I could do without you scaring the shit out of me.'

'No, not like that,' he says, as if what *I've* said is ridiculous. 'In a more sophisticated way.'

'Oh, I see. You mean you'll be one of those *sophisticated* spectres?' I turn down the corners of my mouth and nod, like the concept is a familiar one.

'That's right. I'll pop up when you need me, not before. I mean, there'd be no point 'anging round your gaff otherwise. You don't have much need for posh bog roll when yer dead. Especially when you've no fags in t'ouse.'

'Bloody morbid topic of conversation, this.'

'Nah, bugger that for a game o'soldiers,' he continues, ignoring my comment. 'I'll haunt the boozer instead. That's a better idea. I can 'ave a few crafty pints and ogle Donna's jugs all I want.'

'For God's sake, Dad!'

'Sorry, lovie, don't mean to be vulgar.'

I love it when my dad uses words like "vulgar". It shows how well read he is. In those dark days after Mum left us, when he couldn't sleep, he used to read well into the early hours. If I woke in the middle of the night I'd know from the strip of light illuminating the hallway that he'd still be awake, reading. At least while he was reading, he wasn't crying.

'It's okay. Just promise me if you're going to watch over me, you're subtle about it. Otherwise I might shit miself.'

'Your language is terrible, Ronni. You're swearing like a navvy. I thought you were a cut above these days.'

'You're a bad influence,' I say, standing up and hooking an arm around the carry cot.

Dad waggles his eyebrows. 'I've done my job then.'

I take the lead this time as we make our way over to the edge of the car park.

'Right, see ya then.' I bend down to kiss his forehead. His skin is warm despite the cold air. I get a whiff of fags and Head & Shoulders from his hair. It's thinner than it was, but he's still got plenty of it – another reminder that he isn't old enough to die. *I'm* not old enough to lose my dad. I'm not ready for this. I might have a kid, but in many ways I still feel like one.

I push away the thought. I won't lose my composure in front of him. He deserves better than that. Instead, I grin. I must look like a lunatic because I know that above my grin, my eyes are shining with tears.

'Bye, lovie,' he says, and his voice shakes.

I've *heard* Dad cry before but never witnessed it.

He wipes the back of his hand across his face and sucks in air. 'Bye, lovie, bye,' he repeats, his voice sturdier this time. He reaches into the carry cot in my arms and holds my baby's hand. He circles her tiny palm with his thumb. 'Bye bye to you n'all, little'un.'

A dry lump of what feels like cat fur clambers up into my throat, and I know I need to leave now.

I flash him another of those stupid, inane grins. 'Right, better hit the road.'

He's looking up at me from his wheelchair. His eyes are big – far too big for his thinned-out face and hollowed cheeks. He looks so painfully sad.

It is likely that this is the last time we'll see each other. He knows it. I know it. And yet all I can do is grin like a psychotic Cheshire cat.

I quickly make my way across to my car and secure the baby carrier into its fasteners. I climb into the driver's seat and manoeuvre out onto the main road without looking back. Dad's watching us drive away, of course he is, but I can't risk a glance, because I don't know what I'll do if I catch a glimpse of his sad expression again.

'I had to go,' I say, justifying myself to the bundle in the carry cot on the passenger seat beside me. 'We need to get home to Daddy, don't we? I've got you two to look after now.'

She stirs, then her body spasms and her face contorts as she plunges into an unwelcome wakefulness. A second later, she remembers how to activate her lungs, and the air shatters with her ear-piercing cry. Those big blue eyes are wide open now. Dad never did get to see them.

Chapter Thirteen

26 November 2002 – Woking, Surrey

Raegan

'Hold out your hand.'

Sabrine, tightly packed in her pink quilted jacket, sticks out her arm, palm facing the ground.

'Other way round,' I say and turn her wrist so her palm is facing up. I delve into my supermarket carrier bag, tear off a chunk of the bread inside it and break it into tiny pieces that I place in her mittened open hand. 'It needs to be in little pieces so the ducks can get it inside their beaks.'

'Ducks!' she exclaims, throwing her arm into the air with excitement, and sending the bread bits scattering onto the frosty grass below.

'Yes, sweetheart, ducks. You can feed them in a minute, but you have to keep your arm still first to hold the food.'

She nods, her face a picture of concentration as she sticks out her arm again.

I manage to break off no more than three pieces before she can't contain herself any longer, and throws them into the water.

'Look, Mummy – duck! *Biiig* duck!'

'Oh, that *is* a big duck. In fact, I think it might be a goose.' Ornithology may not be my strong point but if that's a duck, it's on steroids.

The goose glides towards the bread pieces at an alarming speed, and I automatically reach for Sabrine's hand. She giggles, slips her hand away leaving me holding only a mitten and gives a joyous clap.

'Big duck eating my bread, Mummy!'

I watch with growing horror as the goose gobbles up the trio of starters, then flaps its huge wings and scrambles to shore. It heads straight for us, its beady black eyes looking intent on finding its main course.

Oh shit.

I reach for her hand but she flicks me away.

'No, Mummy. I want to give duck a cuddle.'

I throw the Tesco carrier, containing the remaining bread, at the approaching bird. It hits it square on the beak, causing the animal to release a disturbingly loud nasal honk.

I scoop up my daughter's quilted body and lodge her under my arm. She squeals in protest, shouting about cuddling the duck, as I run with her up the grassy mound. Next week's *Surrey Advertiser* headline flashes behind my eyes as I run: "Mother and Child Eaten Alive After Wild Goose Chase".

The tearoom, tucked away in the corner of the park, appears like a mirage. I risk a glance behind me to see if the bird is in hot pursuit, and am relieved to find it with its beak inside our abandoned carrier bag, munching at the contents.

I slow my pace to a power walk, but don't let go of my little girl. I can't have her running back to cuddle the greedy gander. Her vocal protests have turned into sobs.

'It's okay, sweetie,' I say through heavy breaths. 'We're going to go to the nice tearoom for a hot chocolate.'

Her sobs stop abruptly as if someone's just pressed the off button.

'Marshy mallows?'

'That's right. Cream and marshmallows. And if you're good I might even throw in a chocolate brownie.'

'Chocolate!' she exclaims, as Big Duck is shoved off the top spot of her priorities.

In the safety of the tearoom, I sip my peppermint tea and eye my daughter's hot chocolate with envy. It's topped with a mountain of cream and is almost as big as her head. I almost gave into temptation and ordered myself one but managed to scrape together a dollop of self-discipline that lasted long enough for me to place my herbal tea order.

Matthew has been very appreciative of my svelter figure. The two dress sizes I dropped in the three years since giving birth has been largely achieved through a zero carb diet and five hours a week of gruelling exercise. I hate it, but Matthew says being thin makes me look even more beautiful, and if the improvements in our sex life recently have been anything to go by, he means it.

She spoons the cream into her mouth with an *mmm* sound. On having sampled the first delicious spoonful, she's rather too eager with the second, misjudges where her mouth is positioned on her face, and ends up with a smear of cream stuck in her blonde wisps.

I reach across the table with a napkin, and wipe it away.

The misjudgement doesn't slow her down, and she's busy spooning in the next mouthful before I have time to pull away. This time the cream ends up on the sleeve of my jumper. I give a quick look-around the cafe to check nobody is watching, before I put my arm to my lips and lap up the cream like a starving cat. A couple of threads of wool are mixed in with it, but my tastebuds are so grateful for the dairy loveliness it has been a stranger to in recent years, that I don't care.

She sees my cheeky cream dive, and giggles. I giggle too. A tidal wave of love for my daughter drenches me. I've never loved anyone this much. I didn't even know it was possible to love anyone this much until she was growing inside me. She won't ever love me as much as I do her, but that's okay. That's the way it should be.

If anyone ever hurt her I'd kill them with my mama-bear hands. If that goose had touched her, Matthew would be enjoying Big Duck pie tonight.

The sweetness of my sea of emotion is overtaken by a bitter stream, which cuts straight through the middle. Matthew wants to send her to Felbury Girls – as a boarder. It's ages away yet – eight years, in fact, but will I feel differently then from the way I do now?

When I said this to Matthew, he took me in his arms, kissed my forehead and told me not to worry. Of course I'd feel differently, he said, she'd be practically a teenager and so much more independent. She wouldn't need me as much. But maybe it's not all about her needing me; maybe I'll still need her. I can't imagine *not* needing her.

"We have to think about our child in all this," he said, "think about her future". He's right. I have to keep my feelings to myself. This is about her, not me. Felbury is one of the best schools in the country. What could be better for our daughter?

It's testament to how much Matthew loves her that he's happy to spend fifteen-thousand pounds a term on her education. What about other things we could do with that money, I said. Things like go on family skiing holidays. I said that because I'm desperate; desperate to keep her with us. I hate the thought of skiing. I always did hate it, but went along with it for Matthew's sake. Such pretty resorts marred with the expectation of having to fling yourself down a hill at full speed. Matthew, on the other hand, loves it and it would be a great skill for a child to pick up.

"I can already ski," he said, and insisted that a much wiser investment would be our daughter's schooling. I can't think of another argument, not when his is so strong.

I flick away a miniature marshmallow that's somehow become stuck to her cheek. Why am I thinking about all this now? It's too early. If I still feel the same when the time comes, I'll put up a fight, but not now. I should be enjoying my time with my daughter, not worrying about something that may never happen.

Chapter Fourteen

18 September 2018 – M1, Northamptonshire

Raegan

'When were you planning on telling me, Mummy?'

'Hmm?' I check the mirror and realise the van doesn't have a back window, so I look in the wing mirror instead before pulling out to overtake the caravan in front. I'm relieved Sabrine's finally spoken. She's barely uttered a word the whole journey and we've been travelling for almost two hours.

'You told me Daddy had heart failure. You didn't mention he'd killed himself.'

How did she—? My hands start to sweat and the steering wheel slicks beneath them. My indicator taps out a beat – click clock, click clock – at exactly half the speed of my racing heart.

A car horn blares behind me. It snaps me back into the moment. I turn off my indicator, accelerate past the caravan and swoop into the slow lane.

'I-I, I'm sorry, sweetie, I *was* going to tell you, but just later – when things had calmed down.'

'Do you know how I found out?'

I glance over at her. She's not looking at me; she's staring straight ahead out of the windscreen.

'From Octavia's mother,' she offers, without waiting for an answer. 'She said her nephew is at Oxford studying for a PhD in suicidology, and she offered me his number in case I wanted any advice.'

Suicidology. Is that even a subject? Who does that?

'I must have looked like the world's biggest idiot when I looked at her totally confused.'

'Oh God.' I grip the ever slippery steering wheel and experience a sickly swirl inside my stomach.

'Why didn't you tell me in the first place? Why did you have to make some stupid story up? Do you think I can't handle the truth? I'm eighteen. I'm a grown-up. I could be a married woman with a baby of my own, and yet you still treat me like a little girl.'

This time my sideways glance is met with a flashing pair of blue eyes.

'Let's pull into here,' I say, relieved to see a sign telling me Northamptonshire Services is only a few hundred metres away. 'We can have a chat then. I've packed some sandwiches.'

She folds her arms. 'Good idea. We can discuss what a disaster our lives have become in the car park of this particularly grotesque Travelchef.'

'Sabrine, please.'

'Please what, Mummy? What do you expect? You've lied to me for months. I had to find out Daddy killed himself because my friend's mother read the inquest in the paper. I mean, for God's sake!' She flings her hands up, then slaps them down onto her bare thighs, below her shorts.

Damn. Why hadn't I thought about that? I just assumed that no one Sabrine knew would really read the local paper. I should have considered her friends' mothers.

'You're unbelievable!' she says, shaking her head. 'How did you think I wouldn't find out? It's a miracle someone didn't mention it at the funeral. You must have been shitting yourself all day, thinking someone would bring it up.'

'Sabrine. Language!'

'Oh, for Christ's sake, Raegan. I'll say what I damned well like. I am not a kid!'

'Raegan? You're calling me *Raegan* now?' I'm sweating now from the conversation and from squeezing the van into a parking space barely fit for purpose.

'That's your name, isn't it? Or would you rather I call you *Mummy*?'

I smack my hand against the steering wheel. 'I'd rather you called me *Mum*.'

'Fine.' She crosses her arms, then uncrosses them again.

'Fine,' I say. My palm stings. I reach over to the passenger footwell to retrieve a small cool bag. She turns her head to look out of her window and presses her legs up to the car door, away from my arm.

'Would you like a sandwich?' I reach into the cool bag and hand her a clingfilm-wrapped bundle.

She turns to me and snatches it out of my hand, mumbling a thanks.

'So,' I say, trying to find a way into my own tightly wrapped clingfilmed ball. 'Now you know, we can talk about it. If you want.'

'First,' she says, through a mouthful of seeded roll. 'Why didn't you tell me?'

'To protect you.' I give up trying to find a corner of clingfilm I can peel away, and drop the still-wrapped ball into my lap. 'Believe me, I know it was wrong, but I couldn't bear to see you get hurt even more than you already were. I always planned to tell you at some point, but every time I tried, I wimped out.'

She chews, her expression not giving anything away. 'Second,' she says, '*Why* did he do it? Was it something to do with that woman at the funeral?'

Shit!

'Mummy? I mean, *Mum*. Was it?'

I look down at my lap. The pre-made butty feels like a lead weight on my thighs and I no sooner want to eat it than I want Araballa bloody Pentecost to be my new best friend.

'Yes,' I say.

'Was Daddy having an affair?'

'Seems that way.'

She says nothing. I look across at her. She's rolling the empty clingfilm between her palms into a crumby ball.

'I didn't want to have to tell you that, sweetheart.'

'Why? Surely you hate his guts. Don't you want me to hate him too? Wouldn't that help?'

I reach out to touch her hand. I fear she might pull away, but other than squeezing the clingfilm ball, she doesn't move.

'Why would he do that to you?' Tears fill her eyes and one escapes down her cheek.

'I'm still trying to work that one out myself, sweetie, but I'm sure in his head at least he had his reasons. The last thing I want is for you to hate him. He was your father, and he was a good one. Whatever happened between me and him, he still loved *you*. That's what you need to remember.'

She sniffs.

I delve into the pocket of the cool bag and find a few sheets of kitchen roll I packed. 'Here, sweetie' I say, handing her one. 'Blow your nose and let's get on our way.'

'I'm just going to go inside to the loo,' she says, pressing the paper against one cheek at a time.

'Good idea. I'll come with you.' My bladder isn't in need of emptying, but for some reason I can't bear the thought of watching her walk away from me.

"Autumn Dessert Ideas Your guests Will Love". "Give it Some Welly – Cool Boots For Cooler Days". "Spooktacular Make-up Tips – Be The Belle of the Halloween Ball".

I sigh, scanning the front cover of the glossy magazines on the shelf in WH Smith as I wait for Sabrine to come out of the loo. This time last year I would have been seduced by articles on those subjects – things that mattered to me then. My longing for a return of those days brings on a physical ache deep inside my gut. How I wish I still had that life – was still that person, whose greatest dilemma was whether to serve Salted Caramel Roulade or Poached Pear Surprise when Matthew's kettlebell chums and their wives came round for dinner.

The contrast between then and now is so stark it's like two lives lived by different people. These days, my biggest dilemma is less about poached pear and more about being piss poor. What I really need is an article on "How to Look On The Bright Side When Your Life Has Turned to Shit". Unfortunately, *Good Housekeeping* doesn't appear to have covered that topic this month.

More headlines on the shelf above, and below, swim before my eyes. Articles telling me I can drop a dress size simply by adopting yoga breathing exercises into my daily routine (that explains why Tara-bitchface-Grunwald is a dress size *age 9-10*); new apps to help me get my finances in order (pah! I almost laugh at that one); and oh, goodie, a quiz to gauge the health of my marriage. If only I'd read that before my husband got another woman up the duff, I'm sure life would be tickety-boo right now.

I pick up one of the offending magazines and snarl at it. 'Where do you get off telling women how to run their lives?'

'Mum!'

One look at Sabrine's frown tells me she's been trying to get my attention for some time. 'Oh, sweetheart, sorry. I didn't see you there.' I'll have to get used to her calling me *Mum*.

'Why are you talking to yourself?'

I look back at the magazine as if it has the answer. When none magically appears from the pages, I replace it on the shelf and steer Sabrine out of the shop. 'Was I? I didn't even realise. Must be an age thing. Impossibly ancient, you know, forty-three.'

'Great,' she mutters. 'My mother's turning into a total nutcase – that's *just* what I need.'

'Oh, stop it.' I chuckle, and hook my arm into hers as we make our way toward the exit through the throng of people. She doesn't shrug me away, thank goodness, but nor does she tighten her arm to her side to lock my hand in place like she used to.

I try not to dwell on how our closeness has diminished since Matthew's been gone, and instead concentrate on the scene around us. The place is packed. I pick out a group of teenagers with rucksacks brandishing the name of some language school; a young, knackered-looking couple with a toddler in a high chair cheerily filling its face with a rice cake; and a trio of thirty-something women chatting excitedly over coffee – probably thrilled at escaping the mundanity of their jobs, husbands and children for a day promising shopping or spa treatments. Oh, the joy of mundanity.

Where are all these hundreds of people going? What's waiting for them when they get home? Do they know how lucky they are to have money in the bank and devoted partners? In a totally egocentric moment of self-pity, I am certain I win the prize – out of all these people – for the rawest of deals.

'Can you remember where we parked?' I say, looking around the full car park, wishing I'd bothered to make a mental note of our space.

'How can you miss *that* monstrosity?' Sabrine says, pointing over to the right.

'Where?' I say, still unable to spot the Range Rover.

'*There*. You really are going nuts.'

It takes me a few seconds to register what she's pointing at and a second more to piece the last few weeks together and recall the Range Rover has gone.

'Oh yeah.' I force a laugh. 'Silly me.' I squeeze her arm and in response all I get is an eye roll.

I could cheerfully lay down right here, thump my fists on the tarmac and cry that it's not bloody fair. I could refuse to move until the emergency services, or even the Days Inn receptionist, appears and peels me off the ground. Only because I've got Sabrine do I stay on my feet. If I just take things one day at a time – one hour at a time – then I'll get through.

I stop in front of the van and spend at least three minutes looking in my handbag for my key. This attracts more eye rolls and a huff from Sabrine. I smile and apologise as I'm searching, then hold the key up in triumph with a *'Phew!'*.

'Oh, for Christ's sake!'

The male voice coming from the space next to ours in the car park catches my attention. All I can see is a pair of smart dark blue jeans finished off with shiny brogues. The rest of him is behind the open bonnet of his car.

Sabrine looks at me and raises her eyebrows. I raise mine back. I know what she's thinking – she's surrounded by nutters.

'Um, are you all right?' I ask, walking towards the shiny shoes.

A neatly turned-out man, who looks a few years older than me, with cropped dark hair and spectacles peers around the bonnet.

'Oh, sorry,' he says, scratching his head. 'Excuse my language, ladies, terribly coarse of me.'

I smile at his old-fashioned courtesy. 'No problem. Is everything okay?'

'Not really, I'm afraid.' He comes out from under the bonnet and wipes his hands on the cloth he's holding. 'Can't get the bloody thing to start.'

His well-to-do accent makes his mild curse sound almost regal.

'Beautiful car,' I comment, admiring the shiny burgundy Jaguar.

'All style and no substance at the moment, though. And it couldn't have happened at a worse time.'

'Oh dear,' I say.

'Yes. I was on my way to my son's house in Nottingham. He's just started university there, you see. I'm under instruction from my good lady wife to deliver some *essentials*, as she puts it – things we couldn't fit in the car on the first trip up. Essentials—' he repeats. 'Like a nest of woks and a slow cooker. A slow bloody cooker, I ask you! In my day, when you went to university you lived on beans on toast and that was it. We didn't try to be Heston bloody Blumenthal.'

'I wish there was something I could do to help,' I say. 'If I knew anything about engines I'd take a look for you, but unfortunately the only thing I know about cars is how to drive them.'

'Yes, yes, me too.'

'Well, I hope you manage to get it fixed soon.'

'Indeed. Wouldn't want the poor chap going without his miniature wok. How will he survive!'

I chortle at the man's dry humour, and turn to walk back to the van.

'If you were going anywhere near Nottingham I'd pay you good money to deliver it.'

I stop, and look up at Sabrine. She shakes her head, furiously, and mouths *No*.

Good money? Given the state of my bank account, all money is good. And don't we pass Nottingham?

I turn around. Shiny-shoes has got his head back under the bonnet.

'Well, actually,' I say. 'Nottingham is on our route, more or less.'

He pops his head round again. 'Oh, really?'

'Yes. And I'm sure we can make room.' I thumb towards *Hire Me For Ninety-Nine Pounds a Day!*

He seems to consider my offer, then shakes his head. 'Oh, but I couldn't possibly trouble you.'

'Honestly, it's no trouble. Put it like this, your wife probably isn't going to be too thrilled if your son doesn't get his slow cooker. And it'll presumably save you another journey up.'

'Hmm.' The man rubs a finger over his lip, leaving a black smear like a moustache. 'Are you absolutely sure, my dear? I wouldn't want to put you out.'

Behind me, I hear the van door open and slam shut again, conveying quite clearly Sabrine's thoughts on the matter.

'Sure as sure can be.' *Just show me the money.*

'That's terribly kind of you,' he says. He opens the passenger door of the Jaguar, bends to reach inside and emerges with a wallet.

'Here.' He pulls out a wad of notes and hands them to me. It's a big wad – much bigger than I expected. I'm itching to count it out but feel it's far too rude to do so in front of him.

'Is that not enough?' he asks, seeing me looking at the notes. 'Here, take this too.'

He hands me another wad, almost as big as the first.

I open my mouth to object out of learned politeness, but then remind myself of my situation and quickly shut it again.

'That should cover it,' I say, as if accepting cash to deliver goods in a transit van isn't completely out of my comfort zone. 'What's the address?'

'Ah yes, yes.' He reaches back into his car, opens the glove box and retrieves a leather notebook with a slim pen attached to it. He scribbles something down, rips off a page and gives it to me.

'Okay,' I say, glancing at the address, then pocketing the paper. 'Shall we get the stuff in my van?'

'Oh, yes, yes.'

He transfers several boxes of clearly expensive kitchen appliances and pots and pans into the back of the van.

He stands back after loading the last one. 'That should do it.'

'Fabulous.' I shut the van doors. 'We should be there in an hour or so. Would you like to give me your number so I can let you know once we've delivered them?'

'No, no.' He waves a hand. 'I'm a good judge of character, my dear. I have to be because of my job. I trust you entirely.' He laughs, a deep, pleasant chuckle. 'And if you desperately want to run off with all this rubbish, be my guest. I'm sure Tom doesn't know how to use it anyway.'

'Good to meet you,' I say, taking the huge step up into the driver's seat. 'Best of luck getting that car sorted out.'

'Thanks. I'll let Tom know what's happened and that you're on your way.'

I smile and nod, then pull the door shut.

'Great,' says a grim voice beside me. 'I guess that means we'll be taking a detour.'

'Guess it does.' I'm feeling rather pleased with myself at my spontaneous little earner, and even Sabrine's negativity can't quell my smugness.

'Is this what they call *The North*?'

I flash a glimpse at Sabrine, momentarily breaking off my search for number 28 on the residential street we're crawling along. Her upper lip is curled in distaste.

'No, sweetie,' I say, resuming my search. 'This is Nottingham. More like the Midlands.' I'm reminded what a sheltered upbringing my daughter has had and ask myself, not for the first time in the last few months, how much of a good thing that is, especially now our lives have taken the turn they have.

'It's run-down,' she says, craning her neck as we pass a garden adorned with plastic toys.

'Oh, it's not that bad. I've seen a lot worse.' Her comments do not bode well. God only knows what she's going to make of where we're going. It's no more salubrious than this.

'Ah, there it is.' I pull onto the kerb outside number 28, a 1960s style terrace. It doesn't look anything like university digs, but I suppose things change, and suburbia could be the new cool for all I know. 'I'll go and see if I can find Tom,' I say. 'Can you get the back open?'

She doesn't answer, but takes the keys from me with an expressionless face and climbs out of the van. She's barely said a word to me since we left the services and my cheery mood has sunk again. I'm at a loss at what I can do to get the old Sabrine back – the girl who happily chats away to me, her pretty face animated – the girl who loves me. What if she never comes back? What if I've lost her forever because of my own stupidity in not telling her the truth?

'All right?'

A young, lanky man of around twenty emerges from the front door of the house. He's wearing a sports T-shirt that's seen better days and a pair of tight ripped jeans with pockets that his hands are stuffed in.

He's not what I expected, which was a younger version of the smart man in the service station – posh and jolly. From his demeanour and outfit, Tom is neither of these things. But, I suppose, if someone met blonde, leggy Sabrine and assumed her mother was an older version, they'd expect more Ulrika Jonsson and less vertically-challenged me.

'Oh, hi,' I say. 'You must be Tom. I take it your dad called to let you know what happened?'

'What?' He frowns, only for a fleeting second, then his forehead quickly unfolds again. 'Yeah. Yeah, that's right. He told me he'd paid some woman in an old tranny van to deliver my stuff.'

Charmed, I'm sure.

I lament the fate of millennials if this is the extent of their people skills, and pat the side panel of the van, feeling particularly protective of her after Tom's comments. 'Well, more reliable than your dad's Jaguar it would seem, today at least.' I treat him to one of my sweetest smiles. 'Shall we start unloading your kitchen equipment, then? I suspect you might be wanting to start on dinner.'

He grunts and follows me to the back of the van. Sabrine's opened both doors and is standing there, looking glum. Her hands are also stuffed in her pockets, and it strikes me, with their his-and-hers skinny figures, how much the two of them look like old-fashioned wooden pegs; the type infants make fairies out of for the Christmas tree.

'This is my daughter,' I say to Tom, who gives her a cursory nod.

He stands back and surveys the range of boxes. 'Nice,' he says. His lips curl up into a weird sort of smile. I really do not like this man. Not a patch on his father.

I want to get out of here, away from Tom and his disparaging van comments and disconcerting smile. I clap my hands together like a nursery school teacher. 'Great. Shall we get all this indoors then?'

He ignores me, steps towards the van and starts to open one of the boxes.

'I think we should get these inside before you start opening them. I wouldn't want you to lose any of the parts. These things are easy to get out of the boxes but you can never get the blasted things to go back in.'

He ignores me completely and carries on. 'What the chuff is this?' He pulls a white plastic contraption out of the box.

'Ah, that's a spiralizer. My friend's got one. Hers is Lakeland though, so slightly different. Yours is a John Lewis – good make. Here, I'll show you how it works.' I go to take it from him, but he clings onto it.

'No, no!' he shouts, just as the part he's holding comes away from the part I have a hold of.

Something flies out of it and lands on the road.

'Oh, look,' I say, seeing three clear plastic sachets between our feet. 'They've put in some free samples of parmesan for you. Told you it was a good make. Mind you – that's an awful lot of parmesan. You really only need a sprinkling to get the flavour.'

'You stupid bitch!' Tom screeches and bends down to gather up the sachets.

Bitch? How dare he? 'Now, listen. If your father could hear you—'

'Mum, that's not parmesan.'

I turn to face Sabrine, whose eyes are so wide I fear they might be about to pop out of her skull.

'What?'

I'm vaguely aware of Tom beside me pulling the boxes out of the van.

'It's charlie!' she says.

'What?' I repeat, completely confused. 'No, sweetheart, this rude young man is Tom.'

'Fucking pigs!'

I spin around to Tom, ready to give him a piece of my mind for calling us such names, but he's disappearing down the alleyway by the side of his house, as fast as his scrawny tight-jeaned legs will carry him, while trying to balance a coffee-maker and a food mixer.

That's when I become aware of the siren. Pigs. Charlie. Not parmesan. *Oh bollocks.*

'Get in the van!' I yell at Sabrine. I start pulling the remaining boxes out of the van as fast as I can, letting them clatter onto the road. Blenders, pans, juicers, it's all there. The gods of kitchen appliances are going to punish me for this.

When the last one is out, and by my feet is half the stock of John Lewis's top floor, I fling the doors shut. The siren's louder now. It can't be more than a couple of streets away and I'm most likely surrounded by more cocaine than a Columbian drug lord.

Sabrine is still standing next to me, feet rooted to the ground, eyes wide, lips parted.

'Sabrine!' I shout. 'Get in the van.'

She doesn't move a muscle.

'Get in the fucking van!'

She still doesn't move, so I grip her by the arms and rush her to the passenger door, shoving her inside.

Once in the driver's seat, I start the engine with a sweaty, shaky hand and slam the accelerator to the floor.

I swing *Hire Me For Ninety-Nine Pounds a Day!* around the corners of various unfamiliar streets, while she beeps insistently because we didn't stick around to put our seat belts on. Together, the beeps and the police siren are like the beginning of an awful rap track like the ones Sabrine listens to.

I don't know what direction we're going in but am more concerned about getting the hell out of here. After around ten minutes of what I'm sure must be the narrowest streets in Nottingham, I realise I can no longer hear the sirens. *Hire Me For Ninety-Nine Pounds a Day!* is still beeping her objection.

'Put your seat belt on,' I order Sabrine, clicking mine into place.

I'm surprised and also rather pleased she does as she's told.

'Mum!' she says, in a loud whisper.

I shake my head. 'I know, I know. I can't believe I got us involved in that. I'm so sorry. I was stupidly naive. I can't believe I took that man's money to do a delivery. No wonder he was so generous with his payment – it must have been a fraction of what all that was worth. But, why was he taking drugs to his own son?' Realisation dawns and I smack the steering wheel. The old cut I sustained the day I met Arabella throbs.

'Of course! I'm such an idiot. He wasn't Tom's father – he was the *supplier*. And yet he seemed so … nice. Huh! That explains why he was dripping in money. Tom must be his middle man. Bet he was panicking when his car broke down after he'd promised the gear would be with Tom today. Probably had all his buyers lined up. But then a greener than green woman comes strolling along and he thinks all his Christmases have come at once. She's too stupid to ask any questions. She thinks she's delivering nothing more innocuous than a trio of woks and a bloody spiralizer!' I smack the steering wheel again and yelp.

'Mum!' Sabrine hisses again, interrupting my monologue.

I glance sideways at her. She's leaning forward in her seat. Her mouth is open again and turned up into an amazed smile.

'What?'

'You said *fuck*.'

'What?'

'*Fuck*,' she says again. 'You said it. In front of me. You never swear.'

'Yes, sorry about that. I just needed you to get a move on. I won't say it again.'

'I really think you should.'

'What? Why?'

'I'm not a kid any more. I'm an adult now. I want you to understand that. And today, you finally treated me like one.'

She flops back in her seat and her smile widens.

'Right,' I say, somewhat bewildered that all it took to earn my daughter's respect was a vulgar four-letter word. Is that it? Is that the secret of harmonious parenting – swear at them? If only I'd known that eighteen years ago, life could have been so much easier. I wouldn't have had to lock myself in the bathroom to release a tirade of "fuck"s and "bastard"s.

'So, you see – you *can* be cool.' She's shaking her head, that amazed smile still gracing her face.

'I'm pleased you think so,' I say. 'Because I'm likely to be "cool" on many more occasions given that we're now wanted drug couriers.'

Sabrine leans forward again and looks at me. She's not smiling now. 'Will the police be after us, do you think?'

I reach over and give her thigh a pat. 'No. I don't suppose so. Not really. They'll be more interested in Tom, or Charlie as you called him.'

'No, Mum. Charlie is what you call coke.'

'*I* know that. But how do you know that?'

She raises her eyebrows as if I've just asked the stupidest of all stupid question. 'You sent me to private school. Of *course* I know what charlie is.'

'Oh you do, do you?' I'm relieved to see a sign for the M1 and turn in the direction it's pointing. 'What else do they teach you at Felbury – how to make a bong?'

'Oh yes, all that stuff,' she says, no sense of irony in her voice.

'Fifteen grand a term and you come out of there fully educated in street narcotics? Are you kidding me?' Distracted, I join the motorway perilously close to an artic lorry. It thunders past, its driver mouthing an expletive at me through his window. I don't care. It's the least of my problems now I'm imagining my equestrian daughter snorting coke off the back of a pony.

'Oh my God. Is that why you called him *Whitey*?' I almost screech the words.

'What?'

'Whitey. Please tell me you haven't done coke, Sabrine. I knew single-sex education was a bad idea.'

'No, Mum, of course I haven't done coke. I haven't done *anything*.'

'What, not even cannabis?'

'No.'

'Ecstasy?'

'Eurgh. So nineties.'

'Speed?'

'Yes, you're doing far too much of it?'

'What?'

She points to the speedometer, and I realise we are all shuddering somewhat.

'Oh.' I ease my foot off the accelerator.

'I'm not into all that stuff,' she assures me.

I turn to her and raise a single eyebrow.

'Really, I'm not.' Her laugh is laced with exasperation. 'It was mainly the Supes that were into that sort of thing.'

'The Supes?'

'Yeah, you know – the super rich girls. The ones who had massive allowances. They spent it all on designer handbags and coke.'

'And you didn't?' Even I can detect the desperation in my voice.

'No,' she says, defiantly. 'I promise.'

'Okay. I believe you.' I *want* to believe her, but I can't say I'm a hundred per cent certain I do. I glance at her again to check her septum hasn't dissolved since the last time I looked. Two well-defined nostrils put my mind at rest.

'How much further?' she asks, kicking off her pumps.

'Ooh, about an hour and a bit I'd say.'

'God, this place is miles away.' She sighs, and closes her eyes.

She's right. It is miles away. And not just in distance. It's been a long time since I've stepped foot in my father's house, but at least I know what to expect, unlike Sabrine. I can't imagine what our new home will look like through my daughter's privileged eyes. I'm starting to wish I kept one of those kitchen appliances and its spurious contents for myself. I've never been one for drugs, but I think I'm going to need something to get through this one.

Chapter Fifteen

18 September 2018 – Haxton, Yorkshire

Raegan

I pull *Hire Me For Ninety-Nine Pounds a Day!* into the side of the road, grateful there's a space big enough directly outside the house. I'm not used to such a large, heavy vehicle and the reflection in my wing mirror tells me I'm about a million miles from the kerb but it'll have to do.

I plaster a smile on my face and turn to Sabrine. 'Here we are.'

She looks from one side of dark brick terrace houses to the replica row on the opposite side.

'Are you shitting me?'

'Sabrine! Language.'

'So it's okay for you to swear? I never had you down as one of those "do as I do, not as I say" parents.'

'Well—' I search for a reason it's not okay for her to develop a potty mouth. 'I don't intend to make a habit of it. That was an extreme situation.'

'And this isn't?' She looks around again. 'It's like we've landed in a dystopian nightmare.'

'I know you're a keen actress but there's no need to be quite so dramatic,' I say, unclipping my seat belt. 'The people who live here are perfectly nice.' I quietly hope the Barracloughs have moved out since I last lived here because I remember more than one police raid on their place. And the Loughtons weren't any better – rumour had it the woman who lived there, who was rough as hell, was running a knocking shop. That was a long time ago though. Things change. Maybe it's more up and coming now.

By the time I climb out of the van, Sabrine is already standing on the pavement staring up at the house.

'This is where I grew up,' I say, snaking an arm around her shoulder. An unexpected surge of fondness for the place rushes through me.

She widens her eyes. 'You grew up here?'

'Yep.' I nod.

'Did Daddy know?'

'Yes.'

'And Grandma?'

'Oh yes. And she made her feelings about my background very clear.'

'I'm not surprised,' she says, gaping all the way up to the sloped roof and chimney pot. 'Looks like somewhere people get murdered.'

I resist a tut and take the few steps to the front door, leaving her still standing, staring, behind me.

It smells different, is my first thought as I step inside the door. Years of tenants have left their mark; the left-behind molecules of meals cooked and fragrances worn, hang like lost ghosts in the stale air of my once-home, their owners long since departed.

A wave of light-headedness has me holding onto the wall for support. Despite a change of wallpaper, the place still feels familiar, but two decades of transient residents have tainted it, giving me a weird sense of familiarity mixed with being a stranger within these four walls.

The layout of the house is still the same, albeit with more modern decor. As soon as you step foot in the door, you're in the tiny dining area. A few feet away there's an equally tiny living room, and to the left of that, an open-plan kitchen. That's the extent of the downstairs. It's about as far a cry from our six-bedroom home in Guildford as you can get.

The dining table, sofa and other few pieces of furniture are not to my taste, but at least it's furnished. I sold everything from Goring Drive, and even if I hadn't, there's no way our dining table and three-piece suite would have fitted in here.

Sabrine skulks in, her face leaving me in no doubt what she thinks of the place.

'I can't even FaceTime Octavia like I promised,' she wails.

'Why not?' I force myself to shake off my disorientation. The living room curtains have been left shut. I cross the room, sweep the curtain aside, and a blast of sunlight screams into the room.

'*FaceTime*, Mum,' she says, as if the answers are all there. 'It's a video call. It'll mean she sees what a total shi—'

I raise an eyebrow and she stops herself.

'—*hole* this place is,' she finishes.

I walk through the doorless arch into the kitchen and start checking the cupboards. 'We've talked about this,' I say. 'You keep telling me you're an adult, and as an adult I expect you to understand that us not having any money means that moving into a house where we don't have to pay a mortgage, is our only choice.'

'Yes, but I didn't know you'd been brought up on the set of Coronation Street.'

'Ooh, I'd be careful of saying that around here if I were you. This is Yorkshire, not Lancashire.'

'God, you mean there's more than one place like this?'

I sigh. 'This is normal, Sabrine. Not everyone lives in six-bedroom houses. This is real life.'

I swing open the fridge door and inspect the cleanliness level of its insides. It's good to see the rental company is doing their job and had it cleaned since the last tenants vacated.

'Mum, the fridge hasn't even got a water cooler!'

I close the door and turn to face her. 'Look, sweetheart, I know you've been through a lot since Daddy died, but perhaps this move will do you good.'

She wrinkles her nose.

'In many ways you've been a very lucky girl who's had a privileged upbringing. It won't hurt for you to realise that not everyone has a life like that. Some people have it harder. You know, like not being able to afford life's essentials like ponies, holidays in Barbados and fridges with ice dispensers.'

'Why do you always make a joke out of it?'

I place my hands on her shoulders and pull her into me for a hug. 'I'm sorry, sweetheart. I know it's hard for you, what with all the changes and with having to say goodbye to Whitey, but at least you know he's being well cared for. That nice family in Dorking absolutely loved him. You're not going through this all alone though. It's hard for me too.'

'Not *as* hard,' she says, pulling away. 'You've lived here before. It's not such a shock to *you*.'

'Oh believe me, it is.'

She looks down and fiddles with her phone.

'Why don't you go out into the backyard to FaceTime Octavia?' I say. 'Then she won't be able to see our substandard fridge.'

She looks up, her expression brighter. I congratulate myself for my excellent idea for a fraction of a second before I spot the state of the postage-stamp sized garden through the window behind Sabrine's head.

Too late. She spins around, races over to the window and peers out. 'Oh my God. I can't do it there. Octavia will think we've moved to the jungle!'

'Oh, it's just a little overgrown, that's all. Nothing a good mowing won't sort out.' I don't know how to operate a mower. It's another thing I've never had to do. I looked after the inside of our family home in

Guildford – along with the cleaner – while Matthew looked after the garden. He seemed to quite enjoy pushing the mower up and down to create aesthetically-pleasing stripes. After he died I hired a gardener, at least before I realised we were too broke to keep her.

She covers her face with her hands. 'I hate my life so much.'

'Don't say that,' I say, with a forced laugh, and try to pull her hands away.

'I can't believe you've brought us here!' she screams at me, her pretty face turning an angry shade of puce. 'I know we're broke but there must be another way. There must be. You don't understand what it's like for me. You say it's hard for you. How can it be? You've had your life. You're old!'

'Sabrine, I'm forty-three.'

'I know,' she spits through her teeth. 'That's exactly what I mean!'

'I hardly think—'

'I might as well kill myself and get it over with.'

She meets my eyes. She knows what she said was meant to hit a nerve, and she doesn't care.

'I didn't bring you up to be a snob, Sabrine,' I whisper, afraid if I use my vocal cords, my voice – and temper – will snap.

'You sent me to a private school, Mum. What did you think I was going to be – a dinner lady?'

A knock at the door throws us into a stunned silence.

'Hullo!' A voice calls.

We turn around and see we've left the door open and a portly figure is standing at the entrance.

'Hello?' I take the few steps over to the door to see who our visitor is. He's short – only a few inches taller than me. He has a long, white beard, tufts of matching white hair and an ample stomach, which is sheathed in a white Rolling Stones T-shirt and hanging over knee-length shorts. He looks like a Bermudian Santa Claus.

'Hullo,' he repeats. 'I just wanted to check everything was all right here. The lady who owns this place rents it out and the rental company usually phones to let me know if someone is moving in, but I've 'eard nowt from 'em for a while.'

I can't believe he doesn't recognise me.

'By 'eck,' he says, just as I'm about to tell him who I am. He leans forward to get a closer look. 'Well I never.' Recognition takes over his face. He opens his arms wide, beams a smile and wraps me in a bear hug. 'If it isn't little Ronni Fairweather!'

Part Two

Chapter Sixteen

1 December 2011 – Hong Kong
Raegan

'Just going to the bar, darling. Cranberry and soda?'

I smile at Matthew, before he walks off, then turn to watch the Hong Kong skyline shrink as we sail off to the next location on our twenty-one day cruise.

Darling. I love being called that. It can get confusing though. Like when you're in John Lewis and some man shouts "darling" across the store to his wife. Every middle-class woman – me included, I'm happy to say these days – turns around to see if she's the one being summoned.

Sometimes I will Matthew to lose control of his senses and call out "Oi, gobshite!" just to see how many women in John Lewis answer to that one. Ha! As if Matthew would ever do that.

He's a good man, my Matthew. Good choice. Good father. Good job.

I don't know *exactly* what he does, but his title's got the word "director" in it. And he carries one of those thermal portable cups around with him everywhere. The ones directors have, because they're far too busy directing to use a normal mug.

I turn to watch him at the bar. He's suave in his dinner suit. Handsome even. If you squint a bit he's a dead ringer for that bloke who plays Bond. His face is a bit more skew-whiff, but the similarities are definitely there.

Bagged myself a keeper there. An *ender-upper*. Not like that lad, Chopper, I used to go out with in my old life. The Old Life. That's what Matthew calls it. Bugs me a bit when he says it. Like he thinks he's my saviour.

Over at the bar the barman is pouring my cranberry and soda. Didn't belong in The Old Life, that.

'Cranbri' and wo?' Laura spat, at Dad's funeral. 'That's a soft southerner's drink if ever I saw one. No chuffer up North would be seen dead supping that shite!'

'What you got then?' I asked, gesturing at her glass. Looked like cranberry and soda to me. It was the same colour at least.

'Lager 'n' black,' she said, holding it up like a proud parent. Then she necked it in one.

She was probably right. It is a lame drink. Tastes alright though. Not quite a Sancerre, but it'll do. At least Matthew approves. Haven't touched a drop of booze since I had too many that time at his cousin Oli's wedding.

Excruciating was how he described his embarrassment.

Didn't think I'd been *that* bad. So, I puked in a shoe. But it was *my* damned shoe. Shame really. Russell & Bromley. I loved those shoes. Cost a few bob. So, no more booze for me. Not when Matthew's around anyway. I have a couple of glasses of Sancerre from my secret stash if he stays late at the office, which he does more and more these days, come to think of it, but otherwise don't touch the stuff. Don't want to upset the apple cart, and end up back in The Old Life.

Christmas Day 1991. That's when I planned out my New Life. I did it in such minute detail that I had a picture of Matthew in my mind two years before I even met him. When I clapped eyes on him for the first time in the student bar I knew he was the one. Not because it was love at first sight, or because my knees weakened there and then, but because he looked just like the picture I'd formed in my head; tall, athletic, floppy fair hair, shoes instead of nicked trainers. I could tell by the look of this man that he did not drive a van. And if he didn't drive a van, it meant he didn't keep a bucket in the back. This was him. The One. And when he caught my eye, and weaved through the tables heading in my direction, I knew my New Life was about to begin.

The meeting almost didn't happen. When Chopper proposed on the day I was leaving, I had a wobble, and almost said yes. I did love him, but I'd promised Mum I wouldn't make the same mistake as her, and would go off and do something with my life, so in the end I whispered in Chopper's ear that I was sorry but I had to go, and off I went. Now I'm glad. I've got everything I wanted. I wish I hadn't seen Chopper's face when we drove off. But I did. I made the mistake of looking back. Never look back.

Anyway, it all worked out for the best. University meant fancy dinners, and learning which knife and fork to use for which course, and that you always go to the left to get your breadcake.

Bread bun.

Bread roll.

Whatever you're meant to call it. I still get confused, even after all these years.

I got a good job after uni. Assistant to the Commercial Director of an international risk analysis firm. Then Sabrine came along and Matthew said we could afford for me to be a "proper mum", so I gave up the job. It was very generous of him to let me do that. It meant I could spend lots of time with Sabrine while she was still at home.

Even when she went off to school, Matthew said I didn't have to go back to work because none of his colleagues' wives did. He said it would be good for Sabrine when she came back for the holidays if I was at home full-time. I thought he knew best.

And I was never lonely. Not working meant I got a chance to join the Country Club and do plenty of yoga. Yoga. Keeps my muffin top in check. I'm at least two stone lighter these days than I was in The Old Life, although it's a sacrifice. No more Mr Kipling's Viennese Whirls for me.

And I bloody love Viennese Whirls.

All the exercise has made me more flexible though. I can get my leg in all sorts of positions, not that Matthew takes advantage of that – he's a missionary position man. Doesn't like "kinky stuff", as he puts it. Like with life in general, Matthew likes "getting it done" as far as sex is concerned. He hasn't always been like that. Couldn't get enough of me, from all angles, in the early days but these days things are different. I suppose it's his age. And he's got a lot on at work and whatnot. I've always enjoyed our love-making, although I suppose if I'm honest, things are getting a bit samey.

He tends to favour Tuesdays for sex. Don't know why, perhaps his exercise class gets the testosterone flowing. I wait for the routine to begin, then I know we're "on". The clatter of his Rolex being lain on the bedside table, boxer shorts being flung into the washing basket, the light switch snapping off, a quick fondle, the main event, his trademark groan, his sweaty thighs peeling from mine, bare feet padding to the bathroom, and the rush of water from the shower. He always likes a shower afterwards. It would be nice to have a post-sex cuddle, but I am very grateful I have a man with such excellent hygiene standards.

I find it difficult to sleep on Tuesdays after sex, however quickly it's done and dusted. I usually need a couple of games of sudoku afterwards to get me to the land of nod.

That's one thing that *was* good about Chopper – he was amazing in bed. Although most of the time we wouldn't quite make it to the bed. He was selfless, even then when we were barely older than the age of consent.

I spy my phone on top of the table. *Should I?* I glance over at the bar to see Matthew, hand in pocket, deep in conversation with another suited cruiser. Feeling ridiculously guilty, I pick up my phone and select the icon easily recognisable by the big white "F". I have never looked up anyone from The Old Life on Facebook. Okay, that's a lie. When I want to feel smug, I look up some of the planks I went to school with to see what kind of life they've ended up with. With the exception of one, who by some act of God ended up married to a lingerie model and lives in America, it's strangely therapeutic to find that the rest of them, other than Lance and Laura who wouldn't waste their time on Facebook, are living apparently mundane lives with hundreds of kids and a weight problem, frequenting the same pubs we went to as kids – the ones that never bothered asking for ID.

Never before have I looked up Chopper. From time to time I've been tempted, but I've always resisted. I'm not sure what I'd want to find.

I'm not even connected with him on Facebook, but the silly sod hasn't bothered to change his settings so anyone can see all his posts.

I scroll through his comments about football scores (unsurprisingly), until I come across something interesting. It's a video. Another quick glance over at the bar and I'm relieved to see Matthew being handed a glass of red by the barman and cheersing his new fellow cruiser friend. He's occupied. Good.

I press play.

By the looks of things the video was taken in a pub, and by the decor I can tell it's The Royal Oak. Place hasn't changed a bit. Still a hole.

There's a woman sitting on Chopper's knee. It must be his wife. I heard from Laura he got married when he was really young – just a couple of years after I left for university. Apparently it was a girl called Kelly who was in the same year as me at school. I remember her vaguely. Bit gobby. Came from a rough family. I can't say I was jealous when I found out. I'd just met Matthew and was too ensconced with developing my own life to worry too much about what any of the old lot were up to.

In the video, Chopper's bouncing Kelly up and down on his lap. She's got a muffin top all right, and it's wobbling about like nobody's business under her poorly judged crop top. Now there's a woman who hasn't given up on Mr Kipling. She's got a pint of lager 'n' black in her hand and it's flying all over the place. Well, I'm guessing it's lager and black, because I can't imagine Kelly Wallington's the type to be drinking cranberry and soda.

She doesn't seem to care what she looks like. Why should she? She looks happy enough. So does he. Positively beaming, in fact.

She slips off his knee and lands on the floor. All you can see of her through the video lens is the top of her head. She climbs back up and they're both laughing their heads off. I can't help but laugh too. I let out a snort, and there's a *tut* from the table next to me. I look up to see a frigid-looking woman, who's squeezed into an expensive cocktail dress, wrinkling her nose at me. What would Kelly Wallington do in this situation? Flick two fingers up at her and carry on probably. Although a part of me wishes I was, I'm not quite up for that. Instead I widen my eyes and pull a face.

The woman whispers something to her toffee-looking husband, and then – low and behold – they leave. That was surprisingly effective.

The video ends. I press play to watch it again from the beginning, and this time I notice that Kelly and Chopper are flanked by three kids. Throughout the film, the kids are watching their parents while slurping half pints of pop and shovelling bar snacks into their faces. When their mother falls to the floor, one of them spits out a mouthful of masticated crisps as he guffaws. They look happy too.

A tear runs down my face, then another, and another, and before I know it, I'm proper roaring.

I wonder if Sabrine is tucked up in bed in her dormitory. It must be early hours of the morning in England. It's Sabrine's twelfth birthday tomorrow, but the headmistress said it would be too distracting so early into her first year for us to turn up. It might upset her, she'd said. Best not to interrupt her routine, and allow her to celebrate her birthday with friends. So that's what we're doing. I think it was half the reason Matthew suggested this cruise – to take my mind off the fact I wasn't allowed to be with my daughter on her birthday. As if that was going to work.

A need to be with her consumes me.

I loathe myself for going along with Matthew's boarding school decision.

Chopper might be a daft bloody dick head who's got no sophistication. Can't even spell sophistication. But at least he's got his kids beside him. Living life with him.

I, on the other hand, haven't seen my daughter for weeks over and won't see her until she comes home for Christmas.

I grab a handful of the complimentary crisps from the glass bowl on the table, and shove them into my mouth. They taste bloody lovely. The vinegar's a bit sharp on my ulcers, but the pain is worth it. I chew and swallow quickly, then, checking Matthew's not looking in my direction, grab another handful and shove them in.

I eat the lot.

Sod Matthew.

Sod yoga.

Sod Tuesday's post-coital sudoku.

Sod it, he's coming back!

I wipe my mouth with the back of my hand just as he sits in the chair across from me and hands me my cranberry and soda.

'Cheers, darling,' he says. I normally find his well-to-do accent quite sexy, but for some reason tonight it grates.

He holds up his glass of red, and his smile turns into a frown. He's noticed my blotchy face.

'You haven't been crying, have you, Raegan, darling?'

He's always insisted on calling me by my proper Christian name rather than the nickname Dad gave me when Ronald Reagan came to power when I was small. Different spelling, but that never stopped him. After that, I was always "Ronni". Even my teachers called me Ronni. I think most people forgot I'd ever been called anything else.

Not Matthew though.

He says *Ronni* makes me sound like an overweight comedian.

So now I'm Raegan.

'No, not crying, darling,' I lie, in my New Life accent. I used to put it on, but I've been doing it so long now it comes naturally. I'm usually proud of it, but not tonight. 'Something must have set off my allergies.'

Matthew nods, satisfied, and pulls an olive off its stick with his beautiful white teeth. They cost an arm and a leg, those gnashers. Chopper could have bought himself a top of the range Portaloo plus a white stallion to pull it around for what it cost Matthew to have his veneers done.

'Just popping to the bathroom, darling,' he says. Now it's my turn to nod. I watch him walk off until he disappears around the corner to where the blokes' bogs are.

I sip my drink. It's syrupy and sweet, and furs up my tongue.

Then I eye up Matthew's Merlot.

Why not? It's not like one little sip is going to have me throwing up in my shoes again.

I pick up his glass and take a sip. It's rich, and fruity, and very satisfying. I take another sip. Then another. And before I know it, it's all gone. I don't normally like red wine, but it's better than cranberry and soda.

Then I have a brainwave.

I don't mess about. I rush to the bar, and order a Merlot for him and a lager 'n' black for me. It looks just like cranberry and soda. Matthew need never know the difference.

I take the drinks back to the table and sup the lager down in one, then let out a burp that's louder than I expected. I giggle to myself, wondering what Matthew would have said to that if he'd still have been sat there.

The Bee Gees are playing now. Me and Laura danced to this in a club in Leeds the night she pissed in the sink in the ladies' loo. There was a massive queue and she was desperate. She couldn't wait any more, so she pulled down her knickers, waddled to the front of the queue, jumped on top of the sink and peed there and then in front of everyone. There were even a couple of blokes in the queue that night for some reason, not that Laura cared about that. She was a free spirit – did what she wanted.

I was horrified at the time, of course, but thinking about it now has me sniggering.

I could have ended up like Laura, or Kelly. If I'd have accepted Chopper's proposal I might be high on Viennese Whirls, peeing in sinks. I don't want that of course for my life, but maybe, just occasionally, it's liberating.

I take a long gulp of Matthew's wine, caring less if he notices, and stand up. I'm a bit wobbly on my heels, so I shake them off and kick them under the table. I can't dance in them buggers now there's no Chopper with a trolley to wheel me home.

I make my way over to the dance floor, consciously making an effort to walk in a straight line. God knows what Matthew will think when he gets back and sees me strutting my stuff, but if he doesn't like it he can shove his thermal mug up his director's arse.

Right now, right this very second, Raegan Kent-Walters doesn't exist.

Because tonight, Matthew – for one night only – I am, once again, Ronni Fairweather.

Chapter Seventeen

18 September 2018 – Haxton, Yorkshire

Ronni

I fall into Uncle Spud's embrace and bury my face into his ginger freckled neck. He smells of wet potato peelings and engine oil. Retirement obviously couldn't keep him away from his first love – cars. On this day of resentment, panic and upheaval, the familiarity of that scent is so blissful it takes me to the verge of tears. His chest vibrates with his voice, forcing me to pull myself back from the tearful precipice.

'Now then, I bet I can guess who this is.'

He releases me from his bearlike hug and steps past me, into the house, towards Sabrine. 'This has got to be your lass, Ronni. She's the spit of you.' Given that Sabrine is leggy and blonde and I'm only a couple of centimetres away from legally needing to use a car booster seat, I know this is a well-meant white lie.

He wraps his hairy, freckled arms around Sabrine, who stands awkwardly, as still as a statue, arms folded. "Ronni?" she mouths at me, her brow knitted, over Spud's shoulder, and I smile. I'll explain later.

'Well, I haven't laid eyes on you, Ronni, since the day we said goodbye to Lenny,' Spud says after he's squeezed Sabrine to within an inch of her life. 'Great bloke, yer dad. I don't 'alf miss 'im, you know. Especially now Pam's gone.'

I look down at my feet. 'I was so sorry to hear about Aunty Pammy. Laura messaged to tell me, but I just couldn't make it up for the funeral what with the distance and everything that was going on at the time.' Shame seeps through me. Our new hall carpet was due to be fitted the same day they buried Pammy. I could have postponed it but Lucy and Garth from the country club were coming over for dinner the day after and I so wanted it to be down for then, so I'd made do with sending a card and some flowers.

Spud lays a hand on my shoulder. 'Don't you worry, love. I quite understand. I knew you'd be thinking of us.'

The shame pools at my feet, numbing my toes.

'So, what brings you back to Haxton this time? Seen the light and realised you wanna be back amongst decent folk rather than them London softies?' Spud shoots a look back at Sabrine. 'No offence, love,' he says. 'You're 'alf northern, so you're all reet.'

Sabrine raises her eyebrows but says nothing. I'm not convinced she can make out what he's saying anyway. Spud does have a thick Leeds accent. I shook mine off as soon as I could, but listening to him is tempting me on some instinctive level to shorten my vowels again.

'Oh, it's quite a long story.' I will tell Spud the truth. On the journey up I decided there'll be no more lies – I'm just not going to do it here, on the doorstep.

Spud peers around me to see out of the front door. He frowns. He must have spied the van. 'Looks like yer moving in.'

'Yeah.' I take in a deep breath and press my lips together in an attempt at a smile.

He narrows his eyes and searches my face as if trying to process what's going on: van outside, no Matthew. In typical Spud style, he's tactful enough not to push the matter.

'Tell yer what,' he says, giving me a pat with the hand that still rests on my shoulder. 'You can tell me all about it tonight. Why don't you and your lass pop over for tea around sixish? I haven't got a right lot in, mind, 'cos I do my weekly Morrison's shop on Wednesdays and it's only Tuesday, but I can rustle up a spot of bread and a few slices of tongue. It'll save you a trip to the corner shop anyway. It's daylight robbery in there.'

'Thanks Spud.' Gratitude floods through me and I pull him in for a hug.

'Don't mention it, Ronni, love. It's good to see yer. Both of yer.' He scoops an arm around Sabrine and includes her in our hug. He's short but broad, and although he's in his late sixties, he's still strong enough to lock us both in tightly. Sabrine's arms are still folded. For the first time since Matthew died I feel I belong. But the sensation is so fleeting it dissipates as quickly as it arrived, leaving me craving more.

Spud releases us and grins, his cheeks glowing and ruddy from sunshine, making him look more like Santa Claus than ever.

'I'd love to give you a hand with your unloading, but this bloody 'ip's giving me jip these days. I'm on 'waiting list for a replacement, just gotta shift some of this first.' He pats his large stomach which is hanging over the elasticated waistband of his shorts more than I remember.

'Don't worry, Uncle Spud, we'll manage. There's not a lot anyway.'

'Right you are, love. I'll see you at six, and don't bring owt – just your good selves.'

He makes his way out of our door and I notice a slight limp in his gait. The sight gives me a depressing sense of mortality. Sabrine appears behind me, looking over my shoulder.

'I don't understand,' she says.

'Understand what?' I raise my hand to wave at Spud as he limps into his front door.

'Urr, everything that just happened then. Why does he call you Ronni? Why do you call him Spud? Since when did you have an uncle? What in God's name is *tongue*? Please tell me it's not actually tongue. Like a real tongue from a real mouth. And why do you drink tea with it?'

'Let's talk and do.' I gesture for her to follow me, and we walk outside to the van.

'Ronni was my nickname when I was a kid.' I open the van's back door and pull out a cardboard box I seem to remember contains a couple of saucepans and a few mugs. I hand Sabrine the box. 'I used to call him Spud because he was always at the window on a Sunday morning peeling potatoes for the dinner. That was the one domestic chore Pam, that's his wife, would trust him with. His real name is Gus.' I pull out a box containing crockery and head back for the house. Sabrine follows.

'Spud and Pammy aren't my real aunt and uncle, I just called them that. That's what you do round here – you call your parents' close friends aunt and uncle. Don't know why.'

'Weird.' Sabrine lifts the box onto the worktop, using her body to shift it all the way back to the wall so I can fit mine in front.

'Yes, I suppose it is a bit.' I lift the box up onto the top, and she helps me with the final heave. 'What was your other question?' I open and close my fists to try and get the circulation flowing again.

'Tongue.' She pulls a face. 'What is it?'

'Oh.' I wave my hand and turn back towards the door to fetch more boxes. 'It's what northerners call Prosciutto.'

I know I promised not to lie to her again, but this one's for her own good.

'Oh, right,' she says, accepting another box from me that I pull out of the van. 'Why do they drink it with tea? That's a bit odd, isn't it?'

'*For* tea not with tea, is what Spud meant.' I hang an IKEA carrier bag full of clothes over the crook of my elbow and negotiate a plastic tub in my arms. 'Tea here means dinner. Dinner means lunch.' My voice strains with the effort of the weight I'm carrying as I struggle to the door, Sabrine in front.

She shakes her head and places her box on the sofa. 'This place is totally crazy. How is it we've only driven a few hours up the motorway and I feel like I've arrived on a different planet?'

I wipe my dusty hands on my jeans. 'You'll get used to it.'

'Yeah, well I don't want to get used to it.' She heads for the door. 'But I don't seem to get a choice in the matter.'

I wait until she's out of earshot. 'No, sweetheart.' My voice rings out in the empty house. 'You and me both.'

Chapter Eighteen

20 November 1993 – Bangor, Wales

Raegan

'And a glass of Sancerre for the lady, if you will.' Matthew snaps shut the long, slim menu and hands it to the waiter with just the right amount of confidence that says he's perfectly at home here; that even at nineteen years old, this is his world.

'Excellent choice, sir.' The waiter nods as if not just accepting the drinks order but also acknowledging that Matthew is the kind of diner to be respected.

I've never heard of *Sonn Sare* but it sounds like some kind of cocktail. I hope it's fruity. My tastebuds zing at the thought. *The lady*, he called me. Not just *a* lady, but *the* lady. I've only ever been called that before by mothers talking to their children. 'Mind *the lady*, poppet'; 'Look where you're going, you almost bumped into *the lady*.'

Here, in Franks, North Wales' most exclusive restaurant, I feel like a grown-up. Not an adult – I've been one of those since I was eleven. My last day being a kid was the last day my mum was around. After that I soon had to learn adult things, like you have to wash colours separately and milk left out of the fridge tastes like death. Feeling like a grown-up is different. It's being looked at like you're someone that matters.

'You look ravishing this evening, Raegan.' Matthew places his hand on mine and strokes my fingers.

'Do I?' I look down at my cerise pink dress I bought this morning for a couple of quid from Help the Aged and wonder if he's being sarcastic. Is it too short for a place like this? Maybe I should have taken off the ankle bracelet for tonight. Does it give me away as an imposter?

He laughs. 'Absolutely radiant.'

Ravishing, radiant. I love that Matthew has so many synonyms for "beautiful".

I remember the advice given in *More* magazine for how to accept a compliment in an alluring way. I look up at him through my lashes, bat them a few times and smile at him in a way I hope is *coy*. 'Thank you,' I say.

His smile fades. 'Are you all right, darling? Do you have something in your eye?'

'Oh, no, I'm fine.' I lift my head back up, flick my fringe out of my eyes and resolve not to believe anything else I read in the advice columns.

The waiter returns with a glass of red wine for Matthew and a glass of white for me. I wait for Matthew to tell him, no, he's ordered *the lady* a Sonn Sare fruity cocktail, but he just smiles his thanks.

I hide my disappointment as we cheers, but console myself that I have now added to my repertoire that Sonn Sare is a white wine.

'So,' Matthew says, after swirling his wine around the glass, sniffing it and taking a sip. 'What are you hoping to do with your degree? What is it again – business studies?'

'International business studies. I don't know yet. At the moment I'm just concentrating on each essay as it comes so that I pass. Once I do, then I guess I'll look to see what's out there. I'd like to work abroad, maybe Paris or Brussels. I'd have to take some language lessons when I'm there, but it should be fine at the start with English being the main language of business. What about you?'

'My father wants me to take over the family business eventually, but I'm not sure wine importing is for me in the long-term. I prefer to stand on my own two feet and make my own way in life. That's the beauty about a degree in management and communications – it leaves my options open.'

This is why I find this man so sexy. It's not just his piercing blue eyes and toned body – although I have to admit, those things don't hurt – but his independence, his determination to succeed and, oh my God, his perfect sense of style. That's what makes him impossibly attractive.

He leans across the table and gives me a lingering kiss on the lips. Right here in the poshest restaurant in town, in front of all these fancy-pants people, Matthew's snogging me. It's so wickedly romantic I feel as if my bottom's left my chair and is floating three feet above it.

'Ahem!' The waiter's subtle interruption breaks us apart.

'Apologies,' says Matthew to the waiter. Unlike mine, Matthew's cheeks are not showing the remotest sign of a blush. 'But when your date is this sensational, it's easy to forget where you are.'

'Understand entirely, sir,' says the waiter, a hint of a smile at his lips. 'An amuse bouche, courtesy of the house.'

He sets down a bowl in front of each of us. I've never heard of a *mooze boosh* but I'm guessing it must be a fancy chicken soup as it looks that sort of colour.

'Will there be anything else for you or the lady, sir?'

Being referred to in the third person and never directly addressed is starting to get on my nerves now. If I'm going to be a businesswoman extraordinaire somewhere in Europe, I'm going to have to find my voice. 'A bread bun please, to go with the soup.'

Matthew and the waiter both look at me deadpan for a few moments, until Matthew's face breaks into a smile.

'A roll for the lady please,' he says.

The waiter, though still looking confused, nods and walks away.

'This is what I like most about you, Raegan,' says Matthew, linking his fingers through mine.

'What's that?' I'm not sure whether to feel flattered or like an idiot. I've said something inappropriate – again – I just don't know what it is.

'You're so different from any girl I've ever met.'

Given that Matthew's family is loaded and lives in a mansion overlooking Wimbledon tennis court, and he was educated at one of the most famous private schools in the country, this is hardly surprising.

'In what way?' I ask, spooning some of the mooze boosh into my mouth and finding it is cold, and has most definitely not been anywhere near a chicken. I reach for my Sonn Sare and take a large glug to take the taste away. The bitter flavours catch in my throat, making me cough.

Matthew lets out a low laugh and hands me a napkin, which I splutter ungainly into.

'In *this* way,' he says, once I regain my composure. 'You're funny, feisty, and don't try to impress anyone.'

Oh, I try. I just obviously suck at it.

'Thank you,' I say, but this time I don't bother lowering my head and looking at him through my lashes.

For a moment he doesn't speak – he just looks at me like I'm the most exquisite creature to grace the earth. Fuck knows why or how such a miracle should happen, but I think he's falling in love with me. I know I already have with him.

He blinks, picks up his spoon and tries his mooze boosh. I wait for him to comment that it's gone cold or isn't chicken, but instead he *mmm*s.

'Champagne sorbet. Delicious.'

'Oh yes,' I say. I spoon more into my mouth and try out my old trick of holding my breath. It works. 'Delicious.'

'You know, Raegan, I've been thinking.'

'Oh?' I tip back the last of my wine. This Sonn Sare isn't too bad actually. It's not quite lager 'n' black, but you could get used to it.

'We've been on a few dates now. You're like a breath of fresh air in my life.'

Sweeeeeet.

'I think we should go exclusive. Do you agree?'

My spoon clatters as it falls into my bowl. 'Does the Pope shit in the woods?'

Matthew grins. 'Not as far as I'm aware, no.'

'Bears.' I shake my head and feel my cheeks heat up again. 'I mean Popes are Catholic. It's bears that shit in the woods. I mean go to the toilet. They go to the toilet. In the woods.'

'They do indeed.' He's shaking with laughter and can hardly get his words out. 'Shall I take that as a yes?'

I breathe slowly, willing myself to act like *the lady* again. 'Yes.' I smile and pick up my wine glass. I remember as soon as I put it to my lips it's empty, but feign taking a sip, anyway.

'Excellent,' says Matthew. 'In that case, I'd like to invite you to spend Christmas at our family's estate in Herefordshire. It's where we always spend the festive season.'

An estate? I never imagined the Kent-Walters would choose to spend the holidays on a housing estate, but then maybe they have family who aren't as well off and like to spend Christmas with them, as a reminder of how fortunate they are compared to the poorer relatives.

'But I realise you may prefer to return to Yorkshire to be with your father at Christmas.'

'Actually, my dad's going away over the holidays.' Dad did invite me to go to the Costa del Sol with him and Donna, but said I'd have to pay for my own ticket as the cash he'd collected through taxiing only stretched to a week's worth of accommodation and meals out for two and, as he so delicately put it, he "wanted to get his end away".

'So …' Matthew strokes his index finger up my arm to my elbow. 'Does that mean you'll come?'

'I'd love to.'

'That's great. We always go hunting on Boxing Day.'

'Hunting for what?' I say, imagining searching a garden for chocolate Santas to put in a pretty little wicker basket.

'Deer. There are some beautiful fallow.'

'Oh.'

'Have you ever taken a shot before?' He dabs the corners of his already-clean mouth with his linen napkin.

I figure he's not talking about tequila. The picture in my mind of a housing estate fizzles away and is replaced with one of rolling countryside – the kind of estate Matthew is clearly referring to because of course the Kent-Walters do not have poor relatives. Under the table I kick my own shin for being stupid enough for thinking such a thing.

'Erm, no, actually,' I admit. I've never pretended to Matthew that I am from his world, I've just been selective so far with the information I have offered him about my life.

'Then I'll teach you. I'll teach you everything you need to know, Raegan.'

That's gonna take some time.

'I want you'—he gently taps the end of my nose—'funny, feisty, different you, to be a part of my life.'

My heart soars and I can't stop a big, pathetic grin from taking over my face. I lean over and kiss him, with tongues and everything.

'Another drink before the main course, perhaps?'

I jump away at the sound of the waiter's voice. Matthew and I both laugh at being caught again.

'A bottle of Dom Pérignon please. We're celebrating,' says Matthew.

Yes indeed, we're celebrating. Bring on the Don Perry-non!

Chapter Nineteen

18 September 2018 – Haxton, Yorkshire
Ronni

Unlike Dad's house, Spud's remains largely unchanged. Save for the new addition of laminate flooring running throughout the entirety of the downstairs, everything else is more or less just as I remember it, even down to the mottled cream and brown tiles on the kitchen wall, the occasional one punctuated with an image of a bird.

''Ere you go.' Spud leans over the kitchen table to squeeze a bowl of pickled onions into the last available space. His T-shirt rides up as he stretches, revealing a large sphere of belly which presses onto the pile of sliced bread beneath it. When he stands up again, the top slice, already buttered, is stuck to his skin.

'Oops,' he says, and peels it off. 'Waste not, want not.' He takes a bite out of the slice.

I can feel Sabrine's eyes burning into me, willing me to look at her, but I pretend to look around the room. I can't face another judgemental expression from her. I've seen enough of them for one day. Every one of them makes me feel I've let her down and slipped another notch in her estimation.

'Get stuck in,' Spud pipes up, waving the half-eaten bread in the direction of all the food. For a man who hadn't yet done his weekly supermarket shop, he was well stocked. 'You two skinny lasses look like you could do with a good feed.'

'Thanks, Spud.' I help myself to a slice of buttered white bread – something I haven't eaten for years – and let its sugary lightness melt in my mouth.

The taste transports me back to this very place, a long time ago. I reach under the table and run my finger along the underside of the wood. I smile as I feel the scratchy engraving and remember how Laura had sat under the table in a silent rebellion, scratching out the words with a pair of compasses – probably the only time she ever used them.

I smile to myself and wonder if Lance ever did find the statement his sister had written: "Lance is a gay tosspot".

Funny that, although none of us – including Laura – knew it at the time, Lance was in fact gay. I know from Laura that Lance is a successful lawyer in London, living with his just-as-successful gorgeous lawyer boyfriend.

The day I found out, I was almost disappointed. While I never fancied him, I thought he fancied me – maybe because Laura forever teased him about it. It was nice thinking I had an admirer.

'How are Lance and Laura?' I ask.

'Both doing well,' says Spud as he places an oversized mug of tea in front of each of us. 'Lance has just been made partner at that fancy firm he works for, and Laura and Marcus seem to have settled into life in Hong Kong.'

'Oh yes,' I say, remembering Laura's excited text message last year when Marcus had secured his new post. At the time I'd been glad my husband's field of work didn't require him to traipse halfway around the world to find a good job, but the thought of doing that seems far preferable to the situation I'm in now.

'Martha must be starting secondary school soon,' I say, forcing down the jealousy which threatens to consume me. What kind of person is envious of their oldest friend's happiness?

Spud nods and wipes his sweat-laced brow with the back of his arm. 'Just started. She's going to some fancy international school.'

I smile. According to Spud everything is "fancy".

'Don't expect the education will be as rounded as she'd get at Fairhills High,' he says. His expression is wistful, but I can tell by the shine in his eyes that inside he's practically bursting with pride at how both his children have turned out.

I trace my finger again over Laura's thirty-year-old engraving.

'Laura and her lot are coming for Christmas all being well. You'll be able to see her then if you're still about,' says Spud.

I'm about to tell him that short of a lottery win, we'll almost certainly still be about at Christmas, when there's a knock at the door.

'Ah, that'll be Toni and her kids,' says Spud, getting up from the table.

I go to ask him who Toni is but he's already out of the room by the time my mouth is clear of fluffy dough.

'That doesn't look like prosciutto to me.' Sabrine's wrinkling her nose and looking down at the dark pink meat on the plate in front of her.

'It's Yorkshire prosciutto,' I say. 'From pigs hand-reared on organic farms in the Dales. Try it.'

Tentatively, she slices off the tiniest corner like any more might result in sudden death.

She chews for far longer than can be necessary to break down such a minuscule sliver of meat, then shrugs, denoting it edible.

Footsteps pound down the hall, accompanied by a high-pitched squeal, then two faces peer around the door.

'Hello.' I keep my voice soft so as not to intimidate the younger guests.

'Hi.' The older one – the girl – speaks first. She emerges from behind the door, revealing herself to be a pretty, crinkly-haired pre-teen, wearing jeans and a cropped T-shirt. Like her younger brother, who appears to be of primary school age, she has dark eyes and light-brown skin.

'Hiya.' Following his sister's lead, the boy greets us, his big eyes, framed with the kind of impossibly long eyelashes only – and unfairly – found on boys, take us in.

A third, and slightly darker, face appears around the door. Spud must have told her we're here as she's smiling in anticipation.

'Hiya, I'm Toni.'

She's maybe a couple of inches taller than me with slim legs, a thick but not fat waist, and a disproportionately large bust which is proudly on show thanks to a close-fitting T-shirt. Her hair is shaved close to her head in a style which would look utterly horrendous on me, but with her high cheekbones and smooth skin, actually makes me think marine-chic might catch on.

I stand up to greet her, offering my hand. She looks down, as if she's not quite sure what to do, but then accepts my hand and shakes it.

'Rae – um, I mean, Ronni,' I say. It seems wrong somehow to call myself anything other than *Ronni* in this house. 'And this is my daughter, Sabrine.' I turn back to look at Sabrine, who is wearing a faint smile and gives a quick wave.

Spud arrives back in the room, hitching up his Bermuda shorts. He introduces us all, including Pip, who I learn is seven, and eleven-year-old Bronte.

'I thought it might be an idea for all you young people to meet,' says Spud.

God bless Spud, not just for thinking of everyone else, as usual, but for putting me in the same age demographic as Toni, who didn't even look like she'd reached thirty yet, and my own daughter, who is still a teenager.

Tea together is convivial. Toni has a chatty easiness to her and tells us she lives two doors down. Over the course of twenty minutes she offers up more information about herself than I know about my closest friends, while asking us plenty of questions too. I forgot till now that's how it is here. Sit on a bench next to a stranger in Yorkshire and you'll know their life story within five minutes. Sit on a bench next to a stranger in London, and you'll soon have it all to yourself if you try to strike up conversation. I always quite liked that anonymity, but right now it feels good to talk, and to be listened to.

Toni doesn't look at me with shock or pity when I tell her we're here because my husband has died – just with an interested acceptance. I even find myself telling her and Spud that he took his own life.

Sabrine isn't listening at this point. She's in deep conversation with Bronte, who is looking up at her with admiring eyes, the same way a younger sister might look up to the elder. And Pip is cutting eye and nose holes out of a slice of tongue, which he then lays on his face like a mask.

Spud gives me a quick cuddle and offers me his condolences and Toni strokes a hand down my hair in a way that is somehow not at all patronising – just simply, and touchingly, human.

I don't tell them about the other woman, the child, or the gambling debts. It's not the right time for that.

'You don't look old enough to have an eleven-year-old daughter,' Sabrine says to Toni. She's finally relaxing now Spud has declared the double chocolate gateau sufficiently defrosted to eat. For a girl of half-good breeding, Sabrine always did prefer the taste of the cheaper stuff.

'You must have had her when you were about sixteen,' says Sabrine.

I know Sabrine means this as a compliment, and is not expecting Toni to answer that no, she was in fact fifteen.

Sabrine shrinks back into her chair, but there's no bitterness or shame in Toni's admission. She just says it like it is, which I'm starting to realise is her style, and I like her for it.

'When does the hire van need to go back, Ronni?' Spud asks, diffusing Sabrine's moment of mortification.

'I need to ring the company in the morning and they'll come and collect it,' I say.

Spud tears off a piece of kitchen paper from the roll he placed on the table, which he referred to as "posh serviettes". 'What will you do for a vehicle?'

‘God knows,’ I say, leaning back in my chair and stretching my hands to the ceiling. I’m so pleasantly full of pork pie and processed bread, I don’t want to think about that now.

‘Tell you what.’ Spud swipes the kitchen towel across his mouth, but when he takes it away there’s still a smear of chocolate ganache clinging to his white beard. ‘Come down my old yard with me on Monday. The bloke who’s taken it over often gets vehicles to sell on. You never know, he might ’ave just the thing.’

‘That’s really kind of you, Spud. I just can’t afford it at the moment – even a banger. Let’s just say mine and Matthew’s finances weren’t quite as healthy as I thought.’

Spud rubs his moustache, as he always used to do when he was thinking. It sends tiny flakes of pastry spraying onto his plate like a sudden snowstorm.

‘Don’t you worry about that, lass. We’ll ’ave a ride down to ’yard Monday and see if we can’t find you a motor. I can always sort out the engine for ya to save yer a few quid.’

‘Thanks Spud, it’s a date.’ I wrap my arms around his shoulders and give him a squeeze.

‘I can’t believe Toni was only fifteen when she had Bronte,’ says Sabrine after we close Spud’s front door behind us.

‘Yeah, it’s awfully young. I was twenty-four when I had you and that was young enough.’

‘She doesn’t seem the type.’

I notice on the other side of the road there is a dog walker doing the evening rounds. I open my mouth to issue a greeting at exactly the same time the man’s face is illuminated by the orange light from the street lamp. The words catch in my throat when I realise who those sagging jowls and round glasses belong to. It can’t be, can it? Mr Keyton was ancient – and I mean practically Jurassic – when I was a kid. That was thirty years ago. By now he must be … I do a quick mental calculation … one hundred and seventy at least. I glance at the terrier scampering by his side. It even looks like the same bloody dog! Jesus.

‘Mum, you’re not listening.’ Sabrine digs me in the ribs.

‘Sorry, sweetheart,’ I say, turning my head so I could see the retreating dog walker. Perhaps it’s Mr Keyton’s love child. Euw, the thought.

‘Mum, for God’s sake!’

'Sorry, sweetheart, sorry. What did you say?' We reach our door and I fumble in my pocket for the key.

'I said, Toni doesn't seem the type to be a teenage mum because she's so into literature. I'm not saying there's a direct correlation between literature lovers and pregnancy age, but you know what I mean, right?'

'Urgh, yeah.' I wiggle the key in the lock that's been changed to a shiny new one since I last lived here. Finally, the key gives a satisfying *click* and the door opens. 'How do you know she's into literature?'

Sabrine steps into the house after me and kicks off her pumps. 'She told me, when you were doing the washing up with Spud. That's why Pip is called Pip – from the character in *Great Expectations*. And Bronte is called Bronte because—'

'Oh yes, I get it.' I flop onto the sofa, realising just how exhausted I am.

'Cool names, don't you think?'

'Very cool. Hey, I'm pooped. How about I make us both a cup of hot chocolate and we watch a bit of telly together?'

'*Telly*? You're talking funny now we're here. I don't like it.'

I laugh and remove my earrings that are starting to pinch. 'Sorry, sweetheart. I'll try not to from now on.'

'It's just so much change.' She plants herself on the sofa beside me, her bottom lip quivering. 'First Daddy, then leaving Guildford, your hair, and now this.' She indicates the room with her hand, then lets it fall down to her lap. 'I can't cope with you talking funny too on top of all that. It freaks me out.'

I ruffle her hair. 'I understand.'

'Besides,' she says. 'We haven't got a *telly*.'

'Oh no, of course we haven't. I sold them all, didn't I?'

'I don't know why you had to sell all five of them.' Her huffy voice is back.

'Actually.' I lean forward as a thought occurs. 'I didn't. I kept the one out of the gym room.'

'Did you?' Her eyes light up. I remember that look – it's the same one she used to get as a little girl when she realised the tooth fairy had been.

'I did. Haven't a clue how to get it set up, but I'm sure we'll figure it out. Anyway—' I tap her thigh and use all my remaining energy reserves to heave myself up. 'I'll get us that hot chocolate.'

'No, you won't,' says Sabrine as I snap on the kitchen light.

'It won't take a minute, honestly, and I could really kill for one after the day we've had.' I stand in the middle of the room and try to remember in which cupboard I put the mugs.

'No, Mum,' says Sabrine, looking across at me from the sofa into the open plan kitchen. 'I mean we haven't got any of that either.'

With my hot chocolate dreams dashed, I snap the light back off and mouth a silent swear into the darkness.

Chapter Twenty

1 January 1997 – Trysil, Norway
Raegan

'Happy New Year, darling.'

'Happy New Year.' I turn my head to kiss Matthew. It starts as a peck but ends up a long, sexy kiss, which makes me burn between my legs.

Matthew, laying naked underneath me on the sofa, reaches his hand beneath the deerskin blanket which covers us, and squeezes my bare breasts. I feel his hardness dig into the skin of my thigh.

'Again?' He murmurs as he combs a hand through my messed-up hair.

'Mmm-hmm,' I whisper between kisses. 'Five's the magic number.'

'There's just one thing I've got to do first.'

I protest as he gently peels his sex-slick skin from mine and slips away into the other section of our hotel suite.

I imagine he must need a wee. He must be really bursting. Nothing normally deters Matthew from sex. We've been like rabbits since meeting in our first year, and there's no sign of the lust fading. I love the way he always wants me so much.

I sigh with content and snuggle under the blanket. It's colder now without the heat of Matthew's body but the roaring open fire in front of me is doing a good job at combatting that. I smile to myself and gaze out of the large window next to the fire. We decided to leave the curtains wide open while we welcomed in the new year by making love. Our room is high up and looks out onto the piste, which is empty at this time of night. There's a party downstairs in the main lodge, but we're not interested in celebrating with anyone else – just each other.

Outside the sky is black, but with the white of the slopes, and the lodges all studded with hundreds of tiny golden lights, the view is bright and beautiful. Bright and Beautiful. Just like the song. Like how my life has turned out. I sometimes pinch myself to check I haven't imagined it all. I'd had a plan, when I left Haxton, but even the plan didn't look *this* good.

Here I am, Ronni Fairweather, living it up with my gorgeous, attentive boyfriend in an exclusive and expensive Norwegian ski resort for the new year. I can hardly believe it. Plus, after working my arse off and getting a first, I've been offered my dream job in Paris starting in two weeks' time. Matthew's really proud of me. I wasn't sure how he'd take the news as we're hardly ever apart, but he promised to come and visit every single weekend. And he will. I know he will.

I yawn, and the light glinting against the dark green glass of the empty Dom Pérignon bottle on the table catches my eye. Embarrassment swells inside me as I remember that night I first tasted champagne – real champagne, not the cheap fizzy stuff Laura and I used to buy for a couple of quid from the corner shop. It was at that swanky restaurant, Franks, Matthew took me to. I'd got quite drunk, but it didn't stop me remembering the sex. It was our first time and, God, it was amazing.

The thought of sex triggers me to look around for Matthew. I jump as I realise he's sneaked back into the room without me noticing and is crouched on the floor beside me.

'What are you doing down there? Get in here, now,' I purr, sitting up and wrapping my arms around his neck.

'Darling, wait, there's something I want to ask you.'

I stop in my tracks realising his expression is deadly serious. That's when I notice he's down on one knee, and my heart skips a beat. I pull the deerskin over my breasts. It doesn't seem quite right for me to be topless now, even though Matthew's stark naked, with his still semi-erect penis hovering over the fur rug.

'What?' I whisper, but I already know.

He holds up his hand and on his palm is an open ring box. The diamond on the ring inside is huge and sparkly. Bright and Beautiful.

'Raegan Fairweather,' he starts.

It's the first time I've heard his voice shake. Does he really think I might say no?

'Will you do me the greatest honour of becoming my wife?'

Thank God I turned Chopper down all those years ago. If I hadn't, I'd be living in his mother's council house and would never have got to experience this wonderful moment.

'I've asked your father's permission,' he adds quickly. I almost laugh thinking how that conversation might have gone. It must have happened at our graduation. That was the only time my dad and Matthew have met.

Sir, may I have your daughter's hand in marriage?

Aye, lad, does that mean it's your round?

'Raegan.' Matthew laughs, and I detect the touch of nervousness in the sound. 'Will you give me an answer? You're killing me here.'

My face almost splits with my grin. 'Of course I will.'

Matthew cries as he slides the ring onto my wedding finger. I don't know if it's relief or happiness or a mixture of the two, but he actually cries.

This is what I wanted. This is the life I dreamed of.

Chapter Twenty-One

24 September 2018 – Haxton, Yorkshire

Ronni

‘Sabrine, come and see what I’ve got.’

Instead of just one head turning to look at me over the back of the sofa as I arrive through the front door, there are two. ‘Oh, hi there, Toni.’

Toni lifts up her mug in greeting. ‘Hiya, love. I was just telling your Sabrine what there is round ’ere for young’uns to do.’

Sabrine plants her mug on the table, jumps up and practically gallops over to me. ‘Mum, do you know there’s a bus right into Leeds city centre from the bottom of the street? Toni says it runs till about four in the morning and takes you right to the part where all the main bars are.’

‘Oh, really? The transport links must have improved since I was your age, then. It always felt like we were stuck out—’

‘And,’ Sabrine continues, her cheeks flushed. At last there’s a hint of the old Sabrine. I’ve not seen her this animated for months. Hopefully it’s a sign of things to come. ‘There’s even a Harvey Nichols and a Michael Kors boutique.’

‘Well, I’m not sure they’re quite in our price range any—’

‘Toni says the clubs are amazing and—’

‘Okay, okay, that’s great, sweetie. You can tell me all about it later, but first let me show you what I got today.’

I beckon for both of them to follow me out of the front door.

‘Ta-dah!’ I hold out my arms as we stand in a line on the pavement by the small white van. Only silence greets my reveal.

‘So, what do you think?’ I turn to see Sabrine’s expression. One side of her lip is curled in distaste.

‘*Ronni Delivers*?’ she says, reading the signwriting on the side of the vehicle.

‘Yes.’ I try my best to ignore her lukewarm reaction. ‘Spud’s man had this little beauty to sell.’ I give the roof of the van a tap. ‘So I took it off his hands.’

‘I thought we didn’t have any money.’

I’d been hoping she wouldn’t bring that up.

I give my hair a ruffle. ‘Well, I had a little put aside.’

‘Oh God, you used the drug run money, didn’t you?’

Toni’s eyebrows shoot up.

'Ssshh!' I look around to check there are no passers-by. 'Keep your voice down, will you?'

'Sounds intriguing,' says Toni.

I hold up my hands. 'It's not like it sounds.'

'Mum got conned into delivering about a million tonnes of coke to a junkie in Nottingham.'

Toni's eyebrows shoot up further still until they're almost in line with her hairline. 'Well, Ronni, I must admit, I didn't think you were the type.'

'I'm not the type,' I protest. I'm not sure whether Toni's serious or not. Her face is a picture of bemusement. 'But all the little bags were hidden in John Lewis kitchen appliances. How was I meant to know? One was even in a spiralizer.'

'What the chuff's a spiralizer?' asks Toni.

'Well, it's this really nifty device with a handle that you—'

'Mum!'

'Yes?'

'No one cares what a spiralizer is.'

'Toni asked.' I look at Toni. Her head is lowered and her shoulders are shaking. I realise I must sound like a posh twat and shut up. Although she did ask.

'Ronni Delivers,' Sabrine repeats.

'Oh yes, let me explain that. You see, the guy who rents the unit next to Spud's old one is a printer and signwriter. He saw me buying the van and asked if I'd mind doing a small run for him because he's only got a two-seater. Some fancy sporty thing.'

Sabrine tips her head back to the sky and mutters something.

'Anyway,' I continue. 'He's called Baz, or was it Gaz? Doesn't matter. He said if I wanted to make a "bob or two" then he knows loads of people who'd pay me to deliver stuff for them.'

'Stuff?' says Sabrine. 'Not more drugs?'

'No, no, of course not drugs, sweetheart. Products and cargo and things. For people who work in the units in the yard. There are lots of different businesses down there. They all use couriers, but if I could do it cheaper, then there's a good chance they'll use me instead.'

'Right.' Sabrine takes a deep breath in and rubs her eyes. 'But why *Ronni Delivers*? It sounds dodgy. It might make people wonder what exactly it is that you're delivering.'

'What do you mean? I thought I'd keep it open, to show I deliver lots of different things. As long as it fits into the van, then—'

'Mum!' Sabrine cries through gritted teeth. 'It sounds like you might be a mobile prostitute or something.'

'What?'

Toni's lost it now. She had her hand to her mouth but still can't stifle her chuckle.

'Why would anyone make that assumption?' I stare at the van. Baz or Gaz has done a lovely job with the red and black lettering.

'Do you have a massage table in the back that you pull out?'

'Oh, don't be ridiculous, Sabrine.'

'Right,' says Toni, wiping her eyes. 'I need to pick up the kids from school. Why don't you two pop over tonight for a glass or two of wine? We can talk about some ideas for getting the business going, Ronni.'

'Thank you, Toni. It's good to see someone's encouraging.' I flash a look at Sabrine who rolls her eyes.

'No problem, it'll be fun.' She wiggles her fingers in a wave and strolls off.

'Look, sweetheart,' I say once Toni's gone. 'It makes perfect sense. I need a job. My computer skills are way behind and I haven't worked for years, but I *can* drive. Plus,' I add as Sabrine jams her hands in her jean pockets, 'It means we have transport. It'll be handy when you start an apprenticeship and need to get there and back.'

'What?'

'Well, I thought that now travelling is off for the time being you might like to get into the working world, and apprenticeships seem to be the in-thing these days. The yoga teacher's son did one in accountancy and now he's got a job at KPMG.'

'Accountancy? Are you kidding? I'm awful at maths.'

'Nonsense, you got an A at GCSE, and your A-level results were fantastic.'

'Yes, for drama and photography.'

'Accountants need to be very rounded these days. Employers are recognising that now.'

She throws her arms in the air. 'For goodness' sake, I don't want to be a bloody accountant!'

'Hmm, well, there's teaching, but you don't really want to get into that, not with all those knives they have in schools now. What about advertising? That's similar to drama, isn't it?'

'Mum, stop. Please just stop. Since when did you start making these kinds of decisions for me?'

'I just think it makes sense.'

'Makes sense to you maybe, but don't I get a say in what I do with my life?'

'Yes, of course, sweetheart, but you don't want to sit around all day watching *Loose Women*, do you? I mean, I know we've only been here a week, but—'

'For your information'—she spits out the words with such force that a drop of her spittle lands on my cheek—'I've got myself a part-time job.'

'Have you?' Now it's my turn to be surprised. It never occurred to me that Sabrine would look for a job. I always assumed, once I knew we were moving here, that she'd continue with her studies. She's never had a job. We didn't even make her do chores in exchange for the generous amount of pocket money she received.

'Yes, as a matter of fact I have. I got it today, actually.'

'What kind of job?'

She takes her hands out of her pockets and folds her arms across her chest. 'Bar attendant, forward slash'—she draws the slash in the air with her hand—'waitress at The Royal Oak.'

'Oh, Sabrine, no. You're not working in there.'

'Why not?'

'Because it's a total dive, that's why.'

'Spud says you used to work behind the bar there when you were young.'

'Yes, well, that's different.'

She glares at me.

'Oh, you think we're not different, you and I?' I ask.

She doesn't answer, just looks down at me, arching a single eyebrow.

'The kind of people that go in that place, Sabrine, they're not the kind of people you know anything about. Look at you'—I wave a hand up and down at her—'you're gorgeous, and tall, and blonde. They'll love it having you in there – someone to flirt with, prod fun at.'

'Why would they do that?'

'Because you're—because you're ...' *Posh.*

'Posh?'

'No, don't be silly. You're well brought up, privately educated, call it what you like, but you're not like these people, Sabrine. You can do much better than that.'

'And yet'—she flings her arms out to the sides—'here we are!'

'Yes, I know, I know, but it's not forever, just until I can earn enough money to get us out of here.'

'Oh, come on, Mum. How much *cargo* do you think you're going to have to deliver in that old banger to do that?'

'She might have a few years on her but she hasn't got that many miles on the clock.' I spot a patch of rust on the bonnet I hadn't noticed before.

'Get real,' she hisses. 'Even if you chug up the motorway day and night, you can't possibly make enough money to get us as far as Leeds train station, never mind all the way back to Surrey. Face it, we're stuck here.'

'For now, maybe, yes. But that still doesn't change the fact that my daughter is not going to be serving the deadheads who frequent The Royal Oak.'

She snarls at me. 'That's what you think. Have you ever considered that I might actually *want* to contribute to our household income?'

The stone of shame that I'm becoming all too familiar with these days, settles in the pit of my stomach. 'That's very kind of you, but you don't have to do that, sweetheart. I'd much rather you focussed on building a decent future career for yourself and let me worry about the money side of things.'

'We've done enough worrying, Mum. Ever since Dad died, things have been total crap.'

I open my mouth, but she holds out a hand for me to stop. 'Don't even try to deny it,' she says. 'You know it's true. I want to do something positive to help us both out. And if I do manage to save enough to go travelling – even if it's just for a couple of months – then at least I'll be able to say I've got some bar work experience. It should make getting a job out there easier.'

'For God's sake, Sabrine, you're not the kind of person who could cope with working behind a bar!'

She stares at me and for a moment I think she's going to cry or scream or something, but instead her words are cold and calm. 'Thanks, Mum. Thanks very much for underestimating me.' She turns on her heel and struts away, crossing the road to the pavement opposite.

'Where are you going?'

'To the pub for my induction,' she calls back without looking at me. 'Luckily they don't think I'm too posh to pull pints.'

'Sabrine, Sabrine, wait. Come on, please, let's sort this out.'

She doesn’t wait. She continues in the direction of the pub, just as I used to do at her age, dreaming of the day I wouldn’t have to do it any more.

Chapter Twenty-Two

22 August 1998 – Nutfield, Surrey

Raegan

'Oh, bugger!' Melanie lays the mascara wand on the vanity unit and rifles through her make-up bag.

This is the first time in the last half hour she's not been brushing, blotting or drawing something on my face, and I take the opportunity to have a swig of my champagne. The bubbles slip straight down to my empty stomach and leave a pleasant burn in my insides. I've starved myself all morning so I can fit into my beautiful, mermaid-silhouette wedding gown. The dress of my dreams. 'What's the matter?' I ask.

'I've only gone and bloody smudged it.' She tightens the cord on her white towelling robe and sighs. 'I don't know why you didn't just take Mummy and Pops up on their offer to hire a make-up artist for your big day. It would have made life a lot easier.'

I knock back another swig. It goes some way to calming my nerves which have been on edge since I was woken up at just before five this morning by a single magpie carolling insistently outside our window. I still can't quite believe that in less than an hour's time over three hundred people are going to watch me walk down the aisle.

'They've spent a fortune already,' I say. 'It didn't seem right to accept anything else.'

'Why are you worrying about silly things like that, Rae-Rae? My folks have got tonnes of money. What are they going to spend it on if not their precious only son's wedding?' She rolls her eyes and I smile. Despite the sibling rivalry between her and Matthew that simmers away in the background, I've always liked Melanie. She's nothing like me – she's liberal, a free spirit, a bit hippy-like really, which is miraculous bearing in mind her upbringing. She's one of the few people who can see her mother for what she really is: an unbearable snob.

Unlike me, Melanie's life doesn't seem affected by what Elizabeth Kent-Walters thinks or wants. And, oddly, her parents seem to accept her unorthodox ways, which currently involves shacking up with her "Cosmic Life Partners" – Star and Sunrise, two women she met in Brighton at a macrobiotic festival – and making a living, teaching "Tranquillity and Restoration" to a client list which includes London's rich and famous.

I don't know how she does it and remains unscathed. I'd like to be a little more *Melanie*. Maybe after today, when I'm officially a member of the family, I will be.

'Well, it's too late now.' I pat her arm. 'And it doesn't matter anyway, 'cos my lovely sister-in-law-to-be is doing a fabulous job.'

Her eyes dampen. 'Aw, thanks, lovely. I was quite surprised you asked me, if I'm honest. I thought you might have wanted Laura to do it, with her being your maid of honour and all.'

I almost choke on my champagne. 'Are you kidding? Laura's wonderful – an absolute whizz with numbers, but not one artistic bone in her body. She admits that herself. I'd end up looking like a clown if I let her loose on my face with a make-up brush. You, on the other hand'—I smile up at her as she flicks a huge brush over my cheek—'are bloody marvellous when it comes to making this'—I point to my face with both hands—'look half decent.'

'Oh, nonsense.' She grins down at me as she works. 'You're already gorgeous. All I'm doing is making the most of these fabulous features of yours.'

'And I can't tell you how much I appreciate it.'

She motions for me to look up. 'My pleasure, lovely. It's wonderful to be a part of my brother's big day. We hardly ever get all the family together any more.' There's a genuine hint of sadness in her voice.

To what extent is this lack of family time my doing? Guilt bites at me. I've hardly jumped up and down whenever Matthew's suggested doing anything that involves his parents.

'Anyway'—she takes a big deep breath in and smiles—'it must be so magical having your father down here too for the wedding.'

She runs a pencil under my bottom eyelid and I battle against the urge to blink.

'Yeah,' I say, hardly daring to move. 'I just prayed he'd be on his best behaviour yesterday for the pre-wedding dinner.'

'Ooh yes.' Melanie giggles. 'He's quite a character, isn't he? He and Pops seemed to get on like a house on fire, but I'm not sure Mummy knew what to make of him.'

'It was all going fine until he made that stupid joke. I could have killed him!'

Melanie, halfway through a swig of her own champagne, almost spits it out as she battles not to laugh. 'Well, I suppose he's in-keeping with tradition. You know – something old, something new, something borrowed, something blue.'

She's almost right, although I'm not sure where "something nicked" comes into it.

'He was bang on the mark with the *something old.*' She nods at the earrings in my ears; the beautiful gold knots that belonged to my paternal grandmother.

'Yes,' I agree. 'But the new, borrowed and blue parts weren't even for me.'

'At least the blue was for Matthew. But I think the joke was lost on Mummy.'

'Yeah.' I cringe, remembering the moment after dessert when my dad had handed Matthew a pornographic magazine, along with some awful joke about marriage being an anti-climax.

'Having said that'—she dabs her thumb in her champagne and swipes the area under my eye where she smudged the mascara—'I like his borrowed tie.'

I nod my agreement, silently pleased he borrowed a pale pink one to match our colour scheme rather than opt for his only other tie – a well-worn black one that has seen three funerals and at least as many court appearances.

'And that suit he showed us he's wearing is very well cut.'

'Mmm.' She's right. It is. I also suspect he acquired it by being in the right place at the right time when it happened to fall off the back of a lorry. "Ask no questions, tell no lies", he'd whispered to me over the petit-fours.

'This champers isn't shifting this bloody mark,' she says, giving up on rubbing my eye. 'Stay right where you are. I'll leg it down to Bunty's room. She's only down the corridor. I'll see if she has any of those cotton wool stick things. That'll do the trick. Won't be a jiffy!'

She flip-flops out of the grandiose bathroom in her hotel slippers.

I hear the click of our hotel room door, followed by her voice as she talks to someone who must be standing there. I can't make out what she's saying other than a few words which include my name and *bathroom.*

My curiosity as to the identity of my unexpected guest is soon satisfied as a thin face with a pinched chin appears at the bathroom door. The face looks even thinner than usual as the blonde bob which usually frames it has been pulled back into a tight chignon.

'Oh, hi Elizabeth,' I say, attempting to sound chirpy even though my heart has just sunk to the tiled bathroom floor. Why did Melanie have to choose this moment to leave the room?

Elizabeth folds her arms, takes a step forward and peers down at me. Sitting on the stool, I'm a foot lower than she is, and feel like I'm looking up at a disapproving teacher.

'You look lovely,' I say when all she does is look me up and down. With my hair up in curlers, and wrapped in a hotel robe which swamps me I haven't quite yet completed the bridal transformation Melanie has planned for me.

Still all I get in return is silence and beady eyes burning into me like lasers. She drums one set of freshly-manicured fingers against her folded arm.

'So,' she says at last. 'You're still going to go through with it, I see.'

'The wedding? Well, yes of course.' I release a trembling laugh. 'Why, um, why wouldn't we?'

She takes another step forward. She's so close to me now that I can see where her light pink lipstick has begun to congeal in a dry patch of skin.

'Because it's the worst *fucking* idea I've ever heard.'

Her emphasis on the curse makes me jump back away from her. I've never heard Elizabeth Kent-Walters say anything more offensive than "bugger", and that was at last night's dinner when the butter was too hard to spread.

'Wh-what do you mean?' I stutter, willing myself to act more "Melanie".

'Oh, come on. As if you don't know.'

'No, I'm afraid I—'

'Spare me whatever nonsense you're about to spout,' she interrupts. 'Do you really think this *debacle* of a marriage will last? My son, who's from a good family and has a proper education and *you'*—she screws up her mouth and looks down at me like I'm pond life—'some common little gold-digger who must think all her Christmases have come at once.'

'Elizabeth!' I spring up from my stool and face her head-on. I clench my fists down by my side and search for the words this classist, bigoted bitch deserves to hear. To my intense frustration, I can't find a single one and, instead of a dressing-down tumbling from my mouth, the only sound I release is a strangled sob.

'It'd be funny really, I suppose, if it weren't all going to end up a terrible mess.' She holds a hand in front of her face and scans her nails. 'And it will. It'll be absolute carnage.' She sighs, places the hand on her hip and glares at me again.

'Haven't you realised that to Matthew this is all a bit of fun? For some reason he likes girls like you. Always has. When he was a teenager he brought home the most *despicable* creature from the wrong end of town. I think he must get some sort of thrill out of it – or perhaps he thinks going around with working class girls is him doing his bit for the community.'

I can't stop the hot tears that are running down my face. I swipe them away, hating to think how they must be ruining all Melanie's hard work.

'That's not true! Matthew and I love each other. It doesn't matter where we come from.' My voice is shaking so much I can hardly get the words out, but I refuse to be silenced by this poisonous woman whose surname I will soon share.

She flicks a finger on the end of my nose. 'Ah, so very sweet. So very naive.' Her voice drips with condescension, and I tighten my jaw. I want to slam my fist against her bony cheek and show her why messing with *this* girl from the wrong end of town is a bad idea. I clamp my arms to my sides and hold back. Having my mother-in-law turn up at our ceremony with a dishevelled chignon and a ripped turquoise skirt suit would not be the best start to joining the Kent-Walters.

'Not to worry, though,' she says, with a flick of her side-swept fringe. 'Matthew will soon get bored of you. Once he realises that dirty little tramps like you can never be taught how to conduct themselves properly, he'll be heading for the divorce courts. And hopefully that'll be before you bring any half-bloods into the world.'

That's it. My temper switch flicks and my restraint dissipates. 'Jesus,' I say through gritted teeth. 'You really are the most—'

'Oh, good Lord, Rae-Rae. What on earth have you done?'

Melanie is standing at the bathroom door, mouth hanging open. I turn to look in the mirror by my side and see two panda eyes staring back at me with rivers of black running down my face. I have trashed the beautiful make-up job she spent half an hour painstakingly applying. When I look back at her she's staring at the two cotton buds in her hand, thinking no doubt exactly what I'm thinking – it's going to take a hell of a lot more than that to fix this mess.

'I think our bride-to-be's got a spot of last-minute nerves,' says Elizabeth. She squeezes past her daughter in the doorway and pats her shoulder. 'Good job you came back when you did, Melly. Looks like you've got a fair bit of work to do and time is ticking. We can't have her walking down the aisle like this, can we?'

Melanie spins around to face her mother. 'Mummy, you haven't said something to upset her have you?'

'Me?' Elizabeth's face is the picture of innocence. 'Why would you think a thing like that? This is your brother's big day. It must go on without a hitch.'

Without getting hitched would be her preference, I'm sure.

Melanie turns her head to look at me and raises an eyebrow.

'I'm fine,' I insist, answering her questioning look. How I'd love to tell Melanie what Elizabeth said to me, but my priority now is not to start a family feud, but to get myself looking good enough to marry the man I am absolutely bloody well determined to marry – whatever his mother thinks.

'I'll go and leave you girls to it,' says Elizabeth in a falsetto sing-song voice that makes me want to rip my ears off. 'I'll check on your father, Raegan, make sure he isn't drinking the bar dry. He was on his third when I came up to see you.'

My lips go instantly dry. The last thing I need today is my dad having a few too many and causing a scene. Oh, how Elizabeth would love that.

The click of the hotel door indicates her exit.

'Right,' says Melanie, brandishing a cotton wool pad. 'We'd better get moving. There's less than an hour to go and we'll have to start from scratch.'

'I'm so sorry, Melanie. All your hard work—'

'Hush.' She swipes the cotton pad over my lips. 'I need you to be quiet and hold on to your wedding jitters for a while, because you, my lovely, are about to become the most spectacular Kent-Walters bride this family has ever seen.'

'Yeff,' I say through stretched lips as she reapplies my lipstick. 'Yeff I am.'

Chapter Twenty-Three

24 September 2018 – Haxton, Yorkshire

Ronni

‘’Ere you go, love. Get that down ya.’

I thank Toni as she hands me a mug. *Oh, it’s cold.*

‘Got no glasses,’ she says, placing a wine bottle into the fridge. ‘Smashed mi last one a couple o’ weeks back. Mugs are reet though, aren’t they? Tastes t’same.’

‘Um, yes.’ I take a sip. It’s cold and crisp on my tongue and instantly my shoulders drop an inch or two.

She thrusts a flimsy plastic tray under my nose. Each of the tray’s circular indentations houses a swirl of beige.

‘Viennese Whirls?’ My reaction must have been more impassioned than I’d realised, as she laughs.

‘Go for yer life,’ she says. ‘’Av a couple.’

‘I shouldn’t. If I start, I won’t be able to stop.’

‘So what?’ She peels one of the beige swirls out of the tray and forces it into my hand. ‘You can ’av as many o’ these as yer fancy – they’re the calorie-free version.’

‘Are they?’ I take a bite, and the buttery biscuit is set upon by my long-denied taste buds. ‘I didn’t know they did such a thing.’

‘They don’t, you daft tart,’ she says, laughing.

‘Oh. Oh well.’ I glance down at the half-eaten biscuit in my hand and weigh up the guilt versus taste factor. The latter wins out and I devour the rest in one bite.

‘Mum, Mum, can we play Labyrinth?’ Bronte scrapes her teeth expertly along the jam and cream layer of the biscuit and looks up hopefully at Toni.

‘No love, not again. We’ve played that four times already today.’

‘Yeah, Labyrinth! Can we Mum, can we, can we? *Pleeeease*?’ Pip’s eyes widen puppy-dog like, and I can imagine it must be very difficult to say no to that face.

‘I’ll play. I used to love that game,’ says Sabrine.

Bronte looks at her like she’s just offered to save the world, and dives into a cupboard in the living room, emerging with a board game which she carries to the kitchen table.

Pip flings the TV remote control onto the sofa and rushes into the kitchen, demanding to be the green counter.

'She's a good lass, your daughter,' Toni whispers to me, making me feel even worse about the spat I had earlier with Sabrine. I asked her when she got back from The Royal Oak how her induction had gone, but all I got in response was a very curt "*Fine*".

'Now those two are entertained, I'm gonna nip out for a fag. Wanna keep me company?'

I nod and follow her out of the back door, taking a seat beside her on the doorstep.

In an impressive feat of multitasking, she lodges her mug between her thighs, balances a tobacco tin on her knees and rolls a cigarette. 'Should give up really,' she says. 'Mucky habit. And I could do to save a few quid.'

I make a sympathetic noise.

'Want one?' She proffers me the tin.

'No thanks.'

'Good for you.' She licks the cigarette paper and seals it. 'We've all got our vices though.' She picks something up from the opposite side of the step from where I am sitting and hands me a cardboard box. 'And I think we both know what yours is.'

I look down at the box and when I notice it contains more Viennese Whirls, we both laugh.

'Didn't see you sneak those out.'

'Go on,' she says. 'Treat yourself. Sounds like you deserve it after what you've been through.'

I accept the box from her, open it and select my biscuit. I nibble the edge, then wash it down with a mouthful of wine, feeling very naughty indeed. Mr Kipling's and Lambrusco isn't exactly the diet I'm used to, but it's surprisingly satisfying. A wave of guilt runs through me. I've worked so hard, sacrificed so much, to achieve my size eight figure. If I'm not careful I'm going to ruin it in one evening. *But who have I got to impress now?*

With a strange mix of relief at having no one to maintain a figure for, and an acute sense of loss that I don't, I polish off another two biscuits.

Toni takes a drag of her cigarette and tips her head back to blow the smoke upwards. 'So, why did he do it then, yer fella? Kill 'imself I mean. Was 'e depressed?'

I stop chewing and look at her. *Doesn't beat around the bush, this one.*

The last person to ask me such a question had been Tara Grunwald in the Co-op, whose eyes had glinted with schadenfreude. Toni's eyes are not glinting with an intention to spread my life's tragedies around the Country Club. In fact, I'm fairly sure Toni has never been anywhere near a Country Club.

'I've wracked my brain asking myself the same question,' I say. 'At first I wondered whether he was depressed and I was in denial, but I don't think that was the case. Matthew was actually fairly cheerful in his own way. According to the inquest, he took his own life due to being in enormous debt and the stress caused by having a secret family. Do you know what, though? I don't think either of those things were the trigger. I think it was the gambling. Matthew liked to be in control, and if he was addicted and *out* of control … well, forget the money and the mistress, it's that that would have driven him to despair.'

She takes a quick sip of her drink without taking her wide eyes off me. 'Jesus.'

I tell her everything – all about my visit to the bank, Arabella Pentecost and the debts to the casino.

'Bleedin' Nora,' she says, once I've finished. 'You couldn't make it up, could ya?'

I sigh. 'Tell me about it.'

'Well, I think you're amazing, Ronni.'

I almost spit out the final dregs of my wine I've just necked. 'Do you? Why?'

'For being so brave. After all that's happened, you've picked yourself up, come up 'ere and are starting a new business. Bloody brilliant, that is.'

I rub my forehead. 'I wish I shared your enthusiasm.'

She throws an arm around my shoulder and gives my upper arm a brisk rub. 'Everything'll work out, you'll see.'

'I hope you're right, Toni, I really do.'

She takes her arm back and starts to refill our mugs.

I hold out my hand. 'Oh God, that's enough for me. I'm feeling squiffy already.'

'What? You've only 'ad one.'

'I know, but I don't drink a lot.'

She ignores my protest and pours the wine until it reaches the rim. Despite my reservations, I take a sip. It's nice, this tête-à-tête. The alcohol must be contributing to my loose tongue, but it's a relief having offloaded it all.

'Anyway, enough about me.' I delve back into the biscuit box, convincing myself I'll have less of a headache in the morning if I have something to soak up the alcohol. 'What about you?'

'What about me?'

'What's your story?'

She flips open the lid on her tobacco tin. 'It's not a very glamorous one, I'm afraid.'

'Doesn't matter.'

'Haxton born and bred, me,' she begins. 'Grew up on the Sunshine Estate.'

'Oh yeah?' I try to keep my tone judgement-free. The Sunshine Estate. Biggest misnomer going that one.

'There's nowt bright and shining about that dump, let me tell ya,' she says, reading my mind. 'Mi dad's from Jamaica, mi mum's from Leeds. I was one o' seven kids.'

'One of seven? Wow.'

'Yeah, I know.' She tips her head back and blows out a fresh lungful of smoke. 'Mi parents weren't 'alf gluttons for punishment.'

I laugh. I love Sabrine to my death but I couldn't imagine having seven of her.

'It wasn't easy growing up with mixed race parents. Even round 'ere. Mi brother grew a beard once and some dick'ead shouted "Filthy Arab Bastard" at 'im. I mean, he could be a right filthy bastard but 'e weren't an Arab. Not that that makes stupid comments like that all right, but we're 'alf Jamaican, for Christ's sake!'

I shake my head. 'Stupid arse.'

'Mmm.' She nods. 'Abuse like that didn't 'elp matters, put it like that. And it 'appened all 'time. You know, I never really felt 'undred per cent anything. Dad used to bang on about how great Jamaica was, but truth was, I've never even been there. I've never actually stepped foot out of Yorkshire.'

'Really?' *I thought everyone at least had a week on the Costa Brava these days.*

'Aye. There wer' a school trip to London once, but I was ill that day.' She stubs out her cigarette in a chipped saucer by the step. It already contains a couple of old butts and a puddle of rainwater. 'They split up when I was thirteen, my parents. Dad moved out, and things got even shitter than they were before, and that's saying summet. There was no arguing any more at least, but Mum took it badly. Some days she wouldn't even bother getting out o' bed. I'm not sure which was worse.'

'God, Toni, that must have been awful for you.'

'Oh aye, it was. Which is probably why when Shane Smith, the little cock he was, came sniffing around me, I saw it as a way out.'

'Is he Bronte and Pip's dad?'

She turns her head to me, sending the pretty hoops in her ears swinging. 'The very one. I didn't know he was a cock then, of course. I thought the sun shone out of 'is arse. He seemed so sophisticated, you know – eighteen, out working, even rented 'is own flat.'

'Yeah.' I sigh. 'We've all been there.' A picture of Chopper's face flashes behind my eyes.

'So, when I ended up pregnant at fifteen I was actually 'appy about it. Can you bloody believe that? I thought *finally*, my own baby, someone to love, who'd love me back. I 'ad to leave school, o'course, and I didn't mind school, was doing all right, but as far as I was concerned it was a small price to pay for getting mi own 'ouse and starting a family I actually *wanted* to be part of.'

'What happened – to Shane, I mean – if you don't mind me asking?'

She turns down the corners of her mouth and shakes her head. 'It was a disaster from the moment we got this 'ouse. Not exactly the picture of 'appy families I'd envisaged. He didn't beat me up or owt like that – 'e just wanted to play computer games all 'time, get pissed with 'is mates – pretend nowt 'ad changed, basically.'

'So why go on to have Pip?'

She lets out a mirthless laugh. 'Last decent thing Shane did for me was give me Pip. I got up one morning to find 'ouse in a complete state. He'd 'ad 'is mates round 'night before and passed out on t' sofa. Place looked like a bomb'd gone off. There were pizza boxes and beer cans all over. There was even a pill on the carpet.'

'You mean—?'

She shrugs. 'Don't know what it wa'. But by the company Shane kept, I doubt it was a paracetamol.'

'Shit,' I say.

'Shit indeed. I just lost it completely then. Bronte was only four – she could easily 'ave picked it up thinking it was a sweet. God knows what could've 'appened. Plus, I knew I was pregnant then. Shane didn't. I 'adn't told 'im yet.'

'What did you do?'

'Lost my shit is what I did. I couldn't stand the thought of looking after Bronte, a new baby *and* a useless tosser who couldn't look after 'imself. I kicked 'im out there and then.'

'Has he ever tried to come back?'

She snorts. 'Like bollocks. Even when I was shoving 'is stuff into bin bags and ordering 'im out, 'e was most bothered about where 'e was gonna live. His mother 'ad fucked off to Tenerife for good by then, so 'e'd nowhere to go. He didn't mention seeing Bronte. Not once. Didn't even say bye to 'er. He 'asn't tried to see 'er since.'

'Presumably he pays you maintenance?'

'You're 'aving a laugh, aren't ya? No, love. To get maintenance, the bloke's gotta 'ave some form of income. And since roles in professional shirking are somewhat 'ard to come by these days, 'e's been *in-between jobs* for best part of a decade.'

'Where's he live now?'

'He's currently lodging on an all-inclusive basis at 'er Majesty's Pleasure.'

'Oh.' Although Toni doesn't seem at all uncomfortable telling me all this, I don't quite know how to react.

'Thought 'e could make a mint out o'dealing, didn't 'e? Stupid twat got caught first time. It made me so glad I got shut of 'im when I did, let me tell ya.'

'I can imagine,' I say, even though I can't. I really can't. Although I grew up here, it's so long ago it's like it was someone else. It's not *me*. None of this is me. Shit. What the hell was I thinking coming up here and subjecting Sabrine to all this? What have I done?

The mixture of biscuit and sweet wine congeals in my stomach. 'What about your family – do you see much of them?' I ask. *Say yes,* I silently plead. Tell me at least part of this story isn't totally depressing.

She shakes her head, sending her hoops swinging again. 'Dad's back in Jamaica. He got married again and 'ad another kid. She's only three. I've never met 'is wife or daughter but we FaceTime sometimes, so I've spoken to them. Mi mum's not so bad now we've all moved out. All but mi youngest brother – think e'll be at 'ome by time e's fifty. Never 'ad a job. Lives off 'dole.'

Oh Jesus.

'I see more of mi' mum these days, now I've 'ad Bronte and Pip. She dotes on 'em. Probably see more of 'er now than I did when I wer a kid. I clean with 'er three mornings a week, see, when 'kids are at school. We work for Tina's Cleaners, you know the company based down in Worthwell – where all 'posh 'ouses are?'

'Tina's Cleaners?'

She laughs and blows out a plume of smoke. 'Yeah, fucking great name init?'

'Yeah. It is a fucking great name.' I start to laugh. It tickles my inside and I laugh more until tears spring out of my eyes.

Toni laughs too – probably because I've completely lost it now.

A rush of warmth for this woman, and everything she has experienced in her young life, envelops me, and through my strangling fear for the future cuts a sharp edge of hope.

'That must be nice,' I say, when I finally manage to control my giggles. 'Getting to work with your mum. And Worthwell's lovely.'

'Yeah, shite job though. Pulling pubes out of plugholes isn't any more fun just because they used to be attached to posh folk.'

I snigger. 'No, I suppose not. What about giving something else a go then?'

'Actually'—she taps my arm—'I've heard Google's looking for a new CEO and thought a single mother from Haxton with no qualifications might be just what they're looking for. What d'ya think?'

I lean my head to the side and raise my eyebrows at her. 'Okay, no need to be facetious. I just thought if you're not enjoying the cleaning, why not do something you *do* enjoy?'

She grunts. 'Who's going to employ me? I need to be realistic. I can only work school hours and then only up to fifteen hours a week. If I do more it fucks up my tax credits. I'd end up worse off.'

'Okay. What would you do if you could do *anything*?' I span my hands out in front of us to gesture that the world could be our oyster.

'Well, I was always good at English at school. I left before my GCSEs to 'ave Bronte so never got to find out if that "A" Miss Soames predicted for me would 'ave become a reality.'

I clap my hands together and beam at her. 'There you go, that's it! You should take your English GCSE.'

'Oh, 'ang on.' She pretends to get up. 'I'll just see'f I've still got mi old school tie and gym knickers, and I'll pack misen off to Fairhills High come Monday.'

She sits back down, and I knock her gently on the arm. 'No, you divvy,' I say, realising it's the first time for years I've said that. 'You can do it at night school.'

'Um, you seem to be forgetting I've got two young children. I can 'ardly just go swanning off on an evening, can I?'

'I'll babysit.'

She looks down at her lap. 'That's dead kind of ya, Ronni, but I don't expect you to do that.'

'But—'

'Honestly. I can't see me going to night school. I'd probably make a massive fool o'misen. And everyone else'd be really clever. I wouldn't understand what was going on.'

'Toni, that's nonsense.'

She stands up suddenly. 'Getting a bit nippy out 'ere. Let's go in. Brew?'

I pause for a moment, wondering whether to push the subject or give it a rest. I don't want to be a flea in her ear.

'Brew sounds lovely,' I say, and follow her back into the house.

Chapter Twenty-Four

2 December 1999 – Royal Surrey County Hospital

Raegan

'I can't believe you went through all that for me – I mean for us – I mean for her. Oh, I don't know what I mean.'

Matthew looks shell-shocked. He's flushed and beside himself with the worry and excitement that began over twenty-four hours ago when I went into labour.

I smile, first at him, then down at our baby's downy head, nestled on my chest, and my heart threatens to burst out of my body, I'm so happy. She's quiet now, sleeping. All that crying she did in the first twenty minutes after being born must have worn her out. She screamed the second she took her first breath, and continued screaming when she was placed into my eager arms, and even when Matthew held her for the first time. Her tiny arms splayed out, and her tiny fists clenched.

I've only ever seen Matthew cry twice before – once when he proposed and once when he got the call to say his grandfather had died. That was different though – a snotty sort of whimper. This is a stream of silent tears through a beautifully pathetic grin. I love Matthew with all my heart but never as intensely as this. And the way he's looking at me – like I'm a goddess who's blessed him with the greatest gift possible – is empowering beyond belief.

He kisses Sabrine's head and runs a finger over her hair. That's what we've called her – Sabrine. It was Matthew's suggestion but I like it too. It sounds French, and the French have extraordinary taste in many things, such as wine and cheese. Plus, it's a nod to the job in Paris I never took. After Matthew proposed, it just didn't seem right, so I made do with an admin job in Guildford instead, at least until we got married, but then we thought what's the point in me getting stuck into my career if we're going to become parents? We agreed I should concentrate on marriage and family first. There'll be plenty of time for me to focus on my career later. It felt wretched at the time, turning down Paris, but like Matthew said, how could we plan a wedding with me across the Channel? He'd been right of course, like my Matthew always is.

'Look at her, Raegan. She's perfect.' Matthew's eyes are shining as he traces his finger over Sabrine's forehead.

'She is,' I agree.

'So beautiful,' he says. 'Just like her mummy.'

Mummy. That's the first time I've been called that. It fills me with warmth, then terror as I remember it's how Matthew addresses his mother.

'She might prefer to call me *Mum*.'

'Don't be silly, darling. All small children say Mummy. It's easier for them to pronounce.'

'Is it? Oh, right.' I hadn't realised that. I would have thought that two syllables must be harder than one but I keep quiet. I don't want to ruin this magical moment.

The door swings open and a nurse sweeps in. The noise disturbs Sabrine, who screws up her eyes and starts to root around on my chest like a sniffing kitten.

'I think baby's hungry,' says the nurse in a no-nonsense fashion. 'Let's try her on the breast. Is this the first feed?'

'Um, yes.'

'Excellent. Nothing better than the mother's milk to give baby the best start in life. Now, let's get her latched on.'

She cups her hand around Sabrine's head and guides her to my nipple. Sabrine's snuffled cry builds and builds until it becomes an all-out shriek. Matthew has taken a step away. I want him to hold me, to reassure me, but I feel silly asking when the nurse is trying to manhandle my breast into Sabrine's mouth. Finally, the tiny hungry mouth finds my nipple, and sucks with so much force it makes my toes curl.

'I think it's time for Daddy to go home and get some rest,' says the nurse. Although her words are phrased in a suggestion, her tone is more of a demand. 'It's getting late and we don't have spare beds here, unfortunately. It's by far the best idea for you to go home and return refreshed in the morning. You'll be more use to Mum then.'

'Yes, good idea,' I say. The thought of being alone with our new baby is terrifying, but I know Matthew needs his rest. With Sabrine sucking contentedly, I finally look up at Matthew, whose face has resumed its shell-shocked expression. It strikes me this is the first time he's realised his favourite playthings are actually attached to my front for purposes other than his personal entertainment.

He picks up his coat, comes over to me and kisses me on the head. 'See you tomorrow, darling. Can't wait to take my favourite girls home.'

A surge of loneliness sweeps over me and I suddenly want to cry. 'Don't go.' I reach for his hand.

'Now, now,' pipes up the nurse. 'Let Daddy go home and get some dinner and some well-needed rest. He must be exhausted.'

He's exhausted? I'm the one who's been in labour for the last day and night. I want to argue but don't have the energy.

'I'll be back first thing in the morning, I promise,' he says. This time he kisses me on the lips, takes one more soppy look at our daughter, and heads for the door.

'Bye-bye,' I say, but he's already gone. I look down at my baby whose eyes are closed. She's sleeping, still attached to my nipple. Then, whether because Matthew's gone and I'm lonely, or my baby's here and I'm delighted, exhausted, relieved, I think of my own mum and I start to cry.

Chapter Twenty-Five

10 October 2018 – Haxton, Yorkshire

Ronni

I throw the sponge into the bucket, which sends grey suds slopping over the side, settle myself on the edge of the pavement and reach for my mug of tea. The van was filthy after my last jaunt up the A1. I can't remember the last time I cleaned my own vehicle. Matthew used to get the valet chap round to the house. God knows why anyone would want to do that day in, day out. I've only cleaned one van and I'm knackered.

'Ah, well, it's done now,' I say to myself. 'For a few days at least.' It's only been a couple of weeks since Ronni Delivers has been in business but I've just completed my tenth job. 'Not bad for a beginner.' I swallow a mouthful of rapidly-cooling tea and fall into a wonderful daydream where I'm sat beside Alan Sugar on the panel of *The Apprentice.*

'Thank you, Sir Alan, I won't let you down,' says the grateful contestant who's just learned they narrowly escaped being fired.

'It's Dame Fairweather you should be thanking,' says Sir Alan. 'For her impeccable business advice and stunning commercial acumen. Have you heard how she began her empire with one little van that her daughter screwed her nose up at?'

The roar of an engine cuts through my fantasy, replacing *The Apprentice* TV studio with the reality of Gladbeck Road.

The motorbike responsible for the abrupt end of my daydream pulls up behind my van. The rider shuts off the engine, lifts off his helmet and ruffles his hair.

He looks down at me and grins. 'Hello Ronni. I heard you were back.'

I do not need a few seconds to place that grin, that hair, that voice. I know instantly who they belong to. 'Chopper.'

He swings his long, leather-clad legs over his bike as I fumble with my mug, trying to unhook my thumb from the handle. Finally, I manage it, and when I stand up he's right in front of me.

For an excruciating moment we stand there staring at each other. I'm not sure whether to go in for a hug, a kiss, a handshake, so I do nothing except stare. His hair is shorter – not floppy like it used to be – and starting to recede at the sides. It suits him. Other than that he looks the same, albeit with a slightly thicker waist – God knows he needed that.

He breaks into a grin and crinkles span out of the corners of his eyes like rays of sunshine. 'Good to see you again, Ronni,' he says, pulling me into a firm hug.

Finally he relaxes the embrace but still has a hold of me. I look into his eyes and am suddenly transported back over twenty years where, on this very spot, he asked me to marry him. And I said no.

'Do you want to, um, come in for a coffee?'

'Sure.'

'Right.' Despite his acceptance, I don't move. How can I when he's grinning at me like this? I'd almost forgotten how transfixing that smile was.

He breaks our gaze and looks across to my van. 'Ronni Delivers?' He waggles his eyebrows. 'She does, does she?'

I realise I'm still in his arms and shrug him off, pretending I'm desperate to pull down my sleeves which are still rolled up from van washing.

'I've started up in business,' I say, 'offering a delivery service, delivering, you know, stationery, crockery, clothing, whatever people want, really. All around West Yorkshire, and into some parts of the North, and, um East, and sometimes, um, even the South. As far as Sheffield, anyway.' The awkwardness of the situation has manifested itself as verbal diarrhoea.

'Never saw you as a white van woman,' he says. 'What with you being dead clever n'that.'

'Well. Needs must at the moment. Anyway'—I straighten my back—'I'm quite enjoying it, actually.' That's not strictly true when I think about last Wednesday when I got a flat tyre, and yesterday afternoon when I got lost somewhere and ended up en route to Manchester, but apart from that it's been okay. Quite satisfying when I think about it.

'Great.' Chopper, with his helmet slung over one arm, strolls towards my front door without waiting for me to lead the way. I like the way he does this. It means he's so comfortable with me he feels it's perfectly normal to walk into my house ahead of me. It's like we're still a couple. My eyes are drawn to his backside, which is tightly hugged in his biker's trousers.

Something stirs inside my tummy. *Shit, what's that?* Surely I'm not getting turned on by Chopper? Sex isn't something that's even crossed my mind since Matthew ...

'Enjoying being back then?' He turns his head around as he speaks and by the way he raises his eyebrows and flashes a lopsided smile, I realise I've been caught perving.

'What?' I flush. 'Am I enjoying being backside? Sorry, I mean, *back*? Yes. Sort of. I mean, under the circumstances—'

Chopper pushes open the door, then stands aside to let me enter the house first.

'Yeah, I heard about your 'usband, Ronni. I'm really sorry, love. It must be hellish for ya.'

'Yeah, well.' I don't want to talk about Matthew. Not today. Not with Chopper. It doesn't feel right somehow. I kick off my shoes and head for the kitchen area. 'Sabrine and I – that's my daughter – we're making the best of things.'

'I can imagine you are. You always were very resilient.' He bends down to unfasten his heavy boots and this time I force myself to look out the window. I fill up the kettle and come around into the living room and sit on the sofa.

He sits beside me. His leather trousers wield with a squeak onto my leather sofa. The thought of it affects me in a way that sends a spear of shame shooting up me. Women who've recently lost their husbands should probably not be thinking along those lines. Or should I be glad I still can? *I can't get my head around all this.*

'Is she in, your lass? Be great to meet her.'

I adjust my collar in a bid to cool myself down. 'Sabrine? No, she's working.'

'Oh? Where does she work?'

The kettle clicks and I'm glad. I don't want to see his face when he learns that the daughter of the woman who shunned him, because he wasn't cut from the right cloth, is now a barmaid down The Royal Oak. I half walk, half jog to the kitchen and shout to him the answer over the noise from the kettle.

'Good pub,' is all he says in response.

'Still two sugars?' I can't believe I've remembered.

'No thanks, love. Just one n'alf please. Watching the waistline. I even went to Weight Watchers with the mother-in-law down church 'all last week.'

I spoon in the required dosage, and carry the mugs over and place them on the coffee table in front of the sofa.

'Donna's done a grand job with it since she took over,' he says.

'Donna works for Weight Watchers?' Now this does surprise me. She was always very proud of her large breasts, the size of which was mainly achieved through a calorie-uncontrolled diet.

'Nah, course not. Since she's taken over 'pub, I mean.'

'Donna runs The Royal Oak?'

'Yeah. Didn't yer know?'

'No.'

'Didn't your lass mention it?'

'No. I don't suppose she realises I knew Donna.' I look down at my coffee, and watch the bubbly white circle in the centre still swirling around after its vehement stir. 'She hasn't mentioned much about the place, actually. Probably because I wasn't particularly happy about her working there.'

'Why not?'

There's no point even trying to explain. Chopper will never understand why working in the local drinking hole is not considered a promising career.

'Just think she should do something with her education, that's all. Anyway, are you still bricklaying?'

'Yeah.' He gives the back of his head a rub.

'And? Going well?'

'S'fine. Y'know 'ow it is. Work's work.'

'Yeah.'

'Mug's game, labouring,' he says. 'It's all fine 'n dandy in summer, but when winter comes'—he sniffs—'you never know if yer gonna get laid off.'

'Must be hard,' I say, while thinking that it's his career choice.

'Aye. Anyhow'—he lays his mug, now drained of contents, onto the coffee table—'better get off. 'Wife'll be wondering where I've got to.'

'Kelly?'

'That's right. How did you know?'

My cheeks go hot at the thought he knows I've once or twice looked him up on Facebook. 'Oh, um, I think Laura must have mentioned it.'

'It's been good to see you Ronni. I've missed ya.'

He's missed me? 'Good to see you too, Chopper. Been a long time. You've hardly changed a bit.'

'You 'ave.'

'Have I?'

'Yer accent's well posh. And your 'air—' He reaches over and strokes a hand over my head. His touch is so gentle, so tender, it makes me shiver. I close my eyes and breathe him in. There it is – that familiar Chopper scent of leather, Hugo Boss, Benson & Hedges.

'Had it cut,' I say, but my voice is a whisper. My upper body is moving towards him – leaning, falling – I'm not sure which. Although my eyes are still closed, I know my mouth is only a fraction away from his as his warm breath tickles my lips. Just a little closer …

'Woah, woah, woah, fucking 'ell, Ronni!'

He jumps up from the sofa. I snap my eyes open with a start. He's standing there, open-mouthed, staring at me like I'm some sex-starved maniac he's just had a lucky escape from.

Shit.

'What the 'ell are ya playing at, woman?'

'Nothing. I, um, thought …'

'Thought what?' His voice is softer now, but he's still staring at me, unblinking, like he can't quite believe what just happened.

'I guess I thought, you know, for old time's sake, we … um … that we …'

'You were gonna stick yer tongue down mi throat?'

'Well, I wouldn't quite phrase it like that, Chopper.'

'Phrase it 'ow you want, love, but that's what yer were gonna do. I told ya – I'm married. Our lass'd 'ave mi balls on skewers if she thought I wer up to owt.'

'Sorry, I, didn't mean, I just wanted to, um, say hello.' Even as the words come out of my mouth I will myself to be quiet. I will the house to develop sudden subsidence so that any second the roof will cave in and end my mortification.

'That would've been some welcome, let me tell you. Jeez!' He drags a hand through his hair.

'Listen, Chopper, I'm confused. I've had a shit few weeks, well, months actually. I'm sorry. Can we please just forget that happened and put it down to'—I shrug, searching for the word, any word, that can make my behaviour seem anywhere near normal—'grief'.

He puffs out a breath. 'Yeah. Yeah, sure.' He retreats to the door, stuffs his feet into his boots without bothering to bend down and fasten them, and scoops up his helmet from the floor. 'Been nice seeing ya, Ronni. I'd better be off. Catch up, later, yeah?'

He doesn't look at me as he swings open the door.

‘Chopper, wait!’ I jump up from the sofa and make short work of the few steps to where he is. ‘Please.’ I grab hold of his arm. ‘I don’t normally act like this. That there, that wasn’t *me*. Honestly. Things are just … difficult … at the moment.’

His frown relaxes. He presses his lips together and smiles. Great. Now even my ex-boyfriend who I haven’t seen for twenty-five years pities me. I’m not sure what’s worse – him thinking me a bitch-face-marriage-wrecker or a poor old lonely cow he feels sorry for.

He leans forward and kisses me gently on the cheek. ‘Take care, beautiful.’ He prises his arm away from me, and closes the door behind him.

I rest my forehead against the door, then bang it as many times as I can stand, chanting the mantra “You. Stupid. Bleeding. Idiot” with every strike. Only when my head throbs with pain do I stop. I stumble to the sofa, sit on it and stare at the black TV screen in front of me. Then a thought occurs which creates a desperate need inside of me.

I race to the kitchen and grab my mobile phone that I’ve left on the side. I stab in my pin number but, in my haste, get it wrong – three times. Finally, I regain some level of control over my fingers and get it right. With a trembling finger, I punch in the first few letters of his name until his number appears on the screen, glaring up at me like a beautiful drug to a desperate addict, seducing me with its promise of providing an instant high; a hit to make everything better, if only for a moment. I hover my finger above the number, hesitating, asking myself whether this really is the answer. *Of course it is.*

I tap on the number and press the phone against my ear, licking my desert-dry lips in readiness to hear the sweet balm of his voice.

I cry with relief when he speaks. It’s like I’ve found a secret channel to a special world; a world where Matthew will never die. How can he be dead when I can still hear him?

‘Hi, this is Matthew Kent-Walters,’ he drawls. ‘Unfortunately I’m unable to take your call right now. Leave me a message and I’ll come back to you.’

No “please”, no “thank you”. Just matter-of-fact. Commanding. Masterful. In those few short sentences Matthew reminds me of all the things I loved about him.

I listen to it again, and again, and again. Only after the fifth time have my sobs subsided enough for me to say what I’ve got to say. I wait for the *beep,* then start to talk.

'I'm so sorry, Matthew, so sorry. I don't know what I was thinking, trying to kiss Chopper. I don't want him. I want *you.* I always wanted you.' I pause. My breath shakes. And my shoulders drop an inch. 'But you didn't want me, did you? Not in the end, anyway.'

I stab the red button to end the call. In the months since he died I've begged Matthew via his voicemail not to really be dead, demanded answers as to why he cheated – with *her*, and declared my never-ending love for him. I've told him I adore him, despise him, can't live without him, am glad he's dead.

The messages I've left on there reflect however I'm feeling at the time; the full spectrum from *how-can-I-go-on-like-this-another-second* to *I-can-just-about-get-through-today.* The constant yo-yoing is exhausting. I know it's not helping. In fact, it's making me worse. Hearing his voice *just one more time* is a bitch of a narcotic, but I'm not ready to give up just yet because maybe the next time I listen I'll hear a clue in his voice – something that makes me finally understand why I wasn't enough for him; why *our life* wasn't enough for him.

But it's never there.

I shove my phone under a pile of post as if hiding a dirty little secret and promise myself that time really was the last.

Chapter Twenty-Six

23 January 2018 – Guildford, Surrey
Raegan

'Goodnight, darling.' Matthew gives me a chaste kiss on the lips, then leans over to snap off his bedside light.

Our bedroom plunges into darkness. I widen my untired eyes to adjust them to the blackness. After a few moments I can just about make out the curve of his head on the pillow. He's facing away from me.

I drum my fingers on top of the duvet and sigh several times. I hope that Matthew might get the message and ask, 'What's wrong, darling?' At which point I can tell him that it's Tuesday and we always make love on a Tuesday. If that's what you can call it. The last few times we've done it, and that's been sporadic to say the least, it's been more like going through the motions. No pre-sex kisses, none of that tender hair stroking Matthew used to do that I loved, no "I love you" s. Just perfunctory sex.

But even that is preferable to this; a husband who has his back to me and who has now started to breathe heavily, not because we're making hot, passionate love, but because he has fallen asleep. How can he sleep so soundly? Today is Tuesday and we haven't had sex. This is the third dry week in a row.

Perhaps he's been so busy at work he hasn't realised what day of the week it is. That theory calms me for a moment, then I realise that even the busiest person must know that three weeks can't go past without having a Tuesday in there.

I fold my arms across my chest and try an extra loud sigh. It disturbs Matthew enough to make him grumble something incomprehensible before he recommences his heavy breathing.

How can he be so calm, so peaceful, when it's clear to me at least that all is not well in our marriage.

Maybe the kettlebell instructor really put them through their paces earlier down the Country Club; perhaps that's why he's so tired.

'Maybe,' I mouth into the darkness. 'But that doesn't explain his mood recently.'

Matthew's always been a constant and controlled type. You know where you stand with Matthew. Over the last few months though he's been moodier than usual. One minute he's on top of the world, picking me up and swinging me around the kitchen, and the next he's been practically biting my head off, like last Thursday morning when he was heading to work and I asked him if he'd prefer steak or salmon for tomorrow's dinner.

'Oh, I don't know, Raegan,' he'd said. 'How do I know what I'll want to eat tomorrow when I haven't even eaten yet today? Can't you make the bloody decision?'

So I'd decided on salmon en croute, and when I served it up he complained, saying he'd been looking forward to steak! I wanted to throw the bloody lot at him but he'd apologised straight after saying he'd had such a tough day and he didn't mean to take it out on me.

He had to go out after dinner, something about collecting some papers from a colleague who lived in Bramley for a meeting the following week. He was gone over two hours which meant he didn't have time to eat the Madagascan vanilla ice cream I'd made for him in my new machine, but when he came back he brought me a gorgeous bunch of flowers, so I didn't whinge about it. I hate it when he calls me a *nag*. He'd even chosen just the right shade of tulip to complement the kitchen blinds, and how many men would have thought of that? He's very particular, my Matthew. Superior at attention to detail.

I've been making even more of an effort than usual to try to maximise my *allure* so that Matthew will feel inspired to resume Tuesday evening antics. Tonight, while he was in the ensuite shower, I slipped on my new lacy negligee, purchased earlier today from the wonderfully expensive lingerie boutique on Plumpton Road. I also spritzed a little Yves Saint Laurent on strategic parts of my body. Alas, he noticed neither, or at least if he did, they weren't enough to cause any hint of arousal.

I've been wondering if he's not attracted to me any more. I know I'm not as young as I used to be, but I look after myself and think for a forty-three-year-old woman I fare pretty well. I certainly put the effort in. Perhaps, though, when you get to my age, thrice weekly yoga classes just doesn't cut it. I paid an extra visit to the Country Club today for that very reason. I hate working out in the gym but if that's what it takes for my husband to notice me, then that is what I will do.

And I did get noticed. Just not by my husband.

The good-looking rugby-type strode in when I was halfway through my route on the torture instrument they call the cross trainer. He was younger than me – around thirty-five, I'd say – with broad shoulders and a killer smile.

He gave me eyes as soon as he saw me. I thought at first he was one of those blokes who knows they're hot and want to make sure all the women know it too, so I ignored him and looked the other way while he headed over to the weights. But every time the torture machine told me I'd burned another twenty calories, I gave myself a little treat by checking out where he was looking, and it was always straight at me.

By the time I'd done 200 calories, I was finding it difficult to wait for the next twenty to come round before I risked another glance. The cheeky blighter even gave me a wink and a wave at one point. I preened myself a bit for him too, giving a few hair flicks and pushing my shoulders back so my breasts looked as buoyant as forty-three-year-old breasts can look.

Once I'd finished on the cross trainer, I opted for the rowing machine. Rowing for me is one step away from self-harm, but it was the nearest machine to the weights and I couldn't resist turning the flirting up a notch.

Never have I been unfaithful to Matthew, and never would I, but the attention from Mr Rugby-Type gave me a thrill I hadn't felt for quite some time. I figured the confidence boost would do me good, so I carried on.

I rowed for much longer than I'd intended – 1200 calories. I barely had the strength to pick up my skinny latte afterwards – but it was worth it. I could tell Mr Rugby-Type was pumping heavier weights than he normally would to show off his muscles. The air between us was charged with sexual energy. It was like a no-contact love affair that had my libido shooting through the roof. It was magic, even though I knew it could never progress to anything more than seriously heavy flirting.

He didn't know that though, and when I was standing by the water fountain, with shaking legs after my epic row, he came by, skin all slick and glistening with sweat.

'Hi,' he said.

'Hi,' I replied.

'You're in great shape, if you don't mind me saying.'

Oh, how I didn't mind.

'I'm gonna head for the shower, then up to the clubhouse if you'd care to join me for a smoothie,' he offered.

I was so proud of the way I handled it – like a woman who had men coming up to her all the time – like a woman whose husband still shagged her on a Tuesday as well as other spontaneous days in the week.

'I'll think about it,' is all I said. Cool as a cucumber I was. I even twirled my water bottle around in my fingers as I said it. And if that's not the sign of a sexy, this-happens-to-me-all-the-time woman, I don't know what is.

He smiled, gave another cheeky wink, slung his towel over his shoulder and sauntered towards the changing room.

My insides sang. I thought I must be so desirable today that the minute Matthew gets in from work he will throw me over his shoulder Tarzan-style and carry me to the bedroom, where we will promptly make love like never before.

Now, turning my head to look at Matthew, whose heavy breaths have turned into a light snore, those thoughts seem like they never belonged to me. Maybe I should have taken Mr Rugby-Type up on his offer of meeting him in the clubhouse. No doubt he had more than a smoothie and a buckwheat flapjack in mind when he invited me. Things might have progressed. We could have ended up sneaking into a cubicle together in the changing rooms, where we would have ripped each other's clothes off, kissed hard and fast like our lives depended on it and had desperate, hungry sex which involved him bending me over the slatted wooden bench while he entered me, panting my name with unabated desire. I would of course have told him my name previously, while we enjoyed our buckwheat flapjacks – no, not buckwheat flapjacks – protein bars, because that is what Mr Rugby-Type consumes and indeed what I consume because I am in *great shape*, thank you very much.

I sink into the fantasy of him making naughty love to me in the confines of the changing room cubicle, and a wave of arousal floods my lower body. Casting a sideways look at Matthew, who is still in the land of nod, I dare to reach my hand down in between my legs. A thrill runs through me as I touch myself and, feeling guilty, but daring, I carry on a little longer, biting my lip to stem my increasingly rapid breaths.

I'm getting brave now, faster, then Matthew sighs, turns over so his head is now facing me. I freeze, in a panic. How am I going to explain why I'm touching myself as he lays beside me? I could tell him I've got thrush and am having a scratch. His eyes flick open for a fraction of a second, before they close again and his breathing deepens once more.

I don't realise I've tensed my shoulders until they drop in relief. Tentatively, I recommence the stroking of myself until I've gone too far to stop. I even risk a little moan, then giggle to myself as Matthew mumbles something sleepily in response.

In my fantasy, Mr Rugby-Type cups my breasts, pulls me into him and murmurs into my hair what a fine, hot woman I am and he can't believe his luck at seeing me on the cross trainer this afternoon. I tell him, in a sexy, husky voice, that indeed he was lucky because normally I only go to the gym on Mondays and Wednesdays, and then he does something fabulously rude which makes my muscles spasm and causes an explosion down below.

Awash with guilt, I nestle down onto my pillow and promise myself never to go to the Country Club on Tuesdays again.

Chapter Twenty-Seven

23 December 2018 – Haxton, Yorkshire

Ronni

'It's smashing seeing you two together again. And back home in Haxton – who'd have thought it?'

Spud bends down to pick up a sausage roll from the plate on the coffee table, exposing the top of his backside crack as he does.

Laura takes the opportunity to prod the bare flesh with her socked foot. 'Oi, you. I thought you were meant to be watching your cholesterol.'

'It's only mi second one,' says Gus, through a mouthful of pastry.

'Second one, my arse.'

Spud wipes his fingers on his jumper – a particularly colourful creation featuring Rudolph and a light-up nose. 'Surprised you've even noticed. You two have hardly paused for breath since we got 'ere.'

'We've got a lot to catch up on, me and Ronni,' says Laura, hooking an arm around my shoulder.

'Yeah, so much so that your poor husband had to take over the cooking from me.' I laugh.

Laura leans forward to catch sight of Marcus in the kitchen. He's busy chopping. With a tea towel slung over his shoulder and wearing my festive apron, he looks perfectly at home, even though until an hour ago he'd never stepped foot inside my house.

'Don't worry about him,' she says. 'He loves cooking but with his crazy work hours he never gets a chance to do it. Anyway, he's got Toni to help.'

'Help? Is that what you call it?'

We both look back in the direction of the kitchen to see Toni, sitting on top of the kitchen unit, swinging her legs and chatting to Marcus in between each crisp she pops into her mouth.

Laura waves a hand. 'He likes to be in control in the kitchen so he's probably banned her from doing anything other than keeping him company.'

'Aye, well, I think it's lovely we're all together in time for Christmas.' Spud ruffles his daughter's dark hair like she's a child rather than a woman in her forties.

She grins and pushes him playfully away with a, '*Gerroff, Dad*'.

Although Laura left Yorkshire just a few years after me, her accent is still detectable. Not that it's held her back. Even though she had to stall her own career, as a result of following Marcus around the world for his, she's just landed a new accountancy position for one of the biggest financial institutions in Asia.

'I thought I was gonna be on my own this year for Christmas,' says Spud, hoiking up his jeans. 'Then bloody loads of yer turn up. Even 'kids are gerring on a treat.'

He turns to look at the table I've laid out ready for the party feast that awaits. Sabrine is sitting very still on one of the chairs as Bronte paints her nails, and Pip, with his tongue stuck out in concentration, performs his first French plait under the guidance of Laura's daughter, Martha, who appears to be revelling in her role of supervisor.

I open my mouth to issue a warning about not getting nail varnish on my nice new Christmas tablecloth, but quickly close it again, figuring a spoiled cloth is a small sacrifice for keeping them all happy.

'I must say, Ronni,' says Spud. 'You've surpassed yourself with these sausage rolls. Beautifully flaky.' He snatches another from the plate and scurries away towards the kitchen to avoid Laura's protests.

'He's such a bugger!' she says, reaching for her glass.

'Don't worry about it.' I laugh. 'It is Christmas.'

'I do worry about him, though, especially now Mum's gone and we're so far away.' She takes a sip of her wine. 'It's so nice knowing you're around, Ronni. It makes me feel a lot better knowing he has a friend keeping an eye-out for him. And thanks so much for having him over for tea all the time. I'm not convinced he can look after himself all that well.'

'It works both ways. Spud's been an absolute rock since we moved back in. I don't know what we would have done without him.'

'He likes to help out. I think he gets lonely now he's on his own. 'Can't blame him really. He and Mum were inseparable.'

Her voice wobbles and I give her a squeeze.

'Do you ever feel we took them for granted, our parents? You know, when we were young; thinking they'd be around forever,' she says.

I rub her arm. 'You miss your mum a lot, don't you?'

'Yeah.' She sniffs. 'Can't complain though. I had mine a lot longer than you had yours. Do you ever—?'

I shake my head and lean forward to place my glass on the coffee table. 'Nope.' I don't want to talk about that. Not when I'm feeling more relaxed and happy than I have for months.

Laura hooks her arm around the back of the sofa and surveys the room. 'This place makes me think of your dad everywhere I look.' She suddenly bursts out laughing. 'Do you remember after a Thursday night out how he used to drive us home from Leeds at four in the morning because that's when his shift finished? The clubs turfed out at two, so we'd drink about a gallon of tea in that horrible twenty-four hour greasy spoon while we waited. How many dads would do that? We were only sixteen n'all. *And* on a school night. My parents thought I was sleeping round at yours. There's no way they'd have let me out till that time. Oh, bless ya, Lenny. He was quite a character.'

An image so vivid it's in technicolour appears in my head. The three of us – Dad, Laura and I – on our way back from town in Dad's cab. It's so late, the sun's coming up and the three of us are singing along at the top of our croaky voices to Dad's Status Quo cassette.

'We'd usually bump into the milkman,' I say. What was his name? Don Littlewood!'

Laura nods. 'Yeah. His son was in our year. You know, Craig, the one who got a 'tache before anyone else. Do you remember that his dad told him he'd seen us on our way home, and I had to snog him to make him promise not to dob me in to Lance?'

'Oh, yes!' I collapse into giggles against the back of the sofa. 'I'd forgotten that, but now you mention it.'

'Eurgh, I could never forget it.' She pulls a face. 'It was awful – like having your lips stabbed a million times with a tiny needle.'

'Seriously, though,' she says once we've calmed down. 'Lenny would be proud of you.'

'What, which part? Driving my cheating husband to suicide or ending up driving a white van for a living? I'm not exactly a high-flying accountant for one of the biggest firms in Asia, like you, am I?'

She nudges me playfully on the arm. 'For picking yourself up like you have and getting on with stuff. Not wallowing, you know.'

I cast a glance under the coffee table and spot the corner of Matthew's mobile phone sticking out from under a magazine. 'Oh, don't be too impressed. I do plenty of wallowing, just when nobody's watching.'

'It's a wonder you have time. Dad's told me how busy you've been with the business.'

'It helps keep me out of trouble, that's for sure. Between me and you, Laura, it nearly finishes me off some days. There's more work coming in than I can handle, which is good of course, but I can't afford to turn any work down, and end up running myself ragged. I don't know if I'm coming or going sometimes.'

'Why don't you hire someone to help you.'

I smirk. 'I can't afford that.'

'Can't you?'

I shrug. 'Well, I don't think I can. Seriously, even though the business has got off to a good start, it's a drop in the ocean when I think of the money I need to get us on our feet again and back down south.'

'You're keen to get back then, are you?'

I nod. 'Oh yes. Just as soon as I can afford to.'

She folds her arms and takes on a more serious expression, giving a glimpse of how formidable she must be at work. 'In that case … what do the books say?'

'Books?'

'The accounts, Ronni. Come on'—she gives my arm a gentle swat—'what happened to International Business graduate extraordinaire?'

'Oh. That was such a long time ago. It feels like it happened to someone else.'

'Well, never mind. I can help you. Your books will tell you whether it's good business sense to take someone on. Another person could earn you more money.'

'Yes, I suppose …'

'Of course! Think about it. If you have someone working for you, that's another van on the road – added profitability. You know all this, right?'

'I suppose in theory I do, yes. I've just never had the opportunity to put into practice everything I learned at uni. I've never really thought about taking someone on. I wouldn't know where to start, if I'm honest.'

'Let me take a look at your accounts after dinner. It should be fairly clear as to whether it's affordable.'

'I can't ask you to do that, Laura. You're here to enjoy yourself, not for a busman's holiday.'

'I'm offering,' she says. 'It won't take long.'

'Okay, well, that would be great. If you don't mind.'

'Not at all.' She picks up our glasses from the table and hands me mine. 'That's what friends are for,' she says.

'Someone's at the door!' Pip shouts and promptly lets go of Sabrine's hair. Martha races to save the intricate plait he's dropped.

Although I rise from my seat and head for the door, Pip and Bronte get there first, fighting to be the first to greet the visitor. Bronte beats her brother to it and swings the door open while blowing a triumphant raspberry at him.

'Darling!' Charlotte, looking as perfectly blow-dried as ever, reaches over the kids to fling her arms around me, enveloping me into her beautifully familiar Chanel-scented embrace.

'Oh God, Char, it's so good to see you.' For some inexplicable reason, I feel teary at seeing her for the first time in so long. 'Come in, come and meet everyone. Lynn – you made it too!' Once Charlotte is inside I pull my former neighbour into a hug. 'So pleased to see you. Let's get you in, out of this horrendous weather.'

'Hello, Raegan, dear. How kind it was of you to include me in your invitation. I've so been looking forward to it. I haven't been to Yorkshire since mine and John's honeymoon.'

I usher her in and shut out the rain. 'Everyone,' I announce to the room. Eight faces in my cramped kitchen-cum-living room turn to look in my direction. 'These are my lovely friends from Guildford – Charlotte and Lynn.' There's a murmur of hellos and a few waves and nods. Once Charlotte and Lynn are out of their wet shoes and coats and have drinks in their hands, I take them around and introduce them to everyone individually.

'Delighted to make your acquaintance at this most festive time of year,' says Spud in a strangely formal voice that sounds nothing like his own. I frown at him. He pretends not to notice my quizzical look but promptly turns bright red.

'Charmed, I'm sure,' coos Charlotte.

I suddenly feel like I'm caught in the middle of some sort of weird mating ritual, and excuse myself to show Lynn upstairs to her room so she can freshen up.

'It's so kind of you to invite me for Christmas, dear,' she says, following me up the stairs.

'It's my pleasure. When Charlotte told me you two had become friends, it seemed the perfect opportunity to invite you both up together.'

'We've got you to thank for that.'

'Really?' I snap on the light and Sabrine's small yet tidy bedroom comes into view.

Lynn claps her hands together. 'Ooh, how wonderful. I've never slept on a bunk bed!'

'Oh, you don't have to sleep on the top one. I'm sure Charlotte wouldn't mind—' But Lynn is already swinging one 60-denier clad leg over the top of the ladder.

'I saw it first. I'm taking the top one.' She turns to me and smiles, then begins her descent.

'As you like. Anyway, you were saying …?' My heart skips a beat as the ladder wobbles.

'Oh yes, how Charlotte and I met.'

Relief floods through me as her stocking feet meet the safety of the carpet.

'It was the day you left to come here. I saw her waving you off. She looked so forlorn, poor thing, that I invited her in for a coffee. Such an animated young girl she is. We chatted for ages.'

I smile at Lynn referring to Charlotte, who is in her late fifties, as a *young girl*, but I suppose in Lynn's eyes she is.

'Since then we've met up quite a few times for coffee. And cake. She's got a sweet tooth, young Charlotte, which is remarkable really as she's a mere slip of a thing.'

'Well, I'm glad you've made friends, and that you both came all this way to visit us.' I hand Lynn one of the fresh towels I've left out for her and Charlotte. 'Does your daughter mind that you're not seeing her this Christmas?'

She hugs the towel to her chest. 'I do normally go to Kent for Christmas, but I've paid for Jenny and her family to go skiing this year.'

'Wow, that's generous.'

Lynn shrugs. 'None of them knew what they wanted, so I thought – why on earth not? I'm lucky enough I can afford it. What better way of spending it than treating the people I love? You can't take it with you, can you?'

I shake my head, wishing that knowing what to do with all my thousands was a dilemma I faced.

'It might be the last time they have a family holiday all together. The boys are growing up so fast.' She sighs. 'You get to my age and you wonder where all those years have gone. That's why you've got to make the most of things while you can. You never know what's around the corner.'

'That's for sure.'

She reaches out and clutches my arm. 'Oh, I'm so sorry, Raegan, how insensitive of me. Of course you know that more than most.'

I smile and squeeze her hand. 'Don't worry. I know exactly what you mean.'

'Say when,' I say as I start pouring Baileys into Charlotte's glass. 'Um, Char? Are you going to tell me when to stop?'

'Stop when you get to the top, darling.'

I raise an eyebrow but do as she says.

She holds up the dangerously full glass. 'Cheers, girls.'

Lynn, Toni, Sabrine and I all chink glasses with her.

'Good of your mum to come around and pick up the kids so you can stay late,' I say to Toni.

'Aye, she can be a good egg, mi mam. Not that I ever ask her to babysit evenings. This is the first time I've been out for ages.'

'Sorry it couldn't be somewhere more exciting than my kitchen,' I say.

'It's good enough for me, love.'

'We could go sit in the living room.' The five of us are squished but comfortable in my tiny kitchen. Taking inspiration from Toni, Charlotte and I have joined her to sit on any clear space of kitchen counter we could find, while Sabrine and Lynn are standing and chatting.

'Nah,' Toni says. 'Wouldn't want to interrupt those two. I didn't know Pontoon could get so intense.'

I grin and glance through the archway into the living room where Spud and Marcus are studying their fans of playing cards.

'Good point. And everyone seems happy enough in here.'

It's nice to see Sabrine of all people looking cheerful. Our relationship has been tested to the limit over the last few months and we're still not quite there yet. I don't think she's fully forgiven me for not wanting her to work in the pub. She seems to enjoy it though, so I've learned to keep my thoughts on that matter to myself. We rub along okay day to day at least. I think her grief counselling is making a big difference. We couldn't afford the extortionate fees of Lucy's private counsellor, but there's a wonderful local bereavement charity Spud benefited from after losing Pammy, and they've been brilliant. While I opted against having counselling of my own, I did give in to Spud's insistence that I go along to a couple of Widowed and Young meetings.

I really didn't want to go; thought it would be a load of distraught individuals wallowing in the passing of their perfect partners. How would they react when they learned my husband had been a philandering gambling addict? I couldn't bear the judgemental faces. As it turned out, we had a rather pleasant barbeque one time, and a pub lunch another. We talked about all sorts of things but never the details of our spouses' deaths. I'd go as far as to say I enjoyed myself, but don't feel the need to go again for the time being.

Toni's voice cuts into my thoughts. 'Spud seems to have taken a shine to a certain person,' she says loud enough for the other women to hear.

All eyes turn to Charlotte who is too busy enjoying her liqueur to notice. We all laugh, and she wipes an Irish Cream moustache from her upper lip, which seems a much more natural size these days. 'What?'

'Toni was just saying,' says Lynn, popping a chocolate brazil into her mouth, 'that Spud seems to like you.'

Charlotte waves a hand. 'Oh, don't be silly.'

'I must admit I've never seen Spud so shy,' I add. 'I'll let him know the score. He'll be disappointed, but wouldn't want him trying to flirt all week. No point flogging a dead horse.'

Charlotte shoots me a look. 'Who are you calling a dead horse, Madam? There's life in this old filly yet.'

Lynn giggles like a naughty schoolgirl. The port she's knocking back is definitely taking effect.

'I meant'—I poke Charlotte in the arm—'that you're a married woman.'

'Not for long, I'm not.'

'What?'

'Roger and I have separated. I'm filing for divorce.'

'Since when?'

'Since two days ago when he called me the wrong name when we were making love. Well, when I say *making love*, I mean he was doing the thrusty thing he does and I was engrossed in my book. Not too engrossed, mind you, to notice he called me Sybil.'

'Yuk!' Sabrine looks like she's about to throw up. She hasn't had a lot of wine so I think it's the thought of Roger doing his *thrusty thing*.

'He denied it of course,' Charlotte says.

Toni tops up her wine glass. 'Denied it? How could he do that?'

'He claimed he'd said *nipple*, not Sybil.'

Toni knits her brow. 'Why would he just shout *nipple* in the middle of sex?'

'Said he got a glimpse of mine and it excited him.'

Toni's frown deepens. 'Like a form of sexual Tourette's?'

'Don't worry, I didn't believe his crap for a second. I let him carry on though.'

'You what?' Toni shrieks.

'I only had a couple of paragraphs of my book left and I didn't want to ruin the ending.'

'Jesus.' Toni takes a long glug of her wine.

'Oh, Char,' I say. 'I'm so sorry.'

'So, am I, darling. Especially when I found out who Sybil was.'

'There's a Sybil who works in the local library,' slurs Lynn.

Charlotte nods. 'Exactly. I noticed her name badge when I returned my books the day afterwards.'

'What was Roger doing in the library?' I ask. 'I thought he hated reading.'

'Oh, he does. Turns out he first met her when our photocopier packed in and he needed some urgent copies making. I should've guessed something was amiss when he was only too keen to return my books for me. There was me thinking he was turning over a new leaf and being the loving husband I always dreamed of, when all the time'—he hits her forehead with the heel of her hand—'he was screwing the bloody librarian!'

'So,' I unscrew the lid of the Baileys and Charlotte holds out her glass for a top-up. 'You've finally had enough?'

She nods.

'Have you told him you're leaving him?'

'Yup.' She takes a sip and pulls a face. 'Actually, Raegan, sorry, *Ronni*, as everyone seems to be calling you now – I think I've had enough Irish cream. Could I have a cup of tea?'

I hop off the kitchen counter to take the glass from her and place it by the sink. 'Course, love.'

'I'll do it.' Sabrine turns around and flicks on the kettle, and I throw her an appreciative glance.

'Well,' I say. 'It's about time. How's Dodgy Rodge taken the news that his very patient, and very forgiving wife, has finally had enough of his infidelity?'

'Can you believe'—she straightens her back and places a hand on her hip—'that he begged me, and I mean literally *begged* me, to stay? He promised he'd never touch another woman for as long as he lived. Even offered to check into Betty Ford and get treated. Claims he's a sex addict.'

'Sex addict? Where?' Lynn looks far more delighted at this prospect than she should be.

Toni laughs. 'I think someone else needs a cup of tea!'

'Oh, it's all right for her,' Charlotte says, accepting the steaming mug from Sabrine. 'There's a woman who's got it right.'

I look from my lovely old neighbour to my best friend.

'The lovely Lynn here,' says Charlotte, 'is only bonking the hired help.'

'What?' I screech.

'Oh yes, dear,' Lynn says before she's momentarily distracted by Sabrine replacing the port in her hand with a mug of tea. 'He's very strapping, is George.'

'George?'

'The gardener, dear.'

'Isn't George, um'—I choose my words carefully—'rather on the young side?'

Lynn grins. 'Yes. He's only sixty-five; seven years my junior. Quite the toy boy.'

'It's not true what it says on your jumper then?' says Charlotte.

We all read the words brandished in fluffy white lettering across Lynn's chest.

'No,' says Sabrine. 'You obviously don't get your baubles out just once a year.'

Toni holds up her glass in triumph. 'Good for you, love!'

Lynn's eyes glint. 'My doctor said I should keep my joints moving.' She winks at me and lowers her voice. 'Good for my cholesterol levels, you know.'

'Ronni!'

I'm torn from the chatter Lynn's revelation has created as Laura shouts me from the foot of the stairs.

I scurry over to her. I'd almost forgotten she'd been burrowing upstairs, studying my last three months' accounts. 'What's up?'

'Ah, bugger, bust!'

We both look over as Spud throws his cards onto the table and folds his arms across his belly.

'Look at this,' she says, holding up a sheet of paper on which several figures are highlighted yellow.

'I'm looking.' I am looking, but all I can see is a series of numbers.

She pushes her reading glasses on top of her head, making her hair stick up. 'Do you know what this means?'

'Um, I'm doing okay?'

'More than okay, Ronni. You're doing great and you're only within your first twelve weeks of trading. You could do even better if you take on someone to help. And I'm thinking'—she stabs her finger at the end figure—'given how healthy your business account is looking, and your bookings for the next six weeks, it's prime time to go for it.'

'Do you think?'

'Yes, I do. If you're serious about selling up and getting out of here as fast as you can, you're gonna have to build up this business pretty smartish, which means taking some calculated risks.'

There's a scream of laughter from the kitchen. I turn to look and see Charlotte throwing her head back, laughing and Toni swinging her legs in glee, while Sabrine's face has paled. No doubt Lynn's alcohol-loosened tongue is causing her to give far too many details about George's bush-taming skills.

I turn back to Laura. 'What kind of risks?'

She hands me the sheet. 'It's time to pull a team together, Ronni. A couple of drivers, which shouldn't be too difficult to find around here, plus someone to help you with the logistics – you know, admin, paperwork. It'll have to be someone with a brain on their shoulders.' She takes the glasses off her head and chews one of the arms. 'More tricky a position to fill 'cos they'll be dealing with the financials. It's gotta be someone you can trust.'

I glance back over at the kitchen where Sabrine is shaking her head and laughing, Toni has a hand over Lynn's mouth, and Charlotte's lips are apart in shock.

'I am serious about getting out of here,' I say. I drum my fingers against my chin. 'And I might just know the perfect person to fit the bill.'

Perhaps it was the Christmas spirit that emboldened me to walk straight up to Toni in the kitchen and ask her if she'd work for me, offering her more than she earned in her cleaning job on the proviso she studied for her English GCSE at night school at the same time.

'It's not physical like the cleaning,' I'd said. 'Which means you shouldn't be too exhausted of an evening to study. And if you want to send Bronte and Pip around here for their tea a couple of times a week to give you some space, you can.'

I thought she was going to accept immediately until her face fell, she shook her head and told me in a weak voice, very unlike Toni, she didn't think she could do it.

'Of course you can do it,' I'd said, giving her a shake. 'You can do anything. And once you've got your GCSE, you can take your A level, and then who knows – degree, PhD – we'll be calling you Doctor Toni St John before you can say – I don't know, what would you say? Some great writer's name – Jilly Cooper!'

She fell silent, thought about it for a while, then said, 'Shit, Ronni,' with a face somewhere between excitement and sheer terror. 'Do ya really think I can?'

'I know you can. Now, will you work for me, or what?'

'Oh, fuck it, go on then!'

We told the others and celebrated with more wine and deliberated over what title to give her. Laura had put forward *Senior Strategist*, Charlotte suggested *Personal Assistant*, and Spud had gone with *Master of the Universe.* Eventually we settled with Sabrine's more sensible suggestion of *Logistics Manager.*

It had all seemed like such a great idea at the time, but now, in the early hours of the morning, with the alcohol wearing off and having spent the last two hours staring sleeplessly at the ceiling, the responsibility I've just taken on is dawning.

I should switch on my light and try to read to take my mind off things, but I don't want to wake Sabrine who, having given up her room for the week for Lynn and Charlotte, is asleep beside me.

Oh God, what have I done? What if I can't make the business work like Laura seems so sure I can, and have to lay Toni off? She'll have given up her cleaning job by then and might not be able to get it back.

The plan Laura and I cooked up is to advertise for a couple of drivers; to build the team and develop a business worth selling in as short a time as possible.

'Shit,' I whisper into the darkness. 'Shit, shit and double shit.'

I close my eyes, more to block out the reality than in an attempt to sleep.

'Panic not, mi love.'

I turn to the side and see my dad next to me. We're in his taxi and he's driving. It smells of furniture polish and stale cigarette smoke. He's sitting up straight, not hunched like the last time I saw him, and his face is plumper than it was then – like the dad I remember from my childhood.

'Oh, I'm glad you're driving,' I say.

He looks at me and grins. He still has those two teeth missing. 'You're a good driver, Ronni. You should be – I taught ya.'

'But I don't know where we're going.'

'Yeah, you do. I'm just 'elping you get there, but you'll 'ave to take over the steering soon, lovie'

'What do you mean? Why?'

'I'm not yer bleedin' chauffeur, am I?'

'I guess not.'

'I spent mi life taxi-driving. I don't wanna do it in 'afterlife n'all.'

A tinny musical sound reaches my ears. 'What's that?'

'It's your lass,' says my dad.

'Eh?' I look behind me where the music is coming from. Sabrine is sitting in the back, looking out of the window with her headphones on.

'I can't take over the driving, Dad, not with her in the back.'

Dad laughs. 'Course you can. She needs ya, does our Sabrine.'

Our Sabrine. Now Matthew's gone, I only ever think of her as *my* Sabrine. I like knowing I'm not the only one looking out for her.

'She's 'eadstrong all right.' He takes his attention off the road for a second to flash a twinkly-eyed smile at me. 'Reminds me of someone I know.'

'She's had a very different life from me, Dad.'

'Give 'er the credit she deserves, Ronni. She can handle 'erself.'

'I'm not so sure.'

'You'd be surprised. And anyway, she's got Donna looking after 'er.'

'Donna? You mean big tits and Mini Cheddars Donna?'

'Aye.' Dad grins.

I go quiet for a while. Sit back in my seat. 'I'm sorry I only brought Sabrine to see you once,' I say.

'Don't be daft, lovie,' Dad says. 'I see 'er all 'time.'

'Do you?'

'Course I do. I'm dead not blind.'

'Do you see me too?'

He nods, and waves his thanks at another driver, who lets him go.

'Then how come this is the first time I've seen you?'

'Told ya I'd come and visit when you needed me.'

'Don't you think I could have done with you before today? Seven months ago my husband died. Would have been useful to have a friend then.'

He turns a corner using only the palm of one hand on the steering wheel. 'Yeah,' he says. 'But you wouldn't 'ave listened then.'

'What's different now?'

A little voice pipes up from the backseat before Dad can answer.

'What's that weird car?'

I turn around and see that Pip's appeared next to Sabrine. He's pointing out the window.

We're on a dual carriageway, and on the adjacent lane is a hearse.

'That's a hearse,' I tell him. 'It carries people who've died.'

Pip's mouth forms an "oh" shape, then he frowns. 'How does it know the way to Heaven?'

Dad laughs. 'Great question, young'un. Answer that one, Ronni.'

I watch as the hearse overtakes us and zooms ahead. I instinctively know it's carrying Matthew. 'Um, it's because it's got a special satnav,' I say.

'Just a few more miles, Ronni, and it'll be my stop.'

'No! You haven't told me yet.'

'Told ya what?'

'What I'm meant to do. Isn't that why you're here?'

He shrugs. 'You already 'ave all the answers.'

'Do I?'

'Think about it. Remember 'ow independent you were when you moved away from 'ere?'

'But that was so long ago. I'm a different person now.'

'Don't talk shite, lovie.'

'Think about it, Dad. I only had myself – and, well, you – to worry about then. Now I've got Sabrine, not to mention Toni, whom I drunkenly offered a job to, and I'm about to take on two drivers. I've never done anything like this before. Plus, Matthew's gone and I still don't really understand why. How can I move on when I'm addicted to listening to his message on his voicemail? It's all so messed up.'

'You've gorrit in ya, I know you 'ave. You were all ready to take over the world at one point. You just need to find that Ronni again.'

'I'm not sure I know how. And all my energy goes on getting through each day. How can I take over the world when I can barely get to five o'clock without falling in a heap? Plus, I still haven't forgiven Matthew.' I sigh. 'How can I move on when part of me still hates—*loathes*—him for what he did?'

Dad indicates and swings the car around a bend. 'You'll forgive 'im, when yer ready.'

'I can't imagine I'll ever be ready. Who'll walk Sabrine down the aisle? Who'll give her tips on going for job interviews and buying a house and …?'

Dad brakes and the car starts to slow. 'Like I say, you already know the answer to that one.'

'Do I?'

The car is crawling now. 'Yes,' he says with a satisfied smile.

'You're going now, aren't you?'

He confirms with a nod and my head buzzes with panic.

I grab his arm. 'Please don't. I don't want you to go. I'm not ready to do this all by myself.'

'Gotta go, lovie. My ride's 'ere.' He turns to look out of his window. I lean forwards and see that a shiny white hearse has pulled up next to us.

'Look, another one!' Pip calls from the back.

Dad gives me a wink. 'Aye, and I 'ope they've got that special satnav on.'

''Ang on a minute, Lenny.'

I recognise that voice, and don't need to turn around to know that Toni has now joined Pip and Sabrine on the backseat.

'Yes, love?' says Dad.

'If you're getting out, who's taking us on the rest of this journey?'

'Our Ronni is,' says Dad. 'She knows the way.'

He opens the taxi door and I tighten my grip on his arm.

'Will you come and visit me again?' I ask.

He leans over and plants a kiss on my forehead. 'Only if you need me, but I've got a feeling you won't. Now, get yersen ready. You're driving. And yer gonna do a grand job.'

Reluctantly, I let go of him.

'Hurry up, for God's sake, Mum,' Sabrine shouts, unaware of how loud her voice is over her music. 'My shift starts in half an hour, and I've got to unpack all the pork scratchings.'

'Right. Yes.' I shift across to the driver's seat and wince as the handbrake digs into my left buttock.

Once settled in the seat, I look out of the window to wave at Dad, but the hearse has already driven away and is now just a speck of white in the distance.

‘Okay. Everyone ready?’ I say to my trio of passengers. ‘Better buckle up. It might be a bit of a bumpy ride.’ I take a shaky breath and lower my foot onto the accelerator.

Chapter Twenty-Eight

28 January 2019 – Haxton, Yorkshire

Ronni

I grin at Toni's sing-song voice answering the phone, as I finish writing the details of the rest of the week's deliveries on the white board. In the four weeks since she's worked for me, she's really thrown herself into the role. The customers seem to love her, and I'm sure some of them book with us just to get their regular dose of her friendly but no-nonsense approach.

'That was the bloke you're interviewing today,' she says as she replaces the receiver onto the handset. 'He'll be 'ere in a minute. He was just wanting directions from Rowland Roundabout.

'Righto.'

'Where you going to do the interview? In 'ere?'

I glance around the unit that signwriting Baz-Gaz has very kindly said we can use for three months while he finds himself in Thailand. He wanted someone around to look after his equipment that's stashed in a corner as much as it can be, and we were grateful for the extra space.

'Hmm, maybe, but the phone'll be ringing and it might be too distracting.'

'Take 'im down to Lizzie's Caf' then.'

'Yeah, might be better. What's his name?'

She taps her fingers against her lips. 'Oh, what is it now? Ralph something.' She starts searching through a pile of paperwork on her desk. 'Ralph, Ralph, Ralph … Ralph Fiennes I think it is.'

I burst out laughing. 'Ralph Fiennes, the Shakespearean actor, has applied for a job at *Ronni Delivers*?'

'Well, Ralph summet,' she says, studying a sheet of paper. 'Oh, 'ere it is – Ralph Fogerty.' She holds the paper up in triumph. 'Told yer it was Ralph Summet.'

'Um, hullo.'

We both turn to the sound of the voice. A tall man is standing in front of the open door. His dark, chin-length hair is streaked with grey, and he has a short matching beard.

He looks about my age. No, on second thoughts, a few years older. Definitely more like late-forties. Although in close-fitting black jeans, a plain white T-shirt and brown leather jacket, it's clear his body's in good shape. Not cut to within an inch of his life, but not half bad.

He walks towards me, arm outstretched. 'Ralph Summet about the driving job.'

His voice is so deadpan I'm worried we've actually offended him until I see one corner of his lips twitch.

'Oh, hi.' I shake his hand and feel myself growing hot. I tell myself it's because I'm embarrassed he overheard us getting his name wrong, and not because I find him ridiculously attractive, which I really shouldn't because he's not my type. Not my type at all.

'So, Ralph'—I place one of the polystyrene cups on the plastic table in front of him, and keep a hold of the other one—'what brings you to Haxton? You don't sound like you're from round here.'

He nods his thanks for the coffee. 'Neither do you.'

I sip the sludgy brew and wince. Lizzie's Caf' is handy for a pick-me-up bacon sarni at the start of a busy day, but it isn't known for the quality of its coffee beans. 'I grew up here. For my sins.'

'I like it here,' he says, and looks out of the window as an artic lorry rumbles past.

'Do you?' I can't keep the surprise out of my voice.

He looks back at me. 'Yes. It's close to the city, but there's plenty of green space once you get out of Haxton. I like the mix.'

I take another sip of the sludge. 'Where *are* you from?'

'London.'

'Ah, okay.' I search my brain to think of another question I should be asking. I prepared a few in my head beforehand, but sitting in front of Ralph, they seem to have all evaporated. 'What about your family?' I blurt, and realise instantly that's far too intrusive for an interview.

He raises an eyebrow. 'Family?'

'Did they, um, come with you, when you moved from London?'

'No family.' Deadpan voice is back again.

'No significant other?' I know it's desperately unprofessional to ask, but I can't help myself. Heat creeps up from my chest, all the way up to my cheeks.

'No significant other,' he confirms, and I spot that lip twitch again. Maybe asking hideously personal questions is the way to get him to crack a smile.

Hoping to mask my blush, I turn my head to look out of the window. A man with a too-tight T-shirt stretched over an enlarged stomach is unloading pallets from a lorry.

'No, me neither.' Why I offered that piece of information about my marital status is beyond me. As soon as I do, guilt descends. 'Well, I'm recently widowed, to be accurate,' I quickly clarify. *You're meant to be interviewing him, not giving him your life story.*

'Sorry to hear that.'

I don't look at him. I can't. I keep on watching the man unloading the pallets.

'Strange word that, don't you think? Widow, I mean. Makes you think of all sorts of things – black widow, widow's peak—'

'Widow Twankey.'

That makes me look at him. He's smiling. For the first time since this mortifying interview began, he's smiling. And what a smile.

'Yes. Widow Twankey.' I smile back, grateful for his injection of much-needed humour.

'I'm recently divorced, to be accurate,' he says.

'Oh really? I'm sorry to hear that.'

'No need. It's what me and Emma both agreed.'

That's it – *no need*. No further explanation or information. Just *no need*.

I play with my cup, ripping a small crescent off the rim, to distract me from asking more intrusive questions about his life with *Emma*.

I nod down at his empty cup. 'Another coffee?'

'No thanks.'

'No, don't blame you. Tastes like shit, doesn't it?'

He plays with his cup and shrugs. 'Coffee's coffee.'

We both know that's nonsense, but at least he's trying to be polite. What else should I be asking? Come on, Ronni, remember the questions you prepared. *Can't believe I forgot my bloody notebook.* The waft of fried bacon floats past my nostrils, and my stomach rumbles.

'So, whereabouts are you living?' Why is it that every question I ask sounds like I'm at a speed-dating event. 'We'll need your address. For the paperwork.'

He nods. 'I'm renting the cottage on Robertson's Farm. You know it?'

'Um, no.'

'Not surprised. It's pretty much in the middle of nowhere. About five miles out of Haxton.'

'Oh right.' Living on his own in the middle of nowhere? I vaguely consider the notion he might be on the run from the law, when he interrupts my thoughts.

'I'm happy in my own company.'

'I see.' I'm not sure if he's warding me off or reassuring me he's not a fugitive. I glance down at the slightly grubby table and see he's completely crushed his cup into a flattened circle of polystyrene. My gaze falls onto his clasped hands which show evidence of old and fresh cuts.

He sees me looking down. 'I help out with work on the farm. Part of the deal I struck up with old man Robertson that meant I could live in the cottage.'

'Oh right. Have you had a driving job before?'

'Only driving the tractor around the field when Robertson needs me to. He's getting on a bit now. Has good days and bad days. Other than that, no. I was always more of an office bod – used to be a hedge fund manager back in London.'

I snap my head up to meet his eyes. 'Oh, that's a big change. Why would you ...?'

He pushes the crushed polystyrene cup away with his finger, then raises his clasped hands and rests his chin on them. 'Things didn't work out.' He fixes on a point in the distance behind me. He doesn't want to talk about it, and even though I'm dying to know, I stop myself from prying any further.

Toni waggles her eyebrows. 'You've got the hots for Ralph Fiennes.'

'Sshhh!' I lean to the side so I can see behind her. Thank God! He's still bent over the table at the far end of the unit, signing the paperwork. 'It's Ralph *Fogerty*, and no, I don't have the hots for him.'

'Coulda fooled me. Your face turns the colour of beetroot every time 'e talks to you.'

'It does *not*. He's nothing like my type. Seriously, if you'd have met Matthew – he was clean cut, clean shaven – nothing at all like ...' I nod over at Ralph. '*Him*.'

'Maybe it's time to try something new, Ronni. No one would blame you – he's proper yummy. I'd 'ave a go on 'im miself if 'e were more my age.'

'You've been reading far too much romance. Is that what they're putting on the GCSE reading list these days?'

She points a finger at me. 'Ah, the lady doth protest too much.'

I roll my eyes.

'Anyway'—she folds her arms across her chest—'that's not the question you should be asking.'

'What should I be asking?'

She raises one hand as if holding something in the air and tips her head back, adopting a serious expression. 'To be up for a shag or not to be up for a shag, *that* is the question.'

'Oh, shut up!' I nudge her arm and she collapses into giggles.

'Okay, finished!' Ralph calls.

I jump up and head over to him.

'Thanks.' I take the papers and pen from him and smile, hoping I'm not beetroot red as Toni suggested.

'Ey up, ge' kettle on, Ronni. It's parky as ya like out there.'

I snap my head around to see a grinning figure stepping inside the unit.

'Chopper?'

'All right, beautiful?' He strides over, throws an arm around my shoulder and kisses me on the top of my head.

'What are you doing here?'

'Got an interview, 'aven't I?'

'Have you?' I shoot a look over at Toni in the office.

'Yes,' she calls in her efficient voice. 'You must be Charles Worthington.'

Chopper throws his head back and laughs. 'Charles Worthington? Thought you were looking for drivers, not 'airdressers. Who's 'e?' He nods at Ralph. 'Vidal Sassoon?'

Ralph looks from me to Chopper to me again, but says nothing.

I glare at Toni. 'Charles Worthington? Did you mean *Chopper Wallington*?'

She scratches the back of her neck. 'Might 'ave meant that.'

Chopper leans in to me. ''Ey, Ronni, yer not gonna try and stick yer tongue down mi throat again, are ya?'

Ralph's eyebrows shoot up.

'Chopper!' I pull away from him and lower my voice. 'Do you mind?'

'Soz, Ronni.' He grins. 'I know it's only 'cos I'm irresistible but if our lass knows I'm working for a nymphomaniac, she'll 'ave mi guts for garters.'

'I'm hardly a nymph—' I stop quickly, and turn to smile at Ralph. 'So, Ralph, lovely to meet you. Look forward to seeing you tomorrow at seven-thirty for your first shift.'

'Um, yeah. See you tomorrow.' With a final nod at Toni, he strides away.

I wait for the clatter of the door to signal his exit before looking up into Chopper's face and ramming my hands onto my hips. 'What the hell? That's my new driver!'

'Ah, come on, beautiful. I'm only messing with ya.' His grin fades. 'Seriously, though, yer not gonna try owt, are ya, 'cos Kelly'd go spare if—'

'No, Chopper.' I sigh, put my head down and kick a patch of red paint that's ground-on to the floor. 'Don't worry. I'll do my best to keep my nymphomaniac tendencies under control.'

His grin returns. 'Awesome. So, when do I start?'

I look back up at him. 'You seriously want a job?'

He shrugs. 'Yeah.'

'But you've got a job. You've been a brickie for years.'

He shuffles his feet. 'Yeah, but wanna get out of it. Winter's always shit.'

'Right. But is this a good idea?'

Is there a clause in some HR manual somewhere that says you shouldn't employ your ex-boyfriend?

'Why not?' His question reflects my thoughts. 'I can drive. You know I'm a good grafter.'

Yeah. I know that. 'All right,' I say. 'Let's give it a try and see how it goes.'

He grins, eyes shining.

'Start tomorrow, seven-thirty?'

'Nice one, beautiful.' He takes hold of either side of my head and kisses my hair. 'I won't let you down.' He turns and heads for the door.

'Oh, and one thing, Chopper.'

He spins back to face me.

'Enough of the *beautiful*. Call me Ronni.'

'Sure thing!'

The door clatters and Toni pops her head out of the tiny office door. 'Well? How was Charles Worthington? Did you give him a job?'

'I did.'

'Great.' She flashes a smile. 'Better the devil you know!'

I really hope she's right.

Chapter Twenty-Nine

20 February 2019 – Leeds, Yorkshire

Ronni

I finger the oversized, colourful beads of the necklace in M&S's costume jewellery section. Far more in-your-face than my usual style, but what the hell – maybe Toni's right when she keeps banging on about it being time for a change – and it *is* my birthday.

I hold the necklace up to my collar and peer into the tiny mirror built in to the display. Hmm, not looking too bad actually for forty-four. Sabrine says the extra pounds suit me – fill my face out more – *in a good way*, she says. I've kept my hair short – it's easier than maintaining those bloody blonde highlights. Can't believe I put up with it for so long.

I place the necklace into my shopping basket and turn back to the display. *Ooh, they're lovely.* I pick up a pair of matching dangly earrings and hold one of them to my ear. *Can I get away with those?*

'They're lovely,' says an old lady shopper beside me, her eyes glinting through her bifocals.

I smile at her. 'Aren't they?'

'Treat yersen, love,' she says. 'Yer a long time dead.'

'You've convinced me.' I laugh, and drop the earrings into my basket to join the necklace.

I spot a beautiful pair of glittering earrings. They're bigger than studs and shaped like roses; pale pink and dusted with shimmer. *Sabrine will look lovely in those.* I turn them over to see the price sticker. *Twenty-five quid for a pair of metal earrings!* M&S has upped its game since the last time I came in. I thought it was all aged couples in matching macs, and husbands waiting patiently for their wives to emerge from the fitting rooms in yet another twinset and pearl combo.

'Apparently not,' I say to myself as I drop the rose earrings into my basket. Sabrine deserves a treat; I had next to no money when it was her birthday back in December, so these will go some way to making up for it. *And* she's been working so hard – they're short staffed at the pub so Donna's been giving her a lot of extra shifts. Sabrine reckons she doesn't mind, that it helps her "save for when I go travelling".

I stroll away from the jewellery and into the denim section. A pair of fitted black bootcut jeans catch my eye. I run my hand down the soft denim. *Ooh, to be able to wear those.*

Matthew always hated jeans. Said they were common, so I avoided them altogether. *But these lovelies*. I delve into the waistband for the price tag. *Thirty-five quid. I shouldn't really.* Then again, with Chopper, Ralph and me doing the deliveries, business is moving along nicely. And … I flick through the hangers for my size, which is more of a 12 these days … they'd be perfect for tonight.

Bingo. A 12. I tuck them under my arm. *Now, Ronni, don't make tonight out to be something it isn't. Ralph suggested meeting in The Royal Oak to help you build a website – nothing more. He probably just felt sorry for you when he heard you'd be spending your birthday alone.*

Sabrine's working another double shift, Toni's dead excited about having been invited to a showing of *Hamlet* at The Playhouse by another mature student on her course – his name is Mo and he's a "thinking-woman's crumpet", apparently. I did offer to babysit, but she said her mum's coming round. Even Spud's gone off somewhere for the weekend. So, tonight, it's just me in my new jeans, and Ralph, enjoying a very platonic drink.

The handle of the bulging shopping bag digs into the soft skin of my arm as I concentrate on carrying my tray to an available table. Tea sloshes out of the overfilled teapot onto the tray as I lay it on top of the table. I slide myself onto one of the plastic seats, and place my bag of purchases on the seat beside me. *Yes, you little beauties. Jeans that make my butt look that good do deserve their own chair!*

My frustration diffuses as I eye the iced bun I've treated myself to. Well, it is my birthday. I pour tea into my cup. My impatience has rewarded me with an uninspiring murky liquid, but a hasty sip confirms at least it's warm and wet.

I bite into the bun and doughy loveliness explodes on my tongue. I sink back as far as the hard, rigid chair allows and chew. So, forty-four. I never thought I'd end up celebrating on my own in Leeds' M&S cafe with only a sticky bun and piss-yellow tea for company, but I feel surprisingly undepressed about it. Maybe it's because Sabrine has been a lot chirpier recently. I'm still not desperately happy about her working in the pub, but I've heard she's a favourite among the regulars and doesn't take any shit. Actually, I'm quite looking forward to seeing her in action tonight. It'll be the first time I've stepped foot inside the place in over twenty-five years. Can't imagine much has changed other than the calibre of at least one member of the bar staff.

I check my phone as is habit when one sits down for a break these days, and see absolute zero activity except for a solitary message from Toni saying she hopes my birthday's going well and she's finally decided what to wear for her date with Mo. A photo accompanies the message. It's a full-length selfie she's taken in front of the mirror. She's wearing a plunge-neck black top and a PVC mini skirt. Anyone else wearing such a get-up for the theatre would probably be fined for exhibitionism – there must be a law against turning up like that for a Shakespeare play – but Toni looks gorgeous. I tell her so in my reply.

I pour more tea into my cup and look around the cafe. The only other solo customers appear to be old ladies in the obligatory beige mac, many with tastefully patterned scarves hugging craggy necks. I'm pleased to see not everything has changed.

My gaze is drawn to one lonesome customer in particular. She stands out from the rest due to her more daring choice of coat, which is bright pink bouclé. Unlike most of the more mature customers, her hair isn't short and white; it's a deep chestnut colour, pulled into an elegant chignon.

I take another bite of my bun and continue to assess her. She's the kind of older lady I'd like to be one day – stylish, confident – good for her. She lowers her coffee cup. Wow, she even looks good in that bright lipstick. My gaze travels up her face and when I meet her eyes they're looking right back at me.

Oops. I give an awkward smile and avert my gaze to the more beige woman on the next table, who's far too involved with picking bits of scone out of her teeth to notice me. But there's something about the bright-coat lady that's niggling me, dragging my eyes back to her table. I risk another look. Damn it – she's still looking at me! She must think I'm a crazy person.

I stuff the last bite of bun into my mouth and force my eyes to rest on my teapot. Now, stay there, eyes. Don't be staring at innocent people. Thankfully they oblige, and behind the stark white of the porcelain appears a backdrop of bobbled pink.

'Hello Ronni.'

I look up to see bright-coat lady at my table. She has warm eyes and a gentle smile.

On hearing her voice, it takes me less than a single heartbeat to realise who she is.

My legs, feeling disconnected from my body, pound through the indoor market so fast that every few seconds the smells change – fruit, synthetic perfume, cooked meat, incense. My coat, which I didn't wait around long enough to fasten, billows behind me.

'Lovely pair o'melons, treacle. Nice 'n ripe.' A denim-jacketed market trader is holding up two melons to his chest, grinning at me. His mate guffaws. The normal rules of political correctness don't apply inside these walls. I don't care about that. I'd normally just roll my eyes, or maybe even smile, but after today's encounter, I'm not in the mood for his cheek.

My hand, stuffed inside my pocket, still clutches the receipt on which she wrote her number. I looked away the moment I saw her scratch the first numbers onto the paper. 0033. *France*. So, the rumours were true. *Just here for a visit,* she said. *Come back the same week every year. Never had the courage to do anything more than walk around the city. Never thought ...*

I never thought either.

Could she join me?

No.

Just for a minute, to chat.

Chat? Is that what you call it?

If she could just explain ...

No.

Were there things I wanted to know?

No. Yes. Maybe. But there are too many questions to answer over a pot of tea in M&S cafe. Like is Frank still alive? Is it true they live in a chateau? Did they have any children?

Perish the thought.

Instead of asking anything, I'd got up and left. She'd called after me, but I didn't look back; just carried on. I was halfway down the escalator when I realised I'd left all my shopping on the seat. I mourned the loss of the pretty jewellery and flattering jeans with a curse, but I still didn't go back for them. Let *her* have them. As a memento.

I'm forced to slow my pace when the aisle narrows and a young woman pushing a buggy is coming in the opposite direction. The toddler inside releases an ear-piercing screech. He arches his back in a bid to escape the confines of his portable chair, his face puce with the effort.

Oscar.

It isn't Oscar, of course. Doesn't even look like him, but just because he's a child of around the same age, the thought of Arabella's son drops inside my head with an unwelcome *thud*, accompanied with a stab of conscience and a pathetic, unexplained sense of responsibility. A little boy, robbed of his father, and a bigger girl – Sabrine – who, despite my promises of honesty, still doesn't know she has a brother.

I, a woman without her mother, arrive breathless at the bus station in just enough time to see my bus pulling away from its stop.

Chapter Thirty

22 March 1987 – Haxton, Yorkshire

Ronni

The voices coming from the floor below rise as the row escalates. They're reasonably calm still; only just getting started. Give it five minutes or so and Mum will either be screeching or crying. Or throwing something. She's done that a few times. From what I could make out, I think once she threw the TV remote control at the wall. It certainly didn't work the next day and she made some excuse about the batteries being flat. But even when I took them out, gave them a rub and put them under my armpits for a minute, like Dad had shown me, it still didn't work.

I pull the duvet over my head and shove my fingers in my ear holes until a bit of wax gets under my nails, but I can still hear them. It's like a part of me wants to hear what they're saying to each other – like I have to know the truth even though I really don't want to.

I wish I was Laura. Aunty Pammy pretends to be cross at Uncle Spud, chasing him with her slipper and complaining about his mucky overalls, but I'm pretty sure they don't argue like this.

I used to think this was normal; that everyone's parents had nightly rows after their kids had gone to bed, but when I mentioned something about it to Laura, she just gave me a strange look and said that yeah, her parents argue sometimes. I shut up then. I didn't want her to ask me whether they were getting divorced because I don't know the answer. I wish they would. I don't care what people at school would say about it. At least I could go to bed at night without my heart hammering, just waiting for the argument to start. I wouldn't have to stay up late hoping that one of them might get tired before me and go to bed first, which means there couldn't be an argument at all. That doesn't always work though because I've heard them argue in bed before now. All it achieves is that I'm even more knackered the next day.

'For fuck's sake, Ruth, give it a rest, will ya!'

I squeeze my eyes shut as my dad's voice, calmer than my mum's, wafts up the stairs bringing a sinking sense of dread along with it.

Don't they know I can hear them?

They must do.

Then why do they do it?

Because they don't care what you think.

And they're drunk. Like they often are.

That's another thing I thought was normal for parents – drinking. Slurring. Being drunk. But I've been around the Baileys' enough to know now that not all adults drink all the time.

'Jesus, Lenny, when are you going to realise that our life is shit? SHIT! It's just … fucking … *hiccup* … shit.'

'Well, go out and get a full-time job then, woman. No one's stopping ya.'

'You don't love me!' Mum starts to sob.

I'm sweating now even though I'm not hot. I fling the duvet off me and swing my legs around to sit up. Then I do what I do every row night, even though I never know why I do it – I tiptoe out onto the landing and sit in a squatting position on the floor with my back against the wall. The thin cotton of my nightie is no barrier from the cold plaster and I hug my knees, pressing my hands onto my bear feet for warmth.

'You're just pissed off because we haven't got as much brass as those yuppy mates of yours,' I hear Dad say.

'They're not mates, they're *clients*,' Mum says between weak sobs. 'I clean for them, Lenny. Every day, I have to go into their beautiful homes and clean up after other people. And you have no idea – no bloody idea – how it upsets me. It's degrading, that's what it is!'

Now I'm sitting on the landing I can hear how Mum's slurring her words. She's been on the red wine again. I don't know why she drinks that stuff. She always gets like this. And God knows why Dad gives it to her. He's always the one who opens the bottle and pours her a glass. It's like he *wants* an argument.

'What's bloody degrading about it? They need a service – you're providing it. It's business. Like any other bloody business on the planet, only some people arrive with briefcases and you arrive with a feather duster. Who bleeding cares!'

'I care!'

'Ssshh!' Dad hisses. 'You'll wake up Ronni.'

There's a pause before Mum says something else, but she seems to have taken note of what Dad's said because she's speaking quieter and I miss too many words for it to make sense.

'Well if you don't like it, you know what you can do, don't ya?' says Dad, whose deeper voice carries further.

Mum lets out a sardonic laugh. 'Do you think I wouldn't leave you tomorrow if I could? I can't though, can I? I owe it to Ronni.'

‘Don’t kid yerrsen, Ruthy. Our Ronni isn’t the reason you haven’t left – you know it and I do. The reason you’re still ’ere is because you haven’t found anyone with enough brass who’ll take ya.’

‘You’re an arsehole, Lenny. And you’re drunk. I’m off to bed.’

I spring up and scarper back into my room, jumping into bed moments before I hear my mum’s footsteps on the stairs.

Chapter Thirty-One

20 February 2019 – Haxton, Yorkshire

Ronni

'So, you see, we just write the text in these boxes here.' Ralph pauses to spear the last morsel of cheesecake from his plate. He devours it, then wipes his mouth with a serviette. 'And upload whichever images we want. Easy as that.'

'Wow.' I unwrap the foil from a disc of chocolate and pop it in my mouth. This will definitely have to be my last. I've eaten enough for a small army tonight. Mind you, it is my birthday. 'This whole design-your-own-website thing doesn't look as tricky as I thought.'

'No, it's really not.' He picks up his wine glass. 'Nothing's that hard when you know how.'

Conscious I might have chocolate stuck in the corners of my mouth, I run my tongue around my lips. 'How come you know how to do it. I wouldn't have thought web design was in the job description of a hedge fund manager.'

He shrugs. 'It's been almost a year now since I left the city. I've learned quite a few new skills in that time.'

I nod, as if I understand completely, although I don't, not really. Ralph's been working with us for a month, but I barely know anything more about him now than I did the day we first met – mainly because we've been run off our feet since Christmas, but also because he's not one for volunteering personal information. I'm reminded of the challenge Toni set me to find out more about him tonight. I tutted when she said it, as though I thought it was prying, but now – probably thanks to the Sauvignon Blanc – I'm dying to know more.

'Did you work as a web designer, then?' I ask, helping myself to another disc of chocolate.

'When I left London I decided I needed a complete change. I'd been a slave to the job since graduating. Barely any down-time – a classic case of burnout. I didn't care what I did, I just didn't want to do that any more.'

'So, what did you do?'

'I got drunk, attached a map of Britain to the wall and threw a dart at it. Wherever the dart landed, that's where I was heading, to do whatever manual job I could find. I didn't care what it was, as long as it didn't involve taxing my brain.'

'And the dart landed here? Haxton?'

'That's right. I'd never been to Yorkshire before, but fancied the idea of visiting the Dales. It was certainly far enough away to not bump into anyone I knew.'

I'm about to ask why that's a good thing, when a woman appears at our table, carrying the two glasses of wine we'd ordered.

'Well, well, your Sabrine said you were coming tonight, and here you are!'

I look up and directly at my eye level is a pair of boobs crammed into a tight white top. I tip my head further back until I see her face. It's more tanned, slightly craggier and framed with false flashes, but there's no doubt who it is.

'Donna!'

'Hiya, love.' She bends down, wraps her arms around me and squishes me into her chest. 'It's so good to see yer. How ya doing?'

She releases me and I try not to make my gasp for breath too obvious. 'Fine, Donna, thanks. I'm fine. How are you? I hear you're the landlady these days.'

She fluffs up her already fluffy hair. 'That's right, love. When mi mam died last year she left me some money and I bought the freehold.' She gestures around the room. 'Gutted the place, I did. It's a grand boozer, this, just had a bit of a reputation at first, what with all them wrong'uns who used to come 'ere.' She pushes out her chest, nearly smothering me all over again. 'Different though now, isn't it?'

I look around. 'It certainly is. You've done an amazing job.' And she has. The wallpaper is tasteful and modern, as are the plush seats and oak tables. There's no sign of the tobacco-stained ceiling I remember from my teenage years.

She leans forward. 'And? How was the food?'

I'm about to answer that it was genuinely very impressive, but a waft of her perfume sticks in my throat. I cough, and cough again. I can't get my words out and pick up a serviette from the table to hold over my mouth.

'Absolutely delicious,' answers Ralph on my behalf.

'Yes, it was lovely,' I sputter finally, taking a swig of my wine to soothe my throat. 'Really lovely.'

Donna beams and lays an arm over my shoulder. 'Ahh, bless ya, love. Well, it's lovely seeing ya, and I'm glad yer back. Your Sabrine's as good as gold.' She turns her head to where Sabrine is clearing plates from the next table in the packed pub. 'And Lenny'd be skipping in 'is grave if 'e could see ya back in 'is old 'ouse.' She presses the corners of her eyes, which have moistened. 'I don't 'alf miss 'im, the bloody daft bugger. Taken far too young, 'e was.'

She pauses and wipes her under-eyes with the back of her knuckle, then rests one hand on my chair. 'But 'e were grand for a bloke of 'is age. Very agile, if ya know what I mean.' She nudges my shoulder and laughs.

I force the corners of my lips to curl upwards into what I hope resembles a smile even though I feel slightly queasy.

'Anyway, lovies, I'll leave ya to yer romantic dinner. And 'appy birthday, Ronni love.'

'Thanks Donna.'

She swaggers away and I watch her go, as it means I don't have to look back at Ralph and allow him to see my cheeks burning. This is *not* a romantic dinner. It's his kind offer to show me how to build my own website. It's not even an opportunity to wear those sexy jeans, which are probably still sitting on a chair in M&S bloody cafe.

'It must be nice,' he says.

I can't avoid turning to face him now. 'What?'

'Having people so pleased to see you.'

'Oh, I see. Yes. Yes, it is, I suppose.'

He circles the pad of his finger around the base of his wine glass. 'I don't think I'd get the same reaction if I went back to London.'

I raise my eyebrows. 'No?'

He parts his lips, about to say more, but self-silences by bringing his glass up to meet his mouth.

I don't say anything, allowing him to take a drink in peace.

The silence eats at me. 'Why's that?' I blurt, when he replaces his glass onto the table.

He wrinkles his nose and folds his arms. 'My wife, Emma, wasn't exactly amused when I decided to give up my job. That was the cause of our break-up really.' He gives a wry laugh. 'I had a bit of a health scare. My heart. The doctor said I was lucky that time, but might not be so lucky next. Said I needed to change my lifestyle, not work so much, you know?'

He flashes me a look and I nod.

'I went home and told her I was giving up the job, thought it would be a good opportunity for us to move out of London. We'd long ago decided kids weren't for us, but that didn't mean we couldn't still get that cottage in the countryside we'd always talked about.'

'Sounds idyllic.'

He presses his lips together and rubs the back of his neck. 'Doesn't it? I thought so, anyway. Turns out her dreams had changed since we first got married. She said she didn't want to move away from the city any more and be *poor* as she put it. Think she'd got too used to the trappings of the life my job afforded us. Emma liked going to the hairdresser once a week, having her nails done, meeting her friends for coffee, you know the type.'

Was I an Emma? The thought hits me like a thump to the stomach.

'But when you have a scare like I did,' he continues. 'Well, you don't take chances when it comes to your health.'

'Sure, I can see that.'

'In the end, she gave me an ultimatum – keep her and our high life in London, or give it all up but kiss goodbye to our marriage.'

What a bitch. She couldn't have loved him to put her lifestyle before her husband's health. I would never have done that if Matthew had been ill. Definitely not. *Matthew was ill though*, whispers a hateful voice inside my head. *People who are well don't commit suicide.*

'And you chose Haxton over all that?' I say, forcing away the thought.

He gives me a sharp look. 'I chose my health, Ronni. Anyway, it's beautiful here. It's lush and green, and the people are'—he spreads out his hands as if the landscape of Yorkshire is laid out on the table before him—'real. It's all just real.'

His expression is so tortured and bursting with emotion I wish with all my heart I could see this godforsaken town through his eyes.

'And what about her – Emma?' I ask. 'Do you, um, do you think you made the right decision?'

He drops his arms back on to the table. 'I loved my wife. In the early days we both wanted the same things.' His eyes narrow as if opening fully would allow in too much pain. 'But when it got to the point that she put having her nails done ahead of our future together …' He sighs. 'It just didn't seem worth carrying on. Anyway.' His eyes fully open again. 'Sorry to go on. I must sound totally self-absorbed to you, especially after what you've been through.'

'Not at all. Pain is pain.'

I've never told him about Matthew's suicide, but I know Chopper must have mentioned it when out on deliveries together. Hardly prized for his discretion, Chopper. Not that I mind; it's not a secret. I actually find it easier these days when people know and I don't have to dance around it.

I adjust the position of my leg and our feet touch. I expect him to move his away but he doesn't, and I've left mine there too long for it not to be weird if I suddenly move now. He looks at me. That look, with our feet touching, somehow connects us. Neither of us speaks, but it's not awkward – it's comfortable; it's nice. Very nice in fact.

The synthetic tune of my mobile phone coming to life shatters the moment.

'Oh, sorry, that's loud.' I grasp for it, but the slippery thing slides out of my hand and thumps onto the table. I see the name on the screen and freeze. There's only one reason this person is ringing me. My finger trembles as it hovers over the green button to accept the call.

'She's gone, Rae. She's gone. Oh my God, I can't believe it. I knew it was on the cards, but it still doesn't make it any easier.'

'It's okay, Melanie, love, it's okay. Try to calm down.'

Love. I just called Melanie love. I don't think I've ever called anyone that before. It seems to have the desired effect though, as her sobs become marginally less hysterical.

'Sorry, sorry, it's just – oh, Rae, first Matty, now Mummy, all within a few months. And we've already lost Pops. Once we were four and now I'm the only one left. Oh my God – I'm an *orphan*!'

The hysteria builds once more. I don't attempt to quell it this time. I let her cry at me down the phone – perhaps she needs to – and use the time to do a little jog on the spot to try to keep myself warm. I darted out of the pub in such a rush I didn't have time to grab my coat, and it's freezing out here.

A car passes and I flatten myself as much as I can against the cold stone wall of The Royal Oak to avoid being drenched by a puddle that its tyres make a water feature out of.

'Will you—will you …?' she says.

I strain to make sense of her words through her sobs. 'Sorry, will I—?'

'Help me arrange the funeral? I'm so far away here and, and, and, I can't do it all on my, my own.'

Damn. 'Yes, of course I will.'

'Th-thank you, Rae Rae. I really appreciate it. I know we haven't seen much of each other over the years—'

Yeah, since about 2005 when you went on holiday to Bali and never came back. Shame really. Despite Melanie being nothing like me, I always liked her – reckoned we could have been lifelong friends if she hadn't been too busy lining up her chakras and finding her chi.

'I don't know what I'd do without you Rae Rae, you're such a saint.'

She goes on, and between the hiccups and sniffs I manage to work out that by *helping* her arrange the funeral, she means she wants me to organise the whole thing.

'You mean, you're not actually planning on coming over at all?' I can't keep the astonishment out of my voice when I figure this one out.

'I can't possibly, lovely,' she says. 'The guilt of knowing I'd contributed so much damage to the environment by flying all those miles would play havoc with my alignment.'

'What about the people who fly from all over the world to visit your retreat? Aren't you worried about that?'

'Raegan! How could you even compare the two? My guests have no choice but to come – the universe calls them.'

I stand still on the pavement, open-mouthed.

'Although that's hardly the point,' she says. 'By not being at the funeral I can channel Mummy's spirit easier, and connect with her soul much more effectively than if I'm there in person.'

'Right.' *Load of bullshit. Save yourself the airfare more like.*

'Why don't you take Sabby with you to help you with the emotional journey?' she says. 'I know Mummy has left a generous legacy to her in her Will. Matty had power of attorney once the dementia took hold so the paperwork should be with his solicitor. I guess you'll know who that is.'

Another visit to the solicitor. Another Will, another funeral. The biting winter night air can't touch me now, not when the prospect of doing all that again – dredging up all the memories of Matthew's death – are making me hot and scratchy. Another car rolls past. This one swerves to avoid the puddle, although I wouldn't care if it hadn't. Getting wet and dirty is a triviality now.

'And with dear Matty in the spirit world,' she says, 'his portion of Mummy's inheritance will go to Sabrine. I remember him saying that when he took on the paperwork. He wanted me to know in case – in case anything happened to-to— oh my God! He must have known what fate had planned for him, Rae Rae, otherwise why would he tell me? He knows I'm not money-driven. Oh my goodness. He knew! He knew!' She bursts into sobs again.

'It's okay, Melanie. Please don't get upset, I'm sure—' Her wails drown out my words so I give up on that tactic of trying to calm her.

'Listen,' I say. 'Don't worry about anything.' *Why am I saying this*? 'Sabrine and I will sort out all the funeral arrangements.'

She sniffs. 'Oh thanks, lovely. And you will be there on the day, won't you? To say goodbye to Mummy?'

'Of course we will.'

'Oh, thank you. Thank you so much. This is why my brother had so much love for you – because of your big heart.'

'Right.' *So much love? Perhaps he had a glut of the stuff, which is why he had plenty left over to give to Arabella too.*

The call ends with me making a list of promises to Melanie.

Yes, I'll give her a list of venues to choose from, and yes, she can have final say. Yes of course we can have a vegetarian buffet with plenty of vegan and gluten-free choices. Yes, we can request no flowers and all donations to The Cats Protection League.

I jab the red button to end the call.

I run my hand through my hair, which is damp and brittle from the cold night air. I shove the phone into my back pocket, push the heavy door of the pub open and feel the warmth envelop me as soon as I step inside.

'Everything all right?' Ralph asks when I reach our table. Our plates and glasses have been cleared and there's a pack of Mini Cheddars on the table.

'They're from the landlady,' he says. 'She said they're a birthday present.'

'Oh.'

'Are you all right, Ronni?' he asks again. 'You look like you've seen a ghost.'

'Don't say that.' I sit back down on the chair. 'That's all I need – that woman haunting me.'

He knits his brow together.

'Sorry,' I say. 'I'm not making sense.' I give him a quick run-down on what the telephone call was about.

'Were you close, you and your mother-in-law?' he asks.

I regret my snort as soon as I make it. 'Not exactly,' I say in response to his raised eyebrows.

'She always hated me. I could never really understand why. The last time we met she had dementia – thought I was her mother. It was horrible, but I finally understood why she'd resented me so much over all those years …'

24 June 2018 – Treetops Nursing Home, Guildford, Surrey

Maybe she was right all along. Maybe if Matthew had married someone more suitable, he would be alive and happy. Maybe his death is my fault. I drove him to it because our marriage should never have been. Elizabeth was bloody right all along and I never listened!

'I'm sorry,' I gasp, as the realisation takes my breath away. 'I'm sorry for all of it – for everything.'

She purses her thin lips and reaches forward, grabbing my wrist with a strength a six-stone dying woman should not possess, and digs her nails into my skin so hard I cry out.

'No, Mam, no.' Her tiny eyes widen and plead with me. 'Please not tonight.'

She sounds different. What's she talking about? There's a nasal quality to her voice. My brain races to place it and I realise it's a Midlands accent. From Elizabeth – who's so proud of her Queen's English. I raise my eyebrows in question, but daren't speak. It's a bit freaky, but if she thinks I'm her mother, maybe at least she'll be nice to me for once.

'It's too late, isn't it?' Her voice is higher-pitched, almost childlike. 'You've already said they can come, haven't you?'

She squeezes her eyes shut and turns her head away from me. 'I know we need the money, but please not him. *He's …* rough *… stinks.' The hand she's clutching me with shakes.*

I swallow hard. What the hell …?

She turns back to me, leans forward and strokes my face over and over. She's so incredibly gentle. 'Don't cry, Mam,' she says, her voice softer. 'I miss Daddy too. So does Jean. If he were alive, he wouldn't let …'

A tear runs down one side of her face. The crags and wrinkles of her skin force it to take a haphazard route before it ends its journey on her wizened lip.

'No, stop crying. I'll do it. Even stinky man.'

Is this real or is it the dementia talking? Either way, by the look of her pained face, it's real to her. Every part of me aches to tell her I won't let it happen again, but I don't know if my speaking would frighten her, so I say nothing. I never met Jean. Matthew said his mother and her only sister didn't speak. He hadn't known why.

'Don't worry, Mam.' She's calmer now. 'I have a plan. I've had enough of being their whore.' She smiles, her eyes narrow in a determined triumph.

All I can do is stare at her. Then I remember she's still clenching my wrist, and I wrench my arm from her vice-like grip.

She sits back, clasps her knobbly hands together and rests them in her lap like she's at tea with the vicar and has just commented on the moistness of the Victoria sponge. She turns her head away from me to look out of the window at the manicured gardens below. I know this is the last thing I'll ever hear Elizabeth Kent-Walters say. She always was going to have the last word. I just never thought it would be that one.

'Do you think it was true?' Ralph asks, when I finish recounting what Elizabeth told me – something I haven't shared with anyone until now.

I shrug. 'I don't know. I hope not, but if she was acting, the woman deserved an Oscar. The look in her eyes, Ralph, it was so, so … I can't even explain it.'

'You don't think it was some bizarre way of making you feel sorry for her? Maybe a kind of explanation for how she'd treated you.'

I lean back against my chair. 'If her mother really was pimping out her and Jean, it must have been horrendous, but isn't that all the more reason to show some compassion, rather than treat me like a second-class citizen? She always went on about how great her days at boarding school were. It's the reason Matthew was so keen for Sabrine to go – to follow in his mother's footsteps. And all the time, it was a huge lie. Her background was as far from the polished oak panels of Felbury Hall as you can get.'

'Did her husband and children know about her past, do you think?'

'I'm damn sure they didn't!'

He chews the inside of his cheek. 'It must have eaten her up inside, feeling she couldn't share that with anyone.'

'Hmm. I'm wondering if that's why she and Jean didn't see each other. Maybe seeing her sister would've been too much of a reminder of her past. Not to mention it might have been risking it, bringing Jean into her family. If Elizabeth wanted it to remain a secret but her sister was more open, then it could have led to a massive scandal, and one thing I know about Elizabeth Kent-Walters is that she loved a family scandal, as long as it wasn't her own.'

He rests his chin on his hand. 'Maybe you reminded her of her past somehow and it made her feel uncomfortable.'

I raise an eyebrow. 'What – I reminded her of being a prostitute?'

He gives a wry smile. 'I didn't mean it like that. I meant your background or accent.'

'I know what you meant, and yeah, you're probably right.' I fold my arms across my chest. 'Maybe she feared I'd drag her son back down to the level she'd managed to scramble out of.'

'Are you going to tell Melanie, or Sabrine?'

I tip my head to the side. 'I've thought about it, but no. As much as we didn't get on, I respect that it's Elizabeth's secret and it's not my place to tell anyone – well, I'm telling you, obviously, but you have no connection to her.'

He taps his nose. 'Mum's the word.'

'Do you know'—I drum my fingers on my chin—'finding out her story – assuming it was true, that is – actually made me like her a bit. Although what happened to her I wouldn't wish on my worst enemy, and to be honest she did feel like that at times, it showed me a snapshot of vulnerable Elizabeth. I felt that for the first time in all those years, I knew the real her.'

'And the truth about where she came from.'

I bite my bottom lip. Does resenting Elizabeth for her facade make me a hypocrite? Is she the only one guilty of hiding her past?

'Mum!'

I look up to see Sabrine approaching our table.

'Hi, sweetheart.' I tap her lightly on the wrist. 'Thanks for looking after us tonight. Lovely meal.' I wink at her and lower my voice. 'But not nearly as good as the top class service, of course.'

She smiles. 'I told you you'd like it here if you gave it a chance.'

'And you were right.'

'Mum, listen, we're gonna be a while cleaning up tonight, so I'm going to stay over at Sam's, who works in the kitchen. You don't mind, do you, you know, with it being your birthday and everything.'

'Course not, darling. You girls have a nice sleepover.'

She opens her mouth to say something, then quickly flashes a smile. 'Thanks, Mum,' she says, and turns on her heel.

'Aren't you going to tell her about her grandmother dying?' Ralph asks.

'I'll have to, soon. Not tonight, though. I'll tell her tomorrow. Let her have a good time with her friend first.'

Ralph looks over my head towards the bar. 'Yeah. They both look happy at the prospect. Have you met, um, Sam?'

'No, not yet, but I'm glad Sabrine's making friends.'

'Sure.'

I look around and realise that other than a lone gentleman sat at the corner table with a newspaper and a centimetre of beer left in his pint glass, we were the only people left in the pub. 'Gosh. it must be late. Sorry if I'm keeping you.'

'You're not,' he says, and follows my lead as I rise and retrieve my coat from the back of my chair. 'Look, Ronni, are you okay? I know you and your mother-in-law didn't see eye to eye, but she was a part of your life all the same.'

'It wasn't exactly a shock to hear that she's died,' I say, struggling to do up the final button. 'They said last summer she might not have long left. I'm surprised she held on as long as she did.'

'May I?' He nods down at where my fumbling fingers are still trying to do up the button.

I take my hands away and let him take over. He pops the button through the hole with one attempt.

'Thanks,' I say. 'Actually,' I look up at him. I shouldn't say what's in my head, but hear it come out of my mouth anyway. 'Would you mind if I came back to yours?'

His eyebrows shoot up.

'Just for an hour, I mean. For a coffee. Then I'll go. I just don't want to …'

'Be alone? Or go back home just yet?'

I smile, thankful he understands. 'Both.'

'There's no central heating, unfortunately, but this will keep us warm once it gets going.' Ralph closes the door of the wood burning stove and comes over to join me on the sofa. He sits on the other side, leaving the middle seat between us free.

I hug my mug of coffee and look around the tiny living room. 'It's very cosy in here. I can see why you like it.'

'Ha, small you mean?'

'I don't suppose you need a lot of space, as it's just you.' *Rub it in and remind him of his divorce, why don't you, Ronni?*

He nods and takes a sip from his mug.

We sit in companionable silence for a few moments as the heat from the wood burner starts to creep up my feet and warm me through. It's nice, sitting here with him, enveloped in the well-worn sofa with the aroma of coffee filling my nostrils. I don't feel the need to break the silence, and take my time absorbing my surroundings; the stone hearth, the old-fashioned wallpaper that somehow fits the room perfectly, and the chequered curtains, which are good quality but have seen better days.

'The decor not quite to your taste?' he asks.

'What? Oh, no, it's lovely. I was just thinking – well, it's a bit, you know …'

'Lacking in personality?'

I give a little shrug. 'Hmm. Yes, I guess so.'

He laughs at my embarrassed confession. 'I didn't think there was much point trying to put my stamp on the place when I don't know how long I'll be around.'

I turn to him. 'Oh?'

'The plan was to start here, but not to get tied down to one place. I was a slave to my London desk for over twenty years. Now I've finally broken free, I want to move around when the time's right – see more of the country – even other countries if the opportunity comes up.'

My heart lowers an inch at that news; of course because it would be crazily inconvenient. 'Does that mean I'm going to be looking for a new driver soon?'

'That depends,' he says.

'What on?'

He drains his cup. 'Whether there's anything to stay for.'

He looks across at me and the seat in between us seems to narrow to a sliver. My whole body burns. Those wood burners don't half pump out some heat.

'What about your family? Do you still have your mum and dad? And I thought you had siblings. They must miss you. Do you all get on? It's funny how sometimes families are really close, and other times they're not. At all.' My narrative, the onset of verbal diarrhoea, comes out squeaky. The sound of it makes me cringe and I'm relieved I manage to curtail it when I do.

'I've got an older sister, who's a philosophy professor at a university in Canada, and a younger brother. He's married with two kids and works at Tesco in Milton Keynes. In the bakery department.'

'Oh, right. You all sound very different then.'

He nods. 'Not exactly peas in a pod.'

'And your parents?'

'We lost Mum and Dad a while back. Both to cancer.'

'Oh, I'm sorry.' I don't quite know how to move on from that and fluster around for the words. 'So, do you have much contact with them?'

'No, Ronni, they're dead. I'm not a psychic.'

'No!' I laugh, and put my hand to my forehead. 'I meant your brother and sister.'

He smiles. 'I know what you meant, and no, not really. We all get on fine, and we keep in loose touch – you know – Christmas and birthdays, but other than that, not really. We're all busy with our own lives.'

'Do you get lonely or are you happy in your own company?' *Why am I asking so many questions?* I don't seem to do it with anyone else, only him.

To my relief, he doesn't seem phased by my inquisitiveness. 'To be honest, Ronni, after so many years of bending over backwards to please Emma, it's refreshing not having anyone to answer to.'

I give a small smile and, in the absence of a coffee table, reach down to place my empty cup onto the rug below.

'There is one thing I miss, though,' he says.

'What's that?'

'Feeling needed.'

'You are needed. Ronni Delivers would be buggered without you, that's for sure.'

He stretches an arm behind his head and rests against it. 'That's kind of you to say, but what I mean is being *really* needed by someone – not like a job anyone could fill, but being needed 'cos you're you.' He casts me a glance. 'Does that make sense?'

'I think so,' I say.

'People need *you*,' he says.

'Do they?'

'Yes. Lots of people.'

'Well, I suppose that's because I've got Sabrine. I know she's technically an adult, but sometimes I wonder how she'll get on when she moves out. She put the whites in with a pair of red trousers the other day and wondered why all her smalls turned pink.'

'Of course Sabrine needs you, but so does Spud. He's always popping into the unit for a chat, and Toni – she really looks up to you.'

'Does she?' I gawp at him. I hardly think sassy, go-getting Toni thinks I'm much of an icon.

'Damn right she does. And why wouldn't she? You're hard-working, successful, attractive.'

My sunken heart performs a little jig. *Attractive*?

'And there's Chopper,' he says, cutting into my reverie. 'He thinks the sun shines out of you.'

'Oh, that's sweet, but that's because he and I have known each other a long time.'

'I hear you two nearly got married.'

'I wouldn't go that far! No, we had a thing for a while, but we were so young – kids really. It would never have worked.'

'You get on well now though.'

'Oh yes. He's got a heart of gold. Anyway, he seems very happy with Kelly.'

'That reminds me.' He hooks up one leg and rests it on his thigh. 'She called yesterday to speak to you.'

'Who, Kelly?' My palms tingle. What if she's found out I made a pass at Chopper? Kelly's from the roughest end of town. I wouldn't fancy my chances against her.

'She said she wanted to ask you a question – something about what Chopper was getting up to – said he'd been disappearing off and not coming home till late.'

'I don't see what that's got to do with me.'

The corners of his mouth turn down and he shakes his head. 'Apparently he'd told her he was working late and she wanted to check with you.'

'We don't do many late shifts.'

'No, that's what I thought, but I didn't want to stir things up. Whatever Chopper's up to, I'm sure he's got his reasons. Anyway, my point was that people around here need you. And that must be nice.'

I ponder his words for a moment. 'I've never thought about it like that before, but yes, I suppose it is. They've been a huge help to me, all of them, since I've been back in Haxton. I don't think I could have managed without them.'

He eases himself off the sofa and bends down in front of the wood burner. 'It can't have been easy,' he says. He places another log onto the fire before returning to the sofa. This time when he sits down, he's closer to me, but not quite fully in the middle seat. 'Coming back to Haxton and setting up a business after all you've been through takes real guts.'

I wiggle my toes inside my socks and laugh. 'I didn't have a lot of choice.'

'You had a lot of gumption,' he says without laughing with me. 'Going from the life you had to the one you had to set up must mean swallowing a fair amount of pride.'

'My, my. You seem to know quite a bit about my life before Haxton.'

He reaches out and touches my arm. 'I only know what people who are concerned about you told me. And don't take it the wrong way. I meant it as a compliment.'

'I know,' I say, my mouth dry with emotion.

He takes his arm away, leaving that patch of skin cold.

'It's funny,' he says, with a laugh that doesn't sound like he finds it at all funny. 'My experience was completely the opposite. There's my wife, refusing to turn her back on all those things she loves – expensive restaurants, beauty treatments, lunches with the girls – then I look at you coming back to your roots and making a go of things. You're pretty amazing, Ronni Fairweather.'

'Well,' I say, smiling and looking down into my lap. 'That *is* very complimentary.'

It's nice to hear those things. More than nice, in fact. I like the way his words make me feel and although I really should tell him I'm not the person he thinks I am – that I've actually been spending the last two months scanning Rightmove to see if there are any two-bed apartments I can afford in Surrey once I've sold up, I decide that now is not the right time, not if I want this feeling to last at least until the end of my birthday. And my God, I do.

An unexpected surge of desire courses through me, taking me by surprise. I lost my husband, whom I loved, less than nine months ago – I shouldn't be getting turned on this early into my widowhood. But it feels nice. Normal.

I shuffle nearer to him, closing the gap between us.

He lifts his head, then freezes, leaving his raised arm hanging in the air.

For a second I regret moving into him. I must have misread the signs. My blood curdles with embarrassment. I'm about to scuttle back to my corner of the sofa when he lowers his hand and starts stroking my hair.

It feels like nothing else, and makes my whole body tingle.

He's moving closer. His breath is on my cheek; his faint cologne in my nostrils. It's a combination too tempting to resist. Not that I want to, which is why, when his mouth lands on mine, I part my lips eagerly to receive it. Too eagerly? Should I pull away before the kiss deepens? He wraps his arms around my body. I'll be damned if I'm pulling away now.

I'm not sure whether he guides me to straddle his lap or whether I take it upon myself to do it, but within seconds that's where I am. His tongue is in my mouth, and mine in his. Desperate to feel his skin beneath my fingers, I tug at his shirt buttons, but I'm too excited, and I'm rusty. I haven't done anything like this – with this intensity – for such a long time that I'm all fingers and thumbs.

He breaks away from our kiss, looks down and takes over from me undressing him. It takes him three and a half seconds to undo all the buttons. I know that because I count how long his lips are away from mine. I could cry with relief when he lunges forward to kiss me again, shimmying out of his shirt at the same time. It's rough, urgent, but I can't get enough. Neither can he if the hardness at his crotch is anything to go by. I push my hand onto his groin.

He places his hand over mine and utters something I can't make out.

'What?' I pant between kisses.

He hooks his arms under my bottom and stands up, with my legs still wrapped around his waist. 'Upstairs,' he says again, and I understand him this time.

Chapter Thirty-Two

21 February 2019 – Haxton, Yorkshire

Ronni

I stuff a £20 note into the driver's hand and almost fall onto the pavement in my haste to climb out of the taxi.

'Here, love, what about your change?' he calls out through his window.

I mumble for him to keep it as I shove my door key into the lock. 'Bloody thing.' I jiggle it left, then right, until finally it opens. I dart into the house and, with my coat still on, throw myself onto the sofa. I tug my handbag off my shoulder and rifle through it.

'I can't believe I did it. What kind of a slag am I?' Tears stream down my cheeks and panic rises in me as I urgently look for my phone. I know it's in here somewhere.

It wasn't waking up next to Ralph, a slight ache between my legs, that did it – I felt good at that point. Great. Super. The cat that got the cream. It wasn't his arm snaking around me when he woke, telling me how much he'd enjoyed last night, or our lazy morning kiss – that was all wonderful. It was when I rolled on top of him, hoping, eurgh, how disgusting I am, for a repeat performance. That's when I saw the travel magazine on his bedside table with the picture of Norway on the front. Norway. Where Matthew proposed.

It was like a slap in the face – a bucket of iced water over the head – the wake-up call that came too late. My husband was barely cold in the ground and I was in another man's bed.

I made up some story, of course, about why I had to leave in such a hurry. I can't even remember what it was now – something about getting home before Sabrine. I don't even care. I just knew I needed to get home quickly. To listen to my husband's voice.

My hand clasps around the slippery device and I snatch it out of my bag, punch in the pin and select Matthew's number.

But it's not Matthew's honey-drawl that reaches my ears; it's an accented robot telling me his number cannot be recognised and I should try again. I do try again. I try again so many times that the pad of my finger burns from scrolling and stabbing at the screen. But still I get that fucking robot.

My heart's thumping in my chest and my mind's racing. This *cannot* be happening. It can't be. Think, Ronni, think. A eureka moment comes, flooding me with relief that there is still a way for me to reach Matthew. I squat down onto the floor and search through the pile of magazines and other detritus stashed under the coffee table, hunting for the treasure I know is there. I know it's there because I've kept it just in case.

There it is.

Matthew's mobile phone. I grab it, press my thumb against the button on the side and shake it, as if doing so will make it work quicker.

'C'mon, c'mon!' I plead with the screen as it comes to life with a glow and a chirpy little tune.

I swipe away a fat tear and a string of snot from my face.

What's the number? What's the fucking number?

211?

No.

220

Shit. No.

221. That's it!

I try to select the numbers but my thumb, slick with snot, slips on the screen. I bang the phone against the carpet. *Shitty thing.* It's like being in some horrendous nightmare.

I wipe my hand down my coat, and try again.

This time it makes a noise in response. I press the phone to my ear. 'Come on, come on, Matthew. Where are you?'

The phone bleats three tones down my ear. 'This number is no longer recognised. Please try again.'

That bloody robotic voice is back, telling me the same thing again and again after every trio of tones.

'No. No.'

I haven't thought about Matthew for a few days, not in the same way I used to. This is my punishment. I turn the phone off, then endure the gruelling five second wait of turning it back on again.

'Work this time. Please work this time.'

Tri-tonal bleating and robotic voice inform me again this number is no longer recognised.

I shake the phone and scream so loudly at it that my throat burns. Isn't it enough that the pension fund company Matthew had been paying into his whole working life is quibbling about paying out because he took his own life? Apparently no. It's not enough. Now, just to save a few quid, the company he slaved away at, have cancelled his phone contract without letting me know. Bloody brilliant!

I smack the device again and again against the glass-topped coffee table. 'YOU.' *Smack*. 'BUNCH.' *Smack*. 'OF.' *Smack*. 'TOTAL.' *Smack*. 'ARSEHOLES.' *Smack*.

I stop, panting. My coffee table has two massive gouges out of it, but the phone looks untouched. I hold it in front of my face. 'What are you looking at?'

It slips out of my fingers onto the carpet. I kick it away. It skids across the carpet and smashes into the wall. The screen shatters along with my hopes of ever hearing Matthew's voice again.

Chapter Thirty-Three

14 March 2019 – Guildford, Surrey

Ronni

'Someone's popular,' says Sabrine. She's perched on the end of one of the hotel's twin beds, gazing out of the window at the grim car park view.

I disregard the pyjama bottoms I'm folding to eye my pinging phone. The screen's lit up and I can see it's a message from Ralph.

'Just well-wishers,' I tell Sabrine, as I turn the phone over, face down, on top of the bed. There's something about the way she's acting that I can't quite put my finger on. The last thing I need is for her to suspect anything's going on between me and Ralph. Not that there *is* anything going on. I've tried to keep a professional distance between us since we spent the night together, and he hasn't pushed it, so I'm figuring that's that – two consenting adults who had a bit too much to drink and ended up in bed together. It's not like we're the first that's happened to. So, I wonder why he's texting now. I'm itching to check but will wait until I'm on my own.

I carry on packing my case, folding the black trouser suit I wore yesterday. I put Sabrine's "offishness" down to her grandmother's death at first, but now I'm not sure. She hardly spoke during the journey down, nor yesterday at the funeral. I know Elizabeth's death upset her, but something's nagging at me that there's more to it. We've been getting on so well for the last few weeks, which was a relief after our shaky first few weeks in Haxton, but now we seem to be going backwards again.

I tried to talk to her about it, but she just said I was imagining it. Maybe I *am* imagining it. Maybe having Ralph on the brain, even though I know nothing's going to happen between us again, is driving me nuts. No more sex for me. Ever again. Sexless and sane. That's how it's going to be for me from now on.

A thought pops into my head and I laugh suddenly. 'Do you remember the last time we did the journey up north? We ended up delivering ten tonnes of cocaine to that Tom chap. I wonder if the coppers ever caught up with him.'

She smiles faintly as she zips up her make-up bag, but doesn't comment.

'It's okay, sweetheart, there's no need to worry. I think we got away with that one. If the police were going to knock on our door they would've done it by now.'

She unzips her make-up bag again and peers into it. God knows what's in there, because she won't tear her eyes away and meet mine. 'I'm not worried about that,' she says.

I stifle a sigh. 'Well, it's good news that Grandma Elizabeth left you such a generous trust fund. Even though you won't get it all in one go, it's nice to know you'll get a set amount per year. Probably better that way, actually.'

'Yes,' she says.

'Any ideas what you'll do with it?'

She bites her bottom lip. 'Maybe. Funny how she didn't leave any to you though, don't you think?'

I upend the ceramic pot which contains the complimentary biscuits and stash them into my handbag. They'll do nicely for the journey back. 'Not terribly funny, no.'

'But after Daddy died we had nothing,' she says. 'And Grandma was so *rich*.' She props her chin on her hand. 'Do you think that was the reason she didn't leave you any – because she'd never been poor, so didn't really understand what it was like?'

'Hmm, maybe.'

'I will share it with you, you know, once I have it. I want to make sure you're alright.'

My throat tightens. 'That's very nice of you, sweetheart, but I don't want you to do that. It's your money, and I will be alright. I *am* all right. The business is doing well and at this rate it won't be long before I can sell up and we can get out of Haxton.'

She takes a deep breath, lets it out in a rush of air and looks down at her lap. 'Do you think she'd be ashamed of me?'

I pause, midway in the process of fastening my case. 'What on earth do you mean?'

'Grandma Elizabeth. You know how posh she was – how she always told anyone who'd listen that I went to Felbury. Do you think she'd be horrified if she knew I worked in a pub? Like you were at first.'

'Sabrine, Grandma Elizabeth wouldn't be ashamed of you, and neither am I. In fact, I've never been so proud of you as I have since we moved to Haxton.'

She puts her head back up. 'Really?'

I cross the room to where she's sitting and cuddle her.

'Really, sweetheart. You've grown up into an amazing woman.'

She pulls back and grins at me for a second, then her smile fades. 'I'm not sure you're going to be thinking that for long.'

'Why?'

'I've got something to tell you and you're not going to like it.'

Panic rises inside me as a rush of possibilities enter my head. 'What is it, sweetheart?'

I fasten my seat belt and grip the steering wheel with both hands.

'Mum?'

I look straight ahead, out of the windscreen at the blue Ford Focus parked in front of us.

'Mum.'

It has one of those Baby on Board stickers in the back window. It's gone curly round the edges. How old is that *baby* now?

'Mum!'

'What?'

'Are you mad with me?'

'No.' I pause and drum my fingers on the wheel. 'A little disappointed maybe.'

'Why? Just 'cos I want to stay in Haxton. I know you want to come back down here, but you still can.'

'I'm not leaving you! Not when I've only just got you home.'

'Haxton *is* home.'

'Surrey's home.'

'Mum, I'm nineteen. Sam and I want to move in together soon, anyway. I'm not going to be at home forever, wherever you decide *your* home is.'

'Yeah, that's right. Move in. With *Sam*. The boy that up until last week I thought was a girl.'

'Mum, please don't start that again.'

'Well, perhaps if you'd been honest with me from the start—'

'I never lied.'

'Oh, come on, Sabrine. Letting me believe Sam was a girl is just as bad as lying.'

She puts her head down. 'I suppose so.'

I puff out my cheeks. 'I just don't understand why you'd give up everything, all for some boy.'

'I'm not giving up anything,' she says. 'I'm still *me* wherever I am.'

Then she mumbles something I don't catch.

'What did you say?' I ask.

'I said that's more than can be said for you.'

'And what's that supposed to mean?'

She twists in her seat so she's facing me. 'You're like a different person now we're in Haxton. A nicer one, actually. You're funnier, more relaxed, you even look better.'

I look down at my middle, which has acquired at least one more love handle since the move. 'Do I?'

'Yes. Much better. Healthier. Happier even, some days.'

Happier? How can I be, now my husband's gone?

'I'm just trying to find my own way, Mum.' she continues. 'Please let me.' Her face becomes a blur as my eyes fill with tears.

I place my hand on top of hers. Hers is smoother, warmer. 'Oh, sweetheart. I know you think you're all grown up, but you've still got so much to learn.'

She looks right into my eyes. 'Then let me.'

I swallow. 'I just need time to take it all in.'

She nods her head a fraction. 'Okay.' She sits back in her seat and pulls her seat belt around her. When I don't turn on the ignition, she looks over at me.

I don't look back at her. It's easier to stare at the scuffed bumper of that Ford Focus.

'What's wrong?' she asks.

I take a deep breath in. 'You're right about one thing – you are an adult, and you deserve to know this.' I try to get the next words out, but my throat tightens. I close my eyes. If I don't look at her, maybe it'll be easier. 'Sweetheart, well, you know that Daddy had, um, he had, he was, er having—'

'An affair?'

'Yes.'

'Yes, of course I know. You told me, but that's not your point, is it?'

I lick my bone-dry lips. 'No.'

She waits for me to carry on.

'The woman he was, um, having, that he, um had—'

'An affair with?' Her voice is clear, emotionless.

'Yes. Well, she had a child. With Daddy.'

'Mum, are you trying to tell me I have a brother?'

I hold my breath and nod.
Then it hits me.
How does she know it's a boy?

Chapter Thirty-Four

14 March 2019 – Silent Pool, Surrey

Ronni

'He's a good walker.'

Arabella, beside me on the stone bench, follows my eyeline over to where Sabrine and Oscar are walking hand-in-hand around the lake. She nods. 'Yeah. He seems pretty advanced compared to a lot of the other kids his age.'

'That's good.'

I swing my feet, which don't quite reach the ground.

'She's good with children, Sabrine is,' she adds.

'Yes. She is.'

'How did she take it, when you told her?'

'She surprised me,' I say. 'But then, she often does.'

'Oh.' She coughs, and shuffles her backside a little further back onto the bench. 'I must admit, you two were the last people I was expecting to see turn up at my door.'

'Sabrine wanted to meet Oscar,' I say. 'They are siblings after all. None of what happened is their fault.'

'Still.' She sniffs. 'You were pretty clear you didn't want to see me again.'

'I was mad. A lot's changed since then.'

She shuffles again. 'Like what?'

I shrug, even though she's not looking at me. 'Oh, I don't know, just a lot of things. Anyway'—I delve into my coat pocket, pull out a folded slip of paper and hand it to her—'I wanted to give you this.'

'What is it?'

I nudge it in her direction. 'Take it.'

She plucks it out of my hand as if it might bite, and unfolds the cheque.

'Five hundred quid? What's this for?'

'Buy whatever Oscar needs. They grow so quickly, do kids. Expensive little things.'

She folds the cheque and pockets it. 'I thought you said you were broke.'

'I am. Just less broke than I was.'

'Well, thanks,' she says.

'Don't mention it.'

She flicks her overgrown fringe out of her eyes. 'So, your dad's not gonna find out I'm here with you and have me locked up?'

I look at her out of the corner of my eye. 'What?'

'You said your father was a lawyer and if I came within a mile's radius of you, he'd make sure I paid back all the money Matthew had given me.'

I laugh. 'Did I?'

She turns to me and wrinkles her nose. 'What's so funny?'

'The thought of my father being a lawyer. I think what I actually said was he's an expert in law.'

'Same thing.'

'Hardly! He was an expert in law-dodging, not so much law-following.'

'You mean he's a criminal?'

'Was. Well, small-time maybe, never anything big.'

She folds her arms across her chest, pushing the air out of her jacket like a deflating Michelin Man. 'That scared the shit out of me, that did. I thought he was like Judge Rinder or something.'

'No chance. Besides, he's been dead for the best part of twenty years.'

'Judge Rinder's dead?'

'No. I meant my dad.'

'Oh, thank God for that. I like watching Judge Rinder.' She shoots me a glance. 'Oh, I didn't mean—'

'It's fine,' I say. In the hour we've spent in her company, I've learned that Arabella isn't the offensive type – lacking an inner filter, yes, but deliberately offensive, no. What you see with her is what you get. No airs. No graces. She has a hapless charm about her and as much as I want to dislike her, I can't.

We both fall into silence and look forward at the eerily still, blue-green water of the pond.

'Bloody odd choice of location, this,' she says at last.

'Beautiful though, isn't it?'

The sleeve of her puffer jacket rubs against my arm as she shrugs. 'S'pose so. In a creepy sort of way.'

'Have you been here before?'

On the ground in front of us, her shadow nods.

'Me too,' I say. 'Before we moved up north, I came here a couple of times. I thought coming to the place he chose to die might give me some answers. It didn't though. If anything, it made me more confused.' I press my hands in between my thighs, wishing I'd brought my gloves. Not that I expected this detour.

'More confused?' She turns to me, her brow knitted together. 'Why?'

'Look around.' I gesture at the lake, the copious amount of trees surrounding it, all showing the promise of new, green leaves. There's even the burgeoning yellow heads of a few daffodils braving an early spring opening. 'There's so much life here. How could Matthew come here and not feel he had something to live for?'

She pushes Oscar's empty pushchair with her foot. 'You still don't know why he did it, do you?'

'I know he was juggling two families. And I know he had gambling debts, so yes, I guess I do, but it just doesn't seem'—I shake my head—'it doesn't seem like Matthew. He wasn't someone who gave up on anything easily, so why give up on life?'

She stops rolling the wheel of the buggy, and stubs her booted toe against the blackened leaves on the ground.

'There was something else.'

Her voice is so low I'm not sure I heard her right.

'Something else?'

She looks down at her feet. 'I can't believe you don't know.' She squints up at me. The late morning sun makes her fair eyelashes appear almost white. 'He was up to his eyeballs in debt.'

'Well, I've figured that one out.'

'Yes, but he'd taken out a loan. A big one. A personal one. He'd maxed out his credit cards and everything else, so it was his only other option. He kept saying to me that he just needed one more win at the casino and he'd make it all okay. I tried to talk him out of it, but he was so sure it was his time to win that he just wouldn't listen.'

My hands start to sweat and I pull them out from between my thighs and am grateful for the rush of cold air that hits them.

'He didn't win. Obviously. Blew the lot. Every penny. I've never seen him so down. He'd had big losses before that but nothing on this scale. He was terrified of going home and telling you.'

The sweat creeps under my sleeves and inside my clothes. 'Terrified? Of me? Why?' What was she trying to say? That I caused Matthew's death because he was so frightened of my reaction? But if anyone wore the trousers, it was him. I don't get it. None of this makes sense. My head starts to pound.

'Because,' she says. 'Unlike me, you were married to him. His debts were your debts, as long as he was alive, anyway. He was going crazy about having let you down, told me he was going to tell you everything – confess about me and Oscar. He said he'd been an idiot and was going to beg you for forgiveness.' A shadow falls across her face. 'After all the shit he'd put me through, in the end he chose you.'

The world spins around me and my head feels like it's detached from my body. 'But before you said he was going to leave me.'

She puts her chin down to her chest. Her words, muffled by her huge coat, are only just audible. 'I lied. That's what I wanted the truth to be, but it's not what happened.'

'Then why didn't he tell me like he said he would?'

'For someone Matthew said was intelligent, you really are coming across quite thick.'

Matthew told his mistress I was intelligent?

She tuts like she's finally lost patience with me. 'He did it to protect you, *obviously*. If he died, then the loan – at least the personal one he took out – would die with him. That's why I was surprised that time I came round your house, when you said you didn't have any money and were having to sell the house. I assumed there'd at least be life insurance, or something.'

I spin around on the bench to face her and my leggings snag on an encrusted dollop of bird poo. 'Are you saying he killed himself for me?'

She uncrosses her arms and fiddles with the toggle on her zip. 'Not just for that, but it was a big part. There was also the gambling. I don't mean just the debt – I think deep down he knew it was only money and there was a chance you'd forgive him. But it was more than that – it was what the gambling did to him – to his head.

'I begged him not to go, not to leave me and Ozzie, but all he could say was how much he'd fucked up and how much he loved you and Sabrine. He just told me he was sorry, gave Ozzie a kiss goodbye, and that's the last time I saw him.'

She's crying now. We both are. My tears aren't for me. Whatever she thinks, I want to believe in some way that Matthew was trying to protect me. But I don't believe that's why he ended his life. He did that because he was an addict. To gambling. I couldn't see it at first, but the more I piece things together, the more it makes sense. My tears are for Arabella and Oscar – the family that Matthew decided on his last day, would sit in second place.

'I suppose he did tell me he loved me, but that something was wrong,' I whisper. 'In his own way. I just didn't realise what he was trying to say.'

Chapter Thirty-Five

19 June 2018 – Guildford, Surrey

Raegan

Matthew reaches around me to pick up his keys from the kitchen top.

'Going already?' I ask, cupping the gloopy empty eggshell in my palm. 'I was just making you some breakfast.'

He kisses my cheek and I catch a waft of toothpaste from his breath.

'Sorry, darling, I've got a sales meeting first thing. I'll grab something on the way.'

'Oh.' I look down at the now ownerless eggs in the perspex jug. They stare up at me rather sadly with their single yellow eyes like orphaned Cyclopes. 'That's a shame. I got some lovely free range organic duck eggs from Waitrose. I was going to poach them for you and toast you some of that seedy bread you like. Do you want marg?'

'Raegan, for goodness' sake. I told you, I can't this morning.'

I tighten the belt on my satin dressing gown. 'Okay, okay. There's no need to get shirty.' I open the bin cupboard and throw the eggs in. They momentarily cling on to the side of the black bin liner before they give up the ghost and slide down to the dark depths to join Matthew's dinner from last night that congealed long before he got home. 'I don't know why I bother.'

Behind me he mutters an expletive, and his keys clatter on the table. 'Give me a break, why don't you?'

I spin around and fold my arms across my chest.

'Give you a break? You're not the one doing all the cooking for someone who's never around to eat any of it. Work, work, work. That's all you're doing at the moment. I've hardly seen you recently what with you always getting in so late.'

He sighs and presses both hands over his eyes. 'Sorry, darling. I don't mean to take it out on you. Everything's just a bit stressful at the moment.'

He pulls his hands down his face, dragging on the rims of bloodshot eyes. *He works hard for the life we have, I know that.* I slink over to him and wrap my arms around his neck. 'I know, darling, I know.' I push my chest against his, although he doesn't wrap his arms around my waist like I want him to, just lowers his head. I kiss his forehead. It's hot and salty.

'How about,' I purr, 'you and I spend some time together this evening. I'll make us something nice and we could have an early night. It *is* Tuesday.' I giggle. 'If you know what I mean.'

He puts his hands on my waist and eases me away. 'Yeah, maybe,' he says, retrieving his keys from the table.

My shoulders sag.

'Listen, darling, I've got to get going. Have a good day.'

'Wait!' I pull his suit jacket off the back of the chair. 'Have you forgotten something?'

'Oh yeah.' He reaches forward to take the jacket from me. 'Thanks. Have a good day.'

'Bye darling,' I say, opening the fridge door and pulling out the bag of spinach for my morning smoothie.

'Raegan?'

I peer around the edge of the fridge door to see him standing in the open doorway, hand on the door handle. 'I just, um, wanted to say … goodbye.'

It sounds so formal compared to the "see ya!" he always normally issues that I almost laugh.

'I want you to know that I, um, that I love you,' he adds.

I grin. Maybe the idea of Tuesday night shenanigans has perked him up. 'I know, darling.' I smile and turn around to the smoothie blender. 'I love you too.'

'Raegan?'

I turn around and see he's still there. Poor man looks exhausted. I know, I'll give him a massage tonight with that new Spatronics coconut oil. He'll love that.

He starts to say something, then stops himself. For a moment he just looks at me, then suddenly he bounds over to me and wraps his arms around my waist, holding me tight.

'What's got into you?' I laugh. 'I thought you had an early morning meeting.'

'I do,' he muffles into my neck, before pulling away and looking into my eyes. 'I just wanted to say I'm sorry.'

I stroke the back of his neck where he's let his hair grow longer than normal. 'For what?'

'Being a twat. I don't deserve you.'

I tap his arms. 'Don't be silly. It's not your fault they're working you too hard. How about'—I smooth down his shirt collar where it's not folded quite right—'you and I start packing tonight for the holiday? We can do it together like we always used to. It'll be fun. I'm sure Sabrine will want to do her own next week when she's back. I can't believe this holiday has finally come round. Mind you, we'd better make the most of it. It might be the last time Sabrine will want to come with us.'

I swear there's still a trace of sadness in his eyes, but maybe I'm imagining it, because he smiles and kisses the tip of my nose. When he pulls away his forehead is creased. 'Do you know where we keep the passports?' he says.

'What? No. Somewhere in your filing cabinet, I presume, but I normally leave you to get those out.'

His forehead smooths out, but not completely. 'That's right. They're in the second drawer down. At the back.'

A frisson of excitement shoots through me. 'I can't wait to get on that plane! And if Sabrine finds a few kids her age, we might get some time to ourselves. It'll be like a second honeymoon.'

'Yeah,' he says, with only the faintest of smiles. 'Remind each other of why we fell in love. You could be my feisty little Ronni Fairweather again.' His smile fades. 'Whatever happened to her?'

I cock my head to the side. 'She married you,' I say quietly. 'And her life changed for the better.'

'The better?' he says. 'Do you think?'

'Yes. Don't you?'

He doesn't answer – just shrugs and takes me in with his bloodshot eyes.

'That's the first time you've ever called me *Ronni*,' I say.

'Maybe that's where I went wrong.'

I shake my head. 'What?'

'Nothing, darling.' He gives me a final kiss on the cheek and lets me go. 'Gotta get going.' He pulls away and heads for the door, where he pauses and turns back to face me. 'Bye-bye Ronni Fairweather,' he says.

'Bye, darling,' I call with a wave. With thoughts of the holiday dominating my brain, I smile and turn back around to throw a handful of spinach into the smoothie maker.

The kitchen door closes behind me as Matthew leaves.

Chapter Thirty-Six

14 March 2019 – M1, Northbound

Ronni

Sabrine's asleep now. Her head's resting against the passenger window and her mouth's open. We've been travelling for over two hours since leaving Arabella and Oscar. It was a meeting that was emotionally exhausting for me, so goodness knows how Sabrine must be feeling. I turn down the volume on the van radio so as not to disturb her.

'Oscar looks so much like Daddy,' she'd said when we first got back into the van. She was right. He did. I remember a funny thing Matthew used to do with his eyebrows that I noticed Oscar doing. It had freaked me out at first, but then it made me laugh.

It's not like I wasn't used to seeing flashes of Matthew in my own daughter's face; his mannerisms in her. Being reminded of him didn't sadden me, not like it did when he first died. Sometimes I even managed to think of the good times we had. There might not have been so many in recent times, but there had been plenty over the years we were together.

Sabrine finally opened up to me when we set off for home – for Haxton. Turns out, she'd been in the house the day that Charlotte had told me about Arabella. I thought she was still out at her friend's – hadn't heard her return early. She's known all this time that Matthew's affair had resulted in a child. She hadn't told me she knew for fear of upsetting me all over again. She'd even let me believe she'd only learned of Matthew's affair when I told her myself that time in the service station car park. It was easier that way, she said. Poor Sabrine. A girl of eighteen shouldn't be carrying that kind of weight on her shoulders. And certainly not to protect her mother's feelings.

I take my eyes off the road just long enough to glance across at her. She looks so young when she's asleep. Like the eleven-year-old I waved off to school with a fake smile on my face, before I burst into tears the minute her back was turned. And now that same girl wants to make a life for herself in Haxton; the very town I clawed my way out of.

The traffic slows abruptly and I brake. The jolt wakes Sabrine up with a sharp intake of breath.

'Sorry,' I say. 'More roadworks.'

She stretches her back. 'Are we nearly there yet?'

I smile to myself. It's been a few years since I've heard her say that. 'Another forty miles or so to go. You're lucky. You've slept most of the way.'

She tips her head to one side, then the other and winces. 'I'm not feeling all that lucky. My neck's killing.' She reaches for her bottle of water and has a long drink.

'Better?' I ask, as the traffic progresses to a crawl.

She nods and wipes a droplet of water from her lower lip. 'Mm-hmm. Better for the drink, better for the sleep and better I've met Oscar.'

'Good.' I reach over and tap her knee. 'And I feel better now it's all in the open. No more secrets now. Agree?'

'Agree,' she says. 'Does that include me knowing about you and Ralph?'

My foot slips on the accelerator and I quickly steady myself. 'What *about* me and Ralph?'

'Oh, come on, Mum. I know you spent the night at his on your birthday.'

'How do you— how do you know that?' I flash her a glance and she giggles.

'Actually, I wasn't sure, but you've pretty much just confessed.'

'I haven't confessed anything.'

'Then why have you gone red?' she says in a sing-song voice.

'I haven't gone red, have I?' I flip down my sun visor, slide open the mirror and see two flushed cheeks in the rectangle of glass. I flip it back up. 'Look, it was nothing. Just a one-off.'

She performs a mock gasp. 'You mean, like a one night stand?'

'Sabrine! Don't use that kind of language.'

She laughs, clutching her stomach. 'Relax, Mum, you are over the age of consent.'

'Please,' I say, spotting a sign that tells me we're forty-five miles from Leeds. Far too far. I want to get out of this conversation now. 'Stop talking like that.'

Her hilarity increases with my awkwardness, and she pulls her knees up to her chest as she laughs even harder. 'It's fine, Mum. I don't mind. You deserve some fun, because I suppose you're not *that* old.'

'Oh, thanks very much.'

'And Ralph's not bad-looking, for an old guy.'

'Right.' I pause, taking in what she said. 'So, are you saying, that if Ralph and I did have, an, um *friendship*—'

She laughs again, and I ignore her.

'—that you wouldn't mind?'

'No. Why would I mind?'

'Well, I just thought …'

'Mum, I'm not twelve years old. I do want you to be happy, you know.'

Emotion swells within me and my eyes start to sting.

'Does this mean the two of you are going official?' she asks.

Not with the cold shoulder I've been giving him. 'I doubt it.'

'Why?'

I'm about to answer when my phone screen lights up, catching our attention. I switched it to silent a couple of hours ago when Ralph tried to call. I didn't want to disturb Sabrine when she was sleeping, but nor did I particularly want to speak to Ralph. Things have been so awkward recently that I don't know what to say.

'Haven't you got that connected to your van?' Sabrine asks.

'It's my personal phone, not my work one. I haven't sorted out the goldtooth thingy on this one yet.'

'*Blue*tooth, Mother. Never mind. I'll get it.' She snatches up the phone and clocks the name on the screen. 'Speak of the devil.'

Ralph! I reach out to stop her but she lunges out of my grasp.

'Hi Ralph. It's Sabrine. Mum's driving and she hasn't managed to sort out her goldtooth yet.'

She giggles silently and I roll my eyes.

'What? When?' She sits up in her seat and her expression changes to deadly serious.

My heart pounds. 'What?' I mouth. A rush of hideous possibilities flashes through my head. *Is Ralph hurt? Oh, God, please let him be okay.*

'And how is he?' Sabrine asks.

Sweat forms under my armpits and I force myself to drop away from the car in front, whose boot I almost ended up in.

'Yes, of course. I'll let her know.'

She pulls the phone away from her ear and ends the call.

'What's happened?' I ask. Pins and needles spring to life in the end of my fingers.

'It's Chopper,' she says. 'He's in hospital. He's had an accident.'

As soon as we park up at home and Sabrine goes inside, I sit in the van and reach for my phone. I let out a curse. There are two unopened messages, three missed calls and a voicemail. All from Ralph. With my phone on silent, I didn't know he'd called that many times. Guilt dishes me a slap to the face. What was I thinking? Too embarrassed to speak to Ralph when all this time he was calling to say that Chopper was lying in a hospital bed.

I select his number and wait an excruciating four rings for him to answer, my heart pounding several times within each of those rings.

Ralph is off with me, I can hear it in his voice, even though the call is barely a minute long. He says he'll be round in ten minutes to pick me up and take me to the hospital; says he knows which ward Chopper's in and it's easier if we go together. No, he doesn't know how bad the injuries are. All he knows is that Chopper came off his bike last night. He'll explain more on the way. I numbly agree and end the call. All I can think about is Kelly and her kids. I know what it's like to lose a husband, and I hope with all my might Kelly isn't about to find out what that feels like.

'What happened?' I ask before I've even done up my seat belt.

Ralph waits for me to fasten myself in before pulling away. His hair is more dishevelled than usual and faint bags have formed beneath his eyes.

'I don't know the details, only that he came off his Kawasaki somewhere near the city centre at about two in the morning. I don't think anyone else was involved. He was unconscious when they brought him in. I haven't heard from Kelly for a while so I don't know if he's woken up yet.'

'Oh, God.' Fear clogs my throat. 'What was he doing haring around Leeds at two in the morning?'

'Don't know.'

'He can't still be unconscious, can he?'

He grinds the gear. 'I've been trying to contact you all day, but you weren't answering.'

'I know. I'm sorry.' I ramble the story of my visit to Arabella, spilling out the whole story about her and Oscar, and about not wanting to wake Sabrine on the journey back. It's the first time I've told him about Matthew's affair.

'Ronni, I'm sorry,' he says, his jaw relaxing slightly. 'I didn't know you were going through all that.'

'Yeah, well, it's done now. It's Chopper and Kelly I'm thinking about at the moment.'

We spend the rest of the short journey in silence, broken only when I point out an elusive parking space in St James's Hospital car park. I follow him inside, to the lift and along several corridors until we get to a reception desk. I hang back as Ralph talks to the man behind the desk. If it's bad news, I don't want to hear it from a stranger.

'We're allowed to visit but just for ten minutes,' says Ralph when he's finished talking to the man.

Does that mean he's awake? I want to ask Ralph but he's already several strides in front of me. I quicken my step to catch up and reach him when he's by a closed-curtain cubicle brandishing the name Kenneth Wallington. Kenneth? Did I ever know Chopper's real name was Kenneth? I'm not convinced I did. Even his mother calls him *Chopper*.

Ralph peers through the curtain, then turns to me.

'Listen, Ronni. You might be in for a bit of a shock. It probably looks worse than it is—'

I reach past Ralph to grab the edge of the curtain and pull it open wide enough to step inside.

'Jesus, Chopper!'

Both his arms and one leg are in plaster. His face is red and puffy, and is punctuated with two hooded, black eyes.

'Ey up, Ronni.' He goes to wave, then winces.

Kelly, sitting on Chopper's bed, looks up at us. Her eyes are red and smudged with make-up. 'Ronni?'

I nod.

'I tried to call you a couple of weeks ago.' She sniffs and raises a trembling hand to hoist up one of her bra straps which has slipped beneath her one-shoulder top. 'You never called back.'

'Oh, I'm sorry, it's just I've been, um, busy with, um …'

'I was worried about 'im, see. 'E's been out all hours making deliveries on that bloody crotch rocket of 'is.'

I frown.

''Is motorbike,' she says. 'I wanted to ask ya if it wer possible for 'im not to work so many nights. 'E were knackered – working all day on 'vans, then all night on 'bike. I know we need money, like, but there's gotta be a limit, even for folk like us.'

'I don't understand,' I say. 'We don't do bike deliveries.'

'Aye. I know that now.'

I shake my head. 'Sorry. I don't quite understand. What on earth happened?'

'He's been a right twat, that's what's happened,' Kelly says. 'Tell 'er, Chopper. Go on.'

'I've been doing a few'—he coughs and clutches his chest—'emergency night runs.' He coughs again.

Kelly places a hand on top of his. 'I'll tell 'er.' She swivels around to me. 'Daft apeth's only been zooming around on 'is bike till all hours delivering blood, 'asn't he?'

I squint, trying to make sense of all this. 'Oh, you mean donor blood? To hospitals?'

'Yeah. After a full day at work n'all. Thinks e's a bleedin' vampire. Didn't tell me 'cos 'e thought I'd try n'stop 'im from doing it. Bleedin' right I would've.'

Chopper looks up at me from under his hooded lids and smiles a swollen-lipped, wonky smile. 'It's 'cos of our Aidee's accident that I done it,' he says.

''Is younger brother,' Kelly says as she sees me frown.

A picture of a smaller but just as gangly version of Chopper flashes past my eyes. 'Oh yes, course. I remember now.'

'Went bombing down Figging 'ill 'e did on 'is bike, a few years back. They 'ad to pump 'im full o'donor blood to keep 'im alive.'

''E's fine now,' says Kelly. 'Well, 'e's a bit slow on the uptake, like, but I don't think that 'ad owt to do wi' accident.'

'Nah, 'e'll never win Mastermind, won't our Aidee, but e's a good lad,' agrees Chopper. 'I never really thought about it all that much at 'time, but just lately.' He coughs. 'I'm probably going soft in mi old age.' He splutters and coughs again.

Kelly reaches over to his bedside table and picks up a plastic cup with a straw poking out of the lid. She guides it in between Chopper's lips. He takes a sip, dribbles most of it down his chin and starts up again. 'I reckon it's my turn to do summet in return. You know, give summet back.'

'And look at 'bloody state of 'im now.' Kelly cocks her head at Chopper. 'Trying to be a knight in shining armour. Can't even wipe 'is own backside.'

I look from one plastered arm to the other. 'Yes, that might be, um, challenging.'

'In sickness and in 'ealth,' Chopper says, eyes twinkling at Kelly.

'Oh, aye. It'll be muggins 'ere.' She begins stroking his hair and, despite her words, smiles down at him.

He beams, as best he can, back up at her.

He's her hero. No wonder he ran a mile when I tried to kiss him when he's this much in love with his wife.

When was the last time Matthew looked at me like that? Was he my hero?

A hard lump rises in my throat. It takes three swallows to force it down.

'So,' I say, furiously blinking away the threat of tears. 'How are you feeling, Chopper?'

I could have cried with relief when Ralph suggested a drink at The Royal Oak. During the car journey back to Haxton I text Toni, Spud and Sabrine to ask them if they want to join us for an update on Chopper. In the time it takes me and Ralph to get to the pub, the three of them have already arrived.

'How is 'e?' Toni asks, before we even have a chance to sit down.

'He should make a full recovery, thank God,' I say as I plonk myself into the seat beside her. 'Concussion, two broken arms, a broken leg and three fractured ribs, but nothing that won't heal.'

Toni clamps a hand across her mouth. 'Christ. What the 'ell was he doing?'

I fill them all in on Chopper's blood-transporting missions.

'Soft sod,' says Spud, wiping a hand across his eyes.

'He was lucky,' says Ralph. 'But it'll be a while before he'll be back on his feet. We're going to need a new driver for a few months.'

My heart plummets. I've been lucky with staff up to now; couldn't ask for a more trustworthy team than Ralph, Toni and Chopper, but how easy would it be to find a temporary replacement for Chopper at short notice? We had loads of jobs booked in for the next few weeks.

'I might be able to 'elp out there,' says Spud.

I look over at him. 'That's really good of you to offer, Spud, but I don't expect you to do it – you've only just retired yourself.'

'Not me, love, at least not before I get these cataracts sorted. No, I'm on about your Sabrine.'

'Sabrine can't drive,' I say.

'Are you gonna tell her love,' says Spud. 'Or shall I?'

Sabrine takes a quick sip of her drink and looks over at me. 'Uncle Spud's been teaching me to drive.'

'Aye, and she's grand at it,' adds Spud. 'A natural. Ready to take 'er test n'all.'

'I was planning on passing it, then surprising you with the good news,' says Sabrine. 'But as you need a driver now, I could take it sooner.'

All this turning to look between her and Spud is making me dizzy.

I glare at Spud. 'You taught her to drive? You just said you've got bloody cataracts!'

Spud sits upright and strokes his belly. 'Doesn't stop me from giving instructions, does it?'

'Spud's been great, Mum, honestly. He's so patient. No offence, but I don't think I could have learnt with you.'

'Oh? Why's that?'

'You're so, you know, *stressy*.'

I grow hot all over. 'Stressy?'

Sabrine holds out her hand. 'See. That's exactly what I mean.'

I slump back into my chair, and focus on not being *stressy*. 'Okay, okay.' I hold up my palms. 'Spud, thank you. It's incredibly good of you to teach Sabrine to drive.'

Spud nods, relaxes against the back of his chair and runs a hand down his beard. 'Pleasure.'

'And Sabrine.' I turn to her. 'Good for you, sweetheart. I'm proud of you.'

She breaks into a smile.

'But no way do I want my daughter working as a delivery driver.'

'What? Mum!'

Spud folds his arms across his chest.

'Maybe it's not such a bad idea, Ronni,' Ralph says, under his breath to me. 'You know how hard Sabrine works. And wouldn't it be good to keep it in the family? At least you know she's got your best interests at heart.'

'No.' I slice a hand through the air. 'It's not happening.'

Sabrine lets out a gasp of disbelief. 'This is so typical of you,' she says through gritted teeth. 'Remember how you were when I started work at the pub? You didn't want me doing that either.' She pulls a face and puts on a stupid voice. *'For God's sake, Sabrine, you're not the kind of person who could cope with working behind a bar!'*

I tut and shake my head.

She leans forward. 'I get you had high hopes for me and I'm sorry I've turned out such a bloody disappointment to you, but—'

'Sabrine, language, please!'

'Oh, Mum, get real!'

I look around the group. The expressions on their faces show awkwardness starting to creep in.

'This isn't about my language,' she continues, 'or whether my job choice impresses the yoga brigade that, by the way, if you haven't noticed, you're not a part of any more. It's about *me*, and what *I* want.'

'All right, all right.' I wave a hand towards the floor. 'Keep your voice down.'

'No, I won't keep my bloody voice down!' she says, louder than before. Silence falls on nearby tables, while Spud chooses the moment to slurp the last of his coke up through his straw.

'It's time you listened to me,' she continues. 'I told you this morning what I want to do with my life.'

I reach for Toni's vodka, that she hasn't yet added any tonic to, and throw a gulp down my neck. The fumes sting my eyes, and the liquid burns my throat. It clears enough of the fog in my brain to give me a tiny tunnel of clarity.

'Fine.' I say. 'Sabrine, once you've passed your test, you're joining the team.'

I pretend not to see Spud putting his thumb up to her.

The red blotches that have appeared on her cheeks begin to fade and her body visibly relaxes.

'My round,' I say, getting up. 'I don't know about you lot, but after the day I've had, I could do with a rather large drink.'

'I think you did the right thing, you know, saying Sabrine can be a driver for us.'

I look up at Ralph next to me at the pub table. 'I hope so.'

'It must be hard,' he says, 'letting go.'

He clasps a hand around his pint glass, but doesn't lift it from the table. 'You've been avoiding me lately, haven't you?'

I swallow a crisp too quickly. Its sharp edges scratch my gullet. 'Is it that obvious?'

He gives a tight-lipped smile. 'You could say that.'

'Sorry,' I say. 'Things have just seemed a bit awkward since – you know.'

'Yeah.' He nods. 'Listen, Ronni, I'd hate for you to feel uncomfortable around me. I've been thinking. I said to you from the beginning that I wouldn't be here forever, and perhaps now's the time I should move on.'

'Because of me? No.'

My voice comes out louder than I expected. I dart my eyes to the side, but the rest of our group are busy chatting between themselves.

'I felt guilty about what happened,' I say.

'Guilty? Why?'

'Oh, you know, the small matter of my husband dying not that long ago—'

He leans forward. 'Ronni, you can't spend your life—'

I flap my hand. 'I know, I know. But it wasn't just that. I was worried what Sabrine might think too. Maybe she'd see it as me somehow cheating on her dad.'

He doesn't take his eyes off my face – doesn't even blink.

'I know, I know, it's crazy, but all this stuff was flying through my mind. Anyway, she said something to me today that got me thinking.'

'Oh?'

'Yes. She said it was about time I had some fun. And do you know what? She's right. I'm forty-four years old. I don't want to spend the rest of my life feeling guilty or miserable. I *want* to enjoy myself and be happy.'

'So what are you saying?'

'I'm saying,' I begin, 'that if you're up for it – I mean, if you'd *like* to, maybe you and I could hang out, um, more, together.' I sip my drink to help lubricate my suddenly dry throat.

His mouth turns up at the corners.

I hold my breath. Is it a smile because he's happy at my suggestion, or is he about to laugh in my face?

He finally picks up his pint. 'If you want to *hang out* with me—'

My cheeks burn.

'Then I'd be delighted to hang out with you.' He holds his glass up. 'To fun, and enjoying each other's company.'

I tap my glass against his. 'Cheers.'

We both take a drink without breaking our gaze.

'Of course, we're not talking anything serious, are we?' he says.

I shake my head far more vehemently than is probably necessary at that question. 'No, no, of course not.'

'Good. Because I said right at the beginning that I didn't want to get tied down to one place for too long – that at some point I'll be moving on.'

'Sure, sure.' My vehement head shaking becomes vehement nodding. I feel like a wobble head on a car dashboard. 'And you know I'm keen to eventually sell the business. Once I've built it up enough, that is, and it's worth something. Then I want to get back down south as soon as I can. I've been looking at an apartment online actually.'

'Have you? Yes, great. That all works out then.' He starts nodding furiously too. It's like we're competing for the head gestures world champs. At this rate, it's going to be a close call who gets gold.

He leans forward and drops his voice. 'Right. Since that's all worked out, I just have one more question.'

I look at him over the rim of my glass and raise my eyebrows.

'Are we letting everyone know about the fact we're now *hanging out* together, or are we keeping it a secret?'

I lower my glass to the table and grin. 'Oh, I think we can be open about things. We've just got to think about how we go about telling them.'

'I'm one step ahead of you there, Ronni,' he says.

'Really? What do you have in—'

I don't get to finish my sentence because he pulls me into an embrace and plants his lips on mine.

Chapter Thirty-Seven

21 June 2019 – Haxton, Yorkshire

Ronni

I watch out of the flat window as Sabrine laughs at something her boyfriend says. My heart catches but I smile anyway. A poky one-bedroom flat in south Haxton might not be the place I'd envisaged for my daughter but she couldn't be happier, and that's the main thing.

Ralph's stood in the back of the van, passing boxes to Sam, who in turn passes them to Sabrine. They've got quite an effective production line going. I offered to give the kitchen cupboards a wipe down while they're unloading. Sabrine assured me the lettings company had everything professionally cleaned before they moved in. I gave the kitchen a once-over anyway, more to give myself something to do than because it needed it.

'That's the last of it,' I hear Ralph call from the back of the van. He jumps down and shuts the doors. He's been incredible these last few weeks. He knows I've been struggling with the idea of Sabrine moving out, and has been coming by more than usual to help out. I know he's doing it to support me and I'm grateful to him. He even offered to be the guarantor for Sabrine and Sam when I was turned down due to my credit history.

I couldn't ask for a better boyfriend. Boyfriend? Ha. Can you have a *boyfrien*d at forty-four? I suppose *partner* is the modern term, but that sounds more permanent than what we have. We've both been honest with each other. It's not forever. Fun for now, is how Ralph put it, and I totally agree, so that's all fine.

The door opens and the three of them, with a box each, bustle in. The room, even though it hasn't got furniture in yet, is tiny, and the four of us practically fill it.

'All done.' Sam grins. He sets his box onto the floor and brushes his hands against his jeans. 'Thanks for all your help Ronni, Ralph. We can sort it all out from here if you want to get off.'

'No rush.' I bend down and open the box he's just put down and inspect the contents. 'We can help you get unpacked.'

Ralph, suddenly beside me, takes my hand and pulls me up. 'Why don't we let these two unpack in their own time. I expect they want to get the champagne open first.' He winks at me.

'Oh yes,' I say, remembering. I return to the window where I'd left the Sainsbury's carrier bag, and pull out the bottle of Dom Pérignon. 'A little something to celebrate your first home together,' I say, presenting it to them.

'Thanks Mum! Thanks Ralph.' Sabrine hugs us in turn.

'Yeah, thanks guys,' adds Sam, shaking Ralph's hand and giving me a bear hug. 'That's really good of ya.'

We say our goodbyes and somehow I manage to hold back the tears. Sabrine assures me she's only a few streets away and reminds me we'll see each other every day at work. I know all this, and I can't – and won't – explain why it's not the same; why, while I'm thrilled she has Sam in her life, it means that nothing between us will ever be the same again; why I fear that her moving out might reopen the hole in my heart that Matthew's death created. Of course, I say none of that. I hug my daughter, wish her all the happiness in the world and walk out of the door with a wave and a smile on my face. I manage to hold the smile for as long as it takes us to climb into the van and drive off, and only then do I let my face crumple into tears.

I kick off my shoes and, with my jacket still on, flop down onto the sofa, feeling utterly exhausted. Bottling my emotions up in front of Sabrine then bawling my eyes out on the journey back has taken it out of me. I wouldn't blame Ralph for thinking me completely unhinged and bidding a hasty retreat back to his cottage. To his credit he comes in with me and flicks the kettle on.

'You okay?' he asks, concern etched on his face. 'How about I run you a bath?'

His kindness makes me want to cry all over again, but I bite it back and manage a nod. 'That'd be lovely.'

'And I tell you what—' He switches the kettle off. 'What say we forget the tea and open a bottle of wine?'

I give him a watery smile. 'Good idea.'

'Do you want me to stay over tonight?' he asks.

'Yes please,' I say. It's not so much that I mind being on my own. It's more that I want to make the most of what time together we have. It's been three months since our conversation in the pub when Ralph made it clear he'd soon be moving on. He didn't put a date on it, but I don't expect it will be long before he announces he's going. And once the purchase of my new place in Woking completes, then I'll need to head down there to sort things out.

I haven't told anyone about putting the offer in – not even Ralph or Sabrine. I could only afford it because, after months of me fighting it, Matthew's old firm finally agreed to pay out on his pension. It's nothing like the old place, of course. I couldn't afford that if I wanted, not that I do at this juncture in my life. It's a tiny, two-bed flat that needs some serious work and is far enough out of Guildford to reflect on the price tag, but it's cosy and it's perfect for what I'm looking for now. I want to get everything organised before I break the news.

Next door, in the bathroom, water thunders out of the taps into the tub. I peel off my socks, throw them in the linen basket, then tug off my jacket. As I'm about to take off my trousers, I step on something cold and sharp. I lift up my foot, uncovering a crumpled piece of paper. I drop to my knees to pick it up and lean on the bed as I open it out, just to check it's nothing important before I throw it away.

On the paper someone's scrawled a number – a foreign telephone number by the looks of all those zeros. It takes me a few seconds to recall what it is and why it's in my pocket. With a thud in my chest – almost as if my heart's been jump-started – I remember.

I bite my lip and can hardly believe the idea that occurs to me. *Should I? What would I say?*

Nah. Stupid idea. I screw the paper back up and hold it in my fist. My mind whirrs.

What harm would it do?

Slowly, I uncurl the crumpled paper again and smooth it down on the bed so I can decipher the number.

Before I can change my mind, I delve into my pocket for my mobile phone and punch in the number. Blood rushes past my ears as I listen to the alien dial tone.

There's a click and a young woman's voice garbles something I don't fully understand.'

'*Ah, oui, bonjour. Je suis, um, je voudrais parler avec Madame Ruth por favor*. I mean, *s'il vous plait*.'

'*Qui est à l'appareil s'il vous plait?*'

I'm not entirely sure what that means but I'm guessing she's asking who I am. 'Um …' I desperately try to drag up some memories of school French class. How do I say this? '*Je suis la dor-terre*.'

'Je suis désolé, Madame. Je ne comprends pas.'

'*Elle est ma mère,*' I say. 'Ruth is my mother. Please tell her it's Ronni.'

Ralph pops his head around the bathroom door and waggles his eyebrows when he sees my breasts poking out over the bubbles.

I laugh and rearrange the bubbles to cover my modesty.

'Why hide something so lovely?' He hands me the glass of wine he's brought in for me and kneels down onto the bathmat to drop a kiss on my forehead.

I take a sip and smile. 'Wouldn't want you to think I'm a floozy.'

'Bit late for that,' he says, then quickly ducks out of the way as I take a swipe at him.

'Dinner's cooking,' he says, flicking the bubbles off his T-shirt. 'Should be about fifteen minutes.'

'That's good of you, but you didn't have to do that.'

He swirls the water around. The bubbles covering my chest dissolve and he traces a finger from my chin to my navel, making me tingle.

'I wanted to,' he says. 'We're celebrating too.'

'Are we?'

'Yep. Having the place to ourselves. We can make as much noise as we want.'

I laugh. 'I suppose you've got a point.'

He stands up. 'Better go. I'm sure you don't want burnt offerings.'

I sink my shoulders further below the water and sigh. I was going to tell him tonight about the conversation I just had with my mother, and about the decisions I've made since I started my soak, but they're big topics that can wait. I just want tonight to be enjoyable with no serious conversations.

What is it about immersing yourself in hot water that makes the world look so clear? Dilemmas that have been swimming around my head for weeks have tonight been ironed out. For the first time in a year I'm confident about my plans for the future. Of course, it very much depends on what Ralph and Sabrine say, but laying here with only myself for company has made me see things afresh and, unless I've got things very wrong, I can't see why either of them would have a problem with what I've got in mind.

Chapter Thirty-Eight

22 August 2019 – Haxton, Yorkshire

Ronni

I thank Donna and arrange the glasses on the bar so I can pick up all four at once.

‘When am I gonna get your lass back off ya?’ she asks.

‘Sabrine? No chance. Couldn’t cope without her, even now Chopper’s back. We’re run off our feet.’

‘Oh, aye. ’E’s been down ’ere a couple o’ times recently with Kelly and ’kids. Looks right as rain.’

‘Yeah. He’s making a good recovery. Still gets a bit of pain in his legs now and then, but that’s not unusual apparently.’

She rests an arm over one of the beer pumps. ‘Lucky bastard, wasn’t ’e?’

‘Certainly was.’

‘Ah, well. If your Sabrine gets fed up working with ’er mother, lemme know. I’ll ’ave ’er back like a shot. Brilliant barmaid she is. One o’t’best.’

‘Will do.’ I weave my way through the bar and out into the beer garden, where we’ve dragged two tables together to accommodate me, Ralph, Toni, and six of her fellow mature students to celebrate their exam results. They all passed with at least a level 5. Toni’s top level 9 mark surpassed her expectations, but not mine – I knew she’d do well. I’ve never met anyone as passionate about a subject as she is. Ralph and I have already started trying to convince her to take her A-level next. She’s reluctant, but I reckon, with a bit more gentle persuasion, she’ll go for it.

Ralph, in deep conversation with the young, bespectacled chap seated on the stool next to mine, winks at me as I sit down between them. I lean back slightly to allow them to continue talking about “*that scene* in *The Merchant of Venice*”. By the time they’ve finished their lively debate on whether Shylock is victim or villain, I’m starting to feel the back of my neck burning in the sun.

‘Not sharing those, Ronni?’ says Ralph, whose grin I can see through his pint glass.

‘*Oops*!’ I split open the bag of prawn cocktail I’ve been munching to reveal three sorry-looking crisps.

He laughs. ‘You might as well finish them off now.’

I shrug and scoop them into my mouth. My renewed love of salty snacks has resulted in me gaining a dress size in the space of six months, but I quite like the new curves that have come with it, and so does Ralph, so what the hell.

With the bespectacled chap now engaged in another enthralling literature discussion, this time with the blue-haired woman beside him, I lean forward to Ralph. 'Who's he?'

'That's Mo. He's on the course with Toni.'

'Oh, so *that's* Mo? The thinking woman's crumpet.'

He shoots me a quizzical look.

'Never mind,' I say. 'Hark at you – going on about Shakespeare. Didn't know you had a clue about literature.'

He shrugs and his cheeks pinken. 'I wouldn't say I'm an expert, but I like going to the odd play. I haven't seen them all but it just so happens that the last one I saw was *The Merchant of Venice*.'

'So, what did you find out about Mo?'

Ralph drops his voice. 'I'd say he's rather besotted with our Toni by the sound of things.'

I grin. 'Is he really?'

He nods. 'Wouldn't stop talking about her. Kept saying how talented and curious she is. Definitely got the hots for her.'

'That's the one she went to The Playhouse with,' I say. 'She had a great time but doesn't think he's interested 'cos he never asked her out again. Typical Toni – assumed she wasn't good enough for him.'

Ralph pulls a face. 'What?'

'I tried to tell her that was nonsense and that he was probably just shy, and she should ask him out, but you know what she's like. I'll tell her he's interested. She'll be made up.'

We both automatically look over at Toni who's holding an audience with a portion of the group. To a man they're hanging on to her every word.

'Doesn't know how amazing she is, does she?' I say.

'No. She really doesn't. Do you think she'll go on to do her A-level?'

'I'm sure she will once it's sunk in how well she's done. You should've heard her this afternoon when we went down to the college to get her results – "I've failed", "I've let you down", "I'll be a laughing stock". She didn't shut up about it until she opened the envelope. When she saw the grade she thought she'd got someone else's by mistake.'

He laughs and drums his fingers on his stool in time to the beat of the soft rock music playing in the background. 'You always knew it would be good news.'

'Actually,' I say, my heart quickening. 'I've got some good news of my own.'

He leans forward on the table, and raises his eyebrows. 'Have you? What's that then?'

I've been desperate to tell him all week, but it's never felt like the right time. Now, though, in the sunshine and surrounded by happy people, it seems like the perfect moment.

'I've had an offer accepted on an apartment in Surrey.' I think about what this means for the future and, involuntarily, my lips stretch across my face into a wide grin. 'I sign the paperwork tomorrow. I'm going to have to go down there for a couple of weeks and stay with Charlotte while I decide what to do with the place. I got it for a bargain price because it needs a lot of work.'

His lips part, but not into a smile, more an "Oh".

I reach across to hold his hand. 'Don't worry about work. Sabrine's going to have to step up anyway. We only agreed this a couple of weeks ago, but she's going to be a partner. I went to ask her if she'd work some extra shifts while I'm away in France for a few weeks—'

'Hang on.' He frowns 'You're going to France? For a few *weeks*? And you only thought to mention that now?'

'Yes. I was going to tell you sooner, but I wanted to make sure I'd thought everything through first.'

His frown deepens. Under the table I cross my toes for good luck and carry on. 'When I asked Sabrine, she said she'd been wanting to talk to me for a while about using the inheritance money from her grandmother when it comes through to buy into the business. I said no at first. I thought she could do so much better than to part-run a van delivery service, but, well, I thought about it for a while, and realised it wasn't such a bad idea. She and Sam are happy and she's determined to stay in Haxton. Learning how a business runs could be brilliant for her.'

He rubs his upper lip with his index finger. 'I see.'

I take a sharp breath in through my nostrils. This is the bit I'm most nervous about telling him. 'And I've been having a few thoughts. About us. I don't think we should carry on as we have been. I think it's time we—'

He lets out a mirthless laugh. 'Well, Ronni. I've got to give it to you. You sure know how to drop a bombshell.'

'Just let me explain,' I say. 'I know it's come a bit out of the blue, but we always said this wasn't forever. *You* said it, actually. We've always been straight with one another. You knew I wanted to sell the business eventually and go back down to Surrey, but so much has happened since then and I've been thinking—'

He pulls his hand away from mine. 'Sounds like you've been doing a lot of thinking, but not a lot of talking. Not to me at any rate.'

'I realise it's a lot at once, but I really want you to know that—'

He holds up his hands. 'It's my fault,' he says. 'I should have said something sooner, but you seemed so much more settled recently that I didn't think I needed to. I thought we were naturally getting closer anyway.'

'We were – we *are* – which is why I—'

'I realise Haxton doesn't hold a lot of good memories for you,' he cuts in. 'But I thought you'd made better ones in the last few months and got over all that teenage angst.'

'Teenage angst?'

'Well, whatever you want to call it, Ronni, that makes you hate this place so much – the place that's given you so much. I don't get it. I've never got it, if I'm honest, but I thought you'd get over all that and realise what you have here.'

My pulse quickens. 'And what is that exactly?'

His gaze is on my face, but somehow he's looking through me, not at me. 'People who adore you. who support you, who rely on you.' He shakes his head. 'What more is it you want?'

My blood temperature raises several degrees and I talk through my teeth in a bid to keep my volume in check. 'What I want is for you to listen to me for long enough to hear what I have to say.'

'No need. I hear you loud and clear.' He turns his head away, and takes a gulp from his pint. 'Jesus, Ronni. You run a successful business with four people working for you, who couldn't be more loyal. You've built a life for yourself and Sabrine after Matthew's death, and people look up to you for it. And yet all you seem to care about is getting back to your luxurious Surrey life.'

'I beg your pardon?'

He slams his pint down on the table, attracting several glances. 'For Christ's sake, Ronni. Do you need me to spell it out? I'm in love with you.

I just felt like an idiot saying it so soon after I'd insisted I'd be moving on. I don't want you to leave.'

I stare at him, unable to find my voice. I've never heard those words so publicly before.

He stands up and climbs out of the picnic bench.

'Where are you going?' I ask.

'What's the point in me hanging around?' Despite the blazing sun, he drives his arms into the sleeves of his jacket. 'Sounds like you've already made your mind up about what you want. It's all material stuff with you, isn't it, Ronni? My stupid fault. I should've guessed. God only knows why I thought you were any different. Why I thought having all these friends and family around you would make you happy, when all you were interested in was the show.'

I stand up and tip my head back to look straight up at him.

'Are you judging me by your wife's standards?'

'Seems to me'—he shoves his hands in his jacket pockets—'your standards are just as low.'

I gasp. 'I must admit, I never had you down for such an arsehole.'

'Yeah, well.' He scratches the back of his head. 'Maybe I am an arsehole. Maybe that's the problem.' He turns to go, then looks back at me. 'I don't expect you want this particular arsehole working for you any more. See you, Ronni. It was fun while it lasted.'

I don't know what else to do other than stand and stare as he strides away.

'Oh, Ronni.' I didn't even see Toni get up from the table, but somehow she's right beside me, an arm across my shoulders, guiding me to sit back down on the bench. ''E'll come round. 'E's probably just had a few too many.'

'He's only had one.'

'Aye. One too many,' says Blue Hair, leaning forward in front of Mo so I can see her. 'You know what these southerners can be like. Lightweights.'

Toni rests her cheek on my shoulder. 'Knowing Ralph, e'll feel like a right twat in 'morning when 'beer wears off. 'E'll be round yours grovelling before kettle's 'ad time to boil.'

'Men!' outrages Blue Hair. 'Wankers, t'lot of 'em.'

Mo leans even further back.

The fuzz of ripening tears rises up to behind my eyes. That couldn't have gone worse. I wanted to tell Ralph I'd decided to stay in Haxton and the flat in Woking is a refurbishment project I've bought as an investment; that when I return from France, Yorkshire is once again where I'll be calling home, because this is where my friends are, my daughter, my business and, of course, him; that if he'd consider sticking around too that would make my day.

Instead, he's shown what he really thinks of me – that I'm no better than the wife who put her lifestyle in front of his health.

I stand up and frantically search around for my handbag. Toni tries to tug me back down to sitting, but I wrench my arm from her grip.

'Sorry, Toni. I'm sorry. I've got to go. I didn't mean to ruin your day.'

'I don't care about that,' she says. 'I'm worried about you.'

'No, don't. I'm fine.' I swing my handbag over my shoulder. Mo has to quickly duck out of the way to avoid it colliding with his head.

'I'll come with you,' she says, standing up.

'No. Please Toni. I need to be on my own.'

'Are you sure?'

I nod.

She moistens her lips. 'Okay. But if you need me, call me. Straight away. Doesn't matter what time it is.'

'Thanks. I will.'

I turn to say goodbye to Toni's friends and am met with a sea of wide eyes. Over the murmur of goodbyes, Blue Hair mumbles something about "chauvinistic cretins". It's the last thing I hear before I escape the beer garden.

Chapter Thirty-Nine

14 September 2019 – Haxton, Yorkshire

RONNI

I smile and press "send" on the text message I've just written to Charlotte. I must tell Spud she's been asking after him. He'll be thrilled to hear that. And also that she's still single – he specifically asked me that question the other day. That's nine months now – a record for Charlotte.

I lock my phone and sigh. Still so much packing to do and I'll have to finish it tonight. There won't be time in the morning – Sabrine and Sam are coming at the crack of dawn. They want to see me off, bless them. I hope they'll be all right here on their own. I feel uncomfortably powerless to help them on their way into this new era of their lives. I've just got to sit back and let them get on with it. It's up to them now.

'I wonder,' I say to myself as I force myself to stand up from where I'm perched on the corner of my bed and continue my packing. 'Does it ever get easier to accept that you're not responsible for your kids' choices?' I snort. I can't see that day arriving any time soon. I can't even say I've quite got to the point where I don't still consider myself in some part responsible for Matthew's death – that I did nothing to change his mind about taking his own life when he left the house that day. But at least that part of me is smaller than it was. And at least now I feel like I'm a whole person again.

Instinctively, at the thought of Matthew I stop folding up a shirt and finger my wedding ring on my left hand. I've never stopped wearing it. Well, not strictly true – I've taken it off twice before. The first time was the day Arabella came around to our old house and I knew for sure about the affair. I hated Matthew so much at that moment, I thought I'd never wear the ring again. But the day after, in my guilt and confusion, seeing that pale band of bare flesh where my wedding ring had been, left me feeling so bereft, I'd put it back on and had instantly recovered some sense of normality and comfort from it – and both of those feelings were scant in those dark days.

The only other time I'd taken it off was the day of Toni's exam results when I was planning on telling Ralph I'd decided to stay in Haxton and that I'd like there to be a future together for us; that I'd bought a flat down south for visits to see old friends and maybe to rent out one day. Of course, his reaction put a halt to that plan. 'Yep, that chat didn't go so well,' I say to myself. 'But now—' I twist the ring and, with a bit of a tug, pull it off my finger and hold it up in front of me. 'This time, Matthew, I'm taking your ring off my finger for good. Not because I'm still angry at you, because I'm not. I'm really not. And not because of another man, because that unfortunately was a huge misjudgement on my part. No. I'm taking it off because I need to go my own way now. However …' I bow my head and unclip the slim gold chain around my neck. 'I did love you. And you'll always be a massive part of my life, so you can come with me and see where the rest of it takes me.' I thread my chain through my ring and fasten it back around my neck.

'There.' I place my hand over my wedding ring, now placed just below my collar bone, and give it a tap. I pick the half-folded shirt back up and a frisson of nerves and excitement runs through me at what lies ahead.

Chapter Forty

15 September 2019 – Manchester Airport

Ronni

'Are you sure you've got everything you need.'

Sabrine rolls her eyes. 'For the millionth time, Mum, *yes*.'

Sam puts an arm around Sabrine's waist. 'Don't worry, Ronni, love. We'll be fine.'

Since when has it been okay to call your girlfriend's mother *love*? I don't like it. I don't like it at all, but I say nothing. Sam is a nice boy. *Man*. I must remind myself he's a man. He's nearly twenty. He's a nice, sensible boy-man and Sabrine adores him, and that's all that matters. He's quite a staunch northerner, so if he really is *the one*, their children will have northern accents. And live in The North. Maybe that history, that I spent most of my life trying so desperately to stop repeating itself, is on an inevitable loop, and there was nothing I could ever have done to stop it. I'm still not sure how I feel about that, but maybe this trip will help me get my head around it. Is it fate intervening in my best-laid plans? Is this where I've belonged all along? Did it take me two decades away to see that?

Sam kisses Sabrine's cheek and she grins at him.

'I guess I'd better get going then.' I look up, over their heads, at the departures board. It takes me a few seconds to get the letters into focus. *I must book an eye test.*

'My flight's on time,' I say. 'That's good.' Despite my words, my heart thuds solemnly in my chest.

Sabrine, who seems to be able to read my every expression these days, flings her arms around my neck. 'Come on, Mum. Don't back out now. You're going to have a great time, and everything'll be fine at work, I promise. Trust me.'

'I do, sweetheart, I do.' I squeeze her around her tiny waist and bite back my tears. I will not cry. I will *not*. It feels like all I've done over the last eighteen months is shed tears – over Matthew's death, our financial situation, Sabrine moving out, Ralph …

She pulls away from me and smiles.

Sam hands me the rucksack. ''Ere you go then, babe.'

Babe now?

I hold out my hand to take the bag from him.

‘Let me ’elp you get that on,’ he says, coming behind me and threading my arms through the straps. ‘What you got in ’ere – a couple o’ bodies? I thought you were only going for six weeks.’

Blimey, it is heavy. Sam tugs hard on the straps to tighten them around my shoulders, causing me to stumble backwards.

‘Steady, sweetcheeks!’

Sweet—?

He slaps the top of my bag, knocking me off balance again. I turn my head as best I can with this monstrosity on my back and glare at him.

‘Sturdy as a brick shit ’ouse, that is,’ he says, and returns to his spot beside Sabrine.

‘Ooh, you’re going to have such an awesome time, Mum!’ she says, clasping her hands together. ‘I’m so jealous. I was the one meant to be going travelling.’

‘And I would have loved you to. But you wanted to stay here, remember?’ It seems a lifetime ago that Sabrine shouted at me at our old house that she wished I was dead instead of Matthew. Our relationship has had its ups and downs this last year or so, but at last it feels like we’re going to be fine.

‘Yeah, I know.’ She beams up at Sam – one of the few men actually taller than her, and he kisses her hairline.

It melts my heart just a little bit.

She reaches an arm out and touches mine. ‘And you won’t regret making me a partner, I promise. She won’t, will she, Sam?’

‘Nah, ’course not. We’ll ’ave built it up into an empire by ’time you get back. Beat yer ’eart out, Alan Sugar.’

‘It’s *eat* your h—’ I stop myself and smile. ‘Never mind. I hope you do make a go of it. A bloody good go. Remember, though, I’m only a phone call away, so if you need anything—’

Sabrine steers me by the elbow and we begin to walk. ‘I know, I know.’

‘And I’ll be back soon, anyway, so—’

‘Yes, Mum.’

I stop in my tracks. ‘Look after yourselves, sweetheart.’

‘You too.’

I stretch up to embrace my not-so-little girl, then reluctantly prise myself away from her and hug Sam.

‘Don’t worry, babe,’ he says. ‘I’ll take care of ’er.’

Sabrine grins and gives him a tender slap on the back. 'Oi, you. I'm perfectly capable of taking care of myself, thank you very much.'

Yes, Sabrine. Yes, you are.

'Go on then.' She flicks a finger in the direction of *departures*. 'Go and have an amazing time.'

I take a deep breath. 'Okay. See you soon.'

She gives me a little wave and the two of them turn to walk away. Precisely three steps on, she spins around and blows me a kiss. Like I used to do when she was little, I pretend to catch it and hold it to my heart.

She smiles, turns away and, hand-in-hand with Sam, she walks through the sliding doors, out of the airport.

I hover my mobile phone below the scanner at the self check-in machine. An error message appears yet again on the screen and I silently scream inside. This is exactly what I feared. Matthew and I enjoyed exotic holidays together all over the world, but I always left the check-in malarkey to him. How am I going to cope on my own if I can't even check myself in?

I hold the phone back underneath the scanner and will for it to work this time.

'Ronni! Ronni!'

I look around to see where the voice is coming from. I assume it must be Sam and I've forgotten something, but the man running towards me is twice Sam's age, with a short beard and unruly hair flopping over his eyes.

'Ralph?' I say, when he finally reaches me and stands in front of me, panting. 'What are you doing here?'

'I came to see you. Thank God I got here in time. Toni said you were flying off today.'

'I am.' I turn my phone over and look at the time. 'In about three hours.' The memory of the last time I saw him pierces me and I can taste the bitterness in my mouth. 'Like I was trying to tell you, I'm off to France. I'm going to stay with my mum and her partner for six weeks. That's if we all get on okay. I haven't seen her for years, so who knows how things will pan out.'

'Your mum? But I thought your mum was, um, was …' His voice trails off.

'Oh no, no.' I shake my head. 'She's not *dead*. She just left, when I was eleven. She ran off with a chap who lived in the posh end of Haxton.'

He raises an eyebrow. 'There's a posh end?'

I smile despite myself. 'Posh-*er*.'

'You never mentioned anything about your mum when we were …'

'No. Well, it had been so long since she'd been part of my life. I didn't really talk about her much.'

His face falls.

'Not to anyone,' I add quickly. 'Not just you. I bumped into her back on my birthday. In Marks & Spencer of all places.'

'You bumped into your long-lost mother, who lives in France, in Leeds' M&S?'

'Yeah. She said that every year she comes back to England around the time of my birthday. She said she always wanted to get in touch with me but never felt brave enough – thought I'd tell her where to go.'

'But you didn't, obviously?'

I lower my rucksack to the floor and rub my shoulder. 'Actually, I did.' My mind flits back to those gorgeous jeans I never did get back. Perhaps I'll treat myself when I'm in France, at some Parisian boutique, no less.

'Oh?' He knits his brow together.

'She left me her number anyway, and the day Sabrine moved out, I thought— I decided it may be nice if we were part of each other's lives again.'

He nods. And then there's silence between us.

We avoid each other's gaze and stand there like a couple of turnips.

What felt like an age of silence culminates in us both piping up simultaneously.

'So, what are you doing here?'

'Look Ronni, I really want to say—'

He wrings his hands together. 'I want to say that I'm sorry for the way I reacted back in the summer. I acted like a total dickhead.'

I nod. 'Yes. Yes, you did. Total dickhead.'

He shifts his weight onto one leg and runs his hand down his face, pulling his skin so that for a split second he looks like a hound dog. 'No excuses,' he says. 'Apart from it hurts, you know, when you get your fingers burned.'

'I know.'

'But that didn't give me the right to compare you to Emma. You couldn't be more different.'

'Why wait till now to tell me this? I'm just about to get on a bloody plane.'

He rests his hand loosely on his hip. 'Like I said, I'm a dick, or maybe I was scared you wouldn't have accepted my apology.'

'I wouldn't,' I say. 'But I would've enjoyed telling you where to stick it.'

He looks at me and I smile. He smiles back.

'You know,' I begin. 'That day in the pub, I was going to tell you I'd decided to stay in Haxton – that I wanted us to be together like a, um, like a proper couple.'

'Yeah. I know.'

I raise my eyebrows. 'How do you know?'

'Toni told me about an hour ago when she found me knocking on your door. After she'd called me every name under the sun, I finally got out of her that you'd gone to the airport. So I got here as fast as I could. I wanted to apologise before you head off.'

'Right.' I look down at my feet. 'Well, thank you.'

More silence.

'I suppose I'd better get going,' I say at last.

'Six weeks, you say?'

'What?'

'You'll be back in six weeks?' he asks.

I nod.

'Will you come out for dinner with me when you get back?'

I swallow. 'I might.'

'*Might* sounds promising.' He grins. 'Of course, I'd invite you for coffee now but I'm worried you'll tell me to stick that in the same place as my apology.'

'Well, in that case,' I say. 'How about I invite you?'

His eyes shine. 'I could go with that option.'

'Ralph Fogerty, would you like to come for a coffee with me?'

'Ronni Fairweather, I'd love to.' He picks my rucksack up off the floor, swings it easily over one shoulder and takes my hand.

So, book – check. Money to treat myself to a G & T when the cabin crew come through with the trolley – check. What else do I need to sort out before take-off? Phone on flight mode. I pat my jacket pockets to locate which one my phone is in, pull it out and am just about to tap on the aeroplane icon when a message pings up. It's from Ralph. A warm glow envelops me and I smile. I open the message just as the pilot announces that we're moments from take-off.

Wish we could fast-forward six weeks. Can't wait till you're back. Enjoy yourself. R xxx

'Madam, you need to put all devices away now, please.'

I clutch the phone to my pleasantly racing heart and blink up at the air steward, forgetting momentarily why he's there. 'Yes, of course. Sorry.' I switch my phone to flight mode and stow it inside the netting attached to the seat in front.

The plane engine roars to life and thunders up the runway. As its nose rises into the air, I lean back against my chair, allow a grin to play on my lips, and kick off my shoes. For the first time ever in my grown-up life, I'm flying solo.

* The End *

Thank You

Dear Reader,

In many ways, Ronni Fairweather is an anti-heroine. I wanted to create a character who was real and came with flaws, like we all do, but who also had a big heart.

If you did enjoy *The Fall and Rise of Ronni Fairweather*, I'd be most grateful if you would take a moment to leave a review on the platform you purchased the book from or Goodreads. I love to hear from readers, so if you feel like getting in touch, please do so at ginahollands.com.

The Fall and Rise of Ronni Fairweather is a story about independence, belonging and optimism, and yet there's more of a dash of hardship for Ronni along the way – just like there can be in real life. The main message is that life is what you make it, no matter where you are or how much or how little you think you have.

I've written quite a few books now, and every one is different. If you liked this one, please check out my others – details on my website and the pages overleaf.

If you'd like to keep up to date with me and my books, you can find me on most social media sites – details on my 'About the Author' page next. Thank you so much for reading.

Gina x

About the Author

Originally from Yorkshire, Gina now lives by the sea in West Sussex with her husband and son. When she's not working in her job in marketing and PR, or writing her latest book, Gina can be found dancing everything from lindy hop to salsa, shopping (she loves clothes far too much for her own good), eating out (she hates washing up far too much for her own good) or relaxing, which generally involves reading a book someone else has written or indulging in her new hobby of learning to play the piano. She has a sneaky suspicion she may be a musical genius in the making, but isn't about to give up the day job just yet.

For more information on Gina visit:

https://twitter.com/ginaholls

https://www.facebook.com/ginahollands

https://www.ginahollands.com

More Choc Lit and Ruby Fiction

from

Gina Hollands

Little Village of Second Chances

Surely everyone deserves a second chance?

Ex-fireman and edible flower farmer Shay McGillen has plenty of reasons not to give Sarah Pickering even one chance when she turns up in his small Yorkshire village. After all, she is only there to try to convince him and his fellow villagers to sell up so her company can build a bypass. If Sarah thinks she can make Shay give up his farmhouse and his business, she has another thing coming!

But when an unexpected blizzard leaves Sarah stranded in Shay's home, he soon realises that they are far more alike than he could have ever imagined – and perhaps both of them deserve a second chance ...

Available as an eBook, paperback and audiobook.
Visit: www.choc-lit.com for more details.

Yours, Trudy

How many positive words and exclamation marks can you fit into the space of one email?

A lot is the answer, if you're Trudy Drinkwater. As 'Head of People Happiness', her cheery emails are carefully written to boost the morale of her 'fellow finned friends' at Pink Fish Web Design. Yay!

But, in reality, there is very little Trudy has to say 'yay!' about in her home life. Her marriage is all but over, she's in a near constant battle to make her two chicken nugget loving teens eat anything vaguely nutritious, and the days when she and her husband were young lovers with big dreams seem very far away.

Can Trudy keep up the chirpy pretence of her day job, or does she really need a new start and a second chance at true happiness?

Available as an eBook, paperback and audiobook.
Visit: www.choc-lit.com for more details.

Introducing Ruby Fiction

Ruby Fiction is in imprint of Choc Lit Publishing.
We're an award-winning independent publisher, creating a delicious selection of fiction.
See our selection here:
www.rubyfiction.com

Ruby Fiction brings you stories that inspire emotions.

We'd love to hear how you enjoyed *The Fall and Rise of Ronni Fairweather.* Please leave a review where you purchased this novel or visit **www.rubyfiction.com** and give your feedback.

Ruby novels are selected by genuine readers like yourself. We only publish stories our Tasting Panel want to see in print. Our reviews and awards speak for themselves.

Could you be a Star Selector and join our Tasting Panel?
Would you like to play a role in choosing which novels we decide to publish? Do you enjoy reading women's fiction? Then you could be perfect for our Tasting Panel.

Visit: www.choc-lit.com/join-the-choc-lit-tasting-panel for details

Keep in touch:
Sign up for our newsletter for all the latest news and offers: www.spread.choc-lit.com.

Follow us on:
Twitter: @RubyFiction
Facebook: RubyFiction
Instagram: ChocLitUK

Stories that inspire emotions!